A

Eileen MacDonald is a well-respected investigative journalist and author of *Shoot The Women First* - a book containing first person interviews with women terrorists from around the world, and *Brides For Sale* - the story of two British girls sold as child brides in North Yemen. She is the author of two thrillers, *The Sleeper* was her first novel, followed by *The Infiltrator*.

Also by Eileen MacDonald

Brides for Sale
Shoot the Women First
The Infiltrator

The Sleeper

Eileen MacDonald

POCKET
BOOKS

LONDON · SYDNEY · NEW YORK · TOKYO · SINGAPORE · TORONTO

First published in Great Britain by Pocket Books, 1994
This edition first published by Pocket Books, 1998
An imprint of Simon & Schuster UK Ltd
A Viacom Company

Copyright © Eileen MacDonald, 1994

This book is copyright under the Berne Convention
No reproduction without permission
® and © 1997 Simon & Schuster Inc.   All rights reserved
Pocket Books & Design is a registered trademark of Simon & Schuster Inc

The right of Eileen MacDonald to be identified as author of this work has
been asserted by her in accordance with sections 77 and 78 of the
Copyright, Designs and Patents Act, 1988.

1 3 5 7 9 10 8 6 4 2

Simon & Schuster UK Ltd
Africa House
64-78 Kingsway
London WC2B 6AH

Simon & Schuster Australia
Sydney

A CIP catalogue record for this book is available from the British Library

ISBN 0-671-01820-5

This book is a work of fiction. Names, characters, places and incidents
are either a product of the author's imagination or are used fictitiously.
Any resemblance to actual people living or dead, events or locales is
entirely coincidental.

Printed and bound in Great Britain by Caledonian International Book
Manufacturing, Glasgow

To my mother and father with love

Prologue: **The Blooding**

Emilio Calogero had never been happier than in the last few minutes of his life.

He was a week away from his twenty-first birthday, a good-looking boy with blue-black curls and expressive blue eyes. Every Thursday night for the past two months he had been coming to this dingy office in the heart of Turin's industrial district. His task was to help produce the monthly newsletter for *Noi da Soli*, Ourselves Alone, an extremist right-wing organisation that despised the country's democratically elected Fascist politicians as corrupt and faint-hearted. Radical surgery, claimed the group, was the only way to cleanse Italy of its ills, its 'undesirables' – immigrants, Left-wingers and Jews. In seven months, *Noi da Soli* had been responsible for eleven murders.

Emilio had joined, not out of any strongly-held conviction, but in an effort to please his father, a bullying thug in the city's police force.

Within the group he had found a niche. He was intelligent and delicately-made, clearly not Nazi-skin material. But rather than try to batter him into shape as his father had always done, the group's hierarchy nurtured him. They foresaw a time when Emilio, a second year student at the prestigious Business School, could be very useful to them. For now, they asked no more of him than complete, unquestioning loyalty, attendance at all meetings and rallies, and a little administrative work.

In return for accepting him, Emilio's gratitude was beyond words. He was quite convinced that he was prepared to die for the cause.

He simply could not believe it when Valerio Mariana walked into the room. He had only seen him once, and then from afar: a dark, powerful figure on the platform at a rally in Milan. Il Capo himself. His base was Milan and he seldom ventured beyond it – there had been no word that he was in Turin. That he should be here . . . Emilio dropped his pen and rose to his feet, stuttering.

Mariana was a short, almost entirely bald man in his late fifties, whose eyes and mouth were too small for the fleshiness of his face. Most people though, even his enemies, did not see his unattractiveness: his charisma and arrogance over-rode it. He was wearing, as was his custom, an excellently cut suit of a fine, dark grey material, a dazzling white shirt and muted tie.

He smiled at the incredulity giving way to adoration on the boy's face. Such a pretty face. In truth, he had been looking for the editor of the newsletter, but this boy would do well enough, better in fact. Mariana sat himself down at the grey steel desk opposite Emilio's, and motioned for him to do likewise. He adopted his best paternal air: leaning forward, elbows on the table, chin resting on inter-laced fingers. 'Tell me,' he said, and his voice was like honey, 'about yourself.'

Two floors below Xavier had just picked the lock on the outside door. It was not much of a lock; he did not think much of *Noi da Soli*'s security.

The others were behind him on the worn stone steps that led up to the building: Dani and Anya, his comrades in the cell for the last three months, and the British girl, Zoe. She was to be blooded this evening. He gave an involuntary shudder remembering the effects upon himself of his own first killing. Well, it got easier.

He was in charge. He went first, sliding into the hallway. The place was damp, dark and stank of cats. It was empty except for a bicycle and the frame of a filing cabinet. The others filed in silently, Dani closing the door gently behind him. It was suddenly pitch-black and it took a few moments for their eyes to adjust. Xavier took out his gun, motioned for everyone else to do likewise and took the lead in mounting the stairs. They were stone, like the ones outside, so no creaking floorboards could betray them.

The first landing was also in darkness, confirming what

they had seen from outside. The lights had been upstairs, on the top floor only.

The information that they had received, at considerable danger to their informant, was that there was always someone, maybe several people here, doing office work on Tuesday evenings between eight and ten. It was now – Xavier checked his watch – 20.38.

Emilio positively blossomed. Il Capo seemed so genuinely interested in him, so kind. Like a father should be. He had been good enough to say that Emilio showed great potential. Now he was even inviting him to spend a few days with him at his villa in Umbrio. Emilio's cup ran over.

Ascending third in line on the staircase, Zoe Douglas heard the two men's voices. She had just the vaguest smattering of Italian, but she could tell that one voice belonged to a young man. She was holding the pistol in her right hand, down at her side. She could feel its coldness against her palm, and yet it still seemed that she must wake up and find it was all a dream: the gun; the way her heart seemed to jump in her throat; her presence here at all.

She had only been in Turin since noon. Sergio, who had been her sole human contact for the past six weeks, had put her on the ten o'clock ferry from Corsica the previous night.

He had stood with her on the quayside as the boat had docked, disgorging a late flock of tourists. She was a little surprised at his waiting; she would have expected him to have driven off as soon as she got out of the car. She turned to look at him and saw that he was watching her.

Without shifting his gaze, he took the cigarette from his mouth and spoke quietly in English: 'Remember, just hit the target, Zoe. Hit the target.' He tapped her once on the shoulder, turned and walked away.

She had absorbed enough of his teaching by then not to question his orders. She did not let herself think what his words meant, but on the boat she had been unable to sleep. She had sat on the deck, watching the moonlight glitter on the dark water, and had replayed the phrase in her mind until it became a talisman.

She had watched the coast of Italy appear in the pale yellow and pink of the dawn, and had been wrenched by its beauty. She disembarked in a crowd of sleepy families and slowly made her way to the railway station where, as Sergio had told her, she had ample time to catch the express train to Turin. On board, she had at last slept, deeply and dreamlessly and had awakened disoriented at Turin's main station. A young woman of around her own age, twenty-two, had met her on the platform. She had introduced herself, in accented English, as Anya, had brusquely taken Zoe's arm and guided her into a waiting taxi. There was a swift, noisy journey to the Vecchio Centro Storico, the city's student quarter, and then a long climb up to an attic apartment where Xavier and Dani were waiting.

Xavier had fair, crew-cut hair and blue eyes; he looked distressingly like a Hitler youth. He was French and spoke fast, with no consideration for foreign ears.

'Tonight you're to accompany us on a raid of the main Neo-Nazi party headquarters here in the city. We'll take their membership files, destroy computers, any equipment, set fire to the place. OK?'

She knew from his glare that the correct response was a simple nod, but she was determined to put her question: 'There will be no people there?'

'The building will be empty,' he told her shortly.

Anya put a hand on Zoe's arm. 'It will all be over in twenty minutes,' she promised.

They had not talked much after that. Although it was the beginning of October, it was still very hot and there was no wind. Every window was flung wide, but the apartment remained airless. From the building opposite came the sound of rock music and intermittently raised voices reached them from the floor below. There was scarcely any furniture and such as there was, was shabby. Anya had dozed on the sofa; at the wooden table the boys had played cards, smoked a lot.

Zoe had sat, a little bemused, on the floor by the window. On one level her mind was a complete blank, on another a kaleidoscope of the images and sensations she had brought with her.

When she closed her eyes she could see the mountains of northern Corsica, smell the spicy scent of the maquis, hear Sergio's cracking voice as he issued commands. He had taught her to hold the gun steady, to follow the moving target, to aim slightly higher to be sure of a hit, to be a killer . . .

Her eyes snapped open to banish the thought, but she knew it was true. She was a natural; she loved shooting; found it exhilarating and liberating. The physical sensation of firing a weapon was like nothing she had experienced before; the current it sent through her body shook her like a sexual climax. But the purpose of shooting was another matter. Somehow, through it all, she had managed to shield herself from the reality of what she was being prepared for, what she was doing. She was aware, however, that Sergio and the Leadership were not playing games.

Yet that is what it seemed like now. Zoe focused her eyes on the neat, dark pony-tail that hung down Anya's back, two steps above her. She had not queried Xavier's order to bring weapons to an empty building nor, looking upwards from the street outside, the shadows that had played on the wall of the lit room. She blocked the obvious from her mind and concentrated fiercely on the present; on breathing and feeling and moving with the team.

Her right foot came down softly on the top floor landing, making no noise on the stone. Immediately behind her was Dani; Xavier was in front. Now he was standing, not breathing, by the half-open door, the only door up here. His gun came up in his right hand, his left one forming the cradle, supporting it.

They had all flattened themselves behind him against the wall. The paintwork was muddy brown and peeling; flakes fell as they moved against it. Zoe felt her senses heighten to a pitch that was almost painful: her scalp tingled, she smelt her own fear, and the sweat of Anya beside her. Like the others, she raised her gun.

Xavier seemed to dance on his toes: in a soundless leap he was on the other side of the door. He caught them all up in his glance, nodded. They took a collective breath.

Inside the room Valerio Mariana was examining one of his

spotless cuffs. He decided to speed things up. Just as soon as the boy had finished declaring undying devotion to the cause, he was going to ask him out to dinner. Somewhere quiet, discreet of course, and then afterwards . . .

'What was that?' he said suddenly.

The door flew back on its old hinges, knocking the wastebin through the air. A split second later Xavier was in the room, then Anya, then Zoe. They moved as one, their fingers on the triggers, their eyes on the quarry before them.

The words died in Emilio's throat. Mariana screamed, once, at the man whose gun was trained on his heart. It was all he had time for. Xavier fired; the bullet tore through Mariana's breast pocket, smashed into his sternum. Everything in the room seemed suspended, even the silence was stretched out, waiting. Mariana fell forward on to the desk. The last sound he heard was the gurgle of his own bright blood.

Emilio had risen from his chair. He whimpered, knowing his own fate. If he could have articulated what he felt at that moment, it would have been a great cry at the unfairness of it all. Dragging his gaze away from the twitching, dying Capo, his eyes locked onto the small fair-haired girl. She stood less than two metres away, feet apart, holding her gun in both hands, steadying it in line with his chest. He acknowledged, with an odd detachment, that she was beautiful: large grey eyes edged with sooty lashes, small straight nose, and a Cupid's bow of a mouth. He looked into her eyes.

Sergio's chant was playing in Zoe's head: hit the target, just hit the target. She began to squeeze the trigger, narrowing her eyes down the sights for the perfect shot. A tiny sound, a bleat, escaped from the boy's throat. Something like a curtain dropped away inside her mind. She looked into his eyes and saw reflected there all the terror and despair of the last appeal. Her vision blurred. She had joined to save life.

'Bastardo!' shrieked Anya beside her.

'Kill him!' yelled Xavier.

Zoe fired just over Emilio's shoulder. The bullet nicked his shirt, embedding itself in the wood-frame of the window. A moment later she heard Anya's gun, echoing the explosion of her own. She willed Emilio to keep standing, to remain alive.

He never knew that she had spared him. A moment before the awful slamming pain in his chest, he had seen the horror in her face, and he had dared to hope . . .

Anya's bullet pierced his lung first, before entering the right ventricle of his heart. His father had taught him at an early age not to scream, but Emilio had never felt such pain. He gasped and shut his eyes to deal with it, lapsed into blessed unconsciousness.

Zoe's eyes had not left his: she saw the shock and disbelief register before the pain hit and he fell. She could not move; her body was water, floating away from her mind.

'Come on!' Anya was at the door, screaming at her. Still Zoe stood staring.

'Get going!' Xavier pushed her towards the others. 'Get out!' he yelled as she did not move.

Anya grabbed Zoe by one arm; Dani, who had stood guard in the doorway throughout, caught hold of the other. Together they propelled her before them along the corridor, down the steps. Now the stone seemed to magnify all sound: the clatter of their feet, their frantic breathing. Above her head Zoe heard the 'whump' of two more shots as Xavier administered the coups des graces, and then a soft boom as he set the fire.

In the room, Xavier checked the time, paused for one more second, frowning at the older man's face. Then he remembered. 'Got you, you bastard,' he hissed. He grinned and ran, taking the stairs in giant, jubilant jumps.

At first no one noticed Zoe's silence. She had performed well, showing no hesitation when Xavier had ordered her to shoot. In the car, when he had announced who they had just killed, the three of them had all been too high, shrieking congratulations at each other to observe that Zoe had not joined in.

It was only when they had got back to the apartment, called their go-between with the three word message and were all crowded into the little kitchen, Anya insisting on cooking, she and Dani throwing cans of beer in the air, at each other, acting like kids, that they had seen the state Zoe was in: wooden, off in some other world; her eyes not really focusing, ears not hearing.

All of them in the recent past had experienced something similar; they fell awkwardly silent.

Xavier felt the eyes of the other two upon him. As always, they were waiting for him to act.

It was hardly fair: they were all close in age and had joined at almost the same time, but when anything difficult came up, it was left up to him. It was not supposed to be like this – the group's philosophy was strictly non-hierarchical – but Dani, though good with explosives, flinched from any responsibility and refused to take any orders from Anya, his girlfriend. So Xavier had become the leader by default.

He looked over at Zoe again. There was no colour in her face and her eyes were enormous and unblinking; she was deep in shock. He bit his lip: getting blind-drunk had helped him survive the aftermath of his own blooding, but Zoe was a girl. He did not know what to do.

'Anya,' he said softly. 'Talk to her.'

Anya scowled. 'Why me?'

'Please . . . She'll take it better from you.'

'Just because I'm a woman, I suppose.' Anya glared at him, then around at Dani, red-faced and rubbing nervously at his forehead. She shrugged and walked over to the table.

'Zoe,' she said, sounding bored. No response; Zoe sat like a ramrod. Anya tried again, leaning down towards the girl and touching her arm.

'God, she's cold!' She was genuinely concerned now. She sat down and picked up Zoe's hand, placing it against her own hot cheek.

'You're like ice! Listen to me, Zoe. I know how you feel. My first time, I put a bomb in the ladies toilets at a conference centre in Lyons. Dani fixed me up. We called it the baby bomb – the explosive and timer strapped to my stomach and covered by a big jumper. So, I looked pregnant. Who'd suspect a pregnant woman? And it worked! The security was really tight at the conference, but I pretended to faint in the hall and the guards let me in!

'Brilliant, yes? I did well, just like you. I arranged the bomb behind the loo, and walked out, very cool. Then an hour later, I thought about it. I was so sick, wasn't I, Dani? Sick for two days. Can you imagine it!

'Zoe? Zoe, have you heard anything I said? Are you all right?'

Zoe felt as if she was in a mist, floating above herself and the others, looking down on the scene like a curious bystander. She saw the room quite clearly: the chipped cream enamel stove, free-standing on little black feet; the smell of burning fish and oil. She saw Xavier and Dani leaning against a large green fridge, holding their beers, looking at her. Anya, too, was staring.

Zoe was aware that she had to make some sort of response, but it seemed terribly difficult to communicate. With a great effort, she focused on her hand, the one which Anya was holding, saw how brown it was, tanned by the Corsican sun. She vividly remembered how hot it had been there; here she had never felt such cold.

She concentrated on Anya's face, watched her lips move, heard her question, but found it perplexing. How could any of them be OK after what they had just done? How could they laugh and drink, and praise themselves for killing those two men? Had they not heard their screams, seen their terror?

'I don't think I hit him.' She blurted it out, was as surprised by her words as if someone else had spoken.

It was all they wanted from her.

She was engulfed in Anya's arms. 'Hey, we did it together! A team. Who cares whose bullet got that little shit?'

By the fridge, the boys beamed. The dark one, Dani, blushed and held out his beer to her. 'Have a drink,' he said. 'Forget it.'

Xavier was grinning, the relief evident on his face. 'Don't be so modest, Zoe. You did very well. You were cool, you obeyed orders.'

In the street outside a car back-fired. Anya gave her a last pat and went back to the fish, howling that it was burnt. The party started again, louder than before.

Watching them, Zoe understood. They did not want to

know too much; they had their own fragility to guard. No one had seen her alter her aim – or if they had, it was never something to be talked about; the secret was hers to keep.

Dani found the radio, tuned it in to a rock station, turned the volume up loud. It was a song Zoe recognised, though she could not remember the title, or even the artist. Once she had known all the words, memorising them by heart without realising it while she revised for exams, but now . . .

'It should be on soon,' said Dani.

It was 22.19 precisely. The receptionist had worked the night shift on Radio Torino for a year, had done drills for this sort of thing, but now it was real. She trembled with excitement and pleasurable fear, but correctly pressed the right button on the recording equipment. An instant later the silent alarm started flashing in the newsroom, and another alarm, far from silent, was activated at the central police station.

The caller's voice was male, young, and sounded very nervous. He was reading out a statement, the receptionist could tell.

'At 20.43 hours tonight, the Ninth Commando of Never Again successfully carried out the execution of the Fascist pig Valerio Mariana, leader of the filthy Nazi vermin *Noi da Soli*.

'The pig Mariana died squealing. Another Fascist swine was executed with him. The Ninth Commando also triumphed in achieving the total destruction of the disgusting lair of the scum.

'This is one more glorious victory for Never Again. In cleansing the earth of such creatures we are ensuring the safety of millions, for this generation and the future. We are ensuring all people will be free from fear of death and torture, whatever the colour of their skin, their religion, their race or their way of life.

'We utterly condemn the empty, self-seeking mouthings of politicians who declare that Nazis and fascist bastards have the right to speak. They gave them that right while already the first victims of the new Fascism lie in their freshly dug graves. We demand that the governments of Europe, of the

Americas, of the world, root out and destroy the filthy scourge of fascism.

'We also utterly condemn the cowardly and despicable attempts by these politicians to limit immigration. This is a sop to the Fascists, a means by which to appease them. We warn the politicians and the governments who endorse these views and seek to make them law that in doing so they become our enemy. We demand an immediate halt to the strangulation of the rights of the asylum seeker. The consequences of rejecting our demands will be felt in the highest levels.

'Time is running out for the Nazis and for the craven politicians who support them. They do not have long to learn. We reiterate: for every hair that they harm, we will take a head. Tomorrow will never belong to them.

'Never Again will millions go quietly to the slaughter.

'Our voice is the people's voice. The victory belongs to us.'

In the kitchen the music stopped.

'We interrupt the programme to bring you a newsflash.'

The normally flat voice of the presenter was high with excitement. 'Police have just confirmed as genuine a communique received by Radio Torino from Never Again, the anti-fascist extremists . . .'

The man's words were drowned out by cheers and whoops.

Zoe looked from one face to another; watching Dani and Anya hug and twirl and stamp round the table. 'Am I even here,' she thought. 'Or am I dreaming all this?'

She jumped when Xavier gently touched her hair.

'You are in shock,' he told her and she felt absurdly grateful to him for the explanation.

'Shock,' she repeated silently. 'Not mad. Thank God.' The relief obliterated everything else. The sight and sounds of Dani and Anya, now arguing loudly over the fish, simply faded away. Zoe focused solely on Xavier, seeing only him; his spiky hair, young brown face and troubled blue eyes.

Like a shy boy on a first date, he went on stroking her hair then ran his fingers lightly down her cheek. The awkwardness of the movement, his rough fingers on her flesh, suddenly aroused her. She saw the fair stubble above his upper lip and thought it quite perfect; the intensity of her longing for him shook her. It was like nothing she had felt before.

'It is good you feel shocked.' Xavier was speaking slowly and softly, a different voice entirely to the one that had screamed those orders. 'It's natural. It shows you still care.'

He paused; his caressing stopped and he looked over at the others. Zoe knew that he was wondering how much more to say; that it mattered to him what Dani and Anya thought. Herself, she found that she did not care; for the first time that she could remember she felt free of all restraint.

Xavier cleared his throat. 'We have all experienced this shock but we have come through it. You will too. Come.'

Willingly she let him take her hand and lead her from the room. As they passed the stove she saw Anya frown at them and start to say something, but Dani hushed her.

In the bedroom Xavier switched on the light and closed the door. There was a double bed with a bolster and a white sheet; a few clothes lay scattered on the floor. He set her down on the bed, carefully as though she might break, and walked swiftly to the casement-window, shutting out the night-sounds.

His body moved lightly across the floor and he stood before her, hesitating.

'Are you all right?'

She nodded, feeling much older than him. She craved him, could he not tell? All she wanted was to feel his naked skin against her own, to have his lips on hers and absorb every part of him.

He was still staring down at her. 'You are not angry that I lied to you? About nobody being in the building?'

She gazed up at him, wondering at the question. As if anger mattered now.

'It was for your own good,' he said.

He stripped off his white T-shirt and sat at last beside her. He stroked her hair, edged closer, undid the buttons of her shirt, one by one. He bent over her, taking her breasts in his hands, kissing them. She moaned; she wanted him so much it hurt.

'You're so lovely,' he whispered.

She lifted up his head in her hands, kissed his nose, brushed her cheek against his stubble, feeling the softness of his mouth. They fell back together on the bed, struggling out of their clothes, moving hard against each other, easily into rhythm.

'Oh God,' she cried out.

'Hold on, hold on.' They collapsed together into each other's arms, their breathing coming in gasps, their hearts pounding. They fell asleep at once, Zoe's head against his chest.

She dreamed. She was back in that room and the boy with the terror in his eyes was in front of her. She watched his lips move; she tried to hear what he was saying but she could not understand his words and time was running out. The boy opened his mouth wide; there was the crack of the guns, hers and Anya's, and an end to all pleading. There came a long, piercing scream.

Her scream, she was screaming.

'Zoe, Zoe, wake up!' Xavier was kneeling over her, one hand on each shoulder, his face white and scared above her own.

'Xav!' Anya stood in the room. 'Shut her up! Christ!'

Xavier slapped his hand over Zoe's mouth but the scream still bubbled inside her; she could not control it.

'What d'you think I'm trying to do?' he yelled. 'Get those bloody pills!' He turned back. 'Zoe, please, please be quiet. Please, Zoe.'

She began to choke. Anya came running back into the room. She had a silver strip of tablets in one hand, a glass of water in the other. She had spilled most of it. Xavier jerked Zoe upright.

'Zoe, you've got to take these pills. They'll make you feel better, OK? I'm going to take my hand away; you take the pills and drink the water. Understand?'

She was past comprehension. He pulled her mouth open, shoved in the pills and put the water to her lips. He clamped her jaws shut and she swallowed, desperate for air.

'Be calm, be calm,' she heard him say, over and over again until his voice grew further away and his face blurred, and everything went dark . . .

*   *   *

The following morning, Never Again's communique, translated into English, stamped and sealed in a security file, landed with a slap on Barney Turl's desk in London.

Considering the care that the author had taken with it, making sure it contained just the right blend of jubilation, explanation and warning, and the pains taken to time it – two seconds too short for a trace – Barney awarded it scant respect.

He picked up the file, glared at the red 'Immediate' sticker and unwillingly broke the seal. Papers and photographs spilled out. He shuffled through them, picked up the translated text, and cursed it and its writer.

If Never Again went on like this he would have to do a full report for his superior; make recommendations, suggest some feasible plan of action, then an 'overseeing' strategy, so-called. That meant endless meetings and briefings with civil servants, both internally within the Service and externally at the Home Office, as well as with one or two Special Branch people at the Yard.

They would all want to know what the risk was, and that would be where Barney came in, balancing on the tightrope as always. As team leader of ORAF (Operational Risk Assessment (Foreign), Co-ordination and Planning) within the Security Service, it was his job to gather intelligence on all overseas terrorist groups (excluding Irish; there was another department for that), analyse the potential threat to the Realm and advise accordingly.

It would have been fine, he often told himself, if Lavinia Hargreaves, his director, had been a fair-minded individual who appreciated the problems involved in making such assessments: that, however good one's intelligence might be, there was always an element of chance, of trusting one's judgement and experience. But Hargreaves was his worst critic: 'Don't give me hunches; I want percentage risks'. Down to the last fraction, Barney thought bitterly. Sometimes he felt he could never win: too much caution and he would be accused of over-reacting, wasting time, resources and above all, money; too little and something was bound to go wrong.

He glared down at the communique again. Angry words,

and righteous justification; he had seen it all before, hundreds of times. Each group convinced, of course, that theirs was the one true path, the only way forward. Barney was a fair man; he paused in his internal diatribe to consider Never Again's remit. He grunted; at least he had some sympathy for their cause, if not for the means they used.

The same could hardly be said for some of the groups it had been his job to monitor over the last twenty-three years. When he had first joined the European team of MI5, he had daily dealt with the murderous doings of Baader-Meinhof, the Italian Red Brigades, and Action Directe in France. He had not been able to comprehend how these groups had deluded themselves into believing they were fighting for the people, when ninety-nine per cent of the people made it perfectly plain that they were extremely happy living under the 'capitalist confines' of democracy and that they regarded the revolutionaries as nasty, vicious little thugs who should be shot or locked up for life.

Yes, he could understand why Never Again had come into existence. He, more than most, knew how dangerous the new Nazism was; how quickly it had taken root across Europe and how unbelievable it was that Fascism was once more politically acceptable. It was enough to make a man despair, even a middle-aged man like himself.

He stared sightlessly out of the window of his third floor office. It was not a good view: the smoke-blackened back of Vauxhall railway station and the top of a high-rise block of flats. When the Security Service had been rehoused in Thames House beside the bridge on the bank of the Thames, Barney's team had not been included. Office space, apparently, had been at a premium: his department and two others were now accommodated on the other side of the road, beside a railway arch in a pre-war office block that had been due for demolition. Barney did not mind: he found Thames House faintly ludicrous; a building that resembled an elaborate wedding cake decorated with Christmas trees was ill-suited, in his opinion, to the discreet work of intelligence-gathering. Give him a dark, poky office any day.

For Barney – a little jowly now, with his once red-gold hair sprinkled with grey – the glamour of the job had long since worn off. The 8.26am from Berrylands had seen to that. Even Alice, whom he suspected had once found his secrecy exciting, no longer tried teasing him into indiscretion. She told her friends upfront that he was a spook.

He picked up the document again and read the attached Turin police report. The first page was purely factual, noting the discovery of the bodies, cause of death, etc. There was an additional sheet on *Noi da Soli*, its motivation, targets and membership, and a brief biography of Mariana. All in all, unpleasant reading. The report finished with a 'personal' note from the Turin police chief saying that the Italian authorities had little data on Never Again and would welcome information from other countries' security services.

'Bet they would,' growled Barney. He turned to the computer console beside his desk, trolled through the document listings for the relevant file, pressed the return key for Never Again.

The first operations – in September of the previous year – had been petty enough. Firebombings, raids on Neo-Nazi meetings and demonstrations. There had also been a spate of suspicious accidents resulting in quite serious injuries to some Neo Nazi sympathisers; nothing proven, but probably Never Again's handiwork. But then things had escalated fast. A car-bomb in Dusseldorf that killed two Neo-Nazis; the assassination of a right-wing judge in Bilbao; another fatal shooting in Marseille, then the bombing of a meeting of Fascists in Lyons, 1 dead, 18 injured. Three more bombings of similar targets in Hamburg, Antwerp, Bergen, plus numerous 'punishment' beatings, some serious enough to have killed. Net damage: 12 dead, 104 injured. Then this last.

There was no doubt: Never Again was moving up the league and spreading its wings across Europe. It would only be a matter of time before they came to London.

Or recruited a Brit – if they hadn't done so already.

Whether or not it came to anything in the end, it was time to start taking this bunch seriously. He put a call through to his assistant for an early meeting.

*   *   *

'See one of your chaps got himself topped last night.'

Chris Lomax, Editor in charge of Special Investigations of the Sunday paper, *The Clarion*, prided himself on getting straight to the point. In doing so, his listeners were often left trailing behind.

The man he was addressing, a man in his early thirties with dark brown hair and a crumpled white shirt, no tie, looked up from his desk. 'What chaps are you talking about?'

'Chrissake, Anderson! Don't you read the wires? D'you know how much it costs to have AP and Reuters in this newsroom? I do, I can tell you. Management tells me every bloody day! And every bloody day I tell them it's essential for my journalists to have both services. And you, my so-called Chief Investigator, my Man with his Finger on the Pulse, you sit there and say "What chaps?" Christ!'

Matt Anderson let the fury roll over his head. Lomax's temper was legendary: it peaked and was spent in seconds. The man raved, Matt thought, as he continued to read the document before him, in the same habitual way that others coughed or adjusted their collars. He ran a finger round the inside of his own collar; it felt loose, he had lost weight since Louise left.

'Damn you! Are you listening to me?'

Matt grinned up at him. 'I'm all ears, Chris. But what chaps? Arms-dealers, fake gurus, drug-barons or what? Who're you talking about?'

Lomax glowered back. He was not a very tall man; he had white cropped hair and a salt and pepper beard. One of his more repeatable nicknames in the newsroom was The Badger. He was fifty-one and had worked his guts out for *The Clarion* for twenty years, after doing ten in the northern provinces. He was proud of the fact that he had never been to university; he liked to say that he had risen through the ranks the hard way. Just for once, he thought now, it would be nice if someone showed him a bit of respect. Sitting up straight, looking keen and attentive would be a start. He grimaced; if he was hoping for any of that from Matt Anderson, he was in for a long wait.

'All right, smart man, all right. It was one of your Neo-Nazis, as it happens.'

'Oh?' Matt switched on. The document, on the high incidence of childhood leukaemia around a nuclear power station, fell from his hands. His face had adopted what Louise used to call his 'rabbit' look: eyes wide open and watchful, shoulders tensed forward. She used to say she could see his nose twitching.

Lomax noticed too. It was what made Anderson one of the best journalists he had come across. Give him the sniff of a story and he was after it like a bloodhound. It might take him weeks, and the results might be unexpected, but Anderson always brought home the goods in the end. Lomax could forgive a good reporter a lot. He produced a scrap of paper from his pocket and peered at it through his bi-focals.

'Two of them in fact. Uuh . . . Turin last night. Both men shot at close range . . . Blah, blah . . . Bodies burnt beyond recognition . . . dental records . . . Oh! Hey, you'll like this, Anderson. I didn't see this before . . .' He paused to scan the rest of the story.

'What? What didn't you see?' Matt had to resist the urge to snatch the paper out of his hands. He had been late into the newsroom that morning; otherwise he would have read the wires himself. Neo-Nazis were one of his specialities, a subject he had been working on, on and off, for two years.

The previous December he had been the first journalist to find out about Never Again. It had been a sensational story. The new terrorism for the new Europe: anti-fascist. Matt knew that he had only scratched the surface and there was a lot more to come out on the group. If only he had the time to devote to it, he could crack it. The trouble was, he was never given enough time.

'Yep,' Lomax said slowly. 'It's that lot you wrote about, Never Again. Seems it's their first assassination in Italy.'

'Who'd they get?'

'Some chap called . . . Valerio Mariana, and a young bloke, Emil . . .'

'Mariana! Don't you know who he is?'

'No, I don't. And don't shout. You'll frighten the secretaries. So tell me who is, or was, this Mariana?'

'Only the leader of that Nazi lot who burnt down the

synagogue in Milan last year. You know, where the Barmitzvah was going on. They killed most of one family – don't you remember? Two kids and the grandparents.'

'Yeah, now you mention it, I do. Right,' Lomax finally released the scrap of paper into Matt's care. 'Do a few paragraphs on it for Sunday, will you?'

'A few paragraphs?' Matt stared at him. 'You're joking! This is a major story, Chris. Give me a couple of days on it, let me go over there, dig around a bit, see what I get. This is a potential splash.'

Lomax studied him quietly for a few seconds. 'Anderson, your trouble is you think every story is a potential splash. It isn't.

'This one won't be because, one,' he stuck his thumb in the air, 'there isn't any money in the Home News budget to send you to Italy. Two,' his index finger joined his thumb, 'even if there was, I wouldn't send you because you are primarily a Home News journalist and I only let you go Foreign when I, and I repeat, I, think you have a big enough story, and three,' his middle finger shot up, 'and most important, so I'll say it slowly: This is not a British story. Never Again are not British; their victims were not British and the murders did not take place in Britain. And we are a British newspaper so we have little interest in it, do we?'

He smiled brightly. 'So a couple of pars, Anderson, if you please. And I need a lead for Page Five out of you this week too, so get busy.'

Xavier glanced at his watch. It was nearly twenty-four hours since the killings; time was running out, they needed to move on.

'Shit!' He kicked the kitchen door violently. It slammed shut.

Anya looked up from the magazine she was reading. 'Is she not any better?'

'How do I know? She's still asleep. Those pills must be fucking strong.'

Sleep was meant to heal people, wasn't it? Xavier hoped so. He knew what he had to do if Zoe completely cracked up. Never Again could not afford passengers, nor could it risk

releasing someone who might turn informer. He willed her
to snap out of it.

In the bedroom, Zoe woke. Her sleep had been heavy
and her dreams fragmented but vivid. Blinking in the semi-
darkness, she thought that she was in London at her brother's
flat; or in her room on campus or even back in the six-bed
dormitory at school.

She sat up slowly in bed. Her head felt woolly and her senses
dulled and slow. She pulled the thin sheet around her and saw
her clothes lying tangled on the bare floor. She remembered
Xavier and how she had wanted to devour him. She frowned
slightly: she had never been like that before; so hungry for the
simple pleasure of sex. Strange, she thought, she felt nothing
towards him now except fading gratitude for blotting out the
horror that her mind had not been able to accept.

She put her hand up to her face. It was sore and salty with
dried tears. She began to remember more.

From the corridor outside she heard the radio in the
kitchen and, very distantly, the murmur of voices arguing
or just talking loudly. Her mind cleared. She swung her legs
down on to the floor and stood up. She got dressed shakily
and started slowly towards the kitchen to join the others.

She knew that, whatever she had intended, whatever paths
had led her to this place, she was one of them now, on the
side of the killers . . .

Part One

Chapter One

Fourteen months earlier

'Time.'

'That wasn't twenty minutes!'

Zoe rolled over onto her back, fastening her bikini top as she did so. 'It was.' She sat up to apply more Factor 15. It was early afternoon in August and the Greek sun was fierce. Squinting about her, she saw that the beach was nearly empty; just the desperate, the palest remained. 'And you,' Zoe told herself brutally, 'are the palest.' On this, their fourth day, she was slightly pink, and then only in patches. She squeezed the Ambre Solaire onto her tummy and yelped: the liquid was boiling.

Annabelle, already nicely darkening, turned her head and opened one eye. 'You're going red,' she said.

The acquisition of a suntan, they had both agreed at the outset, was an absolute essential. Not that they were frivolous about 'doing' Europe – quite the opposite. Although their student rail tickets gave them almost unlimited travel they were determined to stick to their plan to visit as many former Eastern Bloc countries as possible.

'Before they get just like everywhere else,' Zoe said.

'A McDonalds on every corner.'

'A Body Shop in the precinct.'

The prospect of little food, dodgy transport – their guide-book warned them of 'erratic' timetables in many places – and basic accommodation did not bother them; it all added to the excitement of exploration. But white legs and pasty faces were another matter. People would know they were not real travellers.

They were both twenty-one, students at the same university in the West Midlands, Zoe reading English and French,

Annabelle English and German Literature. The trauma of end-of-year exams had left them greenish-looking.

'Sort of pudgy. Unappetising.' Zoe stared at herself in the mirror of her study/bedroom.

'Dorks,' lamented Annabelle. 'That's what we look like – a couple of dorks.'

Zoe was emptying her make-up bag in search of the scarlet lipstick she had never dared wear. 'Colour! We must have colour!'

'And men! We must have men!'

Thus, one week out of the six was allocated for tanning. Annabelle, dark-haired and olive-skinned, was quite confident that would be long enough. Zoe, blonde and grey-eyed with that Scottish fairness so easily alarmed by the sun, doubted it. From what she remembered, she took weeks and weeks to tan. Well, she could always buy fake.

'OK. Where?'

In the end, they had chosen Greece because it was at the right end of Europe, and the little island of Aegina simply because it was the first stop the ferry made from the mainland. As soon as they had disembarked, they had been engulfed by islanders, offering rooms. The one they chose was in a family's villa, overlooking a pistachio orchard and within ten minutes of the beach.

Zoe lay down again to bake. She would have liked to have carried on reading her book, a Ruth Rendell mystery, but as she was now, flat on her back, it was too awkward to hold. And it was so hot. I could go for a swim, she thought, then cursed. It would mean reapplying the sun-cream. Getting a tan, she told herself crossly, was sheer bloody murder.

At the end of the week, they argued. Annabelle had met Mark, an Australian science graduate and musician who was spending the entire summer on the islands.

'Why don't we do the same thing? We could spend days on the beach and go round the bars with Mark at night. He wants a couple of girl-singers. We could earn some money.'

'No way. We're going to Albania and Poland and Moscow, remember?'

'Yeah, but a couple more weeks here wouldn't hurt.'

'You can do what you like but I'm leaving tomorrow.'

'Oh for God's sake, Zoe, don't be such a Puritan! You could have a really good time if you let yourself. There's loads of men on their own in this place.'

'I want to travel.'

'You want to be a nun!'

Zoe went quiet at that and Annabelle felt mean. For some reason she had never understood, Zoe had never had much luck with men. In the two years of their friendship, she had, to Annabelle's knowledge, only had a couple of brief affairs: a Law student in the first year and a post-graduate a few months ago, but nothing long-term or terribly serious. Perhaps she had wild flings at home but Annabelle suspected not. It was a mystery: Zoe was undoubtedly very attractive – prettier, she admitted, than herself – enviably slim and good fun in her own rather reserved way. Annabelle guessed that might be her problem; the quiet manner could be mistaken for aloofness or disinterest. She herself, at first, had dismissed Zoe as a snob; it had taken her a term or so to realise she was just shy and private.

'Very private,' Annabelle considered. She was probably Zoe's closest friend and yet she knew hardly anything about her background except that her parents were quite old and lived in the Scottish Highlands and her brother had a flat in London. She was aware that Zoe, like herself, had had a year off before starting university but Zoe had never really disclosed what she had done: 'I lived in Edinburgh and went to France for a bit,' was all she had said. She made it sound so dull! Whereas Annabelle had made sure within her first week that everyone on her course had known that she had spent 'the most marvellous year' nannying in the States.

Annabelle gave herself a mental shrug. She and Zoe were very different, that was all. Perhaps that was why they got on so well. Whatever, Annabelle had not meant to hurt her feelings. She would ask Mark to pay Zoe some attention.

As it happened, Mark resolved the matter himself that night by taking the ferry to Santorini. He left a message for Annabelle with his landlady: he had a girlfriend at home in Sydney and thought it was time he moved on.

'Bastard! Going off like that! As if I wanted him anyway!' Annabelle blushed then laughed. 'And me thinking I was such a good judge of character! So where to? Albania or Bulgaria? Your choice.'

They went to Albania, taking a series of trains from Athens. The backwardness of the new democracy stunned them; horses and carts were very much in evidence, cars were scarce and an unimaginable luxury for the vast majority of the population. People were not starving but there were hardly any goods in the shops and buying soap took most of one morning.

They found that, in Albanian terms, they were extremely wealthy but that money did not guarantee very much. For the price of a dormitory bed in Athens, they booked into a 'Five Star' hotel in Tirana and discovered that their room had no lock on the door or curtains at the windows. Water came on only for two hours, between ten and eleven at night and six and seven in the morning.

Their railcards were not much use inside the country. At the main railway station, a charming Tourist Information Officer informed them that there were problems with the track in the southern part of the country.

'We'll go north then.'

'Ah. It is not good to go north. Not so good food.'

'Oh, we don't mind. We'll take some. What time is the train?'

The young woman looked worried. 'Not certain. Perhaps this evening, perhaps tomorrow. Perhaps,' she smiled at them, 'you would like to stay in Tirana?'

After two days they succeeded in catching a train west across the border into Macedonia. They ran out of food and for a day lived on Polo-mints and Coca-cola. When they arrived in the Bulgarian capital, the new hotels and abundant, well-stocked shops seemed intoxicatingly prosperous. They ate out in a couple of restaurants, spent too much money and drank a lot of Bulgarian wine.

'What's the date?' asked Zoe on their third morning in the city.

'Uh, the sixteenth. Why?'

'D'you realise we're nearly half way through? We've only got three and a bit weeks left. We can still see a lot, but we'd better get a move on.'

They agreed: the next five days had to be pure travel and the countries blurred into each other. Of Romania they remembered a night spent in a dormitory-style bedroom shared with a dozen others, male and female; an evening at the railway station in Bucharest where dozens of street-children slept rough. They had both cried to see them: some no more than toddlers, thin to the point of starvation and filthy. They had given them all that they could: apples, chewing gum, Biros and a little money, but they had both felt hopeless and guilty too that they had so much while these children had nothing.

The Ukraine seemed to stretch on and on: mile after mile of countryside so green it made Zoe feel bilious. Sitting upright – the only position she found comfortable – she tried counting trees, then cows. She gave up when she reached a thousand of each. There was a soft grunt from Annabelle; looking over at her, she saw that her friend had fallen asleep.

Zoe studied her. Annabelle looked so peaceful, utterly engrossed in sleep; her dark hair a tangled mess, not a frown or a crease-mark in sight, lips slightly parted, breathing steadily. Zoe wondered if Annabelle realised how lucky she was and how much she, Zoe, longed for her easy self-confidence and the ability she had, and did not even seem to be aware of, of getting on with people. Zoe did not find it at all easy to mix and form friendships.

She guessed that shyness was in her genes. Her mother had lived at home with her parents in Edinburgh, working in desultory fashion in a small museum, until she had met her father, a minor landowner and banker, at a friend's wedding. It had been rather romantic, love at first sight and marriage within six months. They had made their home in the austere, somewhat remote vast stone house that stood on the edge of a glen in the Spey valley that had been home to Zoe's father's family for several generations. He and his new bride had few friends; they were blissfully happy with each other and it was twelve years before they had their first child, a boy, Alasdair. One child, they had always said, and rather tactlessly continued to say, was more than enough. Hence Zoe's conception seven years later was a mistake.

'Heavens, I was forty-two – too old for babies – when you came along!' Zoe's mother was fond of exclaiming. Even now, Zoe thought, her mother sometimes looked surprised when she saw her.

If she was shy by nature, the trait had been carefully nurtured by her upbringing. As daughter of the Laird – ridiculous title, especially when nearly all his land had gone in death duties, and he was 'Laird' only of a couple of small farms and the field where the village played Shinty – she was viewed as a special child by the three teachers at the Church of Scotland primary school.

'Zoe, dear, tell the class about your parents' skiing holiday in Verbier. About how your mummy saw Prince Charles with his new girlfriend. Come along, dear, come to the front.'

And she would have to stand by the blackboard, stuttering and looking at the resentment in her classmates' faces.

Playtimes were a nightmare. She was seldom hurt physically, but emotionally it was a different matter. Most adults remember one or two occasions when they were the butt of the school bullies but for Zoe, looking back, it had seemed an almost daily occurrence.

At home, with the exception of Agatha, her nanny, she was on her own. Alasdair had been sent to boarding school before she could properly remember him and her parents, though fond of her in their own way, preferred their own company. Quite often, on Friday afternoons she would be greeted on her arrival home from school by the sight of her mother and father packing themselves into the Landrover.

'Daddy and I are going off for the weekend, darling. Agatha has said she doesn't mind staying with you. All right? See you Sunday then. Give mummy a kiss. Be a good girl. We'll bring you back something lovely! Big smile, byeee!'

Zoe grew into her solitariness, and would go for long walks on her own, a small figure tramping though the glen, hailed by the occasional shepherd or fisherman. She lived inside her imagination, inventing friends and adventures; she grew to be self-reliant, rather secretive and socially awkward.

Boarding school at eleven was a terrible shock. The establishment, single-sex and old-fashioned, was on the Scottish Borders near Kelso. All the other girls seemed so huge and self-assured; everything was alien and seemed hostile. Once again, Zoe was bullied, but this time the bullies seemed better at it, crueller with their remarks, and there was no escaping home at the end of the day. She was unable to see that many of the new girls were given the same treatment. Her sense of being different – peculiar – deepened. She withdrew and built a protective shell around herself, living inside it with her dreams. Out of boredom initially, but then real enjoyment, she studied phenomenally hard. Literature and languages became the loves of her life; a poem could make her feel bathed in a warm golden light. Her teachers enthused about her sensitivity and perception; her peers called her snooty and a swot.

Her lifeline had been Alasdair. Over the years, during school holidays they had become friends. Even as a boy of ten, Alasdair had been very protective of her, his 'baby' sister; now, Zoe smiled to herself, he still treated her as if she was about six.

'So what d'you think of boarding school?' he had asked her after first term.

She had just looked at him.

'Oh. That bad. Don't let them get you down, Zo. It won't last forever.'

He was right, of course. School had ended eventually. She had been offered a place at an Oxford college – great prestige for the school, their first Oxbridge success – but at the last moment and scarcely knowing why, she had turned it down. Instead she opted to take a year off and go to a red-brick university in the Midlands.

'Have you completely taken leave of your senses?' The headmistress had been quite puce with rage.

For the first time Zoe had experienced the intoxicating power of emerging adulthood. She outstared the woman. 'No. I can do what I like. I'm not a child any more.'

'I shall write to your parents. They'll make you see sense.'

But her parents, thankfully true to form, had not been duly concerned. 'Do whatever you like, darling,' her mother had said on the phone. 'We're very proud of you,' she had added as an afterthought.

Zoe had meant to do so much in that year off. She was going to travel, maybe as an au pair, go to Paris and then on to Rome; perhaps stay with Alasdair for a bit in London, visiting all the art galleries she had never seen, all those theatres and cinemas. Everything had suddenly looked so exciting, so bright. She was going to put school and her loneliness behind her; launch herself into the world and make friends, have boyfriends, be popular . . .

The train began to slow down; a station was at long last approaching. Zoe grimaced: her year-off, her 'year of experience' had hardly turned out as she had planned.

'Hey. Where are we?' Opposite her Annabelle had woken up and was blinking at the landscape. 'How long have I been asleep? I haven't missed anything, have I?'

'Only a couple of countries. Don't worry about it.'

They disembarked at Vilnius, capital of Lithuania, partly to honour their original plan of visiting the first USSR state to declare independence and partly because they were sick to death of the train that they had been on for thirty-two hours.

They found the old Communist hotel their guidebook recommended, near a bridge by the River Vilyna, dumped their bags and went out walking.

Even in early afternoon sunshine much of the city had that drab, uniform Soviet look they had already seen so much of and which depressed their spirits. A splendid baroque cathedral, its golden dome glowing in the greyness, came as a surprise; they went slowly round it, savouring the rich heavy colours of its religious paintings and icons. Emerging in the late afternoon, they discovered the old quarter: cobbled streets, mediaeval city walls and inside one ancient building – a shrine to the Blessed Virgin – they saw pilgrims dressed in black painfully ascending holy stairs on their knees, their fingers telling rosaries as they did so.

'I wouldn't have thought any of this would have survived,' Zoe said softly, in deference to the atmosphere. 'I thought the Communists stamped out all religion.'

There was a tiny cough behind her.

'It was considered to be as a museum, if you please.' The speaker was a man of around thirty, wearing a dark suit, white shirt and tie. He was hovering in shadows by the doorway. He took a step in their direction, smiling hopefully. 'You wish a guide?'

'Oh no, sorry, we're students,' Annabelle began automatically.

Zoe nudged her. She had seen the defeated, rather desperate look in the man's pale face and could not bear it; it reminded her too much of the street-children. His suit, she saw, was of very thin material, in places it looked transparent and it literally hung on his sparse frame.

'We don't have much money,' she ventured tentatively.

'Zoe! We can't afford a guide.'

The man took another step forward. Closer to, he seemed sallower and hungrier. 'I am not very much. Fifteen dollars? With car, twenty. Beautiful countryside of Lithuania. For whole of the day. Yes?'

'Yes,' Zoe agreed. Beside her, Annabelle tutted and sighed loudly.

The man beamed, seized Zoe's hand and pumped it up and down. 'Thank you, Madam ... Miss, thank you. My name,' he touched his breast pocket, 'is Juonas. I am ... I was In-Tourist guide for six years. Now independent. My English is good, yes? For no money today I will show you the museums of Vilnius. As thank-you gift. Please, to follow.'

By nine o'clock that evening Annabelle was seething. They had only just managed to get rid of Juonas and were back in their hotel room.

'Four hours! Four bloody hours of museums! And it's not as if there was anything worth seeing in them anyway!'

'I'm sorry, Belle. I'll pay for him.'

'And we've got him all day tomorrow! "I am being here at eight in the morning," he says! And he's so boring: all that detail: "One more interesting note, young ladies. It is a not known fact that here, in this spot, in 1703 the ninth Duke of Lithuania passed by!" Zoe, honestly! Why not sack him?'

'Oh, Belle, we couldn't! Look how thin he is. It's not his fault he's so awful; it's all that In-Tourist Soviet stuff. He thinks it's how a guide should be. You know, "Foreigners have to be educated". Poor Juonas, he hasn't worked all month. He needs us.'

'Huh! Needs our money you mean. The reason he hasn't worked all month, Zoe you innocent child, is he's awful. Your trouble is, you're too soft.'

'Think of his wife and little baby.'

Between museums, Juonas had told them all about himself: his years studying English at university; acceptance and training as an In-Tourist guide; marriage to the daughter of the local Communist Party leader; birth of first child; sudden loss of job and security after Independence; struggle to survive and now Leda was expecting their second child in December.

Annabelle scowled. 'All right, all right. I'm the wicked witch. But don't think I'm showing intelligent interest tomorrow. He's all yours; I'm just coming for the ride.'

The next morning, seeing Juonas standing in the lobby exactly where they had left him and wearing exactly the same clothes, it passed through Zoe's mind that he had been there all night: patiently, uncomplainingly waiting for them to reappear.

Their car, a pale blue Skoda with orange rust-marks, was waiting for them outside. The driver was an ancient-looking man hunched like a spider behind the wheel; he said nothing to them but started the engine as soon as the doors were opened.

Juonas installed Annabelle and Zoe in the back. From the front seat, he turned to face them, smiling and, Zoe noticed despondently, looking full of energy. 'To start we first are visiting two castles. The first was builded in the 14th century and is most noting for its high-sided walls . . .'

His voice went on and on. He had a way of speaking, Zoe noticed, that would have handicapped the most interesting conversationalist: his intonation was all wrong, accentuating the wrong syllables but with a determined 'tum-te-tum' beat. She found herself longing for temporary deafness.

The morning passed with tortuous slowness. At the second castle, Annabelle refused to get out of the car, claiming ear-ache. Juonas looked puzzled; Zoe felt like screaming.

It was a stiflingly hot day and by noon the heat inside the Skoda was overwhelming. In the back, the seats were melting; she and Annabelle were wearing T-shirts and shorts and the plastic stuck painfully to their legs. They were on their way to Panerai Forest, 'another beautiful spot', according to Juonas. All Zoe could see, stretching ahead on either side of the road, was thousands upon thousands of pine trees.

Annabelle nudged her sharply in the side. 'Look,' she said, pointing out of her window. 'That's where I want to be. In that. Tell him to stop.'

It was a large, dark pool, fringed prettily with trees, and set a little way into the forest. Zoe saw a handful of people swimming in it, looking cool and having fun.

'Go on. Tell him.'

Zoe took a deep breath. 'Juonas?'

His head whipped round. 'Young lady?'

'Juonas, we were wondering if we could go for a swim? Just to get cool before we go to the beauty spot? It would not take very long ...'

She trailed off; the man's face was sagging with disappointment and she suddenly feared he might weep. 'Oh, don't worry Juonas,' she lied quickly. 'It doesn't matter.'

Next to her, Annabelle humphed audibly and glared.

'We don't even have swimming things with us,' Zoe whispered, but Annabelle did not answer. Zoe glanced at her watch: only another eight hours to go.

They all sat in silence after that. The car turned off the main road onto a rough wide track that cut a swathe through the trees. Overhead the branches met, blocking out the sunlight.

The road ended abruptly in a vast tarmacked car-park that was empty apart from themselves. It looked rather forlorn, Zoe thought, as if it was waiting for the In-Tourist coaches that did not come any more.

Juonas was already outside, opening her door. 'Now we are visiting the memorial to the Glorious Dead of the Soviet Union', he announced brightly.

Zoe tore her legs off the back seat and got out. 'I thought you said we were coming to a beauty spot.'

'Beautiful memorial spot.'

The forest edged the car-park on three sides; along the fourth, running out of sight, was a single railway track. Zoe walked over to it: the rails were rusted and some of the wooden sleepers had rotted to nothing; the line had obviously not been used for some time. She squinted along the track into the distance: it had been precision-made, straight as an arrow. She wondered idly where it had once gone to or come from.

Annabelle's voice made her jump. 'Any chance of catching an Express out of here?'

Zoe giggled. 'Ssh! He'll hear you.'

'God, you're right. And he'd probably know every detail of every train that's ever passed this way and tell us all about it.'

By the edge of the forest, Juonas waved enthusiastically. 'Ladies! Young ladies! We start.'

'Goody, goody,' said Annabelle. 'Come on, then. Let's get it over with.'

Juonas was standing beside a large lump of rock. Closer to, Zoe saw that it was some kind of sculpture; she could make out the figures of people, their arms and legs entwined. Carved into the stone was an inscription in Russian.

Juonas cleared his throat. 'Oh, make it a short one, Juonas, please,' she pleaded silently.

'Here we are arrived at another beautiful spot in the country of Lithuania. Here the peoples of Vilnius bring their childrens for picnics.'

'Is there a pool, then?' asked Annabelle.

'Pool?'

'For swimming in. You know, like the one back there.' Annabelle mimed the breast stroke.

Juonas looked worriedly at her, then coughed and turned his attention to Zoe.

'In the war, in this beautiful spot, there appeared the Fascists and their collaborators.'

'Fascists?' Zoe queried. 'Oh, you mean the Nazis.'

'Yes. The Nazis, together with the enemies of the Soviet Union, came here and killed by shootings many people.'

'There was a battle here? Soldiers fought here?'

Juonas frowned and shook his head. 'No, no. Not battle.

Men, women, children, babies were shotted.' He pointed to the monument, and there amongst the arms and legs were indeed the smaller limbs of infants.

Zoe felt her stomach turn. 'Why, Juonas? Why were they killed?'

He looked surprised. 'These were Jews, and Soviet prisoners of war, politicals, gypsies. Also, childrens and old peoples with sicknesses in their heads.' He tapped his own forehead and paused. 'You do not know these things?'

Zoe found herself stammering. 'I didn't realise . . . I mean, I've heard about what happened. The Holocaust. The Jews. And concentration camps and things . . . But I didn't know it was like this . . . I thought people were gassed. I didn't know it happened here.'

'Oh yes, young lady. Many, many thousands. Here, in this spot 230,000 citizens were killed by shootings.' He nodded towards her railway line. 'The Jews and Communists came on the trains from all countries in Europe to be shotted here. The young men walked from Vilnius, the old men and womens and the babies and childrens were taken on trains and trucks.'

He turned his back. 'And now, we will be going to the pits.'

'Pits?'

'Where people were shotted.'

'Oh God,' said Annabelle. 'I'm not sure I want to go to any pits. Zoe, what d'you think?'

Zoe was about to agree and to tell Juonas that this was hardly holiday viewing, when something stopped her. Afterwards, when she tried to remember her reasoning, it became blurred, but in it there had been a mixture of bravery, or maybe bravura, morbid fascination (she had, in all honesty, to admit this), and a voice in her head that said, 'See it. You'll only pass this way once.'

Juonas smiled at her, 'You follow?'

She turned to Annabelle. 'Oh, let's have a look. It can't be that bad. Just another historical spot.'

Annabelle shrugged. 'Well, OK.'

Inside the wood it was dark, and the fresh tang of pine was overpowering. Juonas led them swiftly along a path and

beneath their shoes dry needles snapped like pistol shots.
They walked in single-file, Zoe coming last. 'Was this what
it was like?' she asked herself. 'Did people walk like this in
quiet lines, or did they scream and try to run?' She shivered
and, out of the corner of her eye, saw something move on
her right.

She peered between the trees: surely she had seen someone,
or the shadow of someone? Between the trunks, particles of
dust danced. No, it was nothing, a trick of the light. 'Stop it,'
she told herself sternly. 'Stop spooking yourself.'

Suddenly there was sunlight. They were in a large hollowed-
out clearing, part of it paved with concrete. In the centre rose
a grey, grim finger of stone. Juonas cleared his throat and Zoe
smiled in relief at the noise.

'Here, young ladies, is the spot where the peoples were
instructed to take off their clothes.'

Zoe gasped, touched by the awful orderliness of it.

'You OK?' Annabelle said. 'You look a bit pale.'

'I'm fine. It's just pretty horrible, isn't it?'

Five paths radiated outwards into the trees. Side by side
they followed Juonas along the middle one. He kept up his
commentary:

'The peoples without clothes would be coming on this
road to a pit here.' He came to a stop. They were standing at the edge of a rough grassy dell, perhaps twenty-
five metres across. 'The peoples would be placed at the
tops,' he continued in his curious dulled sing-song, 'then
the soldiers would go back, and shot them.' He paused
and pointed down into the pit. 'The peoples would fall
in, and then more peoples, over them. Sometimes they
would not be killed by the shootings, so the officers would
take the revolver guns and shoot them dead again. You
understand?'

Annabelle was shaking her head from side to side. 'Oh, how
awful,' she said.

Zoe was chalk-white and utterly still, staring numbly down
at the pit. There was only dead bark and needles to see but her
eyes felt transfixed. Then something down there, underneath,
stirred. Her throat constricted: this time it was real, there had

been a movement. With a great effort she tore her gaze away and tried to concentrate on Juonas.

He was selecting his words with care. 'It was good that the peoples killed by the shootings of the officers. If not, their sufferings would have been very bad. After they were shotted, the prisoners-of-war came out of the pits over there,' he pointed to a neighbouring hollow, 'and placed chemicals on them.'

'Why?' Zoe asked, her voice was a croak.

'To make the bodies soft. To make them good for burning. The bodies of the peoples must be burned to make room.'

And the people waiting for their turn in the clearing would see it all, hear it all, those screams of terror and pain, the curtailed cries for mercy. They would know what was coming as they stood naked, clutching themselves and their children, for comfort – no protection.

Suddenly Zoe saw them clearly, the ghosts behind the trees. They came out one by one: first the shadow then the picture of the arms and legs and faces, chests that were breathing and eyes that saw. Old men and young men; a father with a baby in his arms; a small girl picking up the doll that another earlier child had dropped; all moving forward, coming closer, on and on. And now they were upon her: she could have touched them; she felt them passing; heard their pleadings and the low sound of mourning for the lives that they were leaving.

Then she was moving with them, side by side as they stumbled onward, some still hoping, still beseeching. No way out, no way out, and the trees kept growing thinner, and the dell was coming nearer and the noises getting louder . . . Ugly shouts and men in uniform and a desperate thundering in her heart, the hope of last appeal, 'Spare me, Spare me' – cut off by an order, by a snarl to stay in line, 'Hurry!' So she shut her eyes to the deadness in the faces of the soldiers who had learnt to have no feelings for their fellow human beings; only count them, move them forward, keep it going. Gun-barrels prodded the flesh of those who dallied, whom terror made fall.

'Why don't they kill us now, instead of waiting for the line-up?' and the answer came back like an echo: that it would break the sequence, interrupt the flow of life to death.

Now she was at the edge, looking down, seeing the limbs move. She prayed to keep standing upright, be a good target for the bullet, then she heard a whimper and glancing downwards saw a little child right beside her. She stooped to pick him up, turn his head away from horror, heard the volley, saw the pit rush up to meet her . . . knew no more.

Years later, the highly-classified MI5 paper on the phenomenon of Zoe Douglas referred to this incident as being of seminal importance in her development as a terrorist. Of course the haunting that caused her to faint that day did have a profound and prolonged effect upon her. But it is doubtful that, on its own, the experience would have triggered off all the emotional and psychological conflicts that it did, and that those, in turn, would ultimately transform this girl – now lying, literally terrified out of her senses on a forest floor – into a figure of dread.

Perhaps if Zoe had had proper time to recuperate; if she had been able to set the incident in context or dismiss it from her mind; if her psychological make-up and life-experiences had been entirely different, then the touch-paper lit that afternoon might have fizzled out. Such propositions are, of course, hypothetical: to a large extent, Zoe became what she did because of who she was.

But a sequence of events both followed and preceded Panerai so that one might not entirely dismiss the notion that Zoe had become Fate's creature: a dazed Night Wanderer bewitched and bedazzled by the delusive light that led her on, deeper and deeper into those dark woods.

For instance, she could hardly have joined an organisation that did not exist . . .

Five weeks earlier, in a corner suite of the Regency Hotel in New York, a meeting had taken place that was to alter the course of Zoe's life forever.

Nine people were present: two women and seven men. One was black; another Asian; two others were of dark Mediterranean appearance and the rest came under the heading of 'white'. They varied widely in age, from early thirties to sixties, and in religion: Jewish, Christian, Muslim and more were represented. Six had flown in from Europe – from France, Spain, Germany, Switzerland and the UK – two from other parts of the States. The last one, the man now addressing the others with such fervency, had caught a taxi to the hotel from his apartment on the Upper Eastside.

'So we're all agreed?' He threw out the question like a challenge.

The response was hardly a buzz of conversation, either positive or negative. There was, in fact, a long silence and an aversion of glances, but that was not in itself a bad sign. These meetings, of which there had been just two previously, were generally 'stop, go' affairs: long periods of silence followed by very heated, sometimes explosive debate. This was not surprising, given that seven of those present were deeply distrustful of each other.

They had not known each other long enough to be discussing the topics that were on the agenda and, because of the nature of those topics, they could not risk checking up on each other. Each one feared a spy in their midst, for each one had a great deal to lose – their liberty, wealth and position.

Therefore they knew each other's names and nationalities, but not much more than that. Gradually, over the forthcoming months, the tension between them would ease – at times even allowing for brief camaraderie – but the 'norm' was this: circumspection, fear and suspicion.

Amongst all but two, that is. Two men at that table, one British and one the New Yorker who had just spoken, trusted each other implicitly.

Axel Shiner, born in a small Kentish town to parents who had fled persecution in Eastern Europe, was, at 46, considerably the elder. He was good-looking: big-boned with a wide, rather sensual mouth and a well-cut head of dark hair. In the Eighties, as a young commodities broker in the City, he had made a great deal of money which he had invested wisely. It had enabled him to devote his time to the League Against Anti-Semitism, an entirely legal international organisation which monitored and publicised anti-Semitic attacks world-wide. He had been one of the League's most devoted members: inspired at public meetings; thoughtful and attentive on policy matters; invaluable when lobbying Parliamentarians. He gave large donations and travelled widely as a representative of the League at a host of conferences across the globe. It was at a conference in Toronto two years previously that he had met Leon Kleineman.

Leon was thirty-three and of a much smaller, wispier appearance altogether. He had a reedy voice and thinning hair and wore baggy dark suits that seemed to swallow him up. He looked like a victim and he traded on that, describing himself as a Holocaust survivor when he clearly could not have been born in those years. When that fact was pointed out to him, he took it badly, even to the verge of tears.

'My mother lived through Belsen,' he would say. 'Her husband and my little brother and sister died there. Of course I'm a survivor.'

His father, his mother's second husband, was a gentle man, a New Yorker who had cherished the broken woman, married her and tenderly rejoiced at the birth of Leon, ten years later. Materially the boy was spoilt (his father's family was extremely wealthy) and emotionally smothered by his mother. From this woman, originally a native of Cologne, Leon had learned to speak beautiful German. From the wraiths of his two long-dead siblings, he had learnt a living hatred, an eternal watchfulness and a passionate desire for vengeance that stretched out from the past into the future. These qualities, stirred together in one man, produced quite a cocktail: Leon bordered on the manic and was often paranoid, but his very fanaticism was magnetic.

Axel had watched and listened to him, made a few discreet enquiries and, on the third day, invited Leon to hear his plan. A new Resistance, a fighting force that would crush the Neo-Nazi cohorts underfoot; a Resistance with a difference, one that must be launched before the enemy had seized power, a Resistance on equal terms. Leon had wanted to start the group at once; Axel had counselled caution, and waiting for the right moment.

'My friend, we've only got one chance with this thing. We've got to get it right. We don't want to be arrested before we've even begun.'

'Arrested? Who's going to arrest us? We're the good guys, remember?'

'I know that, and you know that, but outsiders might think differently. We've got a lot to do before we're ready.'

They had used the interim to get their financial backers in place and to erect suitable screens for their activities. They set up a company, Dreams of America, which had its main office in New York on the seventh floor of a building off East Fifty-Second Street. On the office door was a brass plaque with the name in modest letters. There was no staff and the office was often locked and empty.

Inside the room, the walls were lined with posters of under-nourished but smiling children from the former Eastern Bloc. Stacked up under the window were piles of glossy brochures, showing these same children, still smiling, as they held up American T-shirts or shook hands with serious-looking adults in what looked like classrooms. The only furniture in the room was a long beech desk, two black leather armchairs and a fax machine set down on the carpet. On the desk were two telephones, one marked 'Dreams', permanently plugged in to an answering-machine.

To the casual inquirer – not that there had been any – Dreams was an organisation beyond reproach. According to the brochures, it raised funds to run skilled training projects and summer camps for young people in former totalitarian regimes. Dreams also had mailing addresses in Seattle, Paris and Bonn. It enjoyed widespread support, its literature stated, and then listed a considerable number of religious, political and youth organisations in several countries. On the final page, under the heading 'The Future', there was even mention of Dreams being given a sizeable EC grant.

Leon and Axel made a good team, fire and earth. On Leon's part there was more than a little hero-worship of the older man; the fellow-sufferer who had called him into battle; the big brother figure that Leon had never known but who had haunted him all his life.

He broke his long-standing engagement to the girl he had

been due to marry in six months time, told his parents that
he needed space and that his father could run the business
without him, and withdrew a large sum of money from one
of his trust funds. He told Axel everything about himself and,
in return, Axel said virtually nothing.

'Your parents . . .' Leon had ventured one day.

Pain had crossed Axel's face. 'They came from Warsaw.
They only just got out in time.'

'The ghetto? They were in the Warsaw ghetto? The
uprising?' Leon's eyes were alight with excitement.

Axel had got up and gone to the window. Outside Leon's
apartment wet snow was falling swiftly down onto the sidewalk
far below. He put his palms on the glass. 'They haven't told
me much. All that suffering, all that destruction. I can't . . .'
His voice had cracked a little.

'Hey, I'm sorry. I should never have asked. Please don't
upset yourself.'

They had met every couple of months, mainly in New York.
At first they had wanted ten backers, but they had eventually
settled for less.

'Quality not quantity, Leon.'

'Yeah, we've got a good mix already. Safer with fewer;
you're right.'

The people they had selected possessed what they decided
were the essentials: considerable wealth, either individual or
corporate; influence either through money, or profession;
squeaky clean hands; a fanatical belief in what they were doing
and the willingness to let others do it for them. They viewed
themselves as defenders of those unable to defend themselves;
crusaders in the eternal war against Fascism, anti-Semitism
and racism; generous benefactors of the Holy Cause. If anyone
had suggested that they were about to pledge themselves to a
new breed of terrorism, they would have been outraged and
accused the speaker of being from the enemy camp.

The meeting was forty minutes old. For much of it Axel had
been talking, calmly and methodically listing aims, intentions
and forecasts. An eavesdropper would have been forgiven
for mistaking it as a low-key pitch for a new flavour of
toothpaste.

'Everything is ready,' he concluded.

'Yeah, let's get on with it,' added Leon, shifting forward in his seat.

At the far end of the table an older man who had sat throughout with his head bowed, looked up. His face had a pink, well-scrubbed look that normally lent him a boyish air. Now, though, he appeared worn-down, aged, more than his sixty-seven years. His brow was furrowed with anxiety as he spoke.

'You are quite certain that every other avenue has been explored? All the political channels?'

He was English; his words were spoken precisely.

There was a snort from Leon. 'Politics! The politicians'll let us burn before they make one move in our favour! Politics, he says! I ask you!'

Axel rolled in smoothly. 'We are aware that this is a very big step we are asking everyone to make. We can assure you, sir, and everyone here present that we have carefully considered every other option. Armed action is the only way forward.'

The pink-faced man did not appear soothed by his words. His mouth opened, then closed again in defeat.

A woman on his right, very well-dressed, in her mid-fifties with grey hair cut stylishly, raised a long index finger. Her English was very good, almost accentless, but she was Swiss, the daughter of a Jewish couple who had fled Vienna just before the Anschluss. 'You have the, er, products and the people you require?'

'Those matters are in hand.'

'So, it will take you how long before you ... it ... can begin?'

'A matter of weeks.'

'So soon?'

Leon slapped both hands on the table. In the tense room it sounded like a pistol shot. He half rose from his chair. 'Soon? Soon? In a couple of weeks, how many more people d'you reckon are going to be killed by these Nazi fuckers? How many more graves you wanna see desecretated before we do something?'

'Leon ...' Axel murmured, with a quieting look. But

Leon was in full spate. 'How much longer are we going to hear that there are second-class citizens and second-class neighbourhoods and golfing-clubs where only WASPS are welcome? How many more people are going to be driven out of their homes on account of their religion?'

'Or colour,' added the only Black present.

Leon frowned over at him. 'Right! Or colour, or being born a Jew or a Muslim.' He glared around. 'What I'm saying is, we haven't got the time any more to sit here discussing things. You've got to give us the go-ahead now, right now. You know what's going on; you know what we're going to do about it. Now's the time.'

He paused and pushed back the fringe of thin hair from his forehead. 'We're all supposed to be together in this,' he said. 'So, we're all agreed?'

The silence lasted a full minute; Leon rocking to and fro, the fingers of his right hand tapping out a beat on the table surface. 'I said . . .' he began again.

Axel cleared his throat and smiled around. 'I suggest a show of hands?'

Some of them moved in their chairs but no one spoke.

'All in favour of the final stage?'

One by one the hands went up; the pink-faced man last.

'Good! We shall begin at once.'

Zoe had come round from her faint quite quickly. As she had lost consciousness, she had pitched forward, but not so far that she had fallen into the dell. Her forehead and nose were bruised, but not too badly – the pine needles had made a fairly soft landing. Her first conscious sight was Juonas's face leaning over her own, then she heard Annabelle's voice, cross with fright: 'It's all right, Juonas. She's only fainted; there's no need to weep about it. Look, she's coming round now. Take it easy, love, sit up slowly.'

By the time they had got back to the hotel and had assured Juonas that it was not his fault ('Not too many historical spot, no, no, Juonas, don't worry'), it was getting dark and Zoe had been glad to agree that she needed to get some sleep.

Annabelle drew the thin red curtain across the windows in

their room. 'I'll see if I can find a doctor if you like,' she offered.

'No, no, it's all right.'

'It was probably just the heat – it was pretty stuffy in there. And we didn't have much to eat at lunch.'

Zoe lay back on her bed and shut her eyes. She was immediately back in the forest; the dark fringes of the pine trees and the blue sky and the shadows . . . She opened them quickly. 'Belle?'

'Yes?'

'You didn't see anything, did you? Anything unusual?'

'What d'you mean?'

'Well, anything moving.'

'Moving?' For a fraction of a second, Annabelle hesitated, then seemed to shake herself. Her voice was determinedly practical. 'There was nothing to move. There wasn't a breath of air in that place, was there?'

'No.' Zoe propped herself up on her elbows to get a better look at her friend's face. She had to find out, had to risk Annabelle laughing at her. 'You didn't see any shadows or people or anything there?'

Annabelle crossed the floor and placed her hand on Zoe's forehead. 'You really have got a touch of the sun, Zoe. There was nothing there, believe me. Just you and me and boring old Juonas, and that horrible pit and about a thousand pine trees. No one else, I promise you.'

'You didn't feel anything? A presence?'

'Oh God! Don't start imagining things! No, I didn't feel a presence. Did you?'

Zoe looked up at her. There was something in Annabelle's expression that told her the door was closed: if she had seen something she was never going to admit it, even to herself.

Zoe took a deep breath. 'No, of course not.'

'Good. "Presence," she says! Don't go freaky on me, you hear? I'm going out to buy us something to eat before that kiosk shuts. You go to sleep, OK?'

She had tried but it was impossible to keep her eyes closed. Even with them wide open, she was afraid of being sucked down into the vortex. It was like a dream she had had as a child:

of herself falling and falling through black air with demons and dragons reaching out to clutch at her and something horrible – she never knew what – waiting for her at the bottom. Only now when she fell, it was pine needles that scratched her, and she could see what was at the bottom of the pit.

She got out of bed and pulled the curtain back. The view was of the yard at the back of the premises: nothing much to see except two huge concrete dustbins and a family of cats fighting in and around them for scraps. Zoe watched absently as she tried to rationalise what had happened to her.

It was as if she had catapulted back in time into a ghostly tableau. She had never given much thought to ghosts before, although her home was supposed to have at least two, a maid and a man who had quarrelled and killed each other. It was not that Zoe disbelieved in them, simply that they had never appeared to her. There was nothing eerie about her home, in spite of it being so quiet and so often lonely.

'But I could feel the evil in Panerai,' she thought. 'It was so strong, as if it had won. The triumph of evil and the killing of good. Everything being turned upside down. Men shooting children and parents carrying their children to death.' She shuddered. 'It was as if evil existed, as if it had become a Thing I could've touched. Perhaps I did . . .'

She pressed her nose to the window-pane. Maybe that was what had happened: the evil done in the forest had tainted the whole place forever. It was in the atmosphere and, if one was sensitive to it, one picked it up. She remembered a day-trip with her school to Culloden, the hills that covered so many dead. It had been a sombre feeling, but not frightening; just a piece of history, however terrible.

Outside, it was growing dusk. There was a burst of noise and light as the door to the kitchens opened, making the cats scatter like tiny clouds. No, Zoe could not really equate the two experiences: Panerai was somehow current, something undead, unfinished. 'But why me?' she asked aloud. 'Why was I taken back to go through that? It's as if those people wanted something from me, or blamed me for something. But they've got nothing to do with me; I'm Scottish Presbyterian not Jewish! Culloden's got more hold on me than Panerai.'

Zoe found that trying to understand the haunting did nothing to alleviate the symptoms. She also discovered when Annabelle returned with the food that her friend's patience had evaporated.

'D'you think ghosts are good or bad?' she asked.

'Oh do shut up about bloody ghosts, Zoe. You're getting on my nerves.'

They ate and went to bed, but Zoe was too scared to sleep. She lay on her soft mattress listening to Annabelle's rhythmic breathing and forced herself to stay awake. There was no bedside lamp, so she could not read but she made herself recite as many speeches as she could remember from *Othello*. Towards dawn, when she was so exhausted that she felt achy and light-headed, she let in the thought that she had pushed right to the very back of her mind.

It was something that Annabelle had said that evening in exasperation and maybe also in fear; Zoe knew there had been no malice in it, and there was no connection, really, with her past, with those other times that she had been branded different. But still those words, 'Don't go freaky on me,' triggered the memories. Freaky, you're a freak. First in the playground, then Tony, now Annabelle.

Tony . . . Zoe turned her face to the wall and let the tears fall. Tony had been right; there was something wrong with her.

He had hurt her so much. A little part of her would always remain amazed at how much one human being could hurt another. Of course, she had been young, eighteen, and a young eighteen at that; she had been so naive, inexperienced. She guessed that was what had attracted him to her. Tony had been a year off forty, and a successful architect in Glasgow. He had seemed so mature, so confident in himself and with other people; as if he had life taped.

They had met at a cocktail party in Edinburgh. It was just a week after Zoe had left school, still on fire with a sense of freedom and excitement at the year ahead.

Attending the cocktail party in the first place had been of tremendous importance to her, signalling as it did an end to shyness and awkwardness. The invitation had been for her

mother – the preview of a new collection at one of the city's
art galleries – but Mrs Douglas had not been interested. She
had been about to throw the card away when her eyes alighted
on Zoe, rather astonishingly no longer a child; in fact really a
very pretty girl.

'Why don't you go, darling? Take my car, spend the
weekend at your grandmother's. They'll be nice people at
the gallery.'

So Zoe had gone, wearing her only 'grown-up' dress, a short
pale blue silk shift that swayed when she moved. Entering the
gallery, on the top floor of a converted warehouse, she had
been horrified at the number of people present and by the
fact that none of them looked under forty-five.

'And you are?' A formidable woman in a long black dress
barred her way.

Zoe blushed and handed over her invitation. 'My mother
couldn't come. She said it would be all right if I did instead.
But if it isn't . . .'

'Oh. Elisabet had a daughter? I thought it was a boy she'd
had. Well, we've lost touch these last ten years. Typical
Elisabet to send a substitute and not think to call me about
it! Well, now you're here, I suppose it's all right. There's wine
over there,' and she turned away to greet a dapper couple in
evening dress.

Zoe had taken a glass of warm white wine from the drinks
tray and retreated to the quietest part of the room, away
from any paintings. 'Stay for an hour,' she told herself
fiercely. 'You don't have to talk to anyone. No one's looking
at you.'

A man had appeared beside her. 'Are you allowed out on
your own?' Tony's first words were a tease. He smiled at her
speechlessness. 'What's wrong? Has your mother told you not
to talk to strange men?'

He had long dark hair swept back off his forehead, hooded
eyes and designer stubble. He was wearing a baggy black linen
suit and open-necked white shirt. She had never seen anyone
so much in control. He talked and she listened, and all the
while she was aware of his eyes upon her, making a casual
inventory. When, at the end of the evening, he touched her

bare arm, she gasped out loud at the sexual charge that surged through her.

She had fallen deeply and wholly in love with him. Her love was mixed with awe and gratitude that he had noticed her and she would have done anything to please him. For ten months she had thought him quite wonderful. It was her first relationship; Tony her first real lover. Until then Zoe's sex-life had consisted of some inexpert fumblings with a boy at a boarding-school disco, the whole episode a memory of acute embarrassment. Sex with Tony was both terrifying and exhilarating. 'I'll teach you how,' he told her that first night. 'My little virgin.'

He had taken her over entirely: bought her new clothes, lots of sexy underwear, shorts and little tops and tight skirts. He 'educated' her in the arts, taking her to exhibitions, theatres, parties. He installed her in his home. Her parents had expressed mild concern at this: there had been a telephone call from her father, but Tony had dealt with it. 'Believe me, sir,' Zoe had heard him say on the phone. 'Your delightful daughter is quite safe in my hands. Her welfare is of paramount importance to me. Why don't you and your wife visit us? Any evening or weekend, just let us know.'

They never had, though. Thinking back now on this lack of parental concern it seemed obvious to Zoe that Tony had been a father-figure for her. She had bathed in his attention, revelling in the knowledge that for the first time in her life an older person cherished and needed her.

As Tony had filled this need in her, so she had fulfilled his as a child-woman. 'Wild child,' he used to call her; 'baby', and she had loved it.

When, after two months, she had told him about her plans for her year off, all the countries she wanted to visit and her university place next October, he had pulled her onto his knee.

He ran his finger down the outline of her left breast, circling her nipple. 'You're not going.'

'No?' She had smiled at him.

'No. You're staying here with me.'

She had been happy to do so; she had enjoyed his control

of her and the feeling that she was surrendering everything to him. She had been the perfect little wife: getting up to make him his breakfast; doing the housework and shopping; always being there for him in the evenings. Very occasionally it would occur to her that she was wasting herself, but when those thoughts came, she would block them out. 'Tony's my life now,' she told herself. 'He's my future. He's all I ever want.'

It had taken her nearly a year to see what was going on. She was his plaything, his little girl, and as long as she went along with that, all was sweetness and light. But let her show any independence of thought, express an opinion contrary to his own, and it was like questioning his manhood. Once, having a drink with some of his friends, she had argued with him over the play they had just seen. When they got home, he had slammed her against a wall.

'You fucking little whore! How dare you show me up? What d'you know about it anyway? What d'you know about anything?'

The end had come fairly swiftly after that, but not swiftly enough. Sex, which she had enjoyed, became awful, an intrusion, another attempt by him to manipulate her.

It was in bed that they had their last row.

'Know what you are?' he said roughly.

She had not answered him. She was trying, without seeming to, to edge to the side of the bed. Tony's rages could be violent.

He grabbed a hank of her hair and jerked her back, hissing the words in her face: 'You're fucking frigid. A fucking little Snow Queen!

'You think yours is so special, don't you?' His voice had risen in cruel imitation: '"Hands off, don't touch me." You'd better sort yourself out, girl, before it dries up.'

All because she could not come on his command, was too scared of him by then to feel anything much.

Then she had made her fatal mistake. Staring up into his face, she had seen the hatred in his eyes and had let him see the fear in her own.

A look of triumph came over him. He pinned her arms to

her sides and climbed on top of her, his whole weight pressing her into the bed; his face an inch above her own.

'Don't worry, little freak. I don't want what's between your legs any more. I don't want to touch it. Nobody else will, either. There's something really wrong with you, you know? Freaky little Zoe who had no friends at school, whose parents don't give a fuck about her. Ever wondered why? No? Well, I'll tell you.' He had paused and stroked her hair in a parody of love. 'No one likes a freak, not even its mum and dad.'

Then he had heaved himself off her, kicked her away from him and quickly fallen asleep. She had lain on the edge of the bed, unable to move, frozen by his words. She was not normal; it explained everything – school, all those lonely years on the border, always an outsider, never part of anything, a freak . . .

Zoe shivered, and pulled the thin blanket around herself. It was only a word, she thought, and Annabelle had meant nothing by it. But feeling as vulnerable and scared as she now did, she let the doubt take shape: freaky. Even her first real friend thought so.

Zoe remembered the fear from that other night, lying awake in Tony's bed through all those long dark hours – much as she was doing now. And, just as she had then, she cried until there were no more tears left. She glanced over at Annabelle; she could see her quite clearly now; still sound asleep. Lucky Annabelle who skipped through life. She would have been horrified to know that a casual remark had cost her friend so much pain.

Zoe glanced at her watch, nearly six o'clock. 'You're not a freak,' she told herself. 'Don't slip back into believing all that stuff. Tony was just a screwed-up, frustrated old bastard.'

She had left him the next day, as soon as he had gone to work. She had written no note, not a word of explanation, and had taken nothing that he had given her. It was not a grand gesture, more that she felt dazed and numbed and needed somewhere to hide.

She could have gone home or to Alasdair's flat in London, but she was too hurt for family sympathy and if at that point her parents had ignored her, she had no idea what she might do. Instead, she had spent a few days with her grandmother in Edinburgh. The old lady was always pleased to see her and seldom asked questions. At the end of a week, Zoe answered an advertisement in the evening paper, and announced that she was going grape-picking in France.

It had saved her. She had worked so hard, day after day in the sun, that she had been too exhausted at night to think. There were eleven other pickers, mostly students, and in the evenings they all ate together and slept in dormitories in a converted barn. Zoe, expecting to be left-out, found the opposite was true: a couple of the boys obviously fancied her, and the other girls were friendly. Over the course of six weeks, the fragile self-confidence that Tony had so neatly shattered, gradually re-established itself. She even began flirting lightly with one of the boys but drew back when he wanted more. She knew it would take her a long time before she could sufficiently trust another man enough to sleep with him.

She had gone home for a week before term started. Her parents had been pleased to see her and tactful about Tony. 'Of course they love you,' Zoe remembered thinking. 'It's just they love each other more. It's nothing personal.'

She had felt that, one by one, she was knocking down the skittles Tony had set up for her. Her first few weeks at university set her back a little. There were so many students and everyone seemed to be friends, no one would want to talk to her . . . She had brought herself up sharply. 'Stop it. Don't start imagining things. Remember France. You're just as normal or abnormal as everyone else. And no one will talk to you if you skulk in the library all day or sit in your room.'

Nevertheless it had taken considerable effort to talk to people in her tutorial group and at lectures. But it had got easier and by the second term, she was part of a loosely-knit crowd who went for coffee together or a drink in the student bar. That was how she and Annabelle – the 'oldies', the only two in the group to have taken a year off – had become friends.

In the other bed, Annabelle stirred. 'Wassa time?'

'Coming up for seven.'

Annabelle muttered something incomprehensible.

Zoe got up and crept along the corridor to the bathroom. She turned on the hot water tap in the bathtub and jumped at the noise of the system kicking itself into life. From below there was a clanking, then the pipes that ran up from the hole in the floor shuddered and moaned. Just for a second they reminded Zoe of the terrible sounds in the forest, but she shut out the memory.

She stared at herself in the mirror. 'You are not going to think about it. You're going to do just what you've done before: block it out. You've got a very active imagination, that's why you saw or thought you saw those people. It's awful what happened, but there's nothing you can do about it. And if you go on thinking about it and talking about it, then you'll become a freak and no one will want you.' She paused for a deep breath. 'And Tony'll have won.'

The mirror was misting with steam; she rubbed it clear again with her pyjama cuff. Her face, white with red-rimmed eyes, looked very determined. 'Don't dare throw everything away. Concentrate on now, and the future, not some horrible thing in the past. OK?'

Matt Anderson pushed his dinghy into the Thames and slid in under the boom. After days like yesterday, the need to sail, to feel the wind on his face, was overwhelming.

They had only been kids, he reminded himself. Young, not very bright kids with no prospects, who had enjoyed bragging to a journalist from a posh paper. Only, it had not all been bragging.

They lived on a vast council estate in south-east London that had the reputation for being one of the most racially violent in the whole of the country. Three days previously a fifteen-year-old Asian boy had been dragged into an alleyway and stabbed twice in the chest by a group of whites. Then they had poured petrol on him, and it had only been the intervention of two neighbours that had saved him from being burnt alive. The boy had described his attackers as being in their late teens, early twenties. Not much older than the ones Matt had interviewed.

They had met him in a lock-up garage behind their estate.

There were six of them, none older than seventeen, all dressed in black jeans, boots and Blood-and-Honour T-shirts. Their shaved heads made them look like young conscripts; the style emphasising ugliness and vulnerability at the same time. They lounged against the walls, saying nothing, watching him. Most of them smoked. They were achieving their intention, Matt thought: they were supremely threatening.

'You want to know who done the Paki?' A youth with a swastika engraved on his cheek asked the question.

Matt had met his stare. 'D'you know who did it?'

'You paying us?'

'No.'

The boy smirked. 'Not telling, then.'

Matt started tacking back towards the small sailing club at Hampton where he kept his dinghy. Many of his sailing friends were scornful of sailing this short stretch of the river at all, but Matt lived a three minute walk away from the club in a flat that overlooked the river and sailing had always been his passion. He had a much sleeker, faster boat that he kept at a reservoir in Staines, but on certain days the prospect of the twenty minute drive there seemed too much, as did the two hour haul down to Southampton.

He passed a small cruiser and two sculls from the boy's public school at Teddington, their coaches shouting orders from bicycles on the towpath. It was a different world from the hopeless brutality of Kirton Park Estate.

'I'm afraid *The Clarion* doesn't believe in cheque-book journalism,' he had told them, and turned to walk out.

'Hang on!'

There had been a muttered conversation.

'All right. We'll tell you anyway. Someone's got to tell the truth, haven't they?'

'So tell me.'

'A load of lads come over from Woolwich to do him special. But we're the ones who said he needed it.'

'Why?'

'He was getting cocky, mouthy, you know? Saying he had the same rights as us. That he was as British as you and me. He'd started going to one of the Commie groups, anti-Nazi something. He needed teaching a lesson.'

'But your mates were going to set fire to him!'

'Yeah? He needed a lesson that he wouldn't forget.'

'And if he'd died?'

'But he didn't, did he?'

There had been no arguing with them. They had been so convinced that their violence was justified, and so frighteningly full of hate. With very little prompting, they had told how it was their six selves who were largely responsible for the terror of every coloured person on the estate. 'Dog shit through their letter-boxes.' 'Pigs blood.' 'Getting their saris off them.'

Matt had stared at this last speaker. The hair was the same, and the clothes, but the voice was high-pitched and the face, when studied closely had fine features: large eyes, well-proportioned lips.

'Oi! That's my girlfriend you're screwing at.'

A girl. Matt had kept staring, and she had blushed suddenly, transforming herself into a pretty teenager.

'Women's lib,' she said, affecting a jeer. 'Ever heard of it, mate?'

Matt watched the pale September sun dance on the brown water and the soft whisper of the breeze as it translated into cat's paws upon the surface.

The girl's boyfriend had smiled at her tenderly. 'We're having tattoos done on Saturday. Swastikas and hearts, matching.'

An elderly man in a wooden Wayfarer passed in the opposite direction. He and Matt waved and exchanged smiles, a gentle code of the river in a gentle world. Matt shuddered at the memory of the previous day, and shut it out of his mind.

Chapter Two

In the days that followed Zoe's experience in the forest, she tried resolutely to block the whole event from her mind and throw herself into the holiday. By mutual consent she and Annabelle had left Lithuania the next morning and headed west for Poland.

'I don't know about you,' she had said as they waited interminably at the border, 'but I've had enough of gloom. How about somewhere a bit more cheerful, maybe Holland?'

'I'd like to stop in Germany for a bit. Keep my language up.'

'OK, fair enough.'

The town that they arrived at six days later had been in former East Germany. It had a three star 'historic' crown in their guide book. There was a tiny, mediaeval church with a stunning fresco, narrow, hilly streets of wooden houses, a large cobbled market-square and dozens of bars and open-air cafes.

They were sitting at one of the cafes.

'Nobody mentioned the drains,' Annabelle declared with some indignation. Zoe giggled. The previous few days had been fun. In Warsaw they had met up with a group of seven Norwegian students, also 'doing' Europe, and had spent two days together, sightseeing during the day and going to bars at night. The haunting of Panerai had slipped further and further to the back of Zoe's mind.

They had reached the town just after noon, booked into a cheap pension and visited the sights, along with hundreds of other visitors. It had not been a pleasurable experience: there had been queues for everything; they had been shoved and jabbed by cameras and camcorders, and prices were prohibitively high. But it was the smell of drains that was unbearable.

Zoe sniffed the air. 'It's not too bad here,' she said.

'No, it's where we're staying that's really pongy. The cheek of that manager saying, "What smell?"!'

'Maybe he's just used to it.'

'Nobody could get used to it,' Annabelle said firmly. She frowned down at the local newspaper she had bought and which she had been painstakingly translating. 'I'm sure there's something here about it. Yes, "Abwasser" is sewage. Hang on, let me get the gist . . . It says here,' she looked up triumphantly, 'that the townspeople are demanding a new sewage system because their old one can't cope with all the tourists.'

'I'm impressed. So why don't they get one?'

'I'm coming to that. Uhh, oh, the usual reason. Shortage of money. "Since reunification, the two main employers . . . a processing plant and something else to do with paint have been shut." Unemployment is – wow! . . . over fifty per cent.'

'Fifty!'

'Yup, that's what it says. Tourism is the only "Wachstums" . . . growth industry, but development is limited due to shortage of cash.'

'Poor people.' Zoe smiled at a passing waiter.

'Yeah, must be awful.' Annabelle sighed and sipped her beer. 'But I think one night's enough.'

'Agreed. So, on to Berlin tomorrow?'

There was a train leaving at seven o'clock the following morning; and it was now beginning to get dark. They finished their beers, vacated the table which was immediately reoccupied, and made their way to the old quarter where they were staying.

The pension was at the bottom of a narrow street that petered out into wasteland. The area that in daylight had possessed, in spite of the pervading odour, a quaint, down-at-heel charm, seemed dismal and even threatening in the late evening. Most of the buildings had a permanently shut-up look; there was no one about and several of the streetlights were broken.

'If my mother could see me now she'd have a fit,' Annabelle muttered. 'Talk about the perfect place for a mugging.'

They increased their pace and crossed the road towards the only lit-up building they could see. Closer to, they heard Eastern-style music coming from an open window at the front. They could not see inside; the window was above their heads, but they paused and listened. A man was singing, more voices joined in, and the sound flowed out into the night. At once the street seemed less frightening.

'St Agnes Hostel for Asylum-Seekers,' Annabelle read out the words from a brass plaque on the building's door. There was a burst of laughter from inside. 'They must be celebrating something. Come on, our place is only down there.'

In their spartan bedroom on the pension's third floor, they argued briefly about open or shut windows. Zoe won: they moved their beds to the opposite end of the room and opened the smallest window a fraction.

Just after one o'clock in the morning, Zoe woke up suddenly. She had either dreamed or had heard something; her heart was thundering and her palms felt sweaty. She sat up, disoriented. It was very dark in the room: only a little moonlight came in through the windows. She strained her ears: nothing. She must have imagined whatever had woken her. She lay back down again.

Glass shattered in the street. A long, piercing scream rang out, swallowed up by laughter. More glass breaking, and shouts. Another scream, more terrified than the first.

'Wassat?' Annabelle woke up.

'I don't know. I . . .' Zoe got out of bed and stumbled over to the windows. Down in the street, away to her right, she could make out the figures of several people. There was a sudden cracking sound, and she could see flames.

'What is it?' Annabelle's voice behind her sounded scared.

'A fire, I think. I can't see.' Zoe found the latch, flung open the window and leaned out. Now she could see more clearly. Five or six men in the street outside; flames billowing out from a building lighting them up. More screams and people tumbling out into the street . . .

Zoe stared. The men in the street were not helping; they were throwing things. They were bending forwards, picking things up, straightening and throwing them at the people coming out. Bricks, it looked like, and lumps of metal. The people were running, and some were being hit and some were falling.

Zoe's eyes fixed on one man: she could see him quite clearly. He was wearing dark clothing, his face swaddled in a bandit-scarf, standing in the middle of the street. He picked up a bottle; she saw him flick a lighter at its neck; he raised it back over his shoulder and hurled it forward in a great sweeping arc at the building.

There was a split second of silence then the bang and whoosh of an explosion. The man shrieked with laughter and his comrades egged him on.

'Sieg Heil! Sieg Heil!' they roared, drunk with success.

The bottle-thrower took a few steps backwards and looked up at the building. His scarf fell away and Zoe saw his face: young, a boy's face, very fair and child-like in the flames. His eyes swept over the windows, and it was then that he saw her looking down at him.

He paused, then grinned and raised his arm at her. She drew back instinctively, but it was not a bottle that he threw at her: only the Nazi salute and a cheeky kiss for fun.

As it went, the attack on the hostel was not a bad one. No one died as a direct result. Only two of the twenty-seven residents, all celebrating the birthday of their patriarch, a seventy-nine-year-old Kurd, were seriously injured. The man's wife, aged eighty-one, suffered a stroke that would kill her in three months' time and a child of three lost an eye due to a splinter of glass. Everyone else escaped with shock, burns and cuts.

The media reported the event in some detail. It was one in a catalogue of racist and xenophobic attacks that had been plaguing Germany since reunification. Politicians and leader writers expressed due outrage and demanded that 'something be done'. An Anti-Nazi demonstration was planned in the town for the following weekend and a vigil against racism was suggested; it would be held in the mediaeval church. However, two days later there was another hostel burning in a town near the Polish border. A Turkish woman and her two young daughters were trapped inside and died. Everyone's attention switched to that.

The police force of the little town did their best to apprehend the culprits, but they did not have much to go on. The victims were too badly shaken to be of much use and they were unable to give anything approaching a decent description.

The young sergeant thought he might have struck lucky with a witness from the student pension next door; an English girl. Her friend said she had seen the whole thing, but when he questioned her, the girl had just stared into space not saying a word. She was probably high on something. Shaking his head in disgust he had let her go.

The details of the incident were logged and entered into the computer at the anti-terrorist police headquarters in Wiesbaden. After that, the file was effectively closed.

The local people declared it had been hooligans from far away: foreigners probably. Still, they were reluctant to donate money for a new, larger hostel on the outskirts of town. The priest of St Agnes could say what he liked; if there were no more asylum seekers, there would be no more unpleasant attacks.

Horst Gemmer had been a policeman for nearly thirty years; the last eight as head of Special Operations attached to Germany's Anti-Terrorist squad in Wiesbaden. He had his own staff and budget, and he was known as the best in his field – that being intelligence-gathering. Most of the material stored in the Terrorist Profile System in the computer downstairs – the same computer that had just logged Zoe's incident – owed its existence to him.

He did not look like a genius. He had an instantly forgettable face: regular features, brown eyes, dark hair. He was of medium height, a little overweight – but then he was fifty-one. He could have been a bank employee, a retailer, or a middle-ranking civil servant.

He was on several hit-lists; he had been shot at and his family had been threatened. Twice they had had to move house. To Gemmer, the danger and the threats went with the territory. In a funny sort of way, it was a compliment; it showed he was doing his job, rattling the cages of the other side. Gemmer was by nature a calm, patient man, seldom provoked to excitation. Just now though, he was tense.

It was early evening. Everyone else had gone home, but he had needed to sit and think things through on his own. He rubbed at the bridge of his nose and gazed down at the photograph in front of him. 'So near, eh?' he asked it.

Beatrix Kessler, Germany's most wanted terrorist, whom he had tracked off and on for over twenty years and whom he had been on the very point of arresting, had vanished. Puff, gone, like smoke.

Five days ago, she had been seen in Germany, in Frankfurt. Unbelievable, he had thought, but then forty-eight hours later there had been another sighting, less than two kilometres away from the first. For some reason Beatrix Kessler had come home.

Gemmer had gone straight to his counterpart in the Anti-Terrorist squad. Together they had notified the Interior Minister, an ambitious man, who had been wildly excited: the catching of Kessler was going to be the best thing that had happened in his eighteen months in office. Gemmer had counselled caution: it might take some time, and a great deal of patience, not to mention money and resources before they found her.

'Anything,' the minister had said. 'You've got carte blanche. Just bring her in.'

They had posted watchers all over the city – teams of them working in shifts, at the railway station, the airport, post offices, shopping malls. Every policeman in the city was issued with her description and the most recent photograph that Gemmer had on file – eleven years old, a snatch-shot showing her profile, looking down with her eyes half-shut, reading something. It had been the only one available. Gemmer himself had walked the city's streets for the first day, peering at the faces of any women the right age – unprofessional, he knew, but he had never been wholly detached about her.

Nothing in the first twenty-four, then thirty-six hours.

By the end of the second day, the Minister had started to panic.

'Your sightings were definite?'

'Definite.'

'How about getting the press in on it?'

'She'd be gone. Or there'd be a bloodbath.'

'Well, how much longer?'

'I can't say for sure. But days, probably, rather than weeks.'

'Weeks! What're you talking about? You've got hundreds of people looking for her, haven't you?'

'Yes, but she may have gone to ground. Or she may have done everything she wanted in the city and . . .' He hesitated.

'And what?'

'Moved on.'

By first thing that morning, when there was still no news, Gemmer had been convinced that was what had happened. He had been in his office at seven, wondering how long the Minister would give him before ordering the stand-down, when the telephone rang. A package had arrived that he must see at once.

A black-and-white photograph in a cardboard reinforced envelope. On the back, the date, August 26th, just three days earlier and the name, Beatrix Andrea Kessler. Gemmer had stared at the face that was altered beyond the mere passage of years: something very different about her mouth, and her cheeks were lower . . . but there had been no time to study her. Attached to the picture by a plain paperclip was an address in a middle-class suburb of Frankfurt.

A helicopter took him to the city. By eight-thirty he was briefing forty members of the rapid deployment team. He wanted her alive, but more than that, he wanted to avoid a bloodbath. They would have to get to her before she could arm herself.

He was driven in an unmarked car to the street in the leafy suburb where the surveillance unit had been hastily dispatched. They were working out of a white van, a kilometre from the post-war block where Beatrix Kessler had a second floor apartment. Directional microphones and cameras had been set up but so far had detected no movement from within.

'Give it an hour,' Gemmer had ordered. More than an hour had been needed to evacuate the rest of the block and get the curious away to places of safety.

Then the team had gone in: six of them abseiling down from the roof, their boots smashing in the windows as their colleagues kicked in the front door.

It had been empty and the bed unslept in. But there had been women's clothing in the wardrobe; food in the fridge and the previous day's newspaper on the kitchen table. Proof that Beatrix Kessler had indeed lived there was immediately provided by a small framed photograph of an elderly woman standing on a bedside table.

Gemmer had picked it up and brought it back to Wiesbaden. It stood on his desk now beside the picture of Beatrix: mother and daughter together.

He stared at the white-haired lady with the gentle face, the very image of a priest's wife.

He let his mind roam back to the day twenty-one years before when Pastor Ludwig Kessler had walked into the main police station in Frankfurt to report the disappearance of his daughter, an only child.

He was a tall, stooping man, with gentle eyes that looked watery behind his spectacles. He held his daughter's note in a shaking hand. 'You see, it's her birthday today. She's nineteen. We were taking her out today to celebrate, but she didn't come down for breakfast. I went up and knocked on her door . . . I found this. I can't think what she means . . .'

Gemmer, then an ambitious young detective recently assigned to Baader-Meinhof duties, had taken the note and read it. 'You are a filthy fascist pig,' Beatrix had written to her father in a large, simple hand. 'Your scum generation are all guilty. You have sought to hide your evil, but we shall expose it. How dare you hide from me what you did to the Jews, the Communists, the gypsies?'

Gemmer had looked up and seen that the pastor was crying. 'I wasn't a Nazi! I was only seventeen years old when the war finished. I did nothing, nothing . . .'

Gemmer had tried to comfort the man, but was aware that his words had sounded unconvincing. He had looked at the coloured snapshot of the missing girl: a slim figure in flared jeans and a tank-top, long hair the colour of a raven's wing and almond-shaped eyes. She was leaning against the wall of a house, smiling at the camera. She looked lovely, and very vulnerable. 'We'll get her back,' Gemmer had promised, but he never had.

Her rise in Baader-Meinhof had been swift. Within a week, on her first 'action', a bank raid, she had killed. A security guard, perhaps fooled by the sweet face, had made a lunge at her. Opening her blue eyes wide, she had pumped bullets into him and watched quite calmly, so the witnesses said, as he writhed at her feet.

The press had christened her 'The Angel of Death' and if at first that name seemed over the top, it grew to accommodate her. At the last known count, she had personally killed nine people, two of them women, and wounded at least twenty-five more.

She had graduated from Baader-Meinhof to running her own group, 'The Spearhead', which had specialised in targeting NATO and military targets with notable success. In the late seventies, she had had almost a cult following amongst the young and those in certain intellectual circles, but then she had orchestrated a fund-raising kidnapping that had gone horribly wrong, leaving the twelve-year-old son of an industrialist severely brain damaged. Popular opinion had changed overnight. Politicians and the media had demanded her blood and the pressure had come down heavily on the heads of the country's police forces.

It had been then that Gemmer had had his brainwave.

He had always kept in contact with the Kessler parents and had become something of a surrogate son for the daughter they had lost. He had known that the mother was suffering from cancer and that she dearly wished to see her daughter before she died.

Why not put the mother on television, begging the daughter to come home? It could be broadcast across Europe, so that Kessler would be bound to see it. It would be bound, at the very least, to unnerve her, make her careless – even if it did not bring her running back to Frankfurt.

Brilliant, said Gemmer's superiors. Do it.

It had been a pitiful, wretched performance. The cancer had ravaged the elderly woman who had wept and begged, stumbling over the words on the autocue. And then, at the end, she had looked straight at the camera: 'Please, darling. They say it'll be all right. The police won't touch you . . .'

Three days later, the pastor's wife was dead. The effort had been too much for her, the doctors had said. And the following evening a bomb had exploded in the canteen of a police station in Dusseldorf, killing one policeman and a civilian and injuring a dozen more. Kessler herself, in a telephone call to the ambulance station, had claimed responsibility: 'For my mother,' she had said.

Her mother's death, the manner of it, had proved a watershed for her. Shortly afterwards, The Spearhead disintegrated but she began freelancing for other groups, both inside Europe and beyond. Her motivation seemed to have died. While she still occasionally did jobs for old friends – a comrade in the Red Brigades or the Belgian CCC – mostly she worked for cash, a great deal of it. She had become a hired gun.

Gemmer sighed and picked up the framed photograph of Frau Kessler that Beatrix had left behind in her apartment. He felt at least partly responsible for what the nineteen-year-old girl had become.

He had monitored her progress down the years. Her notoriety had spread abroad and she was near the top of Interpol's 'Most Wanted' list. Most people, when asked to name famous terrorists, came up with two names: Abu Nidal and Beatrix Kessler.

Three years before she seemed to have disappeared. Dead or retired was the verdict of a dozen countries' police forces. As long as she stayed that way, fine. There were more pressing concerns than lost, inactive terrorists. Except for Gemmer.

To him, the finding of her, dead or alive, was something special, as if the promise he had so rashly made to her father all those years ago still awaited fulfilment.

It had been relatively easy for him to hive off some of his

budget and staff. He had no real boss; he worked alongside the Anti-Terrorist squad rather than as part of it. Bi-annually he had to report directly to Wolfgang Barz, the Interior Minister, with an outline of his projects-in-progress. Apart from that, and barring any national emergency requiring his expertise, Gemmer was left largely to his own devices. After all, he got results.

Thus his unit had been able to keep an unofficial look-out for Beatrix. It had soon become obvious that she was not dead, but it did appear that she had retired. She had been living quietly in East Berlin before the Wall came down and had got out just before the Stasi secret police traded her in to their western colleagues. She had gone to Iraq, moving on to Istanbul a few weeks before the outbreak of the Gulf War. She had been seen several times in that city and a freelance had been despatched to follow her home. His body had been found, with his throat cut, in one of the carpet bazaars. Beatrix moved westwards. First to Constanta on Romania's Black Sea, then Budapest and finally Prague. That had been the last sighting, nine months before, until five days ago.

He stared down at the most recent photograph of her. A middle-aged face, devoid of any make-up, shoulder-length hair gone grey. She was pushing a bicycle across a busy road; looking out for traffic; her thin lips pursed in concentration. She was dressed in drill trousers and a padded jacket and she looked perfectly ordinary, like hundreds of other women. Not like a killing-machine at all.

Gemmer studied the face more closely. It looked battered, as if she had been in an accident. Some of the lines were undoubtedly scars, the results of plastic surgery. Her nose had been broken and reshaped; her nostrils were now rather flared, and her cheekbones were sunken, her neck scrawny. He examined her eyes. There were deep shadows and lines about them now, but the almond-shape was still there, quite unmistakable. He shut his eyes and he could see every part of this woman's face: she had come to haunt him. And now, to have come so close only to have lost her . . .

Gemmer glanced up at the clock. It was past eight o'clock and he ought to be going home. He wondered, as he had all afternoon, who had sent the package that morning, and what their motive had been.

Had Beatrix got news of the plot to reveal her whereabouts and fled? Or had she been snatched? If she had been taken against her will – and there had been no sign of a struggle at the apartment – it had been done professionally and by now she could be anywhere. A dozen groups or governments could have done it, paying her to do their dirty work.

But she had been inactive for so long, who would want her? Gemmer sighed and got to his feet. In the morning he would give orders for the photograph to replace the old one on the 'Wanted' posters. Apart from that, it was back to the beginning again, watching for Beatrix.

Chapter Three

Zoe could not block out the pictures from her mind.

For the whole of that long, terrible night when the hostel had burned and the flames danced and the people screamed, she had felt like a thing possessed: her body shaking, her eyes and ears dead to everything but the sounds and images in her head.

The ghosts from the Lithuanian woods had returned to haunt her. They were outside in that street below where the sirens wailed and the lights flashed; where the glass was breaking and the new Nazis laughed while they took aim and killed. And Zoe had been there, watching from the safety of her window. She had seen it all and done nothing; she had been a powerless onlooker, her weakness seen and mocked by the enemy.

Now she knew there was no escape; that she could not push the horror away back into history; that the same evil done in that forest more than fifty years before had been reborn in the streets of Europe.

She had sat on the edge of her bed all night, being aware of Annabelle's presence, and terribly glad to have her there, but also quite unable to respond to her. Dimly she had known that several other people had tried talking to her and that Annabelle had fended them off.

Now it was two days later and they were close to home. They had travelled all the previous day, spent the night on the train and early that morning had entered France. Annabelle had said if the train made good time they could get an early afternoon ferry and be in London by seven that night. She smiled over at her, but her friend looked away.

Annabelle was willing the train to go faster; to get them home by tonight so she could hand Zoe over to someone else. She had had enough. First Lithuania, now this. She was a twenty-two year old student on holiday, not a psychiatric nurse. She looked over at the blank, faraway look in Zoe's eyes and prayed that she would stay in one piece, not start that awful shaking and moaning again.

Annabelle could not understand why Zoe had flipped out, when she, exposed to exactly the same experiences, had not. What made Zoe so special, so different, that she had to wreck everything?

Remembering that night, Annabelle shuddered. She had been sure that Zoe had been having convulsions – had gone mad, even – and she had had to deal with her, alone in a foreign country. The policeman who had wanted to take a statement had been sympathetic at first, but as time went on, he had got angry. In the end he had been threatening to arrest Zoe for non-co-operation. It had been up to Annabelle to persuade him that she had been wrong; Zoe had seen nothing. Then she had had to get them both out of the place and onto a train, going anywhere in the direction of home. With Zoe in the state she was in, that had not been easy – like dealing with a sleepwalker.

'It would help if you cried,' Annabelle had suggested when Zoe seemed calmer.

'I can't,' her friend had whispered. 'I've tried and I can't.'

'Well, you're not the only one who's had a shock, you know,' she had snapped, without meaning to. Then she had seen the misery in Zoe's face and cursed herself.

That night, when they parted at Victoria, they each felt enormous relief.

'You'll be all right now, won't you?' Annabelle asked, suddenly guilty.

Zoe nodded. 'Thanks, I'm fine.'

'I'll wait until you've got a taxi. You're going straight to your brother's? You're sure he'll be in?'

'Yes. But even if he isn't, I've got a key. Belle, I . . .'

'What?'

'I'm sorry about everything. I can't explain, but I'm really sorry. Thanks for being such a friend.'

Annabelle blushed and would not meet her eye. 'Don't be

daft, that's what friends are for. Here's a taxi. Take care of yourself.'

In the back of the cab, Zoe leaned against the black padded seat and closed her eyes. Thank God Annabelle had gone. Her own wretchedness had not made her impervious to others or their welfare. She had no wish to inflict the way she felt on Annabelle; yet she knew if she opened her mouth she could speak of nothing else. Which was why she had opted for silence after the initial shock of the hostel-burning had worn off.

But now she was going to see Alasdair. Just the thought of how close he was made her feel better; it had been the prosepct of being able to unload everything onto him that had been keeping her going for the past forty-eight hours. Alasdair would understand; he always had. He would get her out of this.

A solicitor with a major London law firm, he lived in a spacious flat just north of Kensington High Street. Zoe had had a room there whenever she wanted it, since her sixteenth birthday. To her, it was more than a bolt-hole; it was home, much more than the granite house where their parents lived and where she had never felt that she truly belonged. Even during her best times with Tony, she had missed her white and blue bedroom and the easiness of a place where she was always welcome and allowed to be herself.

As she paid the cab-driver she looked up at the Victorian mansion-flats and saw that Alasdair's lights were on. Rather than waiting for the lift she shouldered her rucksack and climbed the two flights of stairs. She hoped that her brother would be on his own; that there would not be a bunch of his friends to deal with, or a new girlfriend to meet. She pushed the hair back out of her eyes and rang the bell.

'You're back!' Alasdair's face split into a delighted grin. He gave her a great bear hug and pulled her into the flat.

It was as messy as ever. Ranged down the hallway were piles of newspapers for recycling, the step-ladders and tins of magnolia paint ready for when Alasdair finally got round to redecoration. A little of the terror that had darkened Zoe's soul lifted: everything was so familiar, she could be safe here.

'Let me take that great weight off you! God, Zo, what have

you got in this rucksack? Rocks from the foothills of the Alps? Or is it just presents for me? Come on into the kitchen and sit down. I've opened a bottle of a very nice Sauvignon which you shall share with me. Clear a space for yourself while I get you a glass.'

She transferred a heap of clean clothes from a chair to the table and sat down. Alasdair kept up a volley of conversation as he searched for a clean glass. 'Aren't you back early? What happened? Did you run out of cash? I told you that you could call me if you wanted more money. Damn, I'm going to have to wash a glass. I hope you appreciate this!'

Watching him, Zoe was struck by how young he looked. He had her large eyes and slight frame, and in his jeans and sweatshirt he looked more like an A-level student than a lawyer.

'There, get that down you, and tell me if it isn't the finest thing you've ever tasted.' He put the glass in her hand and smiled down at her, then frowned.

'Zo, my little pet, aren't you meant to be tanned and well, uh, sort of relaxed-looking? If you don't mind me saying, you're looking less than your best.'

'Thanks,' she tried to laugh, but the muscles in her face hurt. She took a gulp from her glass. 'It's – it's complicated . . .'

She told him everything, a little hesitantly at first – both to spare him and herself – but as she went on, the power of the events seemed to recede slightly and she became eager to tell him everything so that he could fully understand.

He listened without saying a word. Only once did he hold up a hand for her to stop: when she was describing her own presence at the pit.

'I've been afraid of going mad,' she finished, looking up at him for reassurance.

Alasdair's face was a study in concern and sympathy. 'You poor kid,' he said gently. 'You've really been through it, haven't you?'

The kindness in his voice was too much: she felt hot tears trickle down her cheeks, and she gave a sudden sob. 'Oh, Al, I haven't known what to do! I've felt so desperate!'

'Don't cry, pet,' he extended an arm and patted her shoulder clumsily. Alasdair had always been at a loss to deal with tears. 'Here, have some kitchen towel.'

She snuffled into it and blew her nose. 'Al, you understand don't you? It's as if all those dead people in Lithuanina have come back to warn me.'

'Warn you?' He smiled at her. 'What are they warning you about?'

'About the Neo-Nazis! That the same thing could happen again unless we all do something to stop it. Don't you see?'

'Zo, calm down. What you imagined in those woods . . . well, it sounds pretty horrible, but you've got to remember you've always had a vivid imagination. That hostel-burning, that was bloody awful, and really bad timing for you. But you've got to put it into perspective: it was a piece of mindless violence by kids probably still at school. It doesn't mean the Nazis are coming back. That stuff couldn't happen again. It would never be allowed and, anyway, the politics of Europe are entirely different. You know that, don't you?'

She twisted the damp tissue in her hands. 'But how about Bosnia? How about the ethnic cleansing and the Fascists getting into power in Italy? How about the National Front in France and . . . and the UK Nationalists here?'

'Whoah! Hey, when did you get so politically active? You'll be telling me you've been on demos next!' He grinned at her.

'Don't laugh at me! I'm not a baby any more!' she protested.

'Sorry, sorry. I'm only trying to help.'

'Don't you see? Someone's got to do something about racism. You don't know what it was like seeing that Nazi boy laughing . . .' She gulped and looked up at him. 'I feel as if I've really got to do something.'

'Do what?' He smiled at her again. 'What can you do?'

'I don't know. I . . . I thought perhaps you might. Isn't there a group I could join?'

'I'm no political animal, you know that. I'm sure there's lots of groups. But you don't want to get too involved in something like this just now.'

She stared at him. 'Why?'

'You've got your final year coming up, remember? You don't want to risk your degree for some half-baked notion that anything you might do will change the way some people are one iota.'

She felt suddenly cold. 'What d'you mean?'

'Racism is an ugly fact of life, sweetie. Especially right now, with all that's going on in the old Eastern block countries. Nationalism and racism get mixed up. People do horrible things. Always have done, always will. That's the way it is.' He got up and drained his wine glass, then he laid a hand on her head like a benediction. 'Part of growing up is accepting things the way they are, Zo.' He smiled down at her. 'And just getting on with life. Now, talking about life, when did you last have a decent meal?'

She dropped her head, not wanting him to see her disappointment or despair. If Alasdair had failed to understand, what hope was there? Worse, did it mean there really was something wrong with her? Why should she be the only one affected; why her but not Annabelle?

'I'm not hungry,' she muttered.

'Well, I am. Go and have a bath and put on something clean and I'll take you out to Mucha Pasta. I'll tell you all about this wonderful girl I've met. She's coming to dinner tomorrow, actually, so you can meet her. She works in an advertising agency, started off there as a typist and worked her way up and now she's a director, which is pretty amazing, don't you think? Considering she's only twenty-seven. That probably seems ancient to you, but it isn't . . .'

In the days that followed, Zoe tried to accept the logic of Alasdair's words: that nothing she might do could change anything. But then, in the face of a passer-by, she would think that she saw accusing eyes and she would shudder, knowing that for her, Alasdair's words were meaningless; she had to do something. She felt gnawed from within, as if she had been bewitched and now her every move was being observed by the caster of the spell.

Alasdair became quite brisk with her. She was not, he said, to sit around the flat 'moping' when he was out at work; she was to see friends and do 'normal' things. If all else failed, he joked, she could always get on with her coursework.

The trouble, Zoe thought as the days passed, was that nothing seemed to matter any more; she was simply going through the motions of being who people thought she was.

She became adept at concealment. Walking back from Kensington tube station one night she bumped into one of her brother's friends, a barrister whom she had met the previous summer at a party. She agreed to have dinner with the man, laughed at his jokes, and even managed to be brittly bright about her European trip, skipping over the bad bits. Afterwards, her jaw ached with tension.

As Alasdair had promised, his new girlfriend, Kerry Lindsay, had appeared the night after Zoe's return. She was a cheerful young woman with a mop of dark curly hair and a burring West country accent. Zoe had smiled when introduced, asked and answered the appropriate questions, then retired at the earliest opportunity to her room, claiming a headache.

She was sure that she was not convincing Alasdair but her acting was better than she imagined. A week after she had got back, she heard him on the telephone to Kerry, saying that she seemed to be 'getting over it'. 'When you're that age, everything's so important,' he had said, with a chuckle and Zoe had writhed with embarrassment and, for the first time, had briefly hated her brother.

She was alone in the flat two days later, when the doorbell rang. Kerry was standing on the doormat. Remembering that telephone conversation, Zoe flushed and stumbled over her words:

'Please, come in. But I don't know what . . . I mean, Al's not here. He's at work. He won't be home for at least another hour.'

Kerry stepped into the hallway and smiled. 'I know. It's you I want to talk to.'

'Me? Why?' She had not meant the words to sound so harsh. She blushed again: 'Sorry. I was in the kitchen, come and have a seat. I'll move these newspapers.'

'Thanks.' Kerry seemed momentarily lost for words. She

opened her mouth and closed it again, then grinned up at Zoe. 'Alasdair's told me all about you.'

'Oh?' Zoe tried not to sound hostile but she felt doubly invaded.

'I don't mean he's been sneaking or anything. He really adores you, you know? Of course you do. Look, you'll probably hate me for interfering, but when Al told me about those things you saw in Germany and that other place, I mentioned it to a girl I work with, who's Jewish, and she said there's somewhere you can go for help.' Kerry paused. 'That's if you still need it. Which I thought maybe you do. You seem so tense; you don't look as if you're sleeping much. Al says to just leave it alone, but I think maybe you could do with some help.'

Zoe said nothing. She stared at Kerry, wondering why she cared.

Kerry ploughed on: 'I promise you, I haven't told Al a word about this. You know what he's like, doesn't like talking about feelings, but I kept thinking about what he said you'd gone through. Then when I spoke to this girl – a lot of her family was wiped out in Poland – she said there was a place that could help you, the London Holocaust Centre. Have you heard of it?'

Zoe shook her head.

'It's mainly for survivors and relatives of the victims, but they offer counselling to anyone who needs it. You could talk to someone who's specifically trained in dealing with what you are experiencing, someone who's used to people like you.'

That last phrase went home like a shaft. 'People like you,' Zoe thought. 'So that's what it's come to; I'm being dismissed as a nutter.' Nothing showed in her face, though, except polite interest.

'I wrote down their address and phone number,' Kerry went on. 'If you need to, will you give it a try?'

Zoe took the slip of paper. 'Thanks. It's nice of you to bother,' she said.

Later that night, after Alasdair had returned and taken Kerry out to see a film, Zoe sat and stared at the address she had been given. Somewhere in Pimlico: somewhere where the relatives and survivors of that terrible time went to be comforted. Not a place for outsiders, Zoe thought. Not to be used as a drop-in centre for people who had no real right to feel so disturbed, who were not Jewish and who had never even known a Jewish person. To go there would be an intrusion into grief; especially for one who had witnessed what she had witnessed and done nothing. Zoe made her decision and tore the paper into tiny shreds.

The following evening, Alasdair came home to an empty flat. He found Zoe's note on the kitchen table.

'A friend called this morning and offered me a lift back to uni this afternoon. Thought I'd take him up on it, so I can get some essays done and use the library before term starts. I tried to call you at work to let you know but your secretary said you were in meetings. I'll call in a day or so. Thanks for looking after me so well. Lots of love, etc . . .'

He called Kerry. 'Move in with me,' he said. 'Tonight. We've got the place to ourselves. Yes, she's gone back to college.

'What? Well, she must have been feeling better to have gone, mustn't she? Hey, it's up to me to worry about her. She's my sister. Just get over here.'

Chapter Four

Zoe felt that she was in a bubble – one of those germ-free bubbles they used in hospitals – touching against life but not joining in. It suited her that way; it protected her from attack.

She had been back at university for three weeks and had established a routine. Each day she washed and dressed, attended lectures and seminars, ate a little, slept a little. Enough to get by, to look OK on the surface. People were still a bit of a problem, their concern and questions prodding at her, exposing her as someone different, a 'weirdo'.

She had overheard Annabelle describing her as that to someone else on their corridor. It had saddened her but not as much, she realised, as it should have done. She and Annabelle had been great friends – Zoe's first real friend – and to hear herself being described by her in such a fashion should have been devastating. Instead, after the initial hurt, she had felt relief: Annabelle was one less person to maintain a front for.

Zoe was finding all close relationships very difficult. She occasionally had the eerie sensation of watching herself on stage and feared that anyone who came too close might see the same thing. That was why she had fled London, from Kerry's concern and questions, and the fear that Alasdair might see through her performance. It was better to keep people at a distance, holding perfunctory, polite conversations.

She spent her free time in the library, although not doing her coursework. Instead, in the History section, she read about the Holocaust and, on the ground floor, where the daily newspapers were kept, she absorbed the activities of the Neo-Nazi movement.

When she tried to rationalise what she was doing, her thought processes blurred. Part of it, she knew, was mixed up in her constant struggle to bury her emotions. Repeated exposure to the horrors would deaden her, she hoped. Weirdo that she was, she told herself, it made sense to her. And over the weeks, it seemed to be working.

There was a book that she had found, called *The Final Solution: A Photographic Record*. The pictures were graphic and uncompromising: the gas ovens of Auschwitz; inmates in uniform crushed against barbed wire; the cattle trucks; weightless, stiff bodies being hurled into fires; the death marches. Here and there a camera had caught something particularly arresting: the simple bewilderment on a child's face; the hopelessness of a mother; the misery in the eyes of a man made old.

Numbed, Zoe had flicked over the pages, but one photograph had arrested her. It showed a group of naked young women, obviously about to be shot, huddled together in a shallow pit. They were trying to hide their nakedness, whether out of modesty, or a desire to shield themselves from the camera, or from bullets or perhaps just the cold, Zoe could not tell. The lens had captured one woman full-frontal, trying to shelter herself with her arms. The expression on her face was a mixture of pleading, disbelief, and most horrible, a timid smile – a pitiful remnant of a distant life – for the photographer.

Staring at that face, unable to take her eyes from it, Zoe had felt physically ill. She had had to steady herself against the metal bookshelves and breathe slowly and deeply until the nausea had passed. But that had been three weeks ago: now she could look at the picture and it registered zero on her emotional chart, or very nearly. It was as if a part of her had died and the rest of her knew that the time for grieving was past, that that part was better off dead.

She realised that if she could do without her emotions, or at least bury them deep within her, then neither they, nor anything else could hurt her again. She would be able to function perfectly normally and people would stop worrying about her. And her theory might have worked, she thought, if only it had not been for the activities of the Neo-Nazis and her reaction to them.

Every day, it seemed, there were new outrages. An Asian

woman raped by a gang of white youths; firebombs in mosques in Birmingham; a Jewish cemetery defaced in north London. The foreign pages were, if anything, worse: virtual no-go areas for coloured people in the south of France; the murder of an anti-Fascist politician in Italy, and in Germany, the Far Right, driven underground, had assumed a glamour that was attracting the bitter, unemployed young.

She was aware that the activities themselves were not new. In the past she had been briefly horrified, but dismissive of them: after all, they had nothing to do with her life. Now she could only wonder at herself for ever thinking that way. Each Neo-Nazi attack was a fresh agony for her; it was the one thing that, like an electric shock, jolted her back to life, sending a charge through her deadened feelings. The rage would twist inside her like something in torment, but leave her drained with frustration. What was the good of anger with no outlet?

Junie Carson saw the man watching her on the second day of the 'think-tank' in Amsterdam. He was in his mid-thirties, with longish dark hair and a thin brown face. He wore a scuffed black leather jacket and lounged slack and at ease in his chair. His eyes were slatey-blue. Junie blushed and looked away, then looked back. He was still staring.

She was a plain girl, an only child who, at twenty-five, still lived at home. She was short, with a surplus of very white flesh and coarse, dark hair cut straight across her forehead. She wore rather heavy-looking glasses; her mother said contact lenses would be wasted on her.

Junie was assistant secretary of the AFF (Anti-Fascist Front) in London, a group she had joined four years previously after being stopped in the street by an eager young man who wanted her to sign his petition. Her membership was her sole piece of rebellion; her mother thought she went bell-ringing every Tuesday evening. She considered that her appointment to the Committee three months before was probably the best thing that had ever happened to her. She chose to ignore the obvious: that she was a gofer for the Secretary and someone to blame for anything that went wrong, from poor attendance at rallies to missing stationery.

She had little success with men, but she did have vanity. The man's attention was like a finger running down her spine. She timed herself – five minutes – before she looked again. His chair was empty and she could not see him anywhere. She bit her cheek; she had only been imagining his interest.

At the end of the morning session, she walked out into the warm October sunshine. The rest of the London contingent was having a working lunch from which Junie was excluded but she told herself she did not mind; she would use the time to visit Anne Frank's house. Then she heard a man's steps behind her and, turning, saw it was him.

'We need to talk.' He was not English. German or French – Dutch, of course. It would make sense. She blinked up at him; he was tall, six feet at least. Close to, he looked even better: a blue shadow around the jaw, a wide mouth, and those wonderful eyes that bored into hers. Her tummy flipped over and an ugly red flush raced up her neck.

He frowned at her. 'About work for the Cause,' he said.

He marched a little ahead of her, not looking back, confident that she would follow, and it did not cross her mind to do otherwise. She panted after him.

The man knew the city well. He led her over two canal bridges, then turned right into a maze of small streets. At the end of one, he stopped outside a brown bar and glanced in both directions. He was inside before she caught up.

He was at the back, sitting at a corner table, watching the door. He kept watching it as she slid awkwardly into the bench-seat opposite. Then he leaned forwards and spoke softly: 'Everything we speak is secret.'

She blinked at him in wonder.

'You will not tell anyone. Not in your group, not your boyfriend, no one. OK?'

'I don't have . . . OK.'

He stared past her towards the bar. 'I think perhaps you might be the person for whom I'm looking.'

She gulped noisily.

'But first you must give me some answers.' He shot her a look. 'The truth,' he added.

She could only stare at him. He fired the questions at her

like a sergeant major. Her position in group; reasons for joining; her fears and hopes; even who of the Committee officers she liked, disliked and why. His English was nearly perfect; only the odd phrase, a slight hesitation now and again, gave him away.

He crossed, criss-crossed her life. 'Tell me about your family . . . Occupation of father? Mother? Their beliefs . . . Your job . . . salary . . . pastimes . . .' Where she went on holiday.

He gave her no time to think or hesitate and, as the interrogation continued, she found herself straining to tell him everything: that she had once been engaged – she had been eighteen; he nineteen – and that her mother had made her break it off. When the questions finally stopped, she was exhausted but exalted. No one had ever shown such interest in her before.

She gazed at the man in adoration tinged with fear: had she passed the test, she wondered. Was she still the person he was looking for?

He said nothing for several seconds. In the silence, Junie found her tissue and wiped her glasses. Her throat hurt with desire to please him.

Then he spoke so quietly that she had to strain to catch the words. 'My group is like yours. We also wish to destroy the Nazis. But my group wants more, much more.' Another full-voltage look: 'You get me?'

'Er, yes.' Bigger things, she thought frantically: rallies, demos, campaigns.

He considered his hands, interlocking them, turning them over face-down on the table. Then he seemed to make up his mind. 'We need people. Recruits. All nationalities, German, Italian, Spanish. Dutch.'

He smiled, showing very white, uneven teeth. 'English. We want English too. Twelve people. Young. Six boys and six girls.'

In the last week of November, Zoe's personal tutor asked to see her.

Zoe had always been a dream of a student: intelligent,

hard-working and highly capable. She had been marked for a good 2:1 next summer, but now ... She had not handed in any work all term and, although she attended everything, she did it in a trance, saying nothing, and there was a vacancy about her that was ringing alarm bells. Overall, amongst the staff that taught her, there was a feeling that something must be said: the task fell to her personal tutor, Sarah Whitely.

Dr Whitely was a woman who heartily disliked and disapproved of most of her students, chiefly on the grounds of their youth. Her own had been wretched – a drunken, abusive father and a defeated mother. It had been schoolwork that had saved her, rescued her from the drudgery expected of her and taken her to university. Academically, she had excelled, but she had never relaxed. She had been considered drab and schoolmarmish; in turn, she saw other students as frivolous and undeserving. That opinion had persisted throughout her academic career: so few of the students she had dealings with were, in her opinion, worthy of a university place.

Until now Zoe's academic excellence had saved her, but Dr Whitely was more than willing to believe the worst.

'Is it drugs?' she asked bluntly.

Zoe stared blankly at her, then got up and walked out.

Feeling vindicated by yet another example of student ingratitude, Dr Whitely wrote in her file, 'Student offered assistance. Rejected.' She paused, then added, 'Churlish.' She timed and dated it – to be on the safe side – and absolved herself from any further responsibility.

Zoe had felt the walls closing in; she had had to get out of that room. As she had left, she had seen the disgusted expression on her tutor's face, but it had not stopped her. 'I've changed so much,' she thought as she shoved open the door of the Arts Faculty. 'I used to care what people thought. Now it doesn't matter.'

It was a bitterly cold day and she had brought no coat, but for over an hour she walked around the campus. Fear hammered inside her head; she was endangering her future, wrecking all her plans without knowing what to do, or where to go. It was as if she had stepped off the edge without first finding out how far there was to fall.

She came to an abrupt halt. She was on the first floor of the Student Union building, facing a wall that was also used as the University notice board. Everything was advertised here: lifts to London; cats; course books; leather jackets; religions. Zoe's eyes fixed on one white card near the bottom. In firm black block capitals, she read:

'ANTI-FASCIST FRONT. STOP THE NAZIS NOW. MARCH AND RALLY TRAFALGAR SQUARE DECEMBER 2. BE THERE.'

It was as if someone had spoken out loud to her, offering a thread out of the labyrinth.

Junie had arrived early at the rally. It was seven weeks since Amsterdam, and she was still one recruit short. Maybe the man would not mind, but she did not want to disappoint him, and she had already failed him, quite drastically, in one respect: equality of the sexes.

She shouldered her way through the crowd. Considering the weather – cold, grey and drizzling – it was a good turnout, around five thousand. Surely here, she thought a little desperately, there must be a suitable female, someone who would help redress the imbalance and make it three women to nine men.

It was not her fault, she told herself, that appropriate females had been so much harder to find. Junie knew what most women were like, even ones sympathetic to the Cause – flirty, caring too much about their looks and boyfriends and clothes, not sufficiently dedicated.

She, of course, had been more than willing to offer herself; but the man had not wanted her. Junie skirted a group of noisy Iranian dissidents. She blushed, remembering her humiliation in the Amsterdam bar when for that split second she had thought he wanted to recruit her.

'Me?' she had whispered.

She had seen the rejection, the incredulous look quickly covered-up, before he said the words. 'No. You will bring them to me. A very important role. You are willing?'

Of course she had said yes. She had swallowed hard and convinced herself that what he said was true: her role was of crucial significance. Only occasionally since Amsterdam had she found herself longing for the excitement, the thrill of being on the front-line, of being part of the 'elite' fighting corps that the man had said he was looking for.

He had been so mysterious, so enticing. He had told her a little – a very little, come to think of it – about the group. It was a secret underground army of Anti-Fascists, people who were going to ensure that the Neo-Nazis had a short and bloody existence. Precisely how they were going to achieve this the man had not mentioned and Junie had not asked. She assumed the fighters would be trained in, well, fighting. Punching Neo-Nazis, kicking them, that sort of thing. Perhaps the female recruits would learn judo.

'Do I investigate their backgrounds?' she had asked, pleased with her question.

'No. Only send them to me.'

The group's leaders were in place, he had said. There were ample funds. Weapons and training were not a problem. The only missing ingredient were the soldiers.

Junie ducked her head to avoid the spoke of a careless umbrella. She glanced at the faces around her. If only they knew who she really was, she thought! How their expressions would change! That had been possibly the hardest thing: to keep quiet about her mission, especially to the others in the AFF.

Sometimes she closed her eyes and saw herself doing it; saw the shock on the Committee Secretary's face. But the man had warned her to maintain her 'cover' at all costs.

At odd intervals during the day – at her job as an insurance adviser in Holborn, or at home with her parents, doing the dishes after tea – Junie would get an odd jumpy feeling inside. Why, she was a Mata Hari figure – an agent behind enemy lines, fearless, dedicated. Never, she vowed, would she betray the Cause, not even if they tortured her.

She began taking elaborate precautions when she came home from work to ensure that she was not being followed. She used the telephone as little as possible.

The Dutchman – he had not told her his name – said that a variety of recruits were required. The 'rougher element' as well as college kids. She had waited for an explanation but he had given her none.

She had dealt with the thugs first: five boys whose faces were well known to her, who appeared regularly at rallies, heckling and picking fights. They had been abusive to her when she approached them, then openly disbelieving, but finally greedily eager to accept her offer: a weekend in Hamburg, as guests of a new European Anti-fascist movement, all expenses paid. Their only commitment would be to attend a meeting each day, and a rally in the city on Sunday morning. The boys had exchanged swaggering, wolfy grins. The shortest one with the bad acne had leered at her: 'We're your men, love.'

The four male students were scarcely more difficult. One of Junie's AFF responsibilities was to circulate invitations to forthcoming events to universities, schools and colleges around the country. Normally, a fairly high proportion of an AFF audience came from academic establishments: all she had to do was select a few promising candidates. Her two females had also come from such gatherings.

But the last one had so far eluded her. If she was going to meet the man's deadline and deliver them all to him by the following weekend, she had to find her here. Junie checked the time and felt a moment's panic: the rally would be over soon, and still she had seen nobody who looked remotely suitable.

Hearing a yell from above her head, she looked up. Several people were climbing over the lions, yelling at each other, showing off. No, too young and she had enough riff-raff, anyway.

She started to weave through the crowd (she had become rather good at this, she thought; no one ever gave her a second glance) looking for the right qualities – alertness, interest, a healthy appearance, perhaps anger. Also, the man had suggested, anyone who looked like a loner. They were of special interest to him.

But no one here was on their own; everyone was in groups. Half of them seemed more interested in talking to each other than listening to the speakers. Junie pushed her way through. She saw a smaller knot of students standing around their University Anti-Fascist banner. Five men, two women and a child, well, a girl of about fourteen. Small, no make-up, very pale and pinched-looking, she stood a little way from the others. A younger sister feeling out of it, perhaps. Junie passed her by then stopped. The girl was wearing the university scarf; perhaps she was older, and there was something about her expression . . .

Junie stared, but the girl did not notice; she was utterly rapt by the speech, or was it something more – lost in her own world, her eyes moving as if she saw something other than the smudgy figures on the distant stage. She had an air of complete solitariness, self-containment, of being out of tune. A loner. Junie cast a few furtive glances at the immediate crowd. No one was watching. She advanced upon her target.

'Excuse me.'

No response. Junie thrust her face a little closer and tried again. This time, the girl jumped and took a step backwards.

Junie went into her routine. She smiled nicely: 'I represent a new international group of Anti-Fascist students. In two weeks we're holding our first annual conference in Hamburg . . .'

That night, in her little bedroom in Worcester Park, Junie triumphantly added Zoe Douglas's name to her list.

It had taken all day, but eventually at five o'clock in the afternoon, Matt Anderson got the go-ahead: he could go to Hamburg for the conference provided he did it on a shoe-string.

Chris Lomax had glared at him with what looked like hatred. 'I've just spent two hours begging cash from that bastard upstairs. I had to listen to him whine about lazy journalists and fat-cat editors and impossible budgets. So no taxis, no entertaining, no frills, no nothing. And receipts for everything. Got it?'

Matt beamed like a pools winner. 'Sure, Chris. And thanks. I really appreciate it. It'll be worth it.'

'Yeah, well just bring me back a story. One for next week,

not next month. And something we can use, not something the lawyers'll jump all over. And Anderson . . .'

'Yup?'

'Don't get too hooked onto this anti-Nazi stuff, OK?'

Matt frowned. 'What d'you mean?'

'You know what I mean. I'm not saying you mightn't be onto something, but I can't let you spend too long on it. We don't have the staff to let you go off-rota. So go to Hamburg, sniff about, but remember this is a newspaper, not your own personal research facility.'

Driving home, Matt sent up a prayer for Hamburg. He very much doubted the conference would merit a decent story. Oh, he could always scribble a few paragraphs, but he knew their contents were unlikely to justify a foreign trip. He was not primarily interested in what was said at Hamburg, more who was saying it and who was listening. It was a fishing expedition, and might net nothing. He was sure he had explained that to Lomax. Anyway, it was pointless worrying about it now.

It took him nearly ninety minutes to reach his flat in Hampton; sitting in the tail-back along the Thames embankment, breathing in all those fumes. Perhaps he should buy an apartment in town, get the tube or the bus to the office like everyone else. But then he would have to give up his sailing or reduce it to weekends only and he was sure that was what kept him sane.

He was thirty-one years old and had been a journalist for ten of them, the last as Chief Investigative reporter on *The Clarion*. It had an international reputation for quality and lucidity of thought. Matt knew that he had a plum job; knew too, that if he was right, then he was on to one of the best stories of his career.

For some time he had been writing about the growth of the Neo-Nazi movement in the UK. The British National Party; the National Front; the new but alarmingly popular UK Nationalists, all with their veneer of political respectability; the Blood-and-Honour skinheads, and then the much lesser known, hence to Matt more interesting, splinter factions. He had investigated several: the International Third Position; Third Way and Combat 18, the numbers standing for the initials, AH, Adolf Hitler. Their membership was small, but nasty.

There had been several racist murders, especially around south London. Victims were mainly young, defenceless black kids. There had been dozens of racist attacks too, but then there always had been, and swastikas daubed on Jewish cemeteries, and graffiti on mosques and synagogues ∴. Just how sinister the groups were, how well-planned and orchestrated their attacks, was open to question. It depended on who you spoke to, but without doubt there were links between this hard-core element and the spreading European Nazi movement.

It was while Matt had been monitoring the extent of these links – scouring the foreign pages and wire service for background – that he had spotted something else. A spate of fires and burglaries on Neo-Nazi targets: in Paris a suspect fire at the home of a Le Pen sympathiser; arson attacks on several buildings used by Neo-Nazis across Germany; and burglaries at the headquarters of an ultra-right party in Berlin and Rostock. Matt wrote brief notes on each one.

All the incidents had occurred within a three-week span in September. No one had been caught and no group had claimed responsibility. Surely they were too far-flung, too spasmodic to be anything other than a series of one-offs? A handful of the angrier Anti-Fascist movements in Germany and France striking back? God alone knows, they had every justification. But something in the nature of the attacks niggled Matt. There had always been boot-boys in the Anti-Fascist movement, kids mainly looking for aggro with the other side: the street fighters of one mob versus the other. But these incidents seemed to be of different calibre. He put in a few calls to stringers; spoke to a couple of German police officers. They confirmed what he thought: the incidents had been well-planned and executed; none of the perpetrators appeared to have criminal records, hence they were possibly politically motivated.

Two weeks before, there had been a burglary on a police station in Lubeck. Security files relating to local Neo-Nazis had been taken. It made three paragraphs on the wire service;

no British newspaper used it. Matt telephoned the police captain direct, thanking God for his good German.

The man was flattered by his interest. He laughed at Matt's suggestion, but agreed to keep him informed, or at least to speak to him on a weekly basis. Two weeks later,, he had stopped laughing. He sounded worried. 'It is probably a coincidence,' he told the reporter. 'But Jurgen Wolf was run over last night. Fractured skull, broken legs, shattered pelvis; the car crushed him against a wall and drove off. Wolf? Oh, I forgot you wouldn't know. He's leader of the "German Soil for German People" movement. Yes, Neo-Nazi.'

The policeman hesitated. 'There's something else, Herr Anderson. I don't know if it means anything at all, but two days ago one of Lubeck's deputies got pretty badly smashed up in a mugging attack. I didn't think much of it at the time; we have a lot of muggings, but both incidents coming together like this . . .? I'm going to pass all this on to Wiesbaden, see what they think about it.'

Then, as if in confirmation, the very next day in Dusseldorf two Neo-Nazi sympathisers had died in a car explosion. Again, no one had claimed responsibility.

Matt had hauled Lomax away from the newsdesk into a meeting room. He was barely able to contain his excitement. 'This is organised stuff, Chris. Someone is behind these attacks, I know it. Mossad perhaps. Or it could be a new terrorist group in the making.'

Lomax had been unmoved. 'Coincidences, Matt. We need proof. The Anti-Fascist movement is a holy cow, specially now with all these racist attacks on foreigners. We can't print one word suggesting otherwise until we've got it in concrete with red ribbons on.'

Matt tempted him. 'You can see the headline, can't you? "The New Resistance: *The Clarion* asks, Is Terrorism Finally Justified?" We'd be first with the story.'

'We'd also be the first with a writ!'

Matt had spent a week working hard on his sources within the Anti-Nazi movement. Some were hostile at the very notion of 'their side' using violence; others admitted there was increasing frustration with the reasonable approach. 'We were reasonable with the Nazis fifty years ago,' one old man told Matt. 'And look where that got us.'

A few communities had set up vigilante groups to keep right-wing thugs at bay and it seemed likely that, in time, these groups would overstep the mark. But there was nothing to suggest the kind of orchestrated, selective violence that appeared to be happening in Germany and France.

The previous evening, Matt had met up with Steve, his Special Branch contact, at a pub near Heathrow Airport. Steve downed a pint and a half listening to his theory of a new Anti-Nazi group.

'Don't know,' he said finally. 'If there is, I haven't heard of them. Doesn't mean they don't exist, just maybe they're not here yet. If they are here, they're so small they haven't made so much as a blip on the screen.' He considered something else. 'This lot in Europe; they're a bit shy, seems to me. Usually these groups can't wait to see their name in print. Your lot are playing things very close to their chests, aren't they?'

'So you think I'm wasting my time?'

'Maybe, or maybe you're just a bit early. They haven't got their act together yet, or they're testing the water. I don't know, just a thought.'

Matt had heard about the Hamburg conference when he got back to his flat at just before midnight. Living alone as he had been since Louise had left two months earlier, he was always immensely cheered by the sight of the ansaphone's flashing light.

The message was from Clive, a young Jewish activist who had helped him expose a number of MPs, including a Cabinet Minister, as being members of an extremist, Far-Right movement funded by white South Africans.

Matt had called him straight back. 'Matt, look, I don't know if it's going to be of any use but there's a conference in Hamburg this weekend that sounds a bit weird.'

'How so?'

'Well, the main groups like the Anti-Nazi league, the AFF, the AFA, haven't been invited. I only heard about it today through the grapevine and the word is, it might not be strictly kosher.'

'What? It's not Anti-Fascist?'

'No. Well, nobody knows really. There's American money behind it, but no one knows whose, or which group it's from. Might not mean anything of course, might just be some guy who wants to stay anonymous. But there's some interesting speakers going to be there.'

'Like who?'

'Heard of a man called Zimmerman? New York? He's been in trouble for stirring kids up to attack anyone they think's Anti-Semitic, and I stress "think". Anyone who looks at a Jew the wrong way, or cracks a Jewish joke, might find himself lying in a dark alley with a broken head.

'Zimmerman's meant to be speaking in Hamburg on Saturday night. I thought perhaps that, plus shadowy sponsors, plus all the mystery around it might add up to something you'd like to have a look at?'

Chapter Five

Zoe gazed about her, absorbing the drabness of most of the audience that did, however, seem to correspond so fittingly with the speakers. She supposed that their words might be losing something in translation – certainly the gaps for the translators did nothing to help the flow of the speeches – but the German contingent that made up most of the audience looked as bored as everyone else.

'FIGHTING FASCISM TODAY; LESSONS FROM THE HOLOCAUST' was the topic for that night's meeting. One would have imagined it difficult to make such a subject tedious, but that was what speaker after speaker had thus far achieved. Instead of practical advice on combating Neo-Nazism, there had been a dreary litany of why the Anti-Fascist movement had failed: verbal attacks on politicians; accusations and counter-accusations of ineptitude and malpractice amongst groups and some pretty wild conspiracy theories including Hitler's heirs still being alive and Nazi messages being subliminally flashed onto television screens.

'A total waste of time,' Zoe thought.

It was Saturday evening; the weekend had been hard-going and, for her at least, profoundly disappointing.

The conference had looked so impressive on the outside. It was being held in a modern complex on the outskirts of the city, near the airport. The place was obviously designed to cater for thousands. Far too big for the Holocaust Conference which numbered, Zoe guessed, a maximum of three hundred including the speakers. They had the whole complex entirely to themselves, but were occupying just the top floor of a four-storey building. It was more than spacious enough: apart from the main hall where she was now sitting, there were several workshop-rooms and a small but well-equipped cinema showing continuous Holocaust footage.

The organisers had clearly done their utmost to ensure that everyone was well catered for. Not only were there interpreters for the wide range of nationalities represented – Zoe had heard German, English, French, and Italian spoken – but all the different groups had their own 'Conference Facilator' who was with them virtually twenty-four hours a day. Meals and refreshments had been laid on; there were easy chairs for the very few 'leisure times'; piles of magazines to read and bookstalls to browse over. The hotel where Zoe and the others were staying was comfortable; transport had been laid on; there was even the promise of some free time in the city the following day.

It must have cost a bomb, Zoe thought. It was such a pity that it was all for nothing.

She had really hoped when Junie started talking to her at that grim Trafalgar Square rally the previous week, that at last she was about to meet people who felt as she did, who were convinced that immediate drastic action had to be taken against the Nazis. If that meant giving up her studies and throwing herself into a political campaign, Zoe was more than willing.

'There's nothing more important to me,' she had told Junie seriously, 'than stopping the Nazis. Nothing.' And Junie had smiled and nodded at her, as if she held the answer. But then this . . .

It had all been so dreary. The workshops and seminars had consisted of academic debate. That morning, Zoe had sat through three hours of furious argument over the word 'Holocaust'; the leader of the group insisting that only Jews had the right to the name. Another session had been entirely dominated by an American Nazi hunter, obsessed in tracking down old Nazis and putting them on trial. Zoe could not see the point: there were too many new Nazis about to bother about a handful of geriatrics.

She checked her watch: coming up for eight. Another two hours at least. She sighed, not caring that she was clearly audible, and shifted her weight in the uncomfortable plastic chair. It was pointless being frustrated, she told herself, she just must endure. At least the last few months had accustomed her to that.

She glanced to her left. At the end of the 'British' row were the seats for the lads of the party: five of them in a uniform of ripped jeans and baseball hats. They had provided some light entertainment in the afternoon by heckling a boring French nun. Zoe craned forward: their chairs were empty. She frowned, then remembered, they had probably done what they had been bragging of since they arrived, taken themselves off to the Reeperbahn, Hamburg's notorious red light district.

'You coming, Zoe?' one had asked her at lunchtime. His friends sniggered, egging him on. 'Give you a good time.'

Thinking about them, Zoe considered that it was strange that someone as mousy and strait-laced as Junie had invited the lads at all. She glanced at the woman, sitting to her right. Incomprehensibly, she looked excited, but then she had looked like that all weekend. Perhaps the true cause was the man who sat beside her.

He had met them all at the airport, driven them to the hotel, and had been hanging around ever since. Junie had obviously met him before; she introduced him rather breathlessly as their 'facilitator'.

He was quite attractive but in the designer-stubble sort of way that reminded Zoe too much of Tony. He had cool bluey-grey eyes that managed to appear both lazy and alert at the same time. He had smiled at them all.

'Good evening. My name is Pieter. I am from Holland.'

Zoe saw that even that scant information had surprised Junie. Pieter was clearly not in the habit of divulging much about himself. Curious, actually, when he was so interested in everyone else, asking all sorts of personal questions.

That morning at breakfast, he had interrogated her. 'So, Zoe, you are a rich girl then, with a flat in London?'

'My brother's.' She had tried to freeze him with a look, but his lips had only curled mockingly.

'And you like to be left on your own, I see.'

She had concentrated on her coffee.

'Is that true of all aspects of your life, Zoe?'

Nosey bastard, she thought now. What had it to do with him? What right had he to question her? She should have told him where to get off; to stop hassling her. She sighed again: she really did not care that much.

But she had been aware of Pieter watching her, on and off, all day. Not in a way that suggested he fancied her, more as a teacher would watch an unusual pupil or as a scientist would monitor a test-animal.

In one of the short breaks that morning she had picked up a couple of books from a stall in the reception area. *Psychology of Resistance* was one title; *Armed Justification* another.

'Interesting subjects, Zoe.' His voice behind her had made her jump.

She had looked round and seen him leaning on a pillar, arms folded; that sardonic look on his face.

She had turned her back on him, replaced the books and picked up another at random: *Memories of Hell – the True Story of a Jewish Lithuanian Survivor.*

'Oh God,' she had said, dropping it. It had landed with a smack on the floor.

In a moment he had been beside her, the book in his hand, frowning at the title and then at her.

'What is it? What is it you don't like?' His eyes had been wide, intent on hers, probing down deep into her, trapping her like a rabbit in a car's headlights.

'What happened to you Zoe?' His voice had been soft and kind, beguiling. And for a moment she had wanted to tell him everything. Then she had remembered that no one could help her; no one could understand. If she talked she would only be revealing her weakness.

She had taken a step back, clenching her fists so hard into her palms that they hurt.

'I don't want to talk about it.'

She had stumbled away from him into the empty seminar room. Her palms had been sweating; she had felt raw and panicky, short of breath. She had shut her eyes and seen the forest, opened them and Pieter had been standing in the doorway, watching.

She shuddered. Even the memory of how exposed she had

felt frightened her. She had the eerie feeling that he was watching her now. She bit her lip and kept her eyes on the stage. She would just have to make sure that she avoided Pieter for the rest of the weekend.

At that moment, two people were watching Zoe. One sat behind her, but a little to her right so that he had a good view of her facial expression and could monitor her reactions. He could not watch her constantly as he was supposed to be evaluating two other members of the English party at the same time. In the student notebook on his lap, he scribbled sufficient notes on Zoe – she was subject B – to keep Pieter happy, but in his eyes, the girl was unlikely to get past the first round; she was too inattentive. Subject D, an intense young man studying engineering, was a far better bet. He concentrated mainly on him.

The other person looking at Zoe was Matt. He was sitting on the stage in the press gallery, a double-row of orange plastic chairs, only three of which were occupied. Hardly surprising: it had taken considerable stamina that morning to get past a line-up of security guards that had materialised in the reception area as soon as he uttered the word, 'Press'.

He had been searched, his tape-recorder and camera taken, and then he had been propelled into a small room for a thirty minute, third-degree interrogation by a hard-faced, well-dressed young woman whose lapel badge declared her to be 'Monika – Conference Organiser'. When she had finally handed him a large, white lapel badge with the word 'Journalist' in capital letters in both English and German, she had managed to convey that she would much have preferred to have branded the word on his forehead with a hot iron.

'Can you tell me the name of the organisation behind the conference?' he had asked in his perfect German and with one of his best smiles.

'I will check for you,' she had answered in equally good English. He had not seen her since.

It had been a trying day all round. He and the other journalists, both local people, had been heavily shepherded throughout by a trio of bland, uncommunicative young men who were supposed to be their personal stewards.

'I'd like to interview one of the speakers,' Matt had said at the brief mid-morning break.

'That will not be possible, I'm afraid,' the chief steward had immediately replied.

'Why not?' demanded the younger of the two other journalists.

'The speakers are resting. Would you care to accompany us to the press room for coffee?'

Lunchtime had been as bad: no chance to get into the crowds and mingle. Even if there had been, Matt doubted how much good it would have done. The audience seemed to be divided into small groups with several leaders or monitors who protected their charges zealously from even casual conversations with other groups' members. The speakers were being as carefully shielded; he saw them being led into a side-room and the door firmly shut.

There had been nothing for it but to let the day unravel and, as it had done, Matt had become increasingly frustrated. The quality of the speeches was so bad! He tuned in, briefly, to the words being uttered by the small figure with the red spikey hair currently addressing the audience: Dr Ernst Zimmerman. At least, Matt had thought, remembering Clive's description of the man, there would be a few newsworthy inflammatory quotes in his speech. Perhaps an immediate call to arms, or an outrageous condemnation of the whole German race. But no, since he had started thirty minutes before, Dr Zimmerman had been numbingly dull. His topic was – Matt consulted his notebook – 'An Appreciation of the Achievements of Anti-Semitic Watchdog Committees across the Globe'.

'And now,' Zimmerman was saying in his nasal New York voice, 'I shall turn to the noble work currently being undertaken in the former Soviet Union.'

Matt sighed wearily. Some rabblerouser, he thought. Clive must have got his wires crossed somewhere.

He put down his pen. He knew that the story was not going to be handed to him in one of the speeches; it was going to need some hard-digging behind the scenes. He needed to

catch someone unawares and get them talking, but how to
do that under these circumstances?

It was then that he saw Zoe. He counted: she was sitting
eight rows from the front, someone who looked clean and fresh
amidst all the greyness. She had fair, shoulder-length hair that
in this light looked blonde. Her face was heart-shaped, her
complexion rather pale with a luminous quality to it, giving her
a rather ethereal appearance. She was probably given to long,
meaningful stares and not finishing her sentences, he thought,
but she stirred him nonetheless, bringing all his protective
instincts to the surface. She was wearing a big chunky white,
clean jumper; it swamped her, adding to the waif-appeal.

From here, her best feature was undoubtedly her eyes: huge
and apparently etched in charcoal. And looking very, very
bored. 'Now what,' he said to himself, 'is she doing here?'

Zoe jumped. She had stopped listening to Zimmerman's
speech some time before and had allowed her mind to go
completely blank; now someone touched her arm.

'Zoe,' hissed Junie. She kept her eyes straight ahead. She
whispered out of the corner of her mouth: 'He wants to talk
to you.'

Zoe gazed stupidly at her profile. 'Who does?'

'Pieter! You're to follow him now.'

'What?'

A boy's head from the seat in front swivelled around.

'Sssh!' said Junie. Zoe saw that she had gone bright red in
the face. 'Just get up when he does and go with him.'

'Why should I?'

'Zoe,' from Junie's other side, Pieter softly called her name.
He bent forward and smiled at her. 'I'd like to talk to you.
Come on.' He stood up and several people in front as well
as the whole row behind, turned to look at him. He leaned
across Junie and touched Zoe's shoulder. 'Come on, let's go,'
he said.

Embarrassment made her move; the fear that if she did not
do as he said then everyone would stare at her. She got up, as
red as Junie, and squeezed past her, trying not to bump into
people's knees.

'God, this is awful,' she thought. 'He's throwing me out for not being interested enough.'

He pushed open one of the main doors and they were out in the main lobby. Apart from three security guards standing at the top of the stairs, there was no one else about. From behind her came the twangy tones of Zimmerman; it was good to be out of there at least, she told herself. And even if she was going to be sent home in disgrace, what did it matter?

Pieter led her over to the group of easy chairs and sat down, motioning for her to do likewise.

'So what did you think about the speech?' he asked, his voice neutral. His eyes were boring into hers and his wide mouth was twisted down at one end. It reminded her unbearably of Tony's sneer.

She stuck her chin in the air: 'I thought it was bloody awful if you must know. And I think it's a criminal waste of money if speakers like that are being paid. In fact, this whole conference . . .'

Pieter was watching her quietly, with the same amused expression. 'Yes?' he said.

'. . . has been a complete waste of time.'

'I agree.' He grinned at her. 'Bloody boring. I'm glad to hear you say it.'

She stared. 'But don't you work for them?'

'Them? Who's them?'

'Well . . . whoever's organised all this.' She made a vague gesture around the lobby.

He leaned forward and spoke so softly that she had to strain to catch his words. 'I work for some people I think perhaps you'd like to meet. People who would also find all this,' he jerked his head at the hall, '"bloody boring". Who think something else is needed, other than such words.'

Her heart lurched and she felt her pulse race. 'What sort of . . .?' She swallowed. 'What sort of something else?'

Pieter looked past her at the guards. 'This isn't a good place to talk. Let's go somewhere where we'll be more private.'

He got up but she hesitated. 'I can't just . . . I mean, how do I know who you are?'

'Zoe, I want to talk to you, that's all. I'm not going to

kidnap you.' He looked steadily at her. 'And I'm not going to rape you.'

She blushed furiously but he did not seem to notice.

'I'm not going to do you any harm at all. But if you want to hear more about these people, if you want to meet them, you'll have to come now.' He thrust his hands into his jacket pockets and glanced again at the guards. 'Up to you.'

She got up. This cannot be happening, she told herself, but she felt wildly elated at the same time. 'I'll come,' she said.

The sea-grey Mercedes was parked in the middle bay at the front of the car-park, thus affording the two men inside the best possible view of the conference hall entrance: not excellent, because the outside lights were switched off, but good enough to see anyone leaving or entering.

Around the corner of the building, near the side-doors, a dark saloon car containing two other men, was almost hidden in shadows.

Both vehicles had been in position for the previous ninety minutes; their occupants maintaining intermittent radio contact. Apart from short bursts: 'Nothing?' 'No. All clear', there was silence in the two cars. Conversation was a distraction and for this job, maximum concentration was required. To that end also, to avoid drowsiness, the heaters in both cars were turned down low and the front windows were opened a tiny crack to allow in the freezing December night air.

In the driving seat of the Mercedes, the younger man suppressed a shiver. His eyes ached from their long vigil upon the entrance but he dared not rub them for fear of arousing his companion's contempt. Physical strength was an Aryan characteristic, and there was at least another two hours of this to endure. To show tiredness, pain or fear was a hallmark of the lesser species, the 'Untermenschen' – the blacks, the Muslims, the Jews, the homosexuals. For one such as he, a member of the 'German Soil for German People' organisation, such weaknesses were inexcusable and would quickly lead to expulsion.

So he ignored the cold and, for comfort, touched the weapon that lay on his lap. He thought of the man who was their target that night – he had memorised every detail of the face in the photograph – and he smiled to himself as he imagined the cowardly terror in that face as he blew its life away.

'Movement.'

The young man started. 'Comrade?'

'Movement by the doors.'

The young man frowned. The evening's conference was not due to finish for another two hours; his comrade must be mistaken. Then, squinting, he saw quite definitely the figure of a man, and behind him a smaller person, female, young. The man pushed the door open and the girl followed.

'I thought none of them came out till the end of each session,' he said.

His companion shrugged. 'So maybe they got bored. Can't blame them. Nice looking little bit of crumpet. Maybe he's brought her out to give her one, huh?' He gave a quick snort of laughter.

The young man was watching the couple walk down the side of the building. He was about to answer his comrade when something in the man's face, now lit by one of the car-park lights, stopped him dead. Something in the set of the eyes, and the jaw line ... His head snapped round. The man was six car-widths away, walking fast, the girl hard-put to keep up. He saw the lights of a van behind switch on, off, on.

'That's him, that's him!' He grabbed his gun and flung open the door.

'What're you talking about?' His comrade clutched his arm. 'He'll be with a group of them!'

'I tell you that's him! Let me go! Call the others!'

The cold air sliced at Zoe's face and seemed to cut down into her lungs as she hurried to match Pieter's stride.

This is madness, she told herself. Just because he says he's not a rapist ... She caught up with him and looked up at his face. An intelligent man, she thought, calm and sure of himself, not the face of a maniac.

He was scanning the vehicles, presumably for the white Volkswagen van which had brought them to the conference.

She followed the direction of his eyes and saw the van ahead, with someone sitting behind the wheel. Its headlights flashed on and off again.

'Come on,' Pieter told her again.

From behind, to her left, she heard a car door open. Then, close to, a sudden dull thud. Pieter slewed his head around. She saw sudden fear in his eyes and felt herself falling: he had shoved her forward, hard. Before she could hit the ground, he had hauled her upright and was pulling her after him, running towards the headlights.

There was another crack behind them.

'Please!' she gasped. He was yanking her arm from its socket.

She heard footsteps behind them, and another sound from far behind: an engine screaming, tyres skidding on tarmac. She tried to crane backwards but Pieter was jerking her forward.

The footsteps sounded closer.

'Run!' Pieter howled.

Everything jumbled: she saw the white van racing towards them; the shadow of a man emerging on her left, so close she could hear him breathing; the footsteps abruptly halting; the screech of brakes and the van's door opening. Then the breath was knocked out of her as Pieter seized her under the arms and swung her up inside the van. Other hands grabbed her and pulled her across the wide front seat. A second later, Pieter landed heavily beside her and slammed the door.

'Let's get going!' he roared at the driver.

The tyres screeched and the headlights picked up the outlines of running men; two fell sideways, like skittles, out of their path. But a third figure remained intact, standing a little to one side, his legs apart, arms clasped together in front, pointing at them. Zoe saw a gun in the man's hands, saw it flash a moment before the van lurched to one side and she was flung onto the driver. He pushed her roughly away and they dodged crazily down a column of cars.

'Did he get us?' the driver asked in German.

'No. I don't think so. Shit! Watch out!'

Just ahead, a low, dark car had shot out and swerved to

a halt, blocking their path. Beside her, the driver wrenched the wheel hard down to the left and Zoe felt the rear of the van drift round in slow motion, before the whump and jolt of metal hitting metal.

'Give her gas!' yelled Pieter. The van's engine screamed. For a moment it seemed stuck to the car, then it broke free. They veered off the kerb, bounced down a slope and they were onto the winding slip-road that lead to the autobahn.

Zoe saw that the driver was sweating and shaking. He looked very young, very scared. 'Did we damage them much?' he gasped.

'Yeah. Smashed them into the side of a car.' Pieter swivelled round, checking mirrors. 'But they'll have another car. We've only got seconds. Take this turning up here on the left.'

'Shouldn't we get onto the autobahn?'

'Don't argue! Do what I say.'

The turning was unmarked and Zoe would not have seen it. The driver swung into it. He turned to Pieter. 'Now what?'

'Keep going!' The road was narrow and badly lit. The van careened down it. 'OK,' said Pieter after a few moments. 'Pull right in to the side and turn all your lights off.'

'But . . .'

'Do as I fucking say!'

They sat in the darkness. Zoe could feel her heart thundering, her breathing coming in short bursts, but there was no sense of panic; the events of the last few minutes had quite stunned her.

A minute passed, then another. There was no sound, either inside the van or out. Zoe's eyes adjusted to the darkness. On one side of the road was a field of crops; on the other, at some distance away, low factory-style buildings. After several more minutes, Pieter said in German: 'Okay. I'm going to have a look and see what damage we've got.'

He opened the door and jumped out. Zoe glanced at the driver – blond curly hair, an unformed face – but he looked straight ahead at the road.

Pieter got in again. 'We're all right. Dented that's all, and the breaklight on that side is smashed. Start her up again, and keep going in the same direction.'

The boy did as he was told. 'Where're we going?' His voice trembled.

Pieter sounded calm. 'This is a service road. It sweeps round under the autobahn and back on itself. Follow it and we'll get onto the autobahn, but going in the other direction, away from Hamburg.'

The boy shot him a look over Zoe's head. 'But how do we get to the house?'

'We come off at the first available exit, and take the small roads back.' He glanced at his watch. 'We'll be there in half an hour.'

'How did you know about this road?'

'Otto, I'm surprised at you. I've recce'd this area. I know it intimately.'

Otto pulled a face. 'And those bastards . . .?'

'They'll be well on their way to Denmark by now.'

Zoe's understanding of German was not good, but she had caught the odd word and the effort of doing so had brought her out of her stupor. She turned to Pieter.

'What's going on?' she asked. 'Who were those men, and why were they shooting at us?'

He glanced down as if he had forgotten her existence.

'They were . . .' he shrugged. 'My enemies.'

'But who? I mean, people don't go around shooting at each other.'

'Don't they?'

She stared at him. 'Why?' she said again. 'Why would they shoot at us?'

'They weren't shooting at us, Zoe. Well, not deliberately, I shouldn't think. They were shooting at me. I was their target. You and Otto were just in the wrong place, with me.'

Zoe tried to make the words sink in. 'But . . . you. Why you?'

'Well, I've shot at them.'

Her heart started to thunder again, much louder it seemed than before. Ahead she could see the lights of the approaching autobahn. Horrible thoughts re-entered her head. Perhaps the men in the car-park had been police officers, trying to rescue her. She gulped; her breathing got quicker and she felt suddenly faint.

'Calm down.' Pieter laid a hand on her shoulder. 'No hysterics. You're all right. I've told you, no one's going to hurt you. Deep breaths. OK?'

The tone of his voice soothed her and she did as he said.

'We're going somewhere to talk, then it's up to you what happens. Either we take you back to your hotel, you go to the conference tomorrow and go home. Forget about us, no further contact, or . . .'

He hesitated deliberately.

'Or what?'

'Or you decide to come further with us.'

With you, she thought. With you who shoot and are shot at? 'Who's us?' she said out loud.

'I can't tell you. Not until you've made your decision.'

They stopped at the junction to the motorway. 'Keep in the slow lane and put on the hazard lights,' Pieter told Otto. 'If the police stop us, let me do the talking.'

He turned back to Zoe. 'Maybe what's just happened will help you make up your mind?'

They joined the autobahn. Overhead the lights whizzed by like stroboscopes. Pieter watched the van's mirrors for a few minutes then turned to Zoe again.

'The people who shot at us . . . I don't know with sureness who they are, but probably assassins for a group called "German Soil for German People". Heard of it?'

She shook her head.

'Neo-Nazis. They say they're just nationalists, proud of their country. But they worship Hitler and say only pure-bred German Aryans should live in Germany. We think they're the ones behind a lot of attacks on asylum-seekers.'

'Asylum-seekers?' Her voice stuck in her throat. She swallowed hard, and shut her eyes. She could hear the sounds of terror from the hostel and the laughter of the Nazis; see the mockery in the boy's face as he blew her a colluding kiss.

'Yes.'

Pieter was staring intently at her. 'Yes,' he said again.

'Attacks on asylum-seekers. I feel sure we're going to have a most interesting talk, Zoe, you and I. I think you'd like to talk about lots of things, wouldn't you?'

'I . . .' She felt a lump in her throat. She so wanted to talk to someone who would understand. 'I don't know yet,' she said softly.

Matt stirred in his chair. At long last, Zimmerman had wound up. Not before time, Matt thought, glancing at his watch: the man had been talking solidly for seventy minutes.

An interval of twenty minutes was announced, and Matt got to his feet, looking round for the minders. Throughout the day, at any break in proceedings, the three 'stewards' had materialised at once. However, not, it appeared, on this occasion.

He looked over his shoulder to the side of the stage where he had seen one of the men standing earlier on. There was no one there. Nor, he saw now, was anyone sitting in the front row seat that had been occupied by the biggest minder all day.

He looked down at the audience, beginning to move towards the main doors that led to the lobby and fresh coffee. He saw the unattractive, dark-haired girl who had been sitting next to the little blonde before a man in a black-leather jacket had taken her away. But in the whole hall, he could count only four security guards where before, he was sure, there had been at least a dozen.

He glanced over to where that evening's speakers sat at the back of the stage. He saw Zimmerman talking away to another man presumably due to speak after the break. They were being ushered off the stage, but only by a conference organiser. Again, there were no security guards.

How odd, he thought, that after all the paranoia most of the security guards seemed to have been given the night off. Then it struck him: he was a free agent. He shoved his notebook in his pocket and started down-stage.

'Hey, where are you off to?' one of the other journalists called, but Matt ignored him. At the back of the stage, on the right-hand side, was a flight of steps. At the bottom was a long corridor, with doors on either side and just a couple of metres away, he saw Zimmerman and the others. He stepped back, out of sight.

'I need to use the john,' he heard Zimmerman say loudly.

'Okay, we'll be just in our room here. Don't get lost.'

Matt unclipped his 'Journalist' lapel badge and pocketed it. The door he wanted was helpfully marked; he pushed it open and saw Zimmerman standing at one of the urinals. He joined him. 'Interesting speech,' he lied.

Zimmerman shot him a look. 'It was a pile of crap,' he said, zipping himself up. 'When're you on?'

'Uh, tomorrow. Morning.'

'I'll be on my way back home by then. What speech have they given you?'

Matt thought desperately. 'The Post-Holocaust Phenomenon.'

'Oh yeah? Sounds about as crappy as mine, huh?'

'Right.'

Zimmerman sighed. 'When I think what I could do with those kids out there. It's my talent, y'know? Speaking to people's hearts, stirring their souls, getting them out in the street. But it's not what we're here for, is it?' He took a comb out of his jacket pocket and ran it through his spikey hair. 'I hope the guys find what they're looking for. Me, I think it's crazy. Waste of time. There's plenty of good kids already who'd do what they want. And they've got the track record to prove it. All the guys'd have to do is ask them. Don't you think?'

Matt busied himself with his fly. 'Maybe you're right,' he mumbled.

'Sure I am.' Zimmerman picked up his briefcase from the floor. 'Still, we're being well-paid, huh? And it's their show. Good luck to them.' He reached the door and opened it. 'And good luck to you tomorrow. Be seeing you.'

The van bounced up the ramp and down a steep driveway into a large garage. Zoe heard the door clang shut behind them and Otto cut the engine. A light went on and she found herself staring at two surfboards hanging on a bare brick wall. To her left, beyond Otto, she saw a glass door leading to a lit room.

'OK Zoe, let's go and have our talk,' said Pieter.

'Where are we?'

'At a friend's house. You're quite safe.'

He helped her out and she followed him down the side of their van, past another smaller one. He went first into the room.

There were no windows but another glass door showed carpeted steps leading upwards. In a corner was a sink; next to it a large washing machine, and beside that, a tumble drier. An ironing board was set up, with the iron standing on it, and on a shelf were neat piles of clothing. Along another wall was an old corduroy sofa and in the middle of the room, a low table and two fold-up chairs.

'Sit,' said Pieter.

She felt suddenly panicky and very unsure. 'I don't need to tell him anything,' she reminded herself. 'I can just say that I want to go back.' Then she looked at Pieter – and saw someone who wanted to listen to her; someone who had shot at Neo-Nazis.

'Tell me what you know about asylum-seekers,' he said.

Her heart flipped over, but she started to speak, haltingly at first but soon the words were tumbling over each other and that terrible night became vivid once more in her mind.

'I feel so responsible,' she said. 'I ought to have done something, not just watched. Even though it had nothing to do with me.'

'Hadn't it?' he said quietly.

'No . . .' she stopped. 'What could I have done?'

'Maybe not a lot then. Maybe not now. But in the future . . .'

'What? What could I do in the future?'

He said nothing for several minutes. Above her head, Zoe could hear the sound of a radio being played loudly.

'What else has happened to you, Zoe? What makes you so guilty about what you saw?'

She stared. 'Come on, Zoe, talk to me. I'll understand.' His eyes had a mesmerising quality and his voice was gentle. He was right, she did want to talk. All her barriers went down and she told him everything: how she had felt herself to be there in that Lithuanian wood; hearing the sound of the soldiers' footsteps behind her; feeling the jab of the rifle, seeing the child beside her.

When she had finished, they both sat in silence. Then she said: 'I don't know what to do to stop it all happening again.'

He looked at her levelly. 'I do.'

'Yes?'

'Yes. I would not normally say this to someone at your stage, but you've already seen tonight the sort of work that I'm involved in, haven't you?'

She nodded but she felt once more that the events were unreal: the shooting; her being here; what Pieter was saying to her. 'Would I have to . . .?' she asked.

'You don't have to do anything, remember that. All our people are volunteers and they do many different tasks. But none of them involve handing out leaflets or passing UN declarations or listening to dead boring speeches. We're a little more active than that.' He smiled suddenly at her. 'But I'm going too quickly. You may not be accepted.'

Zoe glanced up at the ceiling.

'No, they're not here. And before we go to meet them, I need some more from you. You're a student aren't you? Studying what?'

He questioned her for more than an hour, dipping and diving into her life, but he did it in such a way that she did not feel invaded. She realised that she wanted to meet these tantalising 'other people' so much, that she only wanted to please him.

'You have a boyfriend?'

'No.'

'A close friend who you tell things to?'

She thought of Annabelle. 'No.'

'So you feel lonely?'

'No, not really. I've always been on my own really.'

'L'étrangère?'

'I suppose. Yes.'

At last he seemed satisfied. 'Well, Zoe. You want to meet these people?'

'You know I do.'

'OK. Wait here.'

He opened the door and she saw him climbing the stairs. What are you doing, her mind asked once more, but she had come too far for easy explanations. She felt that her future was in others' hands now, and that feeling both comforted and excited her.

Pieter came back into the room. He smiled at her. 'All right, let's go. We've got a long journey tonight.'

He took her back into the garage but guided her to the smaller van where Otto was sitting in the driver's seat, smoking a roll-up.

Pieter touched her on the shoulder. 'Zoe, you must travel in the back, OK?'

'Why?'

'Security. You're not yet one of us.'

'But . . .'

'You must start learning to obey orders. Come.'

He pulled the van's back door open. Inside Zoe saw a mattress had been laid on the metal floor and a blanket. Reluctantly she crawled in: there was no window, and the sliding glass partition had been painted black.

'Tap on the window if you want anything and try to get some sleep.'

The door slammed, she heard him getting into the front seat, and Otto starting the van. She lay down on the mattress and tried to identify sounds: faintly, she could hear them talking in German; there was the noise of the engine and the tyres on the road, and the occasional passing car. After a time, she could tell by the increase in speed that they had joined a motorway. An air-vent halfway up the left side of the van let in a little air and the smell of petrol fumes. She tried not to sleep; she wanted to go over the extraordinary events of the night, but she was completely drained. She made a pillow of her sweater, covered herself with the blanket and fell asleep.

She dreamed. She was back in the forest, part of that unending line of dying humanity. She was at the pit's edge, hearing the order to reload. She turned to face the soldier who would next take her life, saw him start and saw the fear in his eyes. She looked down and realised why. She was armed and full of vengeance, and her hands did not falter as she took aim.

Matt lay fully-clothed on his hotel bed, replaying in his mind the conversation that he had had with Zimmerman and trying to keep a rein on his own imagination. There could be a perfectly innocent explanation, he told himself, but in all honesty he could not find it.

There was a hidden agenda to this conference, obviously. The speakers were being paid to be dull, for God's sake. The real work was going on behind the scenes, where the 'guys', whoever they might be, trawled the audience looking for suitable kids for . . . what?

Matt stared at the ceiling. 'Kids who'd do what they want,' Zimmerman had said; the sort of thing that Zimmerman was good at getting kids to do, being violent.

A conference where kids were being recruited for the new terrorism . . .

As soon as Zimmerman had gone, Matt had been tempted to rush off to find Monika, or one of the other smooth-faced 'organisers' and challenge them with what the man had told him. On one level, it would have been worth it, just to see Monika's expression. Then he had reconsidered. He had imagined the woman scarcely batting an eyelid, saying that a speaker's fee was quite customary and that he must have misunderstood Dr Zimmerman's meaning, even perhaps calling on Zimmerman to refute what he had said. Then she would have had Matt thrown out. And that was not what he wanted.

He needed a few more pieces before his jigsaw puzzle was complete; he needed to be at that conference the following day. Generally to see what else he might pick up but specifically to watch that audience like a hawk to see who else might be watching them, and to see if any of them failed to appear after a break.

He had a sudden, uncomfortable thought. That pretty little girl, the blonde. She had been taken out in the middle of Zimmerman's speech. Matt remembered how vulnerable she had looked. He had assumed that the good-looking man who

she had gone with had been her boyfriend. But maybe there
was a more worrying explanation . . .

He would keep a good lookout for both of them in the
morning.

Chapter Six

When Zoe awoke, a little daylight had filtered in through the air-vent. For a split second, she had been confused and panicky, but then she had remembered. Putting her hand out, she touched the metal of the van's side. So, it was true. She looked at her watch, it was 8.20am.

The van was stationary. She strained her ears and heard Pieter's voice, the slam of his door, footsteps crunching on rough ground and a sudden burst of bright light as her own door opened.

'OK?'

She struggled to sit upright and hit her head on the van's roof.

'Are we there?' she asked.

'No questions. We'll be driving around small roads now, So lots of turns and bumps. If everything's OK, no one's following, we'll stop and then you have to do just as I say. If I say "run" you do it; if I say "down" you do it. Right?'

She rubbed at her eyes; they felt gritty. 'Right,' she said.

'Thirsty?'

'A little.'

'Here.' He gave her a can of Pepsi.

'Are we still in Germany?'

'No questions, I said!'

The door slammed closed again and a few seconds later the van took off. They swerved round corners and Zoe was flung against the side, bashing her arm. From what she could hear, she guessed that they must be retracing the same route: the high-pitched cries of schoolchildren, the sound of trains, and a clanging sound that she could not identify, kept being repeated. She also smelled the tang of the sea. By the seaside, but where, she wondered. She could not remember what time it had been when they had left the garage – eleven o'clock or maybe midnight, maybe earlier than that. If they had been driving all night, where would they be now? France, she thought hazily, or Spain. Or maybe they had gone in the opposite direction, Poland or Italy?

Then the van bumped over rough ground and stopped.

It all happened very fast. The door was yanked open and Pieter stood there.

'Out,' he ordered, unsmiling and curt.

They were in a small courtyard littered with rubbish and weeds; on each side rose up storey upon storey of pre-war apartments. Most looked derelict. Through a short passageway Zoe saw the road and a red Fiat car that squatted with its engine idling. The driver glanced in their direction, threw a cigarette out the window and drove off.

Pieter seized her upper arm and marched her into the passage. He halted before a steel security door and punched the entry-phone buzzer. The sound magnified down the passage. A sharp wind blew and she shivered.

There was no reassurance from Pieter now, no easy teasing; he was taut and alert, on duty.

'Ja?' The disembodied voice sounded harsh and threatening.

Pieter put his lips to the grille, spoke softly, 'Frühaufsteherin'. Early bird.

There came an answering click. He pushed her before him through the door, across a concrete hallway, into a foul-smelling lift. It ground its way upward, coming to a juddering halt on the third floor. Her stomach knotted. She tried to soothe herself: this was the new Resistance she was about to meet; she should be feeling thrilled. But the feeling of dread was much stronger.

She was pushed forward again, onto a landing, to a yellow painted door that opened before they had reached it. She was briefly aware of someone else being in the narrow hallway; of a muttered exchange between that person and Pieter, and then they were moving down the dark hall towards a door at the end.

Her heart was thundering but she felt curiously calm as well. There was no time to panic, she realised, even though it seemed the appropriate response to what was happening. It passed through her mind that the condemned must have felt the same way on that last walk to the gas chamber: that they ought to be screaming, but not now, some other time.

Pieter shoved the end door open with his foot. The room seemed to be in complete darkness. She stood there, for a moment seeing nothing and then the shadows took shape. Three figures sitting at a long table, facing her, their backs to the only window in the room. A thin curtain had been drawn across it, providing a screen to any outside watchers, but allowing in sufficient light, just, to see by.

Slowly Zoe's eyes adjusted.

She stifled a scream. They had no faces: only slits where their eyes should have been and no mouths at all. Terrible, deformed creatures ... She blinked and saw three people wearing black balaclava hoods. The very stuff of nightmares; the very image of terrorists.

She did not know what was expected of her, but she knew she was doing all that she was capable of, and that was to remain standing. Her terrible fear was reduced to embarrassment that she might faint and, as the middle figure rose and started to speak, another fear surfaced: that she would not be able to understand what was being said. Something very strange had happened to her hearing: on one level everything was painfully loud – the creak of a floorboard, a car-horn, her own breathing – on another she could not comprehend the words that were being addressed to her.

She stared at the standing figure. It was only a little taller than herself, dressed completely in black, with a similar small frame. The eyes were fixed on her and over the place where the mouth should have been, the mask moved in and out like a heartbeat. Zoe forced herself to inhale more slowly, to concentrate on the words.

'We are the Leadership of the group. Never Again.'

A woman's voice. Zoe swallowed hard. Women were kinder than men, she told herself, and they would not be involved in anything evil. But the voice sounded harsh, guttural, not a kindly voice. Zoe appealed to the eyes in the mask but could tell nothing from them. She needed to see the speaker's mouth, her expression, but the mask hid everything, leaving Zoe utterly exposed.

'We are the operational vanguard of the worldwide mission to crush Fascism and elimin ... eliminate the scourge of Neo-Nazism.'

The woman stopped and glanced down at a piece of paper in front of her. 'She's not English,' Zoe realised. 'She's reading from a script.' That explained the wooden delivery and the lack of any warmth in the voice. Zoe began to feel a little safer.

'You have been ... selected for possible recruitment. You are here to be evaluated. Also to establish the strength of your commitment to the cause.

'If you fail or do not wish to join us, you will be returned by the recruiting officer. Is that understood?'

Zoe knew her voice would fail her. She gave a tiny nod.

'You must convince each of us. One is not enough, two is not enough. Our decisions are made together, as one.'

The woman sat down abruptly.

There was a moment's pause. It flitted through Zoe's mind that one of the other two had missed their cue, and she suddenly wanted to giggle. Behind her she heard a movement and, glancing back, saw Pieter in the shadows. However wrongly, she felt calmed knowing he was there.

One of the other figures, to the woman's right, half-rose. 'Please, take a seat.'

It was a man's voice, English, with a middle-class accent. Its civility in such surroundings sounded false.

Zoe had not seen the chair he pointed at, placed directly in front of the table. She sat, and found herself on a level with the figures and no more than a few feet from them. Proximity was not reassuring: she was acutely aware of their eyes, boring into her, picking her apart. She shuddered.

'We apologise for the secrecy and the extreme precautions to hide our identity.'

The man's voice was not terribly sympathetic. But he sounded very much in control, and used to being obeyed.

'We assure you it's very necessary. The Neo-Nazis would stop at nothing to find and destroy us. You've already been exposed to the methods they resort to.

'We have heard very good things about you, but you must understand that we have still to be very careful until we are absolutely sure of you.'

There was a pause and, unsure what to do, she nodded.

'Although we are the Leadership, we are not hierarchical. We encourage full discussion from grass roots level upwards. We're all comrades and we three form the pyramid. Without the base of the pyramid there could be no top. You understand?'

She gave another nod.

The man leant forward, and interlaced his hands – longfingered and elegant – on the table.

'Let me explain the reason for our existence. The Nazis of today are seizing and warping the minds of youth throughout Europe and the Western world. They are clever, wellorganised – and ruthless. They are appealing, with some success, to fears of unemployment, homelessness and poverty. They are using the nationalism that has sprung up in the new democracies of Europe to increase xenophobia. They point at scapegoats, some old, some new: blacks, Turks, Muslims and Jews. People say, and you will have heard this, Zoe, that the Neo-Nazis are a small minority, but we know from history that this is what was said of Hitler's Brownshirts sixty years ago.

'Of course, the Neo-Nazis are happy that the world should be duped into believing they are small and insignificant. In that way they can build their forces, use their politicians to bring in racist, anti-semitic and divisive laws. By the time the world wakes up to what they are, and what they intend, it will be too late for the thousands of men, women, children, and yes, Zoe, little babies too, who by then will have died at their hands. It could even be too late to stop them at all. It will be a Holocaust, but not like the last one. This one will have no end.

'Never Again will stop them. By whatever means necessary we will kill this new monster. We regret we must use violence but we know our cause is just and that violence is, to our regret, the best weapon to ensure our ends. Our violence is thus sanctioned and justified. Our fighters will not hesitate, for we know the terrible price that was paid in the past for passivity, for so called "moderation".

'You may ask, who do we strike? Well, we do not intend to simply retaliate, measure for measure. We will act against their evil before even one of ours are harmed. Our intelligence network is already in place, and will grow. So we know that we will always hit the right targets; the innocent need never fear us.

'That is what we are, those are our aims, Zoe, and we are in the process of putting them into practice. For this purpose, we need fighters; men and women from every country, from all levels, who are prepared to fulfil this goal.

'We need more recruits. That is why you are here.'

He had spoken fluently and with a calm passion that was deeply impressive. Zoe gazed at him, quite mesmerised. That a man like this, inspired with such a mission, should want her! And that she, who had never fitted in anywhere or with anyone, was being asked to join this group! The sort of group that she had been searching for, without knowing of its existence, for the past four months.

She would be a fighter. Never again would she have to endure the torments of her dreams, or be the powerless bystander. She was being offered the chance to take up arms against the evil and end her nightmares forever; to fulfil her dream of the previous night.

The words were out of her mouth before she knew that she had spoken: 'I would be honoured to join you. Please, it's all I want.'

'Good. Very good.' The man sounded pleased, not surprised. 'Now we need to know . . .'

'Honoured?' The woman barked the word. She leaned suddenly forward, her black hood less than a yard from Zoe's face. 'Like ein soldat you shall be, only to obey orders. Nicht glamourös, verstehen sie? Killings and deaths and hurting. No family, no childrens, no house. This is not Komisch, not a game for childrens, OK?'

Zoe flinched back in her seat. Was the woman crazy? Why was she trying to frighten her with talk of killing and death? And what did children and houses matter when one was fighting the Nazis? She was trying to warn her off, but why?

The man was speaking again. 'My comrade is right in very many ways, Zoe. She is, in a sense, the leader of all of us. She has been a fighter for a long, long time and has faced great hardships. Sometimes, we know that our naivety and, mmm, relative inexperience irritate her.'

The woman made a move to speak again, but the figure on her left, whose existence Zoe had forgotten, placed a hand on her arm. A man's hand, Zoe saw. Young looking skin, stubby fingers, bitten nails. The woman shrugged it off, but before she could speak again, the first man intercepted her:

'It's very true that it's not an easy life we're offering you. You must be one hundred per cent committed, and that may not always be easy. You may be asked to do things that you find very difficult. But as I said, we do not issue demands like gods; all are equal. We would value your opinions, always.

'As for how long you are with us: it depends on how long it takes for us to win. But you are very young and have a lot of time. Naturally, if you wish to leave no one will stop you.

'You must be trained, physically and mentally, to a peak, and then must maintain that level of training in very difficult circumstances. Your life will no longer be your own; we must know everything about your personal life, your plans, your career, your contacts.

'For your part, you must tell no one of your secret life. You will never be able to relax that guard, not for one moment.

'The demands we are going to make upon you are enormous. Do you honestly think you can do all that we ask?'

'Yes.' She blinked at the vision he gave her. 'Oh yes.'

'We shall see. Now, Pieter has explained quite a bit about you already. Your most unpleasant experiences ...' He paused for a fraction of sympathy. '... and your feeling of helplessness.' He paused again. 'A misplaced feeling, if I may say so.'

She felt her stomach lurch. Was what she had told Pieter going to ruin everything? Would the Leadership think her too weak, too negative to join them?

'Thank you,' the man was saying. 'Now we need to

have a full discussion. You will be informed of our decision.'

She felt completely drained and offered no resistance when Pieter led her from the room.

The media had once called her the Angel of Death; the beautiful killer. She had been very beautiful back then – far more so than the British girl and just as convinced of the rightness of her cause.

Beatrix Kessler sighed inwardly. She peeled off the black wool balaclava and fanned her hot face with her hand. She bore no illusions about herself: her life and the surgeons' knives had carved away her beauty long before; her convictions had been drowned in blood, both her comrades' and her victims'.

She no longer believed in anything much. She had wanted only to be left alone, to have a little time without running and killing. To see her father, if only from a distance; maybe, just maybe, to speak to him for one last time before he died. To be able to tell him how much she loved him, and how sorry she was – in the way that she had so wanted, but had been forbidden, to speak to her mother before death had separated them forever.

But her past would not allow her any time. Too many people wanted her 'expertise'. The men sitting on either side of her were only the latest example.

She let her mind wander. They had come to her five months before, buying their way into the 'network' – an informal but highly effective Contacts directory used across the wide spectrum of the revolutionary world. They had paid her minder enough money to rot his brain with cocaine; in return he had deceived her and delivered her into their hands.

She had come round from the drug to find herself in a dingy modern hotel room. Axel, the smooth-talking Englishman, had come straight to the point. 'We're shopping for someone of your calibre,' he had told her.

'We're prepared to pay,' little sidekick Leon had echoed beside him.

They wanted her as their 'Operational Commander'; her

knowledge, skills, contacts. Beatrix had hired herself out many times before; she knew the score. But now she had more money than she could spend – and no great interest in their cause.

She had made no attempt to hide her boredom when they enthused over it. 'Your cause is just like any other,' she had told them bluntly.

Rage had warped Axel's face; she had watched him struggle for control. 'Perhaps to you. But we are offering you something, too: a way out.'

She had stared at him.

He smirked, playing his trump. 'Yesterday we passed certain information about you – your new identity, a recent photograph, the address of your apartment – to certain people at the Anti-Terrorist Headquarters in . . . Wiesbaden, I think it is?'

He had continued smiling and watching her. 'So you see we did you a favour organising your absence from there last night. I expect the police paid you a visit as soon as they got our package, don't you?'

Nothing, not a flicker of an eye or a quickening of her breathing, had given her away. But looking up at the man's smug face, she had vowed that one day she would see him scream before he died.

He had continued in the same tone: 'Now we would not, of course, consider betraying the current whereabouts of a comrade. We would indeed do everything in our power to protect her. But if you decided not to join us . . .'

He had let the threat hang in the air. That was how they had got her and she hated them for it; hated the way they had so skilfully entrapped her and were now twisting her to their will.

She was commander in name only. In spite of the vast amount of money they were paying her, they used her only for her technical knowledge and contacts. In judgement, they considered themselves her superiors.

Take the recruitment of the English girl for instance: that was another example of being forced to dance to their music.

Beatrix had very mixed feelings about Zoe. She was a truthful woman and she acknowledged that a little of her antipathy was based on jealousy and bitterness. Zoe was a little rich bitch, a college kid. Thought she could change the world by weeping. She would not have lasted two minutes in Baader-Meinhof. Baader would have enjoyed destroying her, taking her apart, turning her dreams into living nightmares.

On the other hand . . .

When Zoe had stepped into the room, wide-eyed and terrified, but so quickly eager and trusting of Axel's honeyed words, so full of hope, something buried deep within Beatrix had cried out. A desire to protect the weak, perhaps her maternal instinct long buried, demanded that this girl should be spared; that she should not have to live the life that Beatrix now endured. That was why she had tried, however clumsily, to warn her off.

The men, however, were determined to have her. They were talking across her; Beatrix tuned in again to what they were saying.

Leon was doing most of the talking. Having been forbidden by Axel to speak in front of the girl – for once a wise decision, Beatrix had to admit, the American being too easily excited and prone to blurt things out – he was giving full vent to his feelings.

'She could be really useful to us, y'know? She looks real innocent, doesn't she, all big eyes and that cute accent. No one would ever suspect her, would they? We could get her in anywhere, our own travelling bait! Or wait, wait, why not get her to go the whole way? Yeah, she could fuck her way through the hit-list!'

A terrorist-whore, Beatrix said to herself. She had known a couple of girls who had been used in that way. Difficult job, killing like that. The girls did not last long: the lucky ones lost their looks quickly; a lot of the others went mad, got killed.

She spoke up in German; she had never let on how much English she understood. 'It would be a shame to waste her potential by getting her face too well-known.'

Both men glared at her; she was interfering in their game,

but she could see that they accepted there was some sense in her argument.

Beatrix pushed her advantage hard. 'I think the girl is too highly strung. Too unstable all round; you heard what she said to Pieter, how that killing ground "got to her"!'

She gave an ugly, harsh laugh. 'She's weak and she'll crack under the slightest pressure; she'd give everything away. I vote against her.'

Axel lit one of his small, pungent cigarettes, and exhaled slowly. He watched her with some curiosity, as if he had guessed her motivation. 'I disagree. I think, like our friend Pieter, that the girl has real potential. She could be one of our Elite. I think she should be trained as such.'

Beatrix lost, as she had known she would. In one respect only were they prepared to heed her warning: that the girl could endanger them all if she decided to talk. They agreed that after her initial training, Zoe would have to be 'blooded': she should either be made to kill, or be present at a killing and thus be materially involved in it. That would ensure her silence.

Beatrix quietened her conscience with a faint hope: that the blooding might also awaken the girl before it was too late.

They called Pieter back into the room and told him of their decision. He too looked satisfied, but Beatrix could not despise him in the way that she did the two others. Pieter had experienced the ugly side of the dream: his own hands were bloody and he had put himself at risk in a way that Axel and Leon only talked about.

'Did they manage to clear things up at Hamburg?' she asked.

'Yes. The security guards did a very professional job. They found three bullets; one in the side of a car. But it was OK, it belonged to us. And they got rid of the wrecked car.'

'Were any of those Nazi fuckers still in it?' Leon asked eagerly.

'No. They must have had a back-up vehicle. There was no trace of them.'

'And no one at the conference suspected anything or heard anything?'

Pieter shook his head. 'They were too far away, at the other end of the complex.' He paused. 'We were lucky, I think.'

'Or careless,' Axel slipped the criticism in quietly. 'Let's hope it doesn't happen again. Especially not when we're about to launch ourselves on our public, mm?'

Beatrix saw Pieter clench his jaw. He was white-faced with fatigue and anger but he kept his temper. 'Everything is ready for the action,' he said calmly. 'If you'll let me have the communique, I'll see that it's passed on.'

'We're still working on it,' said Axel. 'You can have it by tomorrow night.'

'Yeah, we're having real problems with the middle section,' said Leon. 'Say, while you're here, maybe you could give us your opinion . . .'

'We'll sort it out between us.' Axel smiled at Pieter. 'Now, I know you're a busy fellow.'

'Sure.' He got up. 'I'll go tell Zoe the good news.'

Twenty-six hours later, Matt was sitting opposite the manager of the Hamburg Conference centre. It had been a piece of luck that the man had agreed to see him but the skill now lay in getting Herr Franz Moller to talk.

The man's first words were not hopeful. 'I shouldn't really be talking to you, Herr, uh, Anderson. Confidentiality of clients you know.' He fiddled with the gold signet ring on his right hand.

He who hesitates, Matt hoped.

Moller looked up and smiled. 'But I know you journalists. You know exactly who was here at the weekend, don't you?'

Matt smiled.

'You were there both days?'

'Yes, sir, I certainly was.' Sunday's session, if anything, had been more boring than the first day. The security guards had been back in force, and he had had no opportunity for unauthorised meetings. He had done plenty of staring at the audience; as far as he could tell, half a dozen had not returned after lunch, but that, he had reminded himself, was not proof of anything. He had not seen the blonde girl again.

'What access you people have! Well, you must know a lot

more about our guests than I do.' Moller leaned forward across his oak-veneered desk. 'Tell me,' he spoke just above a whisper, 'it was Government stuff wasn't it? Intelligence?'

Thank God for conspiracy theorists, Matt thought. Aloud, he said, 'Well . . .'

'Ja, ja. I appreciate, it's sensitive information. But you know, I had a pretty good feeling that's what it was. You know what made me think it?'

Matt shook his head.

'It was the way the man who booked it reacted when I asked him the name of his organisation. I mean, it's usual to ask that question . . .'

'Natürlich.'

'But this man, this government intelligence officer I suppose he was, got very uptight. "That's none of your concern," he said to me. "I'm prepared to pay cash . . ."'

'He paid in deutschmarks?'

'Ja! A whole briefcase-full! He had it on his lap, and when he opened it and I saw all that money! Well, that was another clue, wasn't it? These agencies don't write cheques, do they?'

'No, indeed. So he wouldn't tell you the name of the organisation?'

'No. Well, obviously there isn't an organisation as such, is there? No, he said he was paying cash and he wasn't answering any questions.

'I thought he'd taken affront so I said, bearing in mind he wanted to hire the whole complex for the weekend, that we'd be happy to throw in the services of our own security guards, free of charge. But he turned me down flat.'

'He did?'

'Yes. He said his people had their own highly trained security personnel, and he didn't want my lot getting in their way. They could have the weekend off.' Moller shook his head. 'I mean, I'd have been pretty dumb not to have smelt government business, wouldn't I?'

'When did he come to see you?'

'Ah, let's think. Two weeks ago?' Moller got up and crossed the floor to a filing cabinet. He pulled out a dark green folder. 'Ja, just over two weeks ago. The man's name was

Herr Johannes Leonhardt . . .' He looked up, frowning. 'Do you think,' he said slowly, 'that it was a false name?'

Matt, who had eagerly scribbled the name down, cursed his own naivety. 'I should imagine so,' he told Moller. 'What did he look like, this Herr Leonhardt?'

'Very well-dressed. Quite young, mid to late thirties, I'd say. I think he'd dark hair. But I do remember something about him, that struck me at the time.'

'What was that?'

'I had the impression that he wasn't German. He had a very good grasp of the language, excellent actually, but there was a trace of an accent. I think maybe he was Danish, or from one of the Scandinavian countries.' He returned to his chair.

'So, Herr Anderson, is there anything you can tell me about what they were doing here? I got the impression maybe it was international talks. About to announce a new security initiative for Europe?'

'I don't think you're that far from the truth, Herr Moller.'

The manager looked satisfied. 'No, I thought not. I do have quite a nose for these sort of things. I'm sure I'll read it all in your paper next week. And, uh, Herr Anderson?'

'Sir?'

'Would it be at all possible to mention the name of this centre in your article? And perhaps a line or two on its excellent facilities? Every little mention helps, you know.'

Matt spent the rest of that Monday, before leaving for his flight home at six, on the telephone in his hotel room. First he called the police captain he had originally spoken to in Lubeck and from him got the name of an anti-terrorist officer at Wiesbaden. The man was intrigued but not able to help very much. He pointed out, as Steve had done, that there was still no evidence that an anti-fascist terrorist group existed.

'But how about all these recent attacks on Neo-Nazis?' Matt asked.

'Could be one-offs. I promise you, we don't have a file on this sort of group. No name; no file.'

By Thursday of that week, that statement was no longer true. At peak travel time in the morning, a viable bomb was located in one of the men's toilets at Frankfurt airport, thirty minutes after a warning had been telephoned to the airport management. Even though the device was safely diffused it caused chaos and widespread panic. Later on in the day, a rather long-winded communique, stating the arrival, declaration and demands of Never Again was received by the German national press agency.

It gave Matt the perfect hook for his story the following Sunday. He got the splash and the whole of page nine.

And in Wiesbaden and in London, new directories were opened in the anti-terrorist databases.

Chapter Seven

The change in Zoe was immediate and remarkable and various people were eager to claim responsibility. It was as if someone had switched the lights back on, Kerry said.

'Yes, she seems much brighter, doesn't she?' Alasdair agreed, smiling at her. 'You're so sweet to care. Perhaps she's got a lover?'

Kerry, who thought she knew the real reason but had promised Zoe never to utter a word about it, marked one up to therapy. She nodded. 'Perhaps.'

Within two weeks of the Spring Term starting, Zoe's personal tutor had received startled congratulations from her colleagues.

'Whatever did you say to her, Sarah?'

'I have my methods. And what's more,' she added, firmly snipping off further enquiry, 'I believe in pastoral confidentiality.'

Zoe had spent Christmas at home with her parents and the time had passed quickly and easily. She had spent much of it studying. It frightened her how far she had fallen behind but she had little doubt that she could catch up. She had to; that had been Pieter's instructions.

'You're to get your degree. You're to go back to university and behave absolutely normally. Do nothing to attract attention.

'Are you a member of any Anti-Fascist societies? No? Good, keep it that way. Don't attend any Anti-Fascist rallies, or show any interest in the subject. If anyone asks about your Lithuanian or German experiences, say it was all a long time ago. You can't imagine why you got so upset about it.

'After your exams, provided you're successful, you'll be contacted again. OK?'

She had nodded and smiled. She had still been feeling

dazed by the news that the Leadership wanted her; that she had been provisionally accepted for training.

'They were impressed with you,' Pieter had told her. 'They think you could be of very great benefit to the Cause.'

She had blushed scarlet, and a thought had struck her. 'Those boys, the ones in my group from England; the ones who weren't at the conference in the evening. Has the Leadership accepted them too?'

He had been momentarily taken aback. 'Those boys, uh . . . they're involved at a different level. The Leadership never saw them, and probably never will.'

'Different level?'

'Yes. Now forget them. Concern yourself only in achieving your degree and remembering all the things I've told you. Most important is that you show everyone that you're now a normal, happy girl.'

It had been easy to do what he said. Her equilibrium had returned, and with it a sense of purpose that she had never known before.

She felt that she must be shining with happiness and that everyone must see it. It was as if she had been sprinkled with fairy dust, she thought. She reckoned that being in love could not be any better than the way she felt now; warm and cherished and excited, and so vitally alive in every part. She hugged herself with her secret: everything she did, and everything she wanted to be – in her work, her contact with others, her way of looking at herself – was for the Cause. It became the central spring of her existence.

It was more, she thought, than just having a goal for the first time in her life. It was being accepted that made all the difference. She was no longer an outsider.

In June, when the exam results came through, she stood staring at the slip of paper in her hand. She had been awarded a good 2:1 degree. She was silent while all around her, fellow students shrilled amazement or despair and frowned at the uncertainty of the future. Zoe was smiling, but silent; she knew where she was going, the paper in her hand was her passport to a new life.

*　　*　　*

Her 'orders' – in retrospect it seemed ridiculous to call them that – arrived nearly eight weeks later, in the shape of a page torn from a travel brochure and journey times.

She stared at the picture of the hotel that had been ringed in violent pink ink. It seemed that in the last week of August, she had been booked into The Citadel, a two-star establishment 'perfectly situated' a stone's throw from the ancient town of Calvi on the north-west coast of Corsica.

She swallowed. It was all going to happen after all. The long wait had been difficult, especially when the first month had passed, then another week, then another and there had still been no word. Terrible, plausible doubts had besieged her imagination: the Leadership had changed their minds about her; Never Again had somehow ceased to be; her UK contact had been caught and killed by the Neo-Nazis.

She had hung around Alasdair's flat, jumping whenever the telephone rang. She had been scared to go out in case she missed the call, and she had little to distract her: Alasdair and Kerry, when not at work, had spent a lot of time out, and in August had gone off to Italy on holiday.

Zoe had bitten her nails, eaten cornflakes, read trashy novels and comforted herself with the thought that she must hear soon.

The call had come the previous night just after ten o'clock. The voice at the other end had been barely audible. 'This is Sandra speaking.'

The phrase Pieter had told her to expect. 'You'll receive our holiday details in the post. One of our representatives will meet you during the first four days.'

The voice had been vaguely familiar but she had not had time to place it. 'Shall I just stay at the hotel?' she had asked, but had found that she was speaking to the dialling tone.

On the day of her departure, she scribbled a note for Alasdair, saying she had gone grape-picking with old friends in southern France. She hoped that would do; it would have to, she could think of nothing else at the moment that was acceptably vague. She omitted, as Pieter had told her to do, the date of her return.

* * *

The Citadel Hotel was crowded with many British holiday-makers – mainly older couples, although there was a sprinkling of young families. The rooms were dingy and thin-walled and dinner was served punctually at seven. The guests were asked to keep to their same tables and to remember that anything other than vin de table was extra.

Few complained; most decamped at once for the beach, a narrow stretch of fine white sand just the other side of the railway track.

Zoe was the only person on her own, and this made her feel even more exposed and unsure of herself. She lay on one of the twenty 'luxury' blue and white striped sun-loungers that were for hire in a private section of the beach and tried to look relaxed, but she was jumpy and unsure of how to act. She swam in the crystal clear water and looked up at the mountains, so close and yet so remote in their size. Was someone watching her? If she read a novel, would she be deemed to be too frivolous? Even now, she feared that a careless action might prove her undoing.

She was suspicious of everyone. None of her fellow guests, especially the ones who tried to engage her in conversation – would she like to join them for dinner, pity to see a young girl all alone, how about a hand of bridge? – seemed probable spies. But, she told herself, if they were truly professional, she would never guess which ones were the spies.

To be on the safe side, she snubbed everyone and was aware of causing widespread offence.

On the second morning she walked into Calvi, past the sprawling tourist cafes sitting side by side with gun-shops. Not having seen guns openly on sale before, she stopped at one window. It seemed vaguely disappointing at first: modest air-rifles, camouflage kits and army boots. Then her eyes were drawn to a central display of cruel-looking, curving knifes arranged according to size, and below them, like a string of dancing buttercups, a row of CS gas canisters.

She peered, fascinated. There was enough there to wage a little war.

At the very end of town, regal on its rock promontory, sat the ancient Citadel, calm and remote above the bustle. She walked through the cool covered stone walkway and climbed the tortuous cobbled street up to the summit of the fortress. Amidst the half ruins there, she found a grassed-over turret, climbed to it and stood looking out over the bay: at the town, the sea, the tourists in their hundreds. She refused to give in to doubt; somewhere out there, someone was waiting for her.

It was late in the afternoon of the third day that she was approached. She was sitting at one of the cafes that curved the length of Millionaires' Bay in Calvi. In front of her was a myriad of yachts, gleaming and bobbing like rich childrens' toys on the water. Listening to the cries of sea-gulls and the twang of steel ropes on masts, she had shut her eyes.

'Is this seat taken?' It was a man's voice, speaking French, but with a noticeable accent.

Her eyes snapped open. She saw a tallish man, middle-aged, wearing dark cotton trousers, grey t-shirt and sunglasses. His hair, tightly curled, was going grey, and his face was deeply lined, but the overwhelming impression of the man was his suprême fitness and watchfulness. A great cat ready to pounce.

She could not speak.

The man brought his plastic chair an inch closer.

'Perhaps you could tell me where I may buy a copy of *La Resistance?*'

His voice cracked as if it had been partly broken through over-use.

'Come,' he said.

She got to her feet and followed him.

He led her to the railway station car-park, to a dusty red Peugeot overheating in the sun. As he unlocked the door for her, he told her his name was Sergio, and that he would be taking her back to her hotel where she would get her things and check out.

'Suppose they ask me where I'm going?' she asked timidly.

He shrugged. 'Tell them you've met a friend.'

He drove fast out of town, with one hand on the wheel, dangerously as befitted a Corsican. In fact, he was Italian.

Sergio Brunelli had been with the Red Brigades in their heyday, had had the sense to get out when the rot set in. For seven years he had freelanced amongst the network of revolutionary groups, and through these had met Beatrix Kessler.

On a couple of occasions they had worked together, liked each other, had, as is the way of things, been lovers. He had heard that she had been spirited out to the East, when there had still been a separate Eastern Bloc. Then for the last three years he had had no news of her, and had presumed her dead.

She had got to him the previous winter through the old network. He was living in Corsica, in the mountains where the island's nationalists had their strongholds and safe-houses. He had sought some sort of peace and there he had almost found it.

He had semi-retired; he had bought a place in Corte, the capital, and some land in the northern part of the island. He had made contact with the nationalists, met with them, drank with them. Once or twice he had been approached for advice, and on a couple of occasions, more practical help. In return he had been awarded the protection of the group. It was an ad hoc arrangement, suiting both sides.

He wondered why he had not thought of Corsica before. It was the ideal place to live if one was a man on the run: so much of the island was impenetrable: dense forests, impassable mountains, few roads. In winter much of it was cut off for weeks. Occasionally the police or the army tried a sortie into the undergrowth, but to little avail. The fighters just moved on, travelling across country by routes known only to themselves and the mountain people.

They were a close-knit community, the true Corsican villagers. Many of their sons had gone to fight for the freedom of their country and had never returned. Their people understood the importance of silence.

Corsica had two small airports with bad security, miles of empty, remote beaches and sufficient corruption at the island's ports to ensure that smuggling was part of the way of life. The presence of the Foreign Legion, with its historical base in

Calvi, meant that the island had always attracted interesting people. They were prepared to pay a lot of money for the equipment and skills that Sergio and a few others could provide.

Kessler's suggestion had intrigued him. To take raw kids and transform them into highly-skilled operational fighters, an elite. Others, she had told him, would be responsible for training the cannon-fodder; Sergio need not concern himself with them. She had remembered him well; she had appealed to his vanity. She had also offered a lot of money upfront plus the promise of more to come. He had accepted the challenge.

He had enjoyed himself. He was a good teacher in the arts that he had perfected over twenty years: shooting, simple but effective explosives, killing silently with a knife, with the hands. In eight months, four 'students' had passed through his hands. He had them for six weeks and he taught, brutally, the cardinal rules of the warfare they were to engage in: obedience, secrecy, courage. He had stretched them to breaking point: forcing them on marathons over the mountains, climbing, swimming, some judo. He had deprived them of food and sleep and he had shown no mercy.

One had died during training. The body lay now under the maquis-covered hillside close to the farmhouse. Sergio had felt nothing when he had buried the boy. He had ceased caring about individuals long ago.

He glanced over at his new recruit. She was the first girl they had sent him, and she looked frail and dreamy. But looks, he knew, could be deceptive, and the other candidates had been of good quality; the selectors must be doing something right. The last boy was still at the house now, waiting till the morning before returning home. Sergio was pleased with him, had liked the steely determination in his soul that so nearly hid his fear of pain. He should not have still been there, that was one of Kessler's rules, that the recruits should never meet, or even see each other. But there had been a mix-up over flight-times and there had been no option but to let the boy stay.

Sergio had sent him out early that morning, had calculated he could not arrive back until after dark. There would be time enough to install the girl in her room then meet the boy and hide him away in the barn. He would never even be aware of the girl's existence.

Sergio had tried to figure out why Kessler and whoever else she was working with wanted an elite; what criteria had been used to select them, and what for. He had soon given up. He had never been a great analyst. What mattered was knocking the new recruit into shape.

The boy Anton had returned earlier than expected. He had run where even Sergio had expected him to crawl. He was weary now, though. On the last half mile, down the mountainside to the farmhouse, he had had to drag himself along. It was still daylight, if only just, when he heard the car along the rough track. Seconds later he saw it come into view, saw Sergio first then realised that he had a passenger.

The car came to a stop at the house. Sergio got out, the passenger followed. Some instinct made Anton duck out of sight, saved his life, as Sergio's eyes made a final sweep of the hillside.

But Anton was able to see the passenger quite clearly. She stood pointing up at the sky, calling out the same phrase twice, as if she was expecting a response from Sergio.

Anton knew some English and he could see what she pointed at. She had a lovely, clear voice, and the words stuck in his mind. He was always to remember what she had said.

Chapter Eight

Zoe thought she would die here and Sergio, when he finally came looking, would give her body an experimental kick, then spit on the dry ground and say that he had been right all along: she was useless; she had no stamina; no courage.

It was that last taunt that had kept her going for the past – she counted – twenty-two days. She would never have believed that she could have endured such pain, nor her mind such shock.

She lay on the riverbank, gulping like a landed fish. The rucksack on her back was filled with rocks, adding enormously to her weight. She had just swum the river, not a wide one, perhaps only five metres across, but she had entered the water exhausted from the climb over the first hillside. The river was deep and its current was powerful, and the extra weight had dragged at her, pulling her down.

Two-thirds of the way across she had gone under and it had seemed, for a split second, that drowning would be a glorious shedding of the unbearable. Then, illogically, she had panicked at the thought of what Sergio would do to her if she drowned. She fought for the surface, spluttering the inky water from her lungs.

She was lying on her stomach, her head turned away from the river, her cheek resting on the dry ground as gratefully as on the softest pillow. Just for a minute she let herself succumb to exhaustion; she knew she must get up, go on, because Sergio would be waiting. He would be sitting now, beyond the shade of the vine, in his usual chair, tilting it backwards so his face could catch the morning sun with all its vigour. He loved the sun. On the wooden box beside him would be his coffee, cigarettes, binoculars and stop-watch. He wore no watch; he seemed to know by instinct when Zoe should be at the next sighting place; the merciless glare of the binoculars were always waiting for her, mocking her.

Zoe's world had telescoped dramatically inward since her arrival at the farmhouse. She no longer dreamed of ghosts in Lithuanian woods, or had flashbacks of the hostel-burning; she no longer recalled the stirring words of the Leadership, or felt the warm sense of belonging that the group had given her. The Cause, when she thought about it, had become indistinct. It was difficult to remember that she was there in Corsica to be trained to fight the Neo-Nazis. To her, the only things that now mattered in life were pleasing Sergio, his binoculars and his stop-watch. She had nothing left over for anything else.

Her days were made up of his seconds, and she had come to dread the click as he pressed the stop-button on the watch. If she had failed to fulfil whatever exercise it was – sit-ups, a circuit-run, a climb, a marathon – in the given time, he made her do it again, and on two occasions, three times. Nothing made any difference: not tears, not begging, not promises. He just stood there until she stopped, beholding her with utter contempt. Then he would say, 'Encore une fois,' and the torture would begin again.

Twice during the first four days she had passed out from complete exhaustion. He had done nothing to revive her, just left her to come round on her own. She had realised, and the realisation had been like hitting a stream of ice in a warm sea, that he really did not care whether she lived or died.

Remembering that, she opened her eyes and looked at the time on the waterproof watch he had strapped on her wrist.

In one movement she was on her feet and running; she had precisely eight minutes and forty-five seconds to get to the next sighting-place. Her breath came in great heaves, her arms and legs working like pistons. She had to make the most of the flat ground by the river, she could only run for two minutes along it before her course took her inwards and up the hill. She felt a sudden jabbing pain in her right thigh; looking down she saw that she had cut herself quite deeply on something – a rock, or tree, she had not noticed – but she had no time to examine the wound. The blood mingled with water and sweat in trickles down her bare legs.

She knew the route, had run it daily, and could have done it blindfold; in fact, it would not have surprised her if that was what he demanded of her tomorrow. That morning had been the first day with the rocks. As he had loaded her down, he had smiled and wagged his finger in some ghastly parody of playfulness, 'Not a second extra, you hear?'

She turned right and began crashing her way uphill, seeking familiar handholds amongst the roots of trees. Pine needles pierced her palms, and branches tore at her, but she was heedless of any pain, only cursing the unnecessary delay they caused her. She made it to the double-trunked pine-tree near the top and halted to push the wet hair back out of her eyes. She spared one glance at where she had just come and it struck her that this deep river valley with its swirling mountain-fed river was probably one of the most beautiful unspoiled places in Europe. Unwillingly she smiled: 'unspoiled' was putting it mildly. Densest, most remote, wildest, loneliest, impenetrable – except of course to Sergio and those he took there.

No paths led here and no sunlight could get through the thick overhead inter-lacing of trees. Apart from her own noisy passage, there was no other sound. Perhaps she had frightened away any animals or birds. She might be the only living thing left; the world might have ended and she had been abandoned in that place. She knew that if she had been there under other circumstances, its eeriness would have got to her and made her afraid. But Sergio ruled out fear.

He had told her on that very first day, when she had still nursed a few illusions about him – this great man who was going to arm her against the Nazis – that the most important lesson she had to learn was to be frightened of nothing.

'Nothing and no one,' he had said firmly and with a smile on his lips, as if by that one gesture he was bestowing fearlessness upon her. Then, as he had looked at her, his lips had twisted into what she would have now recognised as his torturer's grimace. 'Except me, of course. For me you are to have absolute terror – hatred as well of course – but terror is more important. That is the key; you will rather die than disobey me.'

He was right of course, she thought, as she plunged on

through the sparser trees on the rounded summit. She was utterly, totally terrified of him, and, of course, completely dependant on him for all things.

For example, she had no idea where she was, only somewhere deep in the mountains about two and a half hours' drive south-east on twisting roads from Calvi. When she thought back to that last part of the drive she vaguely recollected a few tiny villages, most no more than shuttered stone houses grouped in small clumps of twos or threes. Just past one of them, Sergio had turned sharply right, onto a track that wound its way deep into the interior. They had jolted their way in silence, taking one track after another until finally they had come to his valley, the last habitable place before the front-line troops of the mountains.

There was only one house there, of yellow stone with an orange terracotta roof. Beside it was a barn; that was all, for miles upon miles.

If she ran, where would she run to? And what with? He had taken her money, her ticket and her passport. If she failed to escape, to make a complete getaway, she was sure he would kill her. He had not actually said so; he did not need to. Sometimes she was afraid he would kill her anyway, for some reason, or perhaps none at all. She feared he was mad and capable of anything when he sat silently fashioning a delicate carving with his hunting knife, his eyes watching her devour the food he placed before her.

He never ate with her. It was like feeding time at the zoo for him, she thought. At first she had been embarassed, but now she gulped down whatever he gave her, knowing that unless she finished it within a few minutes, he would take it from her.

The pleasure of eating; the graciousness of a prepared meal was just a memory. He only allowed her to eat the absolute minimum to avoid physical collapse: meat, bread, and fruit. And his feeding of her could be erratic. Half-way through the second week, he had started giving her a huge amount of food, more than she could eat, and then nothing for twelve or fourteen hours.

She half-suspected he starved her for his own pleasure, but

his explanation had made brutal sense: 'You are soft with easy living, like a newborn baby demanding food. On the run you may not eat for many days and hunger can make a tongue talkative. It is better to train the body to expect less.'

He would make one hell of an instructor on a health-farm, she thought. You would lose pounds, or die in the process. Again, he had been right. After the first few days of his new regime, when she thought she would die from lack of regular food, her appetite had altered. She had even retched after one meal.

He had been pleased. 'Good. Soon your body will eat only when I tell it to.'

Sleep was another essential she had learned to live without. He had woken her on the first morning when it was still dark by yanking her bodily from her bed. She had still been asleep when he put her on her feet, set a candle on the floor, and told her curtly to get ready and be outside in two minutes.

She had come a long way since that first day. She doubted she could ever be the same again after what he had put her through. On that first morning, he had been waiting for her by the front of the house where the porch-light provided a pool of light on the grass. She was dressed in the clothes that had been left in her room: white shorts and T-shirt. It had been cold and there was dew on the grass and wetness in the air. She had shivered.

'One hundred sit-ups,' he had told her.

She had hesitated, gazing at him, had even – she shuddered now at the memory – giggled in disbelief and he had hit her, palm upwards, flat-handed across the face.

'Two hundred,' he had said.

He still hit her occasionally, as impersonally as he had done then, whenever she hesitated or dared by look or expression to question his authority. The stinging blows knocked her off her feet; she tried to avoid them by remaining impassive whatever he said or did.

It was very hard to believe that he could have anything to do with the Leadership, or Pieter, or the Cause. Sometimes Zoe would try to force herself to remember that Sergio was part of Never Again: her instructor in the skills that would wipe the Nazis from the face of the earth. But it was so difficult to believe that Sergio could have anything to do with goodness. He seemed too evil.

Right at the beginning, on the journey here, she had tried to show him how much she cared for what Never Again was trying to achieve; how grateful she was to the Leadership for having selected her, and also of course – she had blushed with shyness – how grateful to Sergio for being prepared to train her. She wanted to assure him, she said, that she would do her very best.

He had not uttered a word. He had turned to spit out of the window and then stared ahead at the mountain road, dangerously narrow.

She had been nervous and curious and, in spite of his unresponsiveness, she had kept asking questions: how long had he lived in Corsica; how many people had he trained; would there be any other recruits trained with her?

He had still said nothing. She feared that he had not understood her French and she repeated her last question more slowly.

'How did you become involved?'

He had spat out of the window again before turning to her. 'I'm not,' he had said and smiled.

'I'm sorry? I don't understand . . .'

'I'm paid for what I do. I wouldn't do it otherwise.'

She had laughed before realising he was serious.

'But . . .' She had faltered.

He had shoved a cassette into the car's player. Queen's Greatest Hits; he had turned the volume up. Then he had looked over at her again. 'You talk too much,' he had said.

She had said nothing more. She was sure he must be joking . . . Why, he was saying that he was some kind of mercenary! And yet, would one joke about such things? Glancing suddenly at him she had caught him looking at her as a cat would watch its helpless prey. Mentally, she had shaken herself. She was imagining the cruelty in his face where before she had seen only dedication and fearlessness. Whatever he had said, the Leadership had chosen him, as they had her. They would not have sent her to a psychopath.

'Oh, wouldn't they?' she thought bitterly now as she began the descent of the hill. Her feet came down heavily on the dry ground, the rocks keeping a painful rhythm on her back. She turned her ankle, swore out loud at the wrench, but kept going, her breathing coming in bursts.

She chastised herself inwardly: the Leadership could have no idea what Sergio was truly like. They, who believed so much in the sanctity of life, in the right of the individual, would have had no truck with such a man. He had somehow duped them into believing he was as dedicated as they were. It made her angry, or would have, if she had had enough energy left for anger, to think that Never Again's money was being paid to a man like him.

She thrust from her mind what he had told her the night before. That had obviously been a peculiar game he had been playing for his own warped reason and she had fitted in the role of dupe perfectly. It had been the only occasion when, for no apparent reason, he had chosen to treat her as a human being.

But she should have known better than to believe anything had changed; that he would have been any different today from the man she had come to know.

Yesterday afternoon, she had been on circuit training: running round and round the valley where the stone house stood, leaping the stream, crawling under the net that he had pegged to the dry ground, finishing the lap with a rope climb high into the branches of the tall oak tree. The sun had been high and hot as she pounded the route; the sweat pouring from her. At the end of each circuit he had let her drink a litre of water; it had never been enough.

Her hands and thighs had been raw with the burn of the rope; her muscles seizing with cramp; her whole body crying out for food and rest. But she had dared not stop for a moment.

Out of the corner of her eye she had kept watch on him. He had been sitting in his chair of comfortable canvas, his feet up on the wooden box, his eyes unfathomable behind dark glasses. For all the world like a tourist lazing in the sun. Then his feet would jerk up, the binoculars would be in his hands, and he would find her. Even when he had not appeared to be watching, she had sensed him following every move that she had made.

On the second circuit he had hailed her. She had panted up to him, surprised and grateful that this particular torture should have been so short. The smell of his after-lunch coffee, its aroma heightened by the spicy maquis, had tormented her most dreadfully. He had stood, towering over her, waiting until her breathing had eased.

'You made a short-cut.'

She had dropped her gazed to the earth between them. 'I . . . I didn't mean . . .'

His voice had cracked like a whiplash. 'Don't make excuses.' He had paused, regaining control; he hated to lose control. 'You didn't climb to the top of the tree. Did you?'

She had shaken her head, keeping her face down so that he had not seen the tears.

'Begin again.'

So when, on the twelfth circuit, he had called her to him once more, she had started to sob. She had known that she was incapable of starting it all once more: that within two hours it would be dark, with that Mediterranean suddenness of the curtain falling, but that he would still order her to run in it; he had before. It was the unfairness that had got to her; the knowledge that she had not missed anything that time, or at least she was pretty sure that she had not: exhaustion, starvation and sheer bloody terror did funny things to the brain. She had run to him nonetheless.

He had not been there. His chair had been empty; the binoculars lying neatly on the wooden box. Fearfully she had glanced about, wondering what it could mean, what new, devilish game he had devised, and what her punishment would be for failing it? Would he kill her this time, have done for it? She had wondered a lot about death recently. Her body had trembled uncontrollably, in anticipation of what looked set to come.

'Zoe,' he had called softly.

It was the first time he had spoken her name. He had been standing in the doorway of the house, beckoning to her to follow him inside.

In the kitchen stood the rough pine table where he ate
his meals. She had blinked: it had been covered with a cloth
of dazzling whiteness. Upon it had stood wineglasses and
tumblers of pristine cleanliness, plates and cutlery perfectly
set for two. There had even been white embroidered napkins
and, in the centre of the table, an opened bottle of local wine
and a great earthenware jug of water. The smell of roasting
chicken, flavoured with thyme, had spiralled out from the oven
of the old blackened range.

She had stared at it, and then him.

'You wish to shower first?' he had asked her; his tone that
of the tactful proprietor.

She had feared to speak, to risk breaking the spell.

He had smiled at her. 'Time off,' he had said, and his voice
had sounded so different, even a little kind.

Dazed, she had stood under the icy jet of water, then
changed into the clothes she had found lying on her bed:
a pale blue dress, too long for her but pretty, and soft white
canvas shoes. On her pillow, there had been a small pocket
mirror. She had not seen herself all the time that she had been
there. Almost fearfully she had picked it up and looked: her
face was brown and thin, scratched and bruised like the rest
of her, but it was her eyes that had looked the most different:
something had gone out of them, they were no longer trusting,
but wary like a cat's and hungry like those of a wild animal.

She had touched the thin fabric of her dress in wonder. It
had seemed another lifetime ago that she had worn anything
feminine. He had taken all her clothes, everything, when she
had arrived. Each day she found fresh shorts, T-shirts and
underwear, all white, newly washed and precisely ironed,
outside her door. She had never seen the person who
performed such tasks – she could not believe it was him.

Everything had been so unreal that, as she had descended the
stairs, she would not have been surprised to have found him
waiting at the bottom with an axe. But no, he had been seated
at the beautiful table, pouring her a glass of wine. 'Drink a
glass before we eat,' he had said.

He had seemed so different a person. A gracious and
sensitive host anxious to put a shy guest at her ease. He

had kept the topics of conversation general, and he had talked fluently and at length. He had spoken of his love of Corsica: the blue misty mountains and the coolness they offered even on the hottest day; the smell of the maquis that was so wonderful that he feared he could never live anywhere else; the courage and character of the people. In his enthusiasm he had reminded her a little of Juonas.

When she had at last finished eating, he had paused in his monologue, lit a cigarette and filled her wine-glass again. Then he had picked up his own, swirling the liquid round like brandy.

After some silence he had asked her pleasantly enough: 'What would you do if you were ordered to kill?'

Her heart had hammered. This was it, she had thought, the test, and she was bound to fail. How did one respond to such a question, and to such a man? She had struggled to gain control of her voice, but had not been able to. An odd gurgle had been all that had emerged.

But he had not really been listening for her answer; his eyes were far away. 'Not everyone can kill. Did you know that? Oh, we all think we could if the circumstances were right. If one's child was being tortured in front of one's eyes; or one's wife raped; or if it was question of kill or be killed. But I tell you, not everyone would be able to pull the trigger. I know, I've seen it happen. You wait for them to fire, and they cannot. Even when you warn them what will happen if they don't, when you take aim at them, squeeze the trigger, they still can't do it. Odd, isn't it? How some people can, without thinking, and some who are so sure, will never do it.'

He had stopped again, and seemed lost in thought. She had let her mind drift; sleep had been only a moment away when his words had snapped her to attention once more:

'Tomorrow we shall see if you can pull the trigger or not, eh?'

She had stared, willing him to go on, but he had dismissed her. 'Go to bed now,' he had told her, like a father. 'It's a big day tomorrow for you, yes?'

It must have been as a result of that extraordinary evening, or what he had said about shooting, or a combination of both that had made her dream. It had been the first one that she had remembered having since he had brought her to the ranch.

He had been walking in the glen near her home in Newtonmore, climbing up the steep face of a crag that she had known as a child. He had reached the top and found the hidden cave that had been her hideout, where she gone to when home and school had been too much.

She had entered the dream, begging him to leave her secret place, but all that he had done was laugh, and the wind had caught the sound and thrown it back at her. He had stood on the edge of the crag, mocking her. With an energy that she had not known she possessed, she had given him a mighty shove and seen him falling slowly away, his lips still turned up in the taunting smile.

'Good shot, Zoe,' he had cried as he fell. 'I knew you could do it.'

Now, she stumbled over a hidden tree root and cursed herself out loud. That was what happened when she did not concentrate. It was always on this part of the route, the mad dash for Eagle Rock, that she got careless and hurt herself.

Why, she wondered, had he bothered telling her that he would teach her to shoot today? Had it only been to taunt her? Part of whatever elaborate charade he had been playing?

She had not really known what to expect of her 'training'. But certainly learning to shoot, especially after what she had seen at Hamburg, had seemed an essential: the enemy was armed and she must be also. She must know how to hold a weapon, how to aim it and fire it, if only for self defence.

She had always been a little vague on precisely what else she had expected: some knowledge of explosives, for sabotage purposes. And she had supposed fitness training to a certain level, and hand to hand combat perhaps. She had imagined a sort of summer-camp atmosphere where she and other recruits worked together to hone their skills in the war against the Nazis. There would be great camaraderie and sense of achievement.

Instead . . . this. If there had been some reasoning to the monotonous physical and mental torture, she might have stood it better – but what was the purpose of being bullied and battered into the ground? How was that going to equip her to eliminate the Nazis?

There had been elation in her heart that morning. From now on everything would be different. She had woken early, but instead of lying, hoping against hope that he would sleep in, she had gotten up, crept downstairs in the early dawn and gone for a little run. She had smiled to herself as her feet hit the ground: she wanted to please him, to prove that she was worthy of his teaching.

When she had got back to the house, she had half expected that he would have been waiting for her beside his wooden box, and on it would have been the gun that he was going to teach her to use.

In the nick of time, she jumped over a tree-stump that had caught her out many times before. 'Silly cow,' she muttered to herself.

Sergio had been waiting for her, but there had been no gun. He had surveyed her with his habitual look of consummate contempt; his toy soldier to be pulled and twisted into whatever shape he wanted.

'So lively, so early?' he had asked her. 'We'd better get you going at once, eh?'

He had been a bastard ever since; sending her on short circuits for two hours, roaring at her to run faster, jump higher.

Nothing remained of the man she had glimpsed the previous night. He had obviously had some sort of brainstorm, perhaps he had been lonely or thought she was someone else. Who knows; it hardly mattered now. Today the real Sergio was back.

. She stumbled again and swore: for the rest of her time here she would be falling down that hill, swimming the river, crawling under nets. If she ever met a Neo-Nazi she would be able to shock him into submission by the speed with which she could climb a bloody rope.

Through the trees she glimpsed the clear outline of Eagle Rock. It was a largish piece of granite that she guessed had been left over from some ancient age when the mountains had been forming. It lay awkwardly jutting out of the hillside;

from the valley below it looked quite startlingly like the bird of prey.

Still running, she brought her left wrist up in front of her face and looked at the time. She swore again, the rocks had slowed her down. Eleven seconds to reach it, clamber up the back of the Eagle and get to the edge. She had to stand quite still so that he would see her. Once he had claimed he had not, that she had not positioned herself clearly enough.

He had let her off, she remembered bitterly, with two hundred press-ups.

She was not going to make it. She began to pray out loud: 'Please God, please God,' but could articulate no further. She was at the Rock now, took the incline in one leap, fell badly on her knees, kept crawling forwards. She squeezed her eyes shut with the pain, and stood up.

She screamed out loud. A man sat with his back to her, his feet dangling over the edge. Against the morning sun, he made a perfect silhouette. He had not turned at her scream. She screamed again.

This time the figure twisted to face her.

'Stop that stupid noise,' he snapped. Sergio.

It took her a couple of seconds to realise that it was he. He had never accompanied her on the route; he never went anywhere; his place was in the chair by the house.

She had to accept that he must have done the course himself once, because he had given her precise instructions and descriptions before sending her off on her first attempt. But in over three weeks, the furthest that she had seen him move was between his chair and the kitchen.

Something else did not make sense. Only twenty minutes before, when she had passed the first sighting place, he had been sitting in the sun. It was impossible for him to have got here. She stared at him; he looked perfectly clean and unruffled, certainly he had not been charging up hills or swimming mountain rivers.

'If you spent a little less time running about without your head, you would observe better,' he said.

She knew better than to ask questions.

'If you had ever examined this rock properly you would see

the steps that have been cut into the hillside. Such an easy way to get here, don't you think? It would have saved you so much time . . .' He paused, looking with some disdain at her appearance, '. . . and effort.'

He stood up. 'Another thing. Never scream when you are surprised. It gives your position away.'

He walked to one side of the rock, his back to her. Her dream came suddenly back to her: one good shove would do it.

He turned suddenly. 'A nasty fall, it would be, yes? So be careful you do not fall. Leave that rucksack here. You can collect it another day.'

He slipped down onto a lower section of rock that was half hidden by scrub-bushes. Then he crouched and sprang, oddly graceful for such a large man, and vanished behind the underhang. She shucked the weight of the rucksack from her shoulders and stepped down onto the lower ledge. Below her, in the shadow of the Eagle's beak she could see him quite clearly. She gulped: it was quite a leap and, if she missed, a long drop onto the rocks below.

'Now!' he yelled, his voice echoing.

She jumped, stretching her whole body for the landing. Her toes touched the earth, but her balance was wrong. In sickly slow motion, she began arching backwards. His arms shot out, grabbed her and hauled her in. She sat winded and panting on the ground, but he gave her no time for shock. He nudged her with his foot. 'Be more careful. I'll go first.'

The 'steps' he had referred to were in front of them. They were no more than scooped out pits of earth in the hillside, but they were effective. He descended them at speed, using his heels in the hollows, and the branches to steady himself. She slithered less gloriously but safely after him. They were in the valley bottom in less than ten minutes.

He strode purposefully ahead. Following, she wondered at him: two breaks in his usual behaviour in less than twenty-four hours. Something was going to happen. Her pulse sped up: he had meant what he said after all last night.

He led her not to the house, but to the barn behind it. It was a long low building, made of the same yellow stone but with a corrugated roof. She had never been inside, indeed it had always been ostentatiously locked with a padlock and chain. Now she saw that the large wooden door was open. He disappeared inside.

After the bright sunshine, the place was gloomy and smelled musty. He lit a match, and bent over a gas lamp. Its jet hissed and gave off its white, glaring light. He hung it on a hook on the wall.

He was standing beside a blackboard propped upon a trestle. There was a table and two chairs in front of it, and on the table piles of books: a schoolroom.

Zoe scarcely saw it; her eyes were fixed on the opposite end of the room. Ghostly shapes of men floated and twirled, suspended from a beam. Cardboard cut-out figures dancing in the air; their hearts radiating circles in black and white. The shooting gallery.

She turned to Sergio and smiled.

For once he did not crush her.

'Sit down.' His voice was neutral. He began drawing on the board.

She picked up one of the books on her desk. *Special Weapons, Devices and Equipment* was the title. She opened it: it was full of diagrams, some of which were easily recognisable as guns and other weapons, others not. She paused at one page. The drawing seemed to show a cigarette case. 'Pocket Incendiary,' she read. 'Description: a flat black celluloid container filled with a jelled petroleum fuel. Operated by special Time Delay switches (see diagram 124) for igniting fuel after the copper covered glass ampoules are crushed.'

Her eyes widened as she read on: 'Purpose: To start fires at a future time. It is especially useful where a prolonged flame and silent operation are required. It is most effective in cars, houses, furniture, oil wells, fuel and supply depots, factories and warehouses. The shape of the case allows it to be easily concealed upon the operator's person. Can also be left in a target's personal belongings.'

She felt suddenly sick. The hygienic, orderly description was incompatible with its purpose: to kill and maim.

She flicked over a page: a step-by-step guide to planting a

device under a railway line. She shut the book quickly and closed her eyes. These devices; these methods ... these things were not what she had imagined at all. They were more in line with ... well, with terrorism.

The word hit her in the pit of her stomach. She was here to learn how to kill; that was what her training was all about. And in that moment she knew that she could never do it; the Leadership had picked the wrong person.

She was suddenly furiously angry at herself: what had she expected? The Leadership had been quite open with her. She remembered something the man had said about regretting that violence was necessary; and the woman warning her, what was it she had said? 'You'll be like a soldier. Killing and death. Not a game for children.'

Zoe bit her lip. She had been acting like a child, wanting to learn to shoot but not to know what it was for. Had she imagined that Sergio was going to teach her so that they could both go clay-pigeon shooting together? An awful dread swept through her: the knowledge that she was in too far, and had no way of getting out. She felt her skin prickle with fear.

Sergio had finished. He had been watching her: for how long she did not know. But it was too late now to dissemble; he had witnessed her fear.

He kept watching her, like a snake bewitching a rabbit, as his hand reached out for a chair, drew it closer and sat down astride it, his chin resting on its back.

'Scared?' His voice was again neutral, giving no clue.

She could only stare.

'Nobody told you it wasn't a game?'

She remembered Beatrix's warning and felt a chill start in her scalp and crawl its way down her spine.

He contemplated her for a few seconds. 'Everyone is scared when they stand on the edge and regard what they must do. It does not seem real, and then it does, and boom! It's too big.

'Did you look at who the books were written for?'

She shook her head.

He stretched over and picked one up. 'This one is for the American Army, look.'

She looked at the open page. 'Office of Strategic Services

Research and Development Branch, Washington DC'. She frowned and looked at him.

'And this one is a manual for the British; this one for the French. War is a dirty game. You must understand that.'

He got to his feet. 'I give you advice, the same advice they give any new soldiers: remember how much you hate your enemy, huh? It's the New Nazis you hate, is it not?

'Well, remember that, make them your target.'

His eyes narrowed, and there was the briefest hint of a smile about his mouth. 'If that fails, think of me and how much you hate me. That will always work.'

He tossed the white stub of his chalk up in the air, and caught it deftly in one hand. 'Lesson Numero Uno: bullets.'

If, for the first few seconds, he saw that she was not attending, he gave no sign. He had again surprised her with his demonstration of feeling, but she was also amazed at what he had said. She went over his words in her mind, slowly repeating them. He was right, she thought. He had given her the answer; it had been there inside her all along and had not changed. The books on her desk only reinforced it: if the armed forces of her own country, and those of other civilised nations resorted to guerilla tactics in war, then it was entirely justifiable for Never Again to do so.

It depended, she realised, whose side you were on and what cause you were fighting for. When it came to Never Again, one was entitled to use any sort of tactic against the Nazis. Why, it was the same moral predicament she had once heard mooted at a student debate, entitled: 'Would you have killed the infant Adolf Hitler?' No predicament.

A bullet through the head was too good for Neo-Nazis! She felt her chill and fear evaporate; in their place was conviction, determination – even a sense, at long last, of camaraderie with Sergio. He understood her!

'Attend!'

She started.

He was giving her his meanest look. 'The speed with which the bullet leaves the chamber is the equivalent of one thousand miles an hour; eleven hundred feet per second; fourteen tons per square inch.'

He pointed at the bullet he had drawn on the board. 'When the nose of the bullet is carved with a cross – thus,' he erased the cone neatly with his finger, 'we have a much more interesting projectile: the dum-dum bullet. You've heard of this, I suppose?'

She had; she nodded.

'When this bullet hits soft tissue, flesh, for instance, it explodes outwards in a big hole. Like the petals of a tulip.' He clenched his fist and opened it slowly. 'It gives the single bullet a much better chance to hit something vital.'

She shuddered.

'And sometimes the back of the bullet is drilled and the hollow filled with mercury or lead. If one of these specially adapted bullets hits the arm or leg or nearly any part of the body, the person will bleed to death. The fragments of the bullet explode on impact, you see, scattering everywhere. Very, very difficult for the surgeon to remove . . . but perhaps just possible.

'Plastic bullets, of course, are a different thing.'

He paused as if waiting for Zoe to join in for an intelligent debate. Then he appeared to remember her absolute ignorance and sighed. 'Why are plastic bullets so good? Because it is impossible for them to be picked up on X-ray; so impossible to remove them from the vital organs . . . so kaput!

'Of course, there is also the chance that the person dies from poisoning of the blood from the mercury. But most times he dies before. We must hope that your little group has some special bullets for you, eh? So that you can see for yourself what I mean.'

Sicko, she thought, but kept her face a blank.

'For your first lesson, on the paper targets, you will be using bullets that are modified to pass straight through paper. They're called "Wad-cutter" bullets.'

He produced, from his shirt pocket, a brass oblong cylinder and tossed it over to her.

She did not think that it looked like a bullet, not how she had imagined one would look. It was about five centimetres long and its point had been sawn off. She rolled it curiously between her thumb and her fingers, feeling its smooth coldness. It did not seem possible that a little thing like that could kill someone. Forgetting him, she rubbed it against her cheek.

'You like its power?' he asked her, his voice soft and purring. It was the first time she had sensed him sexually; she looked at him and shivered, both excited and afraid.

He held her eyes for a second, and in them she saw a flame light up and flicker. Then his mouth twisted downwards and the gleam died. 'Don't play with bears, little girl,' he growled.

She blushed and dropped the bullet back onto her desk. She was angry and embarrassed: she did not want him, it was he who had drawn her into his lair and then rejected her. Always, in everything, it seemed he had the upper hand. She raised her head, determined for once to defy him, and found herself looking into the barrel of a gun held an arm's length away. She waited for him to kill her.

He pulled the trigger. There was a small click, a milli-second's silence and he gave a short bark of laughter. 'Wet yourself?' he asked pleasantly. 'This is power, my little friend. Here, try some.'

Trembling, she put out her hand for the weapon he offered her.

It was small – not that much bigger than her hand – and silver-coloured. She was surprised by its lightness; it seemed wrong that an instrument of death should weigh so little. She liked its contrasts: the straight cold line of the barrel, the fragility of the trigger and the roughness of the grip. It fitted well in her palm, a part of her. When she turned it upside down she saw the magazine was empty: it was only as deadly as a pretty toy. She was sharply reminded of Alasdair: he had had such a toy as this once; in the garden at home they had fought furiously over it.

'It's a real gun?'

'Oh yes, and real bullets too.' He displayed a magazine of them in his other hand. In it the little bullets jostled like battery hens. Zoe entertained a brief fantasy of snatching the container, ramming it into the gun and blasting his sneering face off.

He appeared to guess her feelings. He smiled. 'Tempting, I know. But first you have to learn a few facts concerning the use of this little pistol. Don't look so disappointed; if you do well today, I'll let you kill me tomorrow.'

In spite of everything he had put her through, he was a good teacher. He abandoned his technique of roaring orders from the sidelines in favour of a hands-on and patient, almost gentle approach. Zoe, always on the look-out for a vicious mood-change, began, as the afternoon progressed, to relax. Sometimes she even forgot her hatred and fear of him.

He led her to the middle of the barn, facing the targets and about ten metres away from them. He positioned her sideways, her feet a hip's distance apart, her right arm extended, holding the gun firmly but not rigidly. Her eyes, he told her, would naturally adjust to the dual role required for shooting: the right concentrating on the sights of her pistol; the left fixing on the target. Then he turned to her hands. 'Use both of them.'

She obeyed, but – a sign of her growing confidence – dared, by a look, to question why.

'You've heard of kick back?'

She shook her head.

'The physical effect of firing a weapon can be very great, especially if you are not very experienced, or are of small stature – like you are. The kickback can knock you sideways, or over onto the ground. Not very good if you are meant to be frightening a Nazi is it? And if you still had your finger on the trigger and it was on automatic, you might shoot a comrade, or your teacher by mistake. You wouldn't want that, would you?'

He showed her how to cock the weapon without taking half her thumb off, and then began a recital of the naming of parts: the safety catch; fire-flash; the slide. She failed to see their importance; she wanted to fire the weapon not identify its components; her eyes glazed. His voice in her ear, low like a snake's hiss, brought her sharply back to reality.

'Don't sigh and look bored, my friend. What I'm teaching you might one day save your life.'

She swallowed. His voice whispered on:

'You'd look very foolish, as well as dead, if it jammed when you were shooting at a Nazi, wouldn't you? So listen to me when I'm teaching you.'

She heard him take a step back and tensed for a blow. But he said, in quite a different voice, 'You think you're ready? Here, load it.'

She took the cartridge and thrust it home, immediately conscious of the added weight. She felt, too, an added surge of power. 'The bullets . . .?' she queried, turning to him.

'They're real, my bloodthirsty little friend. They'd hurt the same as any others.' He walked over to the wall and pressed a switch.

There was a clanking sound and, drawn by an overhead pulley, one of the dancing men came creaking towards her. It stopped twelve paces away. The figure was stark, black and white only, and dressed in a nondescript uniform. The face under the helmet looked cruel, its eyes narrowed, its mouth a thin line; not like anyone's son. One of its hands was reaching for a pistol.

'Un minuto,' Sergio called to her. He approached the cardboard man, held him still and drew upon him. When he stood back, she saw that the heart was circled three times and on the helmet was an ugly swastika. 'That will help,' Sergio called to her from the side. 'Now, go for the target and keep firing until the bullets stop.'

She stood as he had taught her, her hand an extension of her weapon. Her whole body felt in tune, flexible and alert; her shooting arm steady and strong. For the first time she was aware of the physical transformation that the training had wrought in her: she felt the steel line of her muscles running up her legs, up her back, across her chest. Maybe, after all there had been a purpose to the torture he had put her through.

She looked down the sights of the pistol, altering her aim slightly for perfection. She chose the smallest of the concentric circles on the target and held herself absolutely still. Not moving her eyes, she brought back the hammer and released the safety catch. Slowly she pulled her index finger, curled around the trigger, towards her.

She thought her own arm had exploded. She concentrated

on the circles, on controlling her muscles and gradually her arm obeyed her, jerking up less with with each burst. The bullets sprayed out, passing through the air, the target, only stopped by the back wall. The noise went on rolling in echoes, ricocheting and bouncing backwards from the stone walls. Plaster and dust fell, sprinkling their molecules upon the sunlight.

In the middle of it all, Zoe stood, her eyes now closed, her gun arm down by her side. She was savouring the vibration as it travelled throughout her body. It was like nothing she had ever felt before: like a burst of electricity, a tingling in every fibre of her being. When it was spent and leaving her, she still felt its afterglow. Then she opened her eyes as from a deeply pleasurable sleep. The target, hanging in shreds, seemed to have little to do with her.

Behind her came the sound of slow hand-clapping and a low whistle. She turned, expecting sarcasm and abuse, but Sergio's face wore an expression of admiration. When he spoke, it was to himself, in Italian. 'Who would have thought? A crackshot!'

He took the gun from her limp hand, and walked up to the remnants of the man. It was as he had thought: her fifteen slugs had hit the target thirteen times: eight of them within the circles and two of them the bullseye. He had never before witnessed such shooting from a complete beginner. It did not fit; thus far Zoe had kept pace only by sheer determination. Not her fault really: she was too frail. But now this . . .! He had to find out whether it was just beginner's luck. He replaced the target and tossed her a second magazine. 'Do that again,' he ordered her.

She wanted to laugh; it was so easy! This time she adjusted her aim slightly for the effects of recoil: she fired for a lower point and sent four bullets into the centre hole.

Sergio had no doubt now. He raised his eyebrows slightly at her. 'I pity the Nazi-skins,' he said.

His attitude to her changed dramatically after that. For half the day, usually in the morning, he was still a bastard, forcing her to her limit and beyond on circuit training, but Zoe felt that his heart was no longer in it.

In the early afternoon, he was as keen as she was to begin shooting practice, and it often went on until nine or ten at night. He began eating with her and, if he adhered to the strict demarcation lines between teacher and pupil, at least it was that and no longer the role of terrified slave and master. He respected her, or at least her new skill – and she could see that he respected few people.

Zoe loved everything to do with shooting: from the feel of the weaponry, to the sensation of firing, to the smell of the cordite. After the third day they abandoned the barn for the outdoors, and her sense of freedom increased. It was late September now; the days were long and the earth was parched and hard; the soft breeze had left the valley and even the air felt heavy. But the scent of the maquis from the hillsides was like a wild intoxicant. It matched her mood: she took in great lungfulls of it and felt light-headed, filled with expectation.

Against the backdrop of the purple and blue mountains, their summits hazy and growing more distant in the autumn mists, volley after volley of shots rang out. There was no one to hear them: the mountains seemed to enclose her and Sergio in their own private world where the only thing that mattered was dead centre.

He hung new targets for her on the olive trees: old bolsters bound together in pairs, one for the head, one the body, with pinned-on paper circles. The more she practised, the quicker and more accurate she became; it was as if she had been reborn or made new. With a gun in her hand she knew she was no longer a little girl to be dismissed and disregarded; now people would listen to her and take notice.

Sergio, affecting indulgence, let her use every handgun in his armoury: an old Colt revolver, a Smith and Wesson revolver; a German SIG Sauer. He even, on one particularly hot afternoon when her shooting had been nearly perfect, let her use his personal weapon. It was a curious instrument, a black Liberator, a single shot pistol supplied to the Secret Services for undercover, homicide work. She split asunder the dummy's head with that one shot. Her face had been like a child's when she had turned to him for praise.

He had watched her use them all, keeping a mental tally

of her performance with each. Her best weapon was the little Italian Beretta, the automatic. How fitting, he thought; a true ladies' weapon: small, compact, easily hidden in a handbag.

He saw her confidence increase each time she handled a different gun. Kessler had been right again: there was something extremely special about the young British girl.

For Zoe, at last, everything seemed to be falling into place. The punishing physical routine now had a purpose: to enable her to be in peak condition for shooting. She no longer considered any part of her training to be useless: even if it was not obvious to her why she had to swim the ravine river with weights on her back, she knew one day that it would make sense. And something like love entered her soul for Sergio: he might be a bastard, but he had led her to the thing she loved best and excelled at. Perhaps the crown of it all was that her new skill could so obviously benefit Never Again.

It was time for Sergio to collect his instructions. As he had done with previous recruits, he set Zoe a task that would take her at least eight hours – an arduous marathon deep into the mountains, well away from the cottage and any sight of the road. To be on the safe side, he added another five kilos to her pack. She had nearly toppled over. 'You never know,' he had told her, 'when you might have to run with heavy weaponry on your back.'

He had waited an hour after she had gone, then got into his car and headed for Calvi.

He guessed that he would have Zoe for another two weeks, and then they would want her for something, that was the usual way. He would miss her, he thought, with a self-mocking smile. To be more precise, he would miss her talent with a weapon. He had not seen anything like it since . . . he thought back . . . well, since himself actually, a long time ago.

In the Red Brigades, he had been the boy with the gun, the crackshot, twenty years ago. He was still pretty good, except that his eyesight was not quite 20–20 any more. If he could have Zoe for another month, he could really make an assassin of her. He pulled a face in his mirror: he was getting too involved. It was his job to turn the girl into a good all-rounder, not a one-shot killer. There would be time enough in her refresher courses to teach her other skills – as long as, of course, nothing went wrong on her first outing.

He was having a month's rest after Zoe had gone, and he would be glad to leave the confines of the valley and the primitive house. He used it only for training – for its remoteness and inaccessibility – and it was hardly comfortable. His own home in Corte lacked nothing in the way of luxury, but it was not only the pool and the TV set he was missing. It was his bed, and Carla, his woman.

In that respect, Zoe had proved to be quite a temptation.

He saw her in his mind's eye: bloody and sweaty after one of her circuits, standing before him, hating him. He was turned on by women's hatred, always had been. But what had really got him going was the way she was with a gun. There was the thrill he always got from seeing a girl turned into a killer: the sudden empowerment of the weaker sex; the role reversal. But with Zoe there was more to it. He saw that once a weapon was in her hand, everything else ceased to exist: her fear; any awareness that she was now lethal; where she was or who was with her. She clearly did not see even herself, and for him, that was the greatest challenge of all: to break through her dream and take her.

He had held himself back; he had to. If he took her, he would have to kill her because he could not allow her that power over him. And he could not kill her because she was owned by others, by Kessler and her new group. Even if he did, and claimed that it had been an accident, their suspicions would be aroused. There had already been one real accident; he could not afford another. He did not want to kill her anyway; it would be a shame to waste all that talent.

No, however teased he was by her perfect little body – and he'd seen a lot of it over a lot of weeks – she was strictly off-limits. He groaned: God, it was hard on him.

He left the car where he always did, in the car-park by the railway station. Calvi's post office was just over the road on the corner of Avenue de la Republique. There were still enough tourists in the town to drive a man crazy, but at ten in the morning the post office itself was virtually empty. He had come, he told the counter clerk, to pick up any post for Monsieur St-Georges.

The man pushed one sealed yellow envelope under the grille, and got him to sign for it. Sergio took it, unopened, to the cafe across the street – a locals' bar, avoided by the tourists who were put off by its carefully maintained scruffiness and surly staff.

He took a seat at a table on the pavement, shielding his eyes with dark-glasses, and keeping a tense watch on passers-by. Sitting in Calvi, he was at much more risk of recognition by an arms dealer or a government man, than he was in Corte, his usual haunt. He ordered one cold beer; his alcoholic limit during the day whilst on duty. Then he slid his finger under the flap of the envelope, and pulled out the slip of paper.

'Package to be delivered Turin, by noon on 5th October.'

That was all. He screwed it up, took a lighter from his trouser pocket, and burnt the paper until it turned to black powder fragments in the ashtray. He saw that he was angry by the fierce clutch of his fist, and he frowned. The instruction was not logistically difficult: she could take the night ferry on Monday from Bastia to Genoa, and connect onwards by train to Turin. He would have to check times, but that was easy. His fury was that someone was taking her away: he had only five more days with Zoe.

She was afraid: she knew something was about to happen but not what, or when. For the past two days, her training had intensified to fever pitch, and Sergio had been vicious and relentless. It was as if she was being prepared for an examination without knowing the subject.

She had her suspicions, of course. She would have had to have been deaf and blind not to have done.

Earlier that morning he had stood over her as she did one hundred press-ups, her hands hurting on the gritty parched earth. Normally he sat at ease in his chair watching her; to have him so near, hearing his breathing and the tick of his stop-watch, had made her nervous.

His foot had come down hard on the small of her back. She had screamed at the pain, and her body collapsed forward into the dirt. He had kept his foot on her spine, grinding it. She had not been able to endure it; she had moaned in agony but he had kept on.

'How will you deal with interrogation?' he had asked, almost conversationally, then at last had lifted his foot. 'Have you thought about what it is like?'

She had lain afraid to move, in case it goaded him. Her back had felt split in two. She had prayed for him to die, and quickly.

'Torturers like little girls like you. Did you know? They like to do things to them.'

He had paused and she had waited for his boot again, but the silence had lasted. Trying not to move, she had craned her neck to look at him. He had not been watching her; his eyes had been fixed on some far off spot in the mountains. His whole body had suddenly convulsed in a shudder, and he had looked down at her, speaking quietly: 'Everyone breaks under torture. Just a matter of time.'

He had stepped back, and she had watched him striding off in the direction of the barn. She had raised herself slowly to her hands and knees, and then by degrees to her feet. Standing up straight had been excruciating. The most terrifying thing about him, she thought, as she had tried to rub some of the pain away, was that he could hurt her like that just to get a point across. He would probably have forgotten it by now.

She glanced over at the barn. He had been in there for an hour. He never normally allowed her such time on her own; she dreaded to think what he might be planning for her next. Nevertheless, when she heard his voice calling to her a few minutes later, she had run to the barn door. The habits he had taught were hard to break.

He was at the far end of the building, bending over some objects on the trestle table. From where she stood, just inside, she could not see what they were.

'Come and see some new toys.'

He had made an array of them, like the exhibits she remembered on the Nature Table at school. He listed them for her: a British SA 80, a heavy looking weapon, half of it encased in sludge-green plastic; a more elegant-looking

Armalite rifle, standing on a bipod; an Israeli Uzi; a Sterling sub-machine gun that looked like a piece of junk, its barrel riddled with holes. Taken off-guard, she said as much.

He picked it up. With his right hand he held it, jammed in at hip-level; he rested his left on the magazine and swept the gun from side to side. It stopped looking like junk. The whole point of a machine-gun, he told her, is rapid fire; the barrel gets hot; the holes cool it down, stop it burning up.

He laid the weapon down, picked another up, and gave it to her. 'This is for you to start,' he said.

It was truly like a toy, a little black box with a nozzle at the top. She rattled it; it even sounded like a toy. He handed her a magazine, a heavy-looking black metal silencer and a pair of ear-protectors.

'Put them on,' he ordered her, putting on a pair himself. 'These are very noisy weapons.'

She practised outside, all morning and afternoon; sometimes with and sometimes without the silencer. With it jammed on the barrel of the weapons, it was amazing; all she could hear was 'put-a-put-a-put', the mildest tapping. With the silencer off, the noise tore through her body like a cruel whirlwind. Her whole body felt numb and deafened by it.

She wrecked the dummies within the first hour, leaving shreds of ticking and stuffing hanging from the little olive trees. She took ten minutes off, sinking gratefully to the ground. The weapon had grown heavy, and her shoulders and arms ached from holding it. Sergio rigged up the new shooting range out in the middle of the valley. He placed great sacks of flour – ten of them – in a row. Her bullets riddled them, sending the white powder into great, all enveloping clouds.

'I can't see anything!' she yelled.

'Doesn't matter. Keep firing.'

The gun pumped on in her hands. The magazine finished and, as ordered, she immediately re-loaded. Being unable to see what she was shooting at, she looked down at the weapon and its action. 'It's like an eager little bully,' she thought. 'No heed for anything or anyone.' It wasn't like shooting at all; it was simply holding a killing machine. Anyone could do it. There was no skill attached to this; no marksmanship;

no satisfaction in hitting the target. She could be watching someone else, for all the involvement she had in it.

She was thankful when at last the bullets stopped. Very gradually the scene cleared: there was nothing left of the sacks, just little piles of flour lifting and falling in sighs. Watching the movement Zoe was beguiled. The question, therefore, shocked her brutally: what would it feel like, her mind asked, to shoot a real target, a person?

Part Two

Chapter Nine

The girl was now a killer.

Forty-eight hours ago, in Turin, she had been put to the test and by all accounts had acquitted herself well. A little hesitation, a little shock maybe, but both reactions perfectly acceptable. The fact of the matter was that she had obeyed orders and fired. She was blooded now, and one of them. No longer someone in need of protection. End of concern, or should have been.

Beatrix Kessler shut her eyes; it helped block out the jabbering of the other two. The Leadership – she allowed herself a small sneer at the term – were gathered together, in yet another stinking, derelict apartment block, to congratulate and welcome their new member. Zoe would be arriving shortly and, in front of her, they would present some sort of unified front: the men because they considered unity helped strengthen the recruits' resolve and she because it was easier to do so.

However much she hated the idea, she was virtually the man's prisoner, well paid of course, but powerless. For the past year she had been living in a series of safe-houses, in the suburbs of cities and small towns across western Europe. The men came to her for advice, to listen grudgingly to strategy, and for show meetings such as was scheduled for that night. Afterwards they were free to go, but for her there was no such freedom. A team of three minded her – two on duty, one off – at all times. 'Your own personal staff,' Axel had told her, smiling, mocking her. He reminded her of a child poking sticks through the cage of a zoo animal; fearless because there was no need of fear.

She hated Axel, whereas she only despised Leon. Poor, weak Leon, who had once been so fiery, jumping with ideas, some crazy but some good; whose confidence had been slowly sapped by the older man. Leon, who could not see Axel's lust for power; who could see nothing beyond the Cause and hear nothing except Axel's voice.

She glanced over at them now. They were ignoring her as was their custom. Sitting side by side, Axel talking, Leon listening, smiling, nodding, they resembled nothing more than two schoolboys plotting cruel tricks, the big bully and the little sidekick.

She was left to think her thoughts, whatever they might be.

She tried to get them in order. She tried to tell herself that it was too late; that Zoe had put her foot on the path, and now the only way was down. But quite how fast she might spiral down, only Beatrix, at that moment, knew.

Things had been going well for Never Again recently: last month's bombing attack at a Neo-Nazi rock concert had killed two and injured seventeen; then there had been the shooting of Carlos Mendidas, a fascist judge in Bilbao and two nights before, the killing of Valerio Mariana by the Ninth Commando, Zoe's team. Whoever was behind Never Again, she thought, must be extremely pleased with the results they were achieving. Of course, there was always room for improvement . . .

The previous morning, in her role as Operational Commander, Beatrix had despatched a great deal of money – the equivalent of six months' salary for a prosperous businessman – to Sergio, for Zoe's training. The money went through a network of handlers, each knowing nothing more than the next person's codename, and it was by the same route that Sergio had passed her his message. She had got it just before they left the safe-house to come to the apartment for the meeting.

It consisted of only two words, but they were quite sufficient to convey his meaning: Una bandita.

It was the name, the coveted, envied name, bestowed upon Sergio and two or three others way back in the high days of the Red Brigades. The sharpshooter, the marksman, the bandito. Sergio was telling her that Zoe had it, that most rare and precious of talents.

Operationally, it was a gift from God. If Zoe could be used as an assassin it would eliminate the need for many of the 'big bang' operations. Bombs were effective but indiscriminate; they might be good for headlines, but ultimately they were bad for public sympathy. With a bomb, one could never rule out the chance death of an innocent or the maiming of a child. But with an assassin! With an assassin, the number of bombings could be dramatically cut; Zoe would just need to take out the prominent figure on the platform or in the street. Or in her bed.

Beatrix entertained no doubts as to Zoe's future if she disclosed the news: she would be turned into a killing-machine and used again and again until there was nothing left of her. No feelings, no hesitation, no shock, just nothing. She would cease to be an individual; she would be put on the revolutionary pedestal and on the Public Enemy lists; hounded across the world by every police force and security agency in existence. She would be solely what her talent made her, notorious for her last death. In the end, whoever killed her would be doing her a favour.

Professionally, Beatrix knew she had no choice. It was clearly her duty to inform the two men immediately as to Never Again's good fortune. A crackshot, and their very own baby as well, so no problems with security. Beatrix could imagine their reaction; the wild celebrations and congratulations there would be. As always, of course, their praise would extend only to themselves: Zoe had been their choice all along, another example of their superior judgement over-riding her own. They would only, finally and grudgingly, turn to her, for information on how to run someone like Zoe, how to get the right weapons for her, how to maximise all that lovely potential.

But what if she, Beatrix, kept silent? Clearly, Zoe's skill was not flashy, or else there would have been some mention of it in the Turin report. Only Beatrix had contact with Sergio, and even that was indirect. Axel and Leon knew nothing about him. Sergio himself was safe; he knew that his message to her would have been received and whatever she chose to do with it would be her business. As long as he was paid on time, it would not occur to him to ask questions.

Beatrix stared sightlessly at a mildewed patch of wall

opposite. She held Zoe's life in her hands. Either she could
try to shield the girl from destruction, or she could give her a
good hefty shove in the direction of hell. It intrigued her that
she should care, but care she did. It was a little, she supposed,
like being a mother.

She let out a tiny gasp before she could stop herself. Her own
mother's face had appeared vividly in her mind: so trusting, so
twisted in torment on the TV screen, asking such a simple
thing: 'Do come and see me darling. I'm not terribly well . . .'
That dear face, now utterly lost, gone forever.

Beatrix closed her eyes again. She was breaking her own
rule, never to think of these things, but the memories were
awakening and pulling her in.

Sixteen years before, when her mother had died, something fundamental inside Beatrix had died too. The revenge-
bombing of the police station in Dusseldorf had not taken away
the savage sense of loss that had engulfed her; the feeling that
she had been given up, abandoned.

At least it had made one decision easy: Beatrix had had her
abortion three weeks later. Before, she had entertained the
notion of herself as a mother: nurturing the child, loving it
as her mother had loved her, letting the goodness in the child
make her good. But afterwards such a prospect had been quite
clearly ridiculous. How could a woman on the run, a woman
with blood on her hands, give birth to a new life? From loving
the baby inside her, Beatrix had suddenly hated it, seeing it as
a means to entrap her, in the same way as the police had tried
the motherhood bond on her. Getting rid of the baby had been
like having a tooth out; she had felt nothing, she told herself,
but relief.

She had never told the father; indeed, he had never known
that she had been pregnant. He had been beautiful, and so, at
twenty-five had she. They had made love together all weekend
in an apartment in Rome; drawn together both by the physical
elation that had followed a succesful joint 'mission' of her
group and his – the bombing of a new high security wing
of a prison outside Milan – and the necessity of staying out
of sight until the initial furore had quietened down.

By the time that she had realised she was pregnant, she had

moved on, and so had he. Given their lifestyles, the strong possibility that they might never meet again, or that one of them would be killed or locked up, it had never seriously occurred to her to seek him out to tell him. Anyway, she had never been the marrying kind, and nor had Sergio Brunelli.

She had recovered well, she thought, from the abortion. No psychological effects; no nightmares about killing the child within; no grief for the life that might have been. All her grief had been reserved for her mother and there had been none left over for anyone else.

Since then, caring about anyone had not been high on her agenda. That was why it was such a curious sensation for her now to be concerned with what happened to Zoe. She shrugged to herself; it was a novelty if nothing else.

'Beatrix, we asked you for your opinion.' Axel's voice sawed across her mind.

'My opinion?'

The men exchanged petty smirks. Axel spoke again, slowly as if to an idiot. 'We think Zoe should be a Sleeper. Everything indicates it: her intelligence, age and circumstances – a loner, unattached, very committed. She seems to have performed well in Turin, and we understand she was satisfactory in her training?'

She raised her eyebrows slightly. It was enough; Axel was not really interested.

'So. We do not have a Sleeper in England yet. We need one. We propose it shall be Zoe. Unless,' his voice slipped down to sarcasm, 'you consider she should be used for something else? We know you had doubts about her stability. Those fears have now evaporated, we trust?'

She studied him hard. The desire, suddenly, to put a bullet through his smooth, ignorant face, was overwhelming. You, she thought, who have never, and will never, dirty your fingers or darken your souls with the death of others. Who keep safe and holy while others die and kill.

But at least he had made up her mind for her. She smoothed her features to a smile. 'I think the girl would be an ideal Sleeper,' she said.

* * *

There were no masks this time and, on Zoe's part, there was no fear. Fear belonged in the past; to the time before Turin. Now there was no place for it. It was as if she had gone through a great, cleansing fire and fear had been burnt off in the process, along with a lot of other things.

The pictures in her mind – the death march and the pits, the Nazi boy's salute – were no longer so crystal sharp and they had lost some of their power to haunt her. Even the people she was fighting for, the thousands who made up the scapegoat minorities, were blurring slightly at the edges.

She was a soldier now, someone who had obeyed an order, even when that order had been to kill. That was what she had kept telling herself over the past two days when, suddenly when she was not thinking about it, she would see in her mind's eye the face of the boy from the office in Turin; see him plead silently for his life as her finger squeezed the trigger and his body slumped to the floor.

She blinked to shut out the image and concentrated on the three people who sat in front of her. They were somewhat disappointing in their ordinariness. At least the black hoods had bestowed upon them a certain mysterious chic; they had been terrifying yes, but exotic and exciting too. But face to face . . .

The woman was older than she had expected, and looked, as Zoe's mother would put it, as if she had 'let herself go'. Her hair was grey, coarse-looking and too long; her bare face pallid as if she hardly saw the light or had fresh air. She was wearing a crumpled man's shirt and her fingernails were bitten down. She sat, frowning and severe, in the middle, not meeting Zoe's eyes.

The men looked better; at least healthier and tidier. The older of the two, the one whose voice she had immediately recognised from her first meeting, was big and clean-shaven, with strong features and dark eyes. He was wearing a very white shirt and a tweedy tie; overall he gave an impression of immense cleanliness. She guessed that he was in his late forties, or early fifties. He smiled a lot, but not, she thought, from any nervousness; he had a definite air of command. A bank manager, she decided, or a self-made businessman; certainly not how she had imagined a Resistance leader.

The smaller man, sitting on the woman's left, also looked very much the younger in spite of a receding hairline. He had a thin, pointed face and his loosely cut jacket seemed too big for him. He would not meet Zoe's eyes either, but kept glancing over the woman's head at the other man as if seeking reassurance. Not an impressive figure, Zoe thought; weak and jumpy.

As before, the older man did the talking.

'We're very pleased with you, Zoe.'

He was smiling at her, but she was unsure of how to respond. 'Pleased'? How could anyone be pleased with what she had done?

He seemed to guess her mind. He moderated his smile. 'Of course, we do not rejoice in the death of anyone – even our enemies. We feel for their relatives and friends; we suffer in their mourning. But,' he fixed her with a stare, 'we want you to know that in killing those two men your commando ridded the world of two pieces of scum. You must be proud.'

He halted again and this time, hesitantly, she smiled.

He glanced at the woman and, over her head, at the other man. Then he turned back to Zoe, and spoke weightily.

'We have selected you for our Elite. You are to be what we call our "Sleeper" in the United Kingdom. Do you know what that means?'

She shook her head.

'May I?' he said to the woman, but not, Zoe thought as if he was genuinely seeking permission. She wondered why he bothered to pretend they were equals when it was so clear that it was he who was in charge. The woman, she saw, looked rather indifferent to the whole procedure. She nodded and looked down at the table.

'A Sleeper,' the man continued in the same weighty voice, 'is someone who is undercover, who maintains an outwardly normal life and who does not go on operations. In any underground war such as ours, Sleepers are essential.

'Their faces are unknown to the other side, and only a very few people within their own organisation know who they are.

The police and security forces, of course, are also ignorant as to their identity. Because there is no trace of such a person on any police file or computer, that person can get into places and do things that a more active comrade would find impossible.

'Of course, the Sleeper is only used once.' He stopped and stared at her. 'The big one or nothing. What do you think? It's a great honour.'

Zoe thought how easy it was to be programmed by this man. He was so powerful and he expected people to do exactly what he wanted. A true leader, she supposed, while at the same time being aware that she disliked, and even distrusted him. Nevertheless, she heard herself answering appropriately; solemnly thanking him, saying that she would do everything in her power to justify his belief in her. She thought she sounded stilted, but the man looked satisfied.

'It's like a game to him,' she thought. 'He's the player and I'm a chess piece.' Her eyes flickered over to the other man; he was smiling and nodding like an eager puppy. Then, as the man started talking again, her gaze strayed to Beatrix and stopped. The woman was looking straight at her. It was as if she had spoken and Zoe had heard her words: that the men were indeed playing at it; that they had never done what Zoe had and never would; but that she had and she was warning Zoe again of the danger she was in.

Zoe blinked. The woman's eyes were staring past her and she wore a blank, rather bored expression. Zoe frowned; she must have imagined the whole thing, but the message had been so clear. She gave herself a mental shake: she had been through a lot in the previous forty-eight hours; she must hold on to reality.

The man, meanwhile, had warmed to his theme. She listened, a little dazed. He was proscribing the rest of her life.

She was to return at once to London where she should find herself a flat – on her own – to rent. She was not to stay with her brother for any length of time, he told her: 'Bad for security.' She kept her face impassive, but she felt a sour stab at these words; the intrusion of it all; strangers having the right to nose into her life, to pry and make demands.

The man had noticed nothing in her expression. His voice

flowed on: it was important for cover purposes that she have a job, but nothing too onerous, too career-orientated or structured. She was not to worry about money; financial arrangements would be made and she would receive cash at regular intervals. Perhaps a part-time position; a secretary, or a shop assistant, maybe a librarian? In any event, something that allowed her plenty of leeway to take sudden, unexplained breaks.

Her stomach gave a little flip. What exactly would these breaks entail? she wanted to ask. Weekends away as part of a killing team? Shoot someone Saturday, home on Sunday and back to work in her Laura Ashley dress on Monday morning? Hysteria wormed its way inside her, and a terrible desire to laugh, but the man's explanation quietened her: the breaks would be for refresher courses, and for further training in Corsica.

So she would be seeing Sergio again. Partly she dreaded that, but also partly she was glad. Sergio would never know that she had not hit the target, and she realised, with a sudden lurch inside, that she desperately wanted his approval. She, the pupil, needed her teacher's praise; wanted to hear him congratulate her for pulling the trigger, for not being one of those who had failed the ultimate test.

'Now, the sort of further training I'm talking about includes a variety of underground warfare tactics,' the man went on enthusiastically. 'Explosives, the safe handling of them; the manufacture of simple devices – we already have an explosives expert for the more major bombs; the various skills required in planting such devices to ensure maximum damage while maintaining absolute security. You will also be instructed in the techniques that will help you to avoid capture, but in the unfortunate event that you may be captured you will also be shown how to avoid divulging secrets.'

While being tortured, she thought. Why doesn't he say it? At least Sergio with his boot in her back had given her a realistic idea of what to expect. But then, she realised, remembering Sergio's shudder, he had been tortured himself, whereas this man . . .

He linked his clean hands in front of him; his nails, she

noticed, were evenly cut and nicely shaped. He coughed delicately.

'We're prepared to spend a great deal of time and money in further training for you, Zoe. There are, of course, certain strains to the life we are asking you to live, but we know that your commitment to us, to the Cause, will carry you through.'

How do you know? the question popped into her mind. What if I said 'No!', she wondered. What if I said, I've done enough; find somebody else to; I want out . . .

'We have no idea at the moment how long we will want you to "sleep". Perhaps just a couple of months, or it could be years. You might never be called. But always, always you must hold yourself in readiness. Every day you must say to yourself, "I am prepared", and you must be prepared. You think you can do this?'

She stared at his smiling face and felt her resistance evaporate. She nodded and smiled, and he smiled back.

'There will be one person in Britain who will act as your contact. We will do the contacting, not you. And talking of other people, just a brief word on relationships. You are, as I have told you before, a pretty girl . . .' His smile widened, but his eyes, she saw, remained the same: dark, unreadable. 'Now, while we don't expect you to be a nun, we would ask you to be discreet, circumspect, about your boyfriends. It is, um, inadvisable shall we say, to form close friendships.'

He leant forward like an old professor imparting the formula:

'Don't let anyone get too close.'

It would be necessary for her to supply them with full details about herself, and that meant her family and friends too. She was to tell everything – their jobs, their interests, as many of their friends as she knew. 'The wider the net, the better,' he said. No matter how insignificant it might seem to her, one day a chance piece of information might prove absolutely invaluable to the Cause.

'That is all now, I think,' he finished suddenly, startling her.

He turned an inch towards the woman.

'I have covered everything?'

The woman had her eyes shut and appeared to be dozing. Suddenly she snapped them open and Zoe saw for the first time how vividly blue they were. Why, she was once beautiful, she thought in surprise.

'I have a question.' The voice sounded creaky through disuse and the woman's accent was thick.

Annoyance flickered on the man's face. 'Yes?'

The woman looked clearly across at Zoe. By luck or long cogitation, she got the words right. 'Was it worth killing for the Cause?' she asked.

Zoe had not had to answer; indeed the man had seemed keen that she should not. He had covered up the immediate silence with a false, strained laugh. The other man had directed a look of horror at the woman, as if an old tame lion had roared.

The woman, however, had seemed impervious to both of them. She had kept her eyes on Zoe, waiting for the answer, and Zoe herself had suddenly wanted to talk: to tell the woman that no, it had not been worth it. How could the killing of one terrified boy alter the course of Neo-Nazism even a fraction of a degree?

Zoe had opened her mouth to speak, but a signal that she had not seen must have been given. From behind her, Pieter had stepped forward, taken her arm and hustled her from the apartment. A tramp or several had used it; it had smelled badly, assaulting her senses, and it had been good to get outside, although the semi-industrial part of Antwerp was squalid enough. Pieter had walked her swiftly to the car, unlocked it and told her to get in. Then he had left her to talk briefly to two men whose shadows she could see in a van parked opposite the apartment block.

Everything has changed, she thought. The way Pieter treats me, as an equal, someone who can be trusted; the real faces behind the Leadership; the way I can deal with shocks, like that woman's question, without freaking out; how I feel awakened to what people really think, the truth if you like. She recalled some distant phrase from the Bible; St Paul when the scales fell from his eyes. It had been a miracle in his case, though, and in her own . . . well, something entirely different that had wrought the change.

Pieter got in and started the engine. 'Well, Zoe. What do you think of our leaders?'

She eyed him cautiously. 'What d'you think?'

He smiled at her. 'I asked you first.'

'The main one's a smooth bastard who wouldn't know one end of an Uzi from the other; the little one's a wimp, and the woman . . . the woman doesn't belong.'

'Hey!' He shot her a look. 'Quite a full character assessment.'

'Am I right?'

He shrugged and drove on in silence.

She tried again. 'The woman . . . she was trying to tell me something. Like she understood, I mean about the boy . . . about Turin. As if she'd been through the same thing. She has, hasn't she?'

'Yes, she has.'

'And you too?'

'I told you last year I'd shot at people.'

'But did you kill them?'

He hesitated, keeping his eyes on the road. Then: 'Yes. Yes, Zoe, I've killed people too.'

'And did you go through what I've been through after it?'

'Mmm, something similar, anyway. How're you feeling about that now?'

She shrugged. 'It comes and goes,' she said.

'Yes, it will do for a while. You want to talk about it?'

She was tired and shook her head. Pieter switched the radio to a commercial rock station. She was grateful; the music soothed her and made her feel reassuringly normal. Pieter's presence had the same effect. When she had seen him at the city's airport that afternoon, lounging against a pillar, familiar in his black leather jacket, and then catching sight of her and giving her the little salute of welcome, she had felt such relief, a sense of coming home to an old, dear friend. Ridiculous, she knew; she could hardly lay claim to long acquaintance with the Dutchman, but the bond was there, nonetheless. Forged that cold December night in Hamburg when they had run together from the bullets; when he had teased from her troubled mind the pictures that had terrified her, and had given her another picture instead ... herself as the avenger of the innocents. She smiled sadly; she was so much older now. 'Can I ask you a question?' she said suddenly.

'Yes.'

'D'you still kill people?'

He flinched quite visibly.

'No, not now. And to answer your next question, it's mainly because the other side have my description and know who I am, so it's too dangerous for me to go on missions.' He glanced over at her. 'Anyway, I have another job now.'

'The recruiter.'

'Yes. Number one recruiter, go-between and delivery man.'

'Junie? You chose her?'

He laughed shortly. 'There were not many to choose from.'

There was, again, a companionable silence between them. They left the suburbs of the city behind, and took a major road signposted for Rotterdam and The Hague. Zoe felt her eyes grow heavy. She tried to remember when she had last slept naturally, without the aid of the drugs that Xavier had thrust down her throat in the aftermath of Turin. Had it been seventy-two hours? No, longer; she had not really slept on the ferry that had brought her from Corsica to Italy. So long ago, it now seemed, that she had sat on the deck of the boat and watched the moon on the water and the pretty colours of the sunrise.

A little later, when she woke, Pieter was still driving, and it was still dark. A signpost flashed by, but too quickly for her to have read it. 'Where're we going?' she asked.

'Eventually you're going home. Like the man said, to London, to rent your flat and get your little job.'

She wondered whether he was mocking her and scowled. 'Eventually?'

'Yes. First we're going somewhere so that you can tell me each detail of your life.'

'I thought I already told you everything last year.'

'Oh no, that was just touching the surface. This is in depth.'

'What, like the name of my pet rabbit when I was five?'

'That sort of thing exactly.'

They crossed the invisible border into Holland, drove on a short distance before he turned off the motorway and entered a small town. He stopped the car and consulted a map, then drove deftly to a street lined with small, well-groomed modern houses.

'Home,' he said, pulling up at one that looked deserted.

'Your home?'

'One of them. I'll go first. You stay outside.' She saw that he had keys and let himself into the house. Lights went on as he moved swiftly through it, drawing blinds and closing curtains. Then he reappeared beside the car, tapping on her window. 'OK, come in now.'

She followed him up the short gravel path and stepped inside the door that immediately opened onto a large ground-floor room. The furniture looked new and unused; there were no books on the shelves, no pictures on the walls, nothing personal anywhere. 'Where's the bathroom?' she asked.

'Upstairs, I guess.'

When she came down, he was in the kitchen, the kettle was boiling on the stove and he was opening and shutting cupboards, looking for something.

'This isn't your home, is it?' she asked.

He looked surprised. 'My own home? No, of course not. It's just a safe place. We have it for a couple of days.'

'Don't you have a home?'

'Of course. Everyone has a home. But home isn't safe any more.'

'So whose is this place?'

'I don't know. A sympathiser's. Ah, coffee. You want some?'

She did, and she wanted food too. She had hardly eaten since Turin and now she was suddenly ravenous. 'There'll be food in the freezer,' he told her and there was: drawer after drawer of ready-cooked frozen meals. She heated one for each of them in the spotless microwave that stood on the work-surface.

'Don't you think this is eerie?' she asked, between mouthfuls.

'What?'

'Coming into someone's home like this. Just using it all as if we're burglars. Us never knowing the owners, and them never knowing us.'

'It's better that way. Now, if you've finished, we've got work to do.'

In the main room, they sat opposite each other on comfortable sofas. At first Zoe had baulked at some of his questions: 'So how did you feel as a child when your parents left you so often?'; 'Did you feel unloved, unwanted?'; 'Were you jealous of your brother?' Such things were so personal . . .

But then she had looked over at Pieter and seen his warm eyes fixed on hers, understanding her, drawing her out, helping her when a question probed too deep, endlessly patient, endlessly kind. And she had thought that her feelings were safe with him; he would never betray her or use what she said to scorn her.

As it grew later, so she had relaxed more. She had told him about school – he seemed genuinely horrified at the idea of boarding-schools – and about switching universities at the last minute.

He had laughed. 'First sign,' he had said.

'What of?'

'The rebel.'

Then she told him about Tony, how he had shattered her self-confidence. 'He called me . . .' She stopped, wishing she had not remembered.

'What, Zoe? Come on, you can tell me.'

'He called me the Snow Queen, the untouchable.' She blushed, suddenly remembering how she had been with Xavier: hot and eager, demanding satisfaction. There had been nothing icy about her that night, and yet . . . a part of her had remained distinct and separate, unable or unwilling to give herself up. She twisted awkwardly in her chair.

Pieter was watching her. 'Hey,' he said gently, for once misunderstanding. 'The man was an arsehole, that's all. He shouldn't have been screwing little girls.'

It was nearly midnight, and she had been yawning when he

said, 'Now I need to know everything, really everything about your family.'

'My family? Why?'

'You never know when a detail might be really important.'

She stifled another yawn. 'I don't see how . . .'

'Let me decide. You just talk to me.'

If she had not been so tired she thought afterwards, she might have protested more. It was such an odd thing to do: to tell someone who was really a stranger such intimate details about her family. How could it possibly matter to Never Again that her mother loved ballroom-dancing, or that her father's fiercest ambition was to be the owner of the Cheltenham Gold Cup, or that Alasdair's last girlfriend was a secretary at New Scotland Yard.

None of it could be relevant to the Cause, she thought sleepily. It was making her feel vaguely uncomfortable too, the telling of family trivia. It was was rather a distasteful thing to do, she supposed; almost recruiting her family to Never Again as well as herself.

She frowned and struggled to sit upright. 'What's this going to be used for?' she asked.

Pieter's hand stopped scribbling notes. 'Nothing at all probably,' he told her gently. 'Don't worry.'

He resumed his quiet questioning, and she gave in, telling him everything he asked. Eventually, he set the pen aside.

'Is that it?' she asked. She felt more awake than she had for the past couple of hours, she wondered if he had any sleeping pills.

'In a minute. Zoe, you remember in Hamburg last year when we talked? You said you felt like the outsider, "L'étrangère"? You still feel like that?'

She answered slowly. 'Yes, I think so. I never seem to think or feel the way that other people do. Even the other night, you know, in Italy. I was part of a group and we all did it, but I didn't feel one of them. I didn't feel the same way.' She faltered, aware that she might sound disloyal. 'Is that wrong?'

He shook his head and sighed. 'No, Zoe. It's not wrong. It's the way you are. It is because of your, mmm, difference that I chose you.'

'It is?'

'Yes. Sleepers are not ordinary people, even though they must act like that. They are the most lonely, cut-off people in the world. If you already feel an outsider, I hope it should not be so hard for you.' He paused. 'But it will still be difficult. You will never be able to open up completely to anyone, or trust anyone. Do you understand that? Even a lover – you must keep him far away. That is why it was good advice that the Leadership gave you tonight; let no one get too close.'

She felt suddenly very sad. 'I'll never belong, will I?'

His eyes slid away and his voice held a trace of bitterness, and a little pity. 'Oh yes, you'll belong. You already do. You belong to the Cause.'

Senor Pablo Carerra tenderly placed his two little girls in the back seat of his Mercedes, harnessing the baby in, and letting his older daughter fasten her own belt. Isabella, aged five and Aurora, eighteen months, were the most precious people in his life. Today they looked absolutely beautiful: both small and fine-featured like their mother and with her perfect porcelain skin, but dressed the way he liked to see them, in frills and sashes with ribbons in their hair, like little girls should be. His wife put them in dungarees and trainer shoes; it was one of the chief sources of argument between them.

It was Sunday morning and he was taking the girls to see their grandmother, his mother. Normally, even on a Sunday, he would have gone into his office in the affluent Old Quarter of Madrid for a couple of hours to catch up on paperwork and prepare for the coming week's cases. Today, though, he was having a break, a much needed one after the hell of the past eight weeks.

His mother was always complaining that she did not see enough of her grandchildren or her son; her daughter-in-law was always left pointedly out of the equation. So today, when his wife wanted to go visiting her girlfriends in the city, he was going to please everyone: his wife, his mother, his daughters and himself.

It was a joy being with his children. Isabella kept up a constant flow of chatter, and Aurora sang loudly and tunelessly, but to him the voices of angels could not have sounded sweeter. The only sorrow in his life was that his work kept him away from them too much. For a man of his age, forty-one, he was doing extremely well: he was a State Prosecutor and one of Spain's most important representatives in the National Court. It paid well and he was awarded great respect; he was able to give his wife nearly everything she wanted and to ensure that his daughters would be privately and expensively educated. The only drawback was the long hours.

Earlier in the week, a case had finally finished that had taken up most of his life for the past two months. It had been a difficult trial, touch and go, with little firm evidence beyond the quantity of circumstantial, the defendants refusing to admit their guilt, but in the end he had caught one of them out. Another success for him, another pat on the back and hints that his future would soon be even more star-studded, but it had been exhausting. It had meant that he had had to spend several nights in the tiny rented apartment in the city, working all hours, sometimes through the night. His wife had got thoroughly fed-up with it and he knew that promotion meant more separations, more sacrifice. He was not sure he wanted to sacrifice seeing his children grow up. A part of him longed to step off the treadmill and be satisfied with less.

It was an hour's drive to his mother's, not long enough for the girls to become bored or whiney, and that was important. He wanted them to be on their best behaviour; any infraction would result in his mother crowing that it was the bad blood of their mother coming out in them. He wanted the day to be perfect. He knew that his mother would have been up since dawn, cooking for them all and that the day would be spent with her pressing dish after dish upon them, as if at home they were starved.

The motorway was approaching. Senor Carerra checked the girls in his rear-view mirror. Aurora had fallen asleep, head on shoulder, baby curls cascading; Isabella was drawing shapes on the window with a wet finger. She caught sight of his face in the mirror and smiled at him. He blew her a kiss and eased the car forward into cruise. In doing so, he broke the fine thread of steel wire that caused the instant detonation of the small packet taped to the offside wheel-arch of his car.

The explosion catapulted the car across two lanes of the motorway but sprayed shards of metal and glass over a far wider area, resulting in a double pile-up in both directions, the killing of two more people and serious injuries to another eleven. In the Mercedes itself, the bomb ripped out most of the left side of the car, killing instantly Senor Carerra and Aurora, harnessed securely in her baby chair behind him. Isabella, with appalling head injuries, survived only a few hours.

Six hours after the explosion, and an hour after the National Police had finally found Senora Carerra ensconced in the bed of her lover in Madrid's Old Quarter, a group of extremists that most Spaniards had never heard of claimed responsibility. 'Nunca Mas' issued a lengthy statement to the Spanish News Agency saying that State Prosecutor Carerra had been executed for his part in sending two young 'heroes of Anti-Fascism' to prison for life. The young men in question, the statement claimed, had suffered torture and deprivation at the hands of the Civil Guard and had then been subjected to a two month trial during which they had been tricked into giving damning evidence by the 'State's Fascist puppet, Carerra'.

The statement concluded with the words: 'We deeply regret the accidental death of Aurora Carerra and the injuries caused to Isabella Carerra. We wish Isabella a full and speedy recovery.' In spite of their wishes, however, Isabella succumbed to her injuries within the hour.

There was intense public revulsion at the deaths, particularly of the children, and the police forces of Spain were put under immediate pressure to find and punish the bombers. It was fairly quickly established that Nunca Mas was simply the Spanish name for Never Again, the group of Anti-Fascist terrorists which had sprung up initially in Germany a year previously.

At least the statement had cleared up one mystery: why the young 'heroes' had followed and stabbed to death two middle-aged men, who had been drinking quietly together in a bar all evening. It had been established at their trial that the two dead men had had strong Nazi sympathies, but no one, not the police or the men's lawyers, could ascertain why the killers had killed. On being arrested, they had said nothing about belonging to a group; nothing at all, in fact, about their motivation. It had hamstrung their lawyers and irritated the judge.

The police computer in Madrid was quick to fill in the gaps that the Spanish authorities had about Never Again: their last outrage, only three days earlier, had been the cold-blooded murder of two unarmed men in Turin.

The Spanish Anti-terrorist police and security forces were soon in conversation with their counterparts across Europe. In Wiesbaden, Horst Gemmer was informed that he should stop worrying so much about finding an old terrorist; there were too many new ones out there. In London, likewise, Barney Turl was told by Lavinia Hargreaves, his superior, that she found it 'quite beyond belief' that he had so few hard facts on Never Again; that it was obvious to anyone with half an eye that Never Again was the biggest threat to national, as well as to European security, after the IRA, and that he had better produce something tangible on them – 'Not one of your hunches, please Turl' – pronto.

In Turin there was some relief: the police captain there felt a weight lift off him as the international attention and criticism switched elsewhere.

In the anonymous Dutch house, Zoe was so tired of talking that her jaw ached. All day she had only had an hour to herself, and that had been early in the morning when she had awoken stiff and sore from sleeping awkwardly on the sofa. She had discovered Pieter asleep in a bed upstairs and had crept down to raid the kitchen. She had made gallons of coffee and devoured the ham and eggs that she had found in the fridge. It was a novelty to her, being able to eat as much as she liked, not to have Sergio ruling and abusing her appetite.

She had spent a little time prowling round the house, looking for a clue as to its owner. But there was nothing. No coat left hanging, no shoes in a cupboard: everything sterile and untouched.

Then Pieter had come down, and the interrogation had

begun all over again. Some of it had seemed to her to be a mere repetition of the previous day's questions, but she could not be sure. After so much talking, it was hard to know what she had said, and what she had imagined saying. Her mind was sick of the subject of herself and who she knew, and who they might know.

It was nearly six o'clock in the evening. Her words were beginning to jumble and she had been sitting all day. After a month with Sergio, her body hurt with inactivity.

'I can't talk any more,' she said suddenly. She got up and stretched.

He nodded. 'OK. You want to watch TV?'

'I'd rather go for a run.'

'Too risky.'

'A walk then.'

'Sorry. Orders are to stay inside.'

He got up and switched the set on. The screen flashed photographs of two little girls; one with long dark ringlets tied in pink bows, standing with her hands thrust somehow defiantly into jeans and grinning at the camera; the other, little more than a baby and looking like a china doll in a frilly dress.

They vanished; in their place was the mangled remains of several cars spattered across a motorway. The camera lingered on one car that looked as if it had been sliced in half. All of one side was missing.

The commentary was in Dutch. 'A pile-up?' Zoe asked.

'Ssh.'

The scene changed again. A woman being hurried along by two policewomen, letting herself be propelled as if she was a sleepwalker; other officers pushing the crowd back to make way for her; camera crews and photographers in an ugly scrum, elbows and curses flying. Then a close-up. Zoe saw a good-looking woman of about thirty-five dressed in designer jeans and a short cream jacket. Her face was papery-white, her eyes enormous with shock.

Now a press conference: two men in different police uniforms and two in civilian clothes sat behind a long table. The film crews were more orderly; the photographers clicked more quietly; one journalist at a time asked the questions. On stage, the four men batted the answers back and forth. Everything was in Spanish with a Dutch voice-over. One of the uniformed policemen picked up a piece of white paper and began reading from it. Zoe heard 'Nunca Mas'. A journalist interrupted with a question.

The policeman deferred with his colleagues, then shrugged. 'Aleman o Italiano. No esta claro.'

Another question. The policeman consulted his paper. He spoke the foreign words with care, 'Never Again.'

Pieter switched the TV off. There was silence in the borrowed house. Zoe heard the fridge humming to itself and through the back window watched two birds squabble in a tree outside. Life went on, even though the chasm yawned.

This was . . . this was so different from what had happened in Turin; this was murder, there could be no justification. Innocent children had been murdered. Zoe felt the way she had once when she had been small and her mother had taken her shopping in Edinburgh, and in a large department store, had lost her. In that instant all her certainties had gone; there was nothing to hold on to, just the sensation of falling over and over in uncaring air.

She looked at Pieter. He was staring at the floor. She knew at once he had no easy answers and that it was ripping him apart too.

'We did that?'

He said nothing and did not look up.

'Why?'

He told her, briefly.

'But that lawyer wasn't a Nazi!'

'No, he wasn't.'

'He shouldn't have been killed!'

She watched him steel himself. He met her gaze, although not steadily. 'Zoe, we are at war. It is very important to remember that. Put it at the very front of your mind. It's not for us to question orders.'

'But we must question, or else we'll be just like the Nazis! All those people who said they were just obeying orders.'

He looked at her and nodded. He said in Dutch to himself,

'We shall become who we hate.' To Zoe, he said: 'I tell you to put it at the front of your mind for your own sake. Like a soldier anywhere, it's not a good idea to think too much about the individual.'

'But the children!'

He shut his eyes, shutting out the smiles and expelling them in one breath: 'Casualties of war.'

'You can't mean that!'

He stood up and she saw that his hands were clenched. 'It doesn't matter if I mean it. What matters is staying sane. Blocking it. Or else you go under. You understand?'

He sounded angry, but she knew the anger was not at herself.

She followed him into the kitchen where he was making coffee. He had taken his leather jacket off and she saw the black metal of a revolver, nestling in a holster under his armpit.

'Is that why you stopped killing people?' she asked.

His shoulders tensed but he did not turn round to face her.

'Did you stop because it got to you too much? Did you start seeing someone's face inside your head, hear them crying to you not to shoot? Did you? Were you scared of going mad, too?'

He spun round and placed his hands lightly on her shoulders. 'Zoe,' he said gently, 'you're not going mad. I've already told you what you're experiencing is shell-shock. Soldiers get it. It's normal, you'll get over it. But you mustn't dwell on it. You have to remember why you did it, who you're fighting for, OK?'

She stared into his eyes, seeing herself reflected minutely. 'Why did they pick you to do this questioning and the recruiting?'

He dropped his hands and turned back to the coffee grinder.

'You must have done something before Never Again,' she said.

'Of course. Ten years of doing something.'

'What?'

He looked round slowly. 'I was a psychiatrist,' he said.

Chapter Ten

That night German television also carried extensive coverage of the Madrid bombing, along with speculation that Never Again was based in Germany.

One German expert on terrorism surmised that the group might be the next generation of the Red Army Faction, or Baader-Meinhof as it was previously known. 'Their old cause of communism has died,' he told the millions of viewers with great complacency. 'No one wants it any more, not even the young people. But many of our young people want to stop the Neo-Nazis and are fed up with politicians not doing enough . . . so, what could be better for the dead bird than a new egg? From the ashes of Baader-Meinhof, Never Again is risen!'

'Stupid bastard!' The woman's voice was harsh.

Christoph had not heard her come into the room and at once he jumped up from his chair. His stomach knotted and he wrapped his thin arms across his body as if to protect it.

'I'd just switched it on,' he said and swallowed painfully. 'The other little girl has died.'

The woman ignored him. She was listening to the expert who by now had been joined by another. Things were beginning to heat up; the second man was insisting that Never Again was an offshoot of the Red Brigades, with a few Israeli agents thrown in.

'Do you think they get paid for talking this fucking shit?' the woman asked.

Christoph flinched; he did not like swearing, not from anyone, but especially not a woman. But Inge was not like any woman he had met in the whole of his eighteen protected years of life.

She was older than him, about twenty-five he guessed, and nice-looking in a wild sort of way: tall, with a firm strong body and long legs, quite a nice shape in black jeans and a white shirt, and shoulder-length dark hair, really dark eyes and a full red mouth.

When he had first met her, he had imagined kissing those lips, but that was before she had spoken. She had a coarse, ugly voice that she used as a weapon to hurt, terrify and shock. Like some awful monster from a nightmare, she fed on fear and any demonstration of what she considered to be weakness. She had fun with Christoph, who trembled too easily; she used him as a butt for her foul mouth, and Nico, the only other member of the team, joined in, although Christoph knew his heart was not in it. He did not blame Nico. Inge ruled and she was brutal. More brutal than any man he had ever met.

Earlier, when the TV news had first come on with the killings in Spain, she had cheered. She had even called 'Victory!' Then, when the pictures of the children had been shown, and he had felt his own eyelids pricking with tears, she had sat sneering. 'Aah, the little pretties,' she had purred. Then she had turned and caught his look of appalled disbelief, and her face had lit up with cruelty. 'Is the baby going to cry then? Cry for his mutti?'

She did have an ability to find people's weak spots. Since joining Never Again two months before, Christoph had felt homesick, and sick inside at some of the things he and the other two had done. At first he had been foolish enough to let his feelings show; now he liked to think he knew better.

At night, when he lay awake biting his hands and trying to blot out the sounds of her loud love-making with Nico, he prayed to God to get him out of this. He knew there was no walking out; he would need divine intervention. But God had turned his back and Christoph did not blame Him. If he had been in God's place, had witnessed what Christoph had done, he would have his turned his back too. Only . . . only, at least until now he had not killed anyone. Tomorrow morning that would all change.

They – himself, Nico and Inge – were the Fifth Commando. In eight weeks, they had travelled the country: Munich had been his first action; he had stood guard while the other two had knee-capped two little Nazi thugs. He had thrown up watching it: the boys squirming and screaming on the ground, the thud, thud of the silenced bullets; the screams for mercy and a split second later the screams of pain. How she had enjoyed that! Then there had been Stuttgart, Köln, Dortmund and soon now, Bremen.

Dortmund had been bad: he and Nico had beaten that man to a pulp; an oldish man, unarmed, defenceless; the beating had been the man's 'first warning'; he would not recover from his second, they had told him, their words bursting from their lungs as their boots drummed the punishment home into the man's soft flesh. But in the morning, worse was to come; much worse. Inge had promised him that in Bremen he was really going to 'enjoy' himself. He had shivered, well aware of her idea of pleasure.

They had been in Bremen for eight days. They were staying in an old house that Christoph could only imagine belonging to gentle, elderly people like his parents. It had thick, soft carpets on the wooden floors, and heavy drapes at the tall windows. All the furniture was old and dark; Christoph imagined it at night slowly dancing the waltz. In such a place even the TV set looked brazenly out of place.

On the screen, a sombre police spokesman from Germany's Anti-terrorist unit was extending his country's deepest condolences to the families of those killed in Madrid. He wanted to assure the Spanish people that he did not believe Never Again was solely German, but nevertheless he could promise them that the German police were doing everything in their power to track down the perpetrators of the crime. In this, the public could help by being particularly vigilant and reporting anything suspicious; any unusual behaviour by new neighbours; odd comings and goings. 'So far these terrorists have had an extraordinary run of luck,' he informed the camera. 'It cannot hold.'

His words lit Inge's fuse. She screamed, a maddened banshee shriek: 'Yes it can, fuck-pig!' She twisted in the sofa like an animal in torment: 'Wait and see till tomorrow whose luck will hold!'

Christoph had seen her like this before, working herself up into a killing rage. He began to make for the doorway to the hall, but the movement attracted her attention.

'You!' she roared. He froze; like this, she was capable of anything. She let him imagine the worst, kept him dangling, then said quite reasonably: 'Go and get my case, will you? The special case.'

It was in her room, lying on its side at the bottom of the huge double bed that she and Nico shared. Although he knew it was perfectly safe and that it only contained timing devices, command wire and various casings, Christoph still handled the black plastic case as if it were already the thing that its contents would soon create. He looked at his own watch as he carried it downstairs: nearly eleven o'clock, Nico would be back soon with the stuff, and then in twelve hours' time . . .

At eleven o'clock in the morning Christoph had an appointment with Herr Johannes Pohle, chairman of EX-EL Foods in Bremen.

Never Again's intelligence operative in the area had done his homework well. EX-EL Foods, manufacturers of 'quality' tinned food, had just settled an industrial action taken by twelve of its workforce claiming racial discrimination. The twelve, all Turkish 'gastarbeiter', had been fired for demanding a pay increase that would have brought them into line with their white German counterparts. The settlement had been paltry, but the Turks had been desperate after three months without salary.

Now, in a series of newspaper articles, Pohle, anxious to improve the badly tarnished image of his company, had offered to meet any youth-worker in the surrounding area, with a view to offering employment for up to six young people. They did have to be locals, Pohle had said, and – not to put too fine a point on it – of Caucasian descent and, naturally, to hold German citizenship.

Christoph had rehearsed his script and telephoned the company two days before. At first he thought that God was going to be merciful to him: Pohle's secretary had sounded so very unhelpful.

'He's a very busy man,' she had informed him. 'However, I'll see what he has to say. Hold on.'

In the intervening seconds, Christoph had prayed silently, then the secretary had come back on. Her tone had been austere and reluctant: 'Yes he will see you. Monday. Eleven sharp.'

Christoph had papers proving that he was the Careers Adviser of a Boy's Rambling Club in the area. The one problem that Inge foresaw was Christoph's extremely youthful appearance. She had plucked at his cheek painfully. 'We'd better buy you a suit. And darling, do try to keep your voice low. We can't have Herr Pohle mistaking you for a schoolboy, can we?'

His instructions were to let the Chairman do most of the talking – he was supposed to be a garrulous, pompous man, so that should not be too difficult – and secrete the briefcase in the room, beside his chair, or by the desk. It did not much matter where, so long as it was out of sight; there would be enough explosive in it to take most of the office apart.

Inge had laughed, and stroked Christoph's hair: 'But don't let him talk too long,' she had teased. 'Or else the bomb might go off, and you, baby Christoph, would go "boom!".'

Thinking about the morning made Christoph sweat and feel faint. He must not; he steadied himself against the newel post and took deep breaths. Then he carried the case into the kitchen where he could hear Inge banging about.

She was preoccupied, opening and shutting drawers, pulling out pans from beneath the sink, searching for something. She looked up, not really seeing him, and told him to put it on the table. He did so, gingerly.

There was a noise outside. She glanced at the window, listening intently. He listened, too: the sound of a car turning off the road, then the slow advancing crunch of wheels on gravel. A car door slammed and then came single soft footsteps. The handle on the back door turned and opened: Nico.

He came in heavily, pulled out a chair from the table and sat down without looking at either of them. He was a young man, only a couple of years older than Christoph, but definitely a man in appearance rather than a boy. He was breathing quite hard.

'Everything went OK?' Inge asked, with the slightest trace of worry in her voice.

'Ja. Fine. I'm knackered, that's all. All that bloody digging.

It's hard work, you know.' He slid a dirty hand into the side pocket of his coat and produced a small packet, wrapped in many layers of paper and sealed in a plastic bag. He dumped it on the table beside the case.

Inge seized it, weighing it in her hands. 'This'll be enough?'

'More than. Enough for another job. Save me a trip to the site.'

'Orders are . . .'

'Screw the orders! Every time I go to that place, I risk my neck. You want to obey orders, then you do it next time! You take the shovel to the middle of that fucking field in the middle of . . .'

'Shut up! He's not to know where.' She jerked her head at Christoph. 'He's not quite trusted enough, are you darling?'

Normally Christoph would have blushed and stuttered at that and the other two would have diverted their quarrel onto his head. But now he was not listening. He was sure he had heard another noise outside, a noise that he could not explain but that did not fit in. A noise like static, like a two-way radio, cut off abruptly. People outside with radios . . .

'What is it?' Inge demanded. 'Why are you looking like that? Answer me! You going to have a fit? Don't think you're going to get out of tomorrow . . .'

The glass of the window shattered as the first canister came in, exploding its choking gas. Inge screamed, beginning the sound in fear and ending it in rage.

'Polizei!' echoed an amplified voice from outside. 'Throw out your weapons!'

Nico and Inge flung themselves on the floor. Inge began crawling towards the sitting room, where the Uzis were kept, but at the same time Christoph saw her freeing her handgun from her shoulder-holster. Nico followed, his large body slithering awkwardly in its coat like a snake shedding its skin.

Christoph still sat woodenly at the table. Everything seemed to be moving in slow motion. He heard the police warning and the radios clearly now, but he felt so removed from it.

Another canister came in the kitchen window, bounced onto the special black case, seemed about to roll onto the explosive, but finally fell off onto the floor beside his chair. He watched it as if it had performed solely for his benefit, like a remote-controlled car his father had once given him and then played with himself. He stared stupidly down at the canister hissing by his foot. Only in the moment before it exploded did he think to kick it away from him across the floor. It rolled across the stone and hit the tall dresser.

Then the air was thick with it; his eyes were streaming and he began to choke; the coughing brought him round. He fell onto the floor and crawled away from the window, towards the other two.

In the sitting room the TV set was still on. By now a politician had been found to denounce the Madrid Atrocities, as the bombing had already been christened. The rhetoric poured from the man's mouth, calm and oblivious to the events in this house: 'Wherever these people are, wherever they are hiding, I am sending them a message tonight. Your time is running out. You will be hounded down to your lair, and rooted out like the evil menace . . .'

'Fucker!' Inge screamed. She got up on her feet, her revolver stuffed in the top of her jeans; the loaded Uzi in her hands. She aimed at the screen and let the politician have it. She did not have to be a good shot: the TV gave a mighty bang and flash of magnesium and threw out a thousand jagged pieces.

She began to laugh, high-pitched and raucous. Having wrecked the TV, she turned the weapon on the furniture; bits of wood, and stuffing, bits of wire and metal and velvet span and twirled in the room. The bullets skipped and sprayed and ricocheted. Over it all from his hiding place between the door and the sofa, Christoph heard her laughing crazily. He peeked out: she was using her handgun, too, both weapons together like a character from a western.

More glass breaking, the police had followed them to the front of the house.

'Throw out your weapons! Walk towards the light with your hands right above your heads.'

'Pig-shit scum!'

The deafening sound of gunfire, and more canisters, and

the choking gas. Christoph tore off his holster and his shirt and tried using the garment as a mask but it was not much good. He looked down at the holster, with the gun still inside it lying beside him. It did not occur to him to use it; he had no desire to fight. He peered around the sofa again and saw Nico, with another Uzi in his hands, but sitting up on his haunches, his face red and his shoulders heaving in the fight to breathe.

Inge stopped her awful laughing and kicked him hard in the legs. 'Get up and fight, you bastard!' she snarled. She seemed to remember Christoph just then too.

'Baby!' she screamed. 'Come here, baby! Don't be scared!'

'You have one minute to give yourselves up,' boomed the voice from outside. 'Come to the window or the door and show yourselves. Walk towards the sound of my voice. I promise that you will not be harmed.'

'Lying fucker!' Inge yelled. Christoph moved fractionally and saw her pointing the gun at the window. She pulled the trigger, but nothing happened. She swore: 'Another magazine!'

'No, Inge!' Nico looked up at her, and shook his head. 'No, listen. They'll kill us. Don't you understand? We must surrender, please, Inge, please.' He began to weep, great childish sobs that shook his whole frame.

Outside, the policeman said: 'Thirty seconds.'

'Never, never, never!' Inge howled. She snatched the Uzi from Nico, checked to see it was loaded and turned again towards the window.

It was a gaping hole, allowing in the cold winter air and the clear sight of flashing police lights and white ambulances.

'Never!'

Christoph, drawn out in horror from the shadows, saw the whole thing: her standing there, legs jammed apart, one hand firm on the handle of the gun, the other supporting it, and he felt a last admiration for her.

Then a burst from outside and her body arched and was caught up in the bullets: she flew high through the air like a rag doll, spewing out bits of bone and blood. She hit the wall with a sickening thump and Christoph, still staring, saw how dead her face was, its eyes still open but nothing looking through them any more. Her blood flowed swiftly down the wall, staining the old wallpaper like graffiti.

Nico moved suddenly and fatally. He stood up, his revolver in his hand and raised his right arm. Christoph knew what he wanted to do – give himself up – and that the raised arm was confusion and instinct, but it was misunderstood. Nico howled when the bullets hit him, once, twice, three times and, at each impact, his body seemed to absorb the slugs and curl into them, becoming smaller. He sagged on to his knees, he cried nothing coherent, and fell forward onto his face. For several seconds Christoph watched him, twitching and shaking, and then the body was still.

Christoph was alone now. For the first time in weeks he felt strong and in control, and he knew what he was going to do: his death would be compensation for the little girls and their father; he deserved to die. He got to his feet and began walking towards the window . . .

Chapter Eleven

News of the deaths in Bremen began to leak out to the media shortly before five o'clock in the morning. It was too good a story, too perfect in its timing, to await official confirmation. A few hurried telephone calls were made; police contacts were woken in their beds to be told by begging journalists that this was the very last favour they would ever ask. By 04.28 the story was running. It made the last editions of a few daily papers, then radio got it and finally it was picked up by the morning TV stations. By the time most adults had woken up that Monday morning, the TV crews had found the house and reporters had been placed in front of the building where they stood shivering in thick coats against the early cold.

With its shattered windows, striped police tape, hordes of pointing bystanders and bustle of police, officials and sundry experts, it had quickly assumed the air of criminal glamour that marked it out from its sedate neighbours.

The story had everything: high drama, righteous revenge, even sex appeal.

'It is understood that the leader of the three terrorists was a young woman and that it was her obstinate refusal to negotiate with the police here last night that ended in her death and those of her two male compatriots.

'A police spokesman said: "We had no choice. She was beyond reason; it was her or one of our officers."

'The woman died instantly at the scene as did one of her male comrades. The third terrorist, believed to be just eighteen years of age, was taken to hospital with bullet wounds to the head, but died of his wounds at a little after five o'clock this morning.

'The woman, whose body has not yet been identified, is understood to be in her mid-twenties, tall, with dark hair. A neighbour has described how, on several occasions last week, he saw an attractive young woman leaving the house accompanied by one or two young men, and driving off in the car parked behind me.' The reporter indicated a poppy red BMW convertible sitting outside the house, and narrowed his eyes at the camera.

'We understand from police sources that the Never Again cell were planning an imminent attack in the town and it was only the speedy intervention of the police and tactical support units last night that prevented another atrocity on the scale of the Madrid bomb less than twenty-four hours ago.'

Promising to keep viewers informed of any further developments, the reporter gave his name and signed off.

A little later in the morning the news came out about Christoph's intended victim. Herr Pohle suffered a minor attack of hysteria but, quickly realising the potential of the situation, pulled himself together and opened EX-EL's doors to the TV cameras.

He made a very good interview: shaken but determined to soldier on in the face of barbaric attacks by outsiders.

Much later that morning other journalists discovered the elderly woman who lived next door and who had reported 'seltsame Dinge' – odd goings on – at the house. Asked what she meant by 'odd', she had puckered up her mouth into a buttonhole and closed her door firmly.

It was left up to one of the local police officers, a blushing young man, to explain that the old lady had come into the station earlier in the week to report her new neighbours for . . . 'excessive noise during continuous intercourse'. She had been very upset about it, the officer told the sniggering journalists defensively.

She had told him that those young people had just arrived out of nowhere. The owners, the Stachowiaks, had said they were lending their house for a couple of weeks to a group of young musical students who were too poor to go on a proper holiday. But she had not seen one single sign of an instrument. They did not practise; they did not go out anywhere except in their car . . . 'It was a new, expensive car and they were meant to be poor students . . .'

Alarm bells had sounded in the young officer's head and

he had reported the conversation to his Chief. The 'students" car had been checked and found clean. The Chief had shrugged; there was no law against being a student with an expensive car.

Then one of the older officers had remembered hearing something interesting about the Stachowiaks: they had both been in a concentration camp in the last war, not as Jews but because of their trade union links, or was it Communism? The officer could not be sure. But apparently Mrs Stachowiak had lost her baby in the camp; the only child they ever had. Suddenly the suspicion assumed a firmer outline and discreet enquiries had only made it worse.

No one knew where the old couple had gone; they had taken off a couple of weeks ago, quite suddenly in their car. The two clubs they attended regularly, gardening and opera, were most put out: the Stachowiaks were normally so reliable, and they had said nothing about taking a holiday. Indeed, the only person to whom they had mentioned anything was their next-door-neighbour, known as being rather inquisitive.

So when Nico had gone digging in his field near the Dutch border, he had not, as he had presumed, been alone: two heavily armed surveillance teams had been with him, out of sight. When he left, the teams had moved in. It was a fairly small cache of plastic explosives and arms, but it was the final proof needed to raid the Bremen house.

The field itself was watched for several days, just in case, but no one else came digging in the moonlight. On the fifth day it was decided that continual surveillance was too expensive. The cache was subsequently 'discovered' by an off-duty police officer, creating another media sensation for Germany's anti-terrorist squad.

Chapter Twelve

For two weeks after the Bremen raid, there was a lull. By the middle of the third week, when there was still nothing, no attacks, no threats, not so much as a statement from Never Again – either vowing vengeance for their comrades' deaths, or declaring that the war against Fascism would continue – a lot of people started to think that the group was finished. The Bremen cell had been of pivotal importance, and with it wiped-out, the rest of the organisation had collapsed.

Certainly, that was what Chris Lomax thought.

It was Tuesday morning, the start of *The Clarion*'s week, when Lomax was at his most mellow – and, with a whole paper to fill, his most receptive. He agreed to give Matt ten minutes of his time.

Lomax's office had what the building's management described as 'an open, leafy aspect' over the park and it was true that if one ignored the always traffic-jammed road, one could see some trees and railings from the window.

Matt perched uncomfortably on the one easy chair and cleared his throat. 'Chris, I've got an idea for a real cracker.'

Lomax beamed. 'That's what I like to hear. What is it?'

'I'd like to infiltrate one of the Anti-Fascist groups. I think that's the way to get to Never Again. Go in as a recruit. In fact, considering how security-conscious they are, I think it's the only way. It'll mean me being off the rota and out of the office for maybe a couple of weeks, maybe a bit longer. But I think it'll be worth it.'

From the other side of the desk, Lomax regarded him speculatively. 'That's your real cracker, is it?'

Matt knew then that it was no use. He wished he could have turned off the speech that was bound to follow, but Lomax had already embarked upon it:

'Look, Anderson, I've told you this before, but I'll say it

again. You mustn't get too obsessed with stories. It's a tendency you have, you know?'

Matt hated Lomax most when he was in paternalistic mode.

'I'm not saying you're not a good journalist, but you're still young, relatively speaking, and you've got some things to learn. And I think one of the most important things is to know when to leave a story alone, eh? Like when it's no longer a story?'

'Let's have a sensible look at Never Again. No one's disputing that you did absolutely sterling work, first-rate, on them last year. You were first with the story, finger on the pulse, great stuff. And you can't deny that I gave you your head to follow it up, can you?'

Matt looked at the carpet. After his expose of the Hamburg Conference he had tried numerous tacks on delving further into the group. Steve Carrington, his Special Branch contact, had been unusually eager to meet up for a drink. But it had only been to pick Matt's brains, not to divulge any information himself on the group.

The same was true, to a large extent, with Clive. He had been delighted with Matt's story; keen to help, but so far had been unable to come up with any more leads, apart from Zimmerman's New York number.

Matt had tried calling on numerous occasions. Usually, there had been an answerphone; twice a woman's voice had answered, had said that the 'Doctor' was out, and that she would take a message, but Zimmerman had never called back. Then, three weeks before, after the Turin attack but before the Madrid one, he had got Zimmerman himself.

'My name is Matt Anderson from *The Clarion*, a Sunday newspaper published in the UK.'

'*The Clarion*? Didn't they write about the conference last year? Didn't some joker quote something I'd said?'

'Yes, Dr Zimmerman. I wonder if we could have a further chat about . . .'

'Forget it. I don't speak to journalists. Not when I know that's what they are, anyway.' He had hung up.

Telephones were no use in such situations. What Matt needed to do, he knew, was to go over to New York, meet up with the man, get him talking – about anything if he would not talk about the subject – and then slowly bring the conversation round to what he wanted. Matt was a skilled operator but with Zimmerman, he needed to be face to face.

'No chance,' Lomax had said briskly when asked. 'New York for a chat? Forget it. Think, budget, Anderson, budget.'

He had said it after the Bremen raid when Matt had suggested going over to speak to the relatives of the dead terrorists.

And he was saying the same thing now: 'I can't afford to let you waste any more time on these buggers. Not with my budget as it is . . .'

Matt interrupted: 'But if I went undercover, it wouldn't cost anything.'

'We're understaffed as well, or haven't you noticed?' Lomax was beginning to colour and wheeze. When very angry he was subject to asthmatic attacks. Matt watched him consciously calm himself down, taking deep breaths. 'Look, I might consider letting you go off-rota if I believed there was anything in it. But I don't.'

'Sorry?'

'Never Again are caput. Gone. Turned their toes up.'

'You're wrong, Chris. They're going to come back, and they're going to grow. That's why, if I go in now, we'll be streets ahead of the competition by the time of their next attack.'

Lomax swivelled round in his chair to face the park. He spoke to the window. 'You're flogging a dead horse, Anderson, I'm telling you.' He swung round to face him once more.

'If you've been reading the papers or watching the news, or even listening to the radio over the last few days, I'm sure you've heard the same sort of stuff that I've been hearing. Just in case you haven't, I'll tell you what all the terrorist experts – and I repeat, experts – have been saying.'

He loosened his tie. Matt saw that his neck was flushed red. 'They've been saying, these experts, that if Never Again was still functioning they would have would done something pretty spectacular by now. You know, blown up a few old ladies or derailed a passenger train. Something to demonstrate they were pissed off about their pals being bumped off in Bremen. But they haven't done anything like that, have they?'

'No, but it's far too early to write them off. Believe me,' Matt protested.

'Why should I? What d'you know that the world doesn't? Or have you just developed second sight?'

'No, it's just that my sources indicate that this is just the calm before the storm . . .'

'Calm before the storm! There isn't going to be any storm! There hasn't been a peep out of this bunch of bomb-chucking, baby-killing do-gooders in over a fortnight, has there?'

'Well, no. But I don't think that signifies . . .'

'I don't give a damn what you think it signifies! I hired you as a reporter not a bloody analyst! And I've got a pretty good idea who one of your precious "sources" is.'

Lomax had forgotten to keep calm. His face was flushed and his wheezing much worse. 'It's that young hothead from the Nazi-hunting outfit, isn't it? What do they call themselves? Oh yes, "On Guard"!' The voice dripped sarcasm.

'"On Guard", correct me if I'm wrong, have always expressed horror and outrage at Never Again's tactics, haven't they? And distanced themselves to the ends of the earth from them? So how the hell can one of them now claim he's party to their innermost thoughts, tell me that?'

Lomax wheezed to a halt. Matt looked up and saw he was sweating. 'Bloody hell, Anderson. Why d'you do this to me? Why d'you wind me up like this? D'you have any idea what my blood pressure's like?' He produced a handkerchief from his trouser pocket and wiped his face.

'This job'll kill me in the end,' he said, then caught Matt's eye. 'And I'm sure, Anderson, that you'd weep buckets at my funeral.'

He stood up and came around to Matt's side of the desk. Matt braced himself for a fatherly pat on the shoulder, but Lomax opened his door. 'Come on, it's time for news conference. If it's any consolation, it would have had to have been a cracker of the Discovery of Martin Bormann variety to have let you off-rota at the moment. There's a

General Election just around the corner, in case it's slipped your attention. All hands on deck!'

At five minutes to five o'clock on the afternoon of the same day, Zoe unlocked the door to her flat and let herself in.

She stood for a few seconds in the wide hallway savouring, as she did every day, the illusion that this was her own place, her sanctuary. That the carpet, the lamp-shade, the little wooden table with the telephone upon it, the front-door key in her hand, still with the estate agent's label on it, even the plates and knifes and cups and forks in the kitchen were hers. That she had chosen to live here, on the south side of the Thames, beside Battersea Park, was not because of its proximity to the best gun-club in London, or because of its easy jogging distance to a good private gym, but because she liked feeding the ducks and Canadian geese in the park.

That is what she told anyone who asked. The nosy manageress at the book shop at Clapham Junction where she worked each day from ten till four, had said, 'You like birds that much!' and had given her strange looks ever since, but at least the answer had silenced her.

Concentrating on the ordinary, the mundane aspects of life was of tremendous benefit, Zoe had found. Shopping for food at Marks and Spencer, hesitating over Baked Potatoes with Mushrooms or Turkey a la King, helped convince her that she was an ordinary girl, popping in for her supper on her way home from work. That she was somebody leading her own life.

Of course, it was all fantasy. Nothing was hers. Every single item, as well as the flat itself, and the Golf parked in the resident's space outside, was paid for by Never Again. She had as much right to it as any intruder. It was theirs; as surely as she was their creature; as surely as the whole fabric of her life, past and present, belonged to them.

She was their puppet, set up to do their bidding. Sometimes she imagined them pulling at her strings, making her dance, curtsy and sway; watching her every move.

Alone in the flat, especially late at night when she would look out over the park to the pretty lights on Albert Bridge, she would feel their presence sharply. There would be a sudden shadow on the sitting-room wall, or the creak and sigh of a floorboard. She would start, and her heart would pound; she would turn to face Beatrix or open the door and expect to see Sergio waiting. When there was nothing and nobody there, she would not be at peace until she had searched every corner of the flat, frenziedly like a child hunting out night-monsters.

It did not seem a crazy thing to do. One day it will come true, she told herself. I'll come in and they'll all be here, grouped around the kitchen table. Beatrix and the men, Pieter by the wall, and Sergio . . . Sergio somewhere behind me, waiting.

She walked into the kitchen, took off her raincoat and dumped her bag on a chair. The round wall-clock over the sink read one minute to five. She spooned coffee into a mug and switched on the kettle. The seconds ticked up to twelve. She turned on the radio.

'It's PM at five p.m. with Terry Lewis and Barbara Cramer. Tonight, on his election tour in Barnstaple, the Prime Minister attacks the Liberal Democrats' plans for economic recovery as "weedy, wimpy and weak". The Home Secretary promises yet more public accountability of the Security Services, and The Highs and Lows of Life on the Dole: Tower Blocks in Hackney are to be demolished by teams of the Unemployed. The news summary is read by . . .'

Zoe listened for another minute, then switched it off. Her stomach unknotted slightly: one more reprieve: one more day gone by with no mention of Never Again. That made it, she counted, ten days now since there had been any mention of the group on the news.

Feeling hope surge through her, she carried her coffee through to the bedroom. However hopeful she might be, the routine that she had set herself had to be adhered to. She was not quite sure what would happen if she failed to run her five miles every day or go to the shooting range twice a week or the gym every evening – but it would be something terrible she was sure. Zoe had become supremely superstitious.

Tuesday night was circuit-training at the gym; she had half an hour to get there and she could have five minutes in the shower.

This is how I live now, she said to herself as the hot water drummed down upon her head and splattered on her shoulders. Filling every minute with an activity so she did not have to think too much. But every activity had a purpose, and every purpose led back to the Cause and forward to whatever future 'They' had planned for her. As long, of course, as 'They' still existed.

The first time it had occurred to her that she was praying for the demise of the Cause that surely meant more to her than life itself, she had felt suddenly and horribly guilty, as if she had been caught plotting the murder of her family. In a sense they were her family now: they were all linked together: she and Pieter and Sergio and the Leadership. No, she reassured herself, she did not want any of them dead; she just wanted them to leave her alone so that she could stop being afraid of the future.

In the cubicle of the white-tiled bathroom, Zoe shut her eyes and abandoned herself to the hope that Never Again had ceased to be as completely as a dream upon waking.

Every day that passed without reference to them on the TV or radio news, or in the papers, made it seem more possible. She listened to as many news programmes as she could; setting her alarm clock for 6.30 in order to catch the whole of the Today Programme on Radio Four.

It had reaped nasty consequences during her first week back. Twice she had heard Turin mentioned: 'the brutal slaying of two unarmed men, one only twenty years old and the son of a policeman'. There had been a phone-in, called 'The Victims of Terror'. A woman from West Belfast whose children had seen gunmen shoot dead their father said: 'I don't care what their motive was. To kill my man in front of the kids, to hear their screams . . . Murderers, murderers!' Zoe had stood by the sink, her nails dug deep into her palms, her breathing coming in gasps.

'Block it, block it,' she had told herself but Emilio's face had appeared before her; his eyes with that message and mouthing the words she could not understand. It was two days before she had slept after that. By now she had got better at blocking. When the killing-scene popped into her mind, she shoved it out again and thought of some- thing else.

She also tried to stop herself thinking about Neo-Nazi attacks. Listening to and watching as much news as she did, she could not fail to be aware of the racist and Anti-Semitic attacks that were being reported, or so it seemed, on an increasing basis. At first, she had hoped that exposure to such evidence would help her to justify Never Again's actions, and especially Turin, but she only became more confused.

One night on Channel Four News she had watched an interview with a seventeen-year-old Asian youth, beaten unconscious by a gang of skinheads. 'There,' she had told herself, '*he*'s who you're fighting for. He's the reason Never Again has to exist.'

But the fear in the boy's eyes as he recounted the brutal attack had reminded her too much of that other boy's, and her justification had swayed and disintegrated. So it was safer, she had discovered, not to dwell too much on what the enemy was doing; it only led her into dark woods.

She shut her eyes and turned her face up to the showerhead. Nothing since Bremen, she thought again. No attack for over two weeks. Surely that must mean . . .

The Leadership had been so shocked by the deaths that they had decided to call it a day; the cells had all been disbanded; Sergio had been told he could find some other group's recruits to terrify, or go back to wherever he came from; Pieter had got a job as a psychologist and was sitting at the head of a couch, listening to people's problems, and the Sleepers . . . Well, the Sleepers would realise that everything was over when they received no orders and the bank drafts stopped coming.

In many ways, she considered that that was one of the scariest moments of all: when Never Again had proved that they were all powerful, that they held her in the palm of their hands, and that they could reach her anywhere.

Until then, back in London in the rain and cold, with delays on the tube back from Heathrow and taxi-drivers that called her 'love', it had all suddenly seemed too ridiculous. It simply could not have happened. None of it. The feeling was so strong that on the first night back, Zoe had convinced herself that it had not happened; that it had all been some kind of weird dream.

The next morning, after Alasdair and Kerry had left for work, it had still been unbelievable. In a strange, elated mood, she had telephoned the bank and asked for a balance on her account. She knew exactly how much had been there before she went to Corsica: £347.29.

While she had hung on, the first doubts had assailed her. 'Please God, please God,' she had prayed suddenly. 'Let it be the same.'

'Miss Douglas? Your account was credited with £30,000 yesterday. Yes, I can tell you that. Just a minute . . . uuh, yes, it's a numbered account held at a bank in Zurich. I'm sure that means more to you than to me! Miss Douglas, have you yet had a meeting with one of our financial advisers? I really do feel that you might benefit . . .'

Thirty thousand pounds. Zoe had put the phone down and seen that her hand was shaking. Everything was true then: Sergio and Turin and the dead boy, and what the Leadership had said to her; what they expected of her, what they were investing in her, all that money and training, all leading towards the 'Big One', whatever and whenever that was.

She had spent that day worrying about how she was going to break the news to Alasdair that she had to move out. She would have to lie to him about wanting her own space and she would have to invent some job that would pay enough for rent. Her soul had cringed at the thought of lying to him.

But that evening he had looked nervously at her, poured them both a glass of wine and blurted out: 'You're welcome to stay for a couple of weeks, Zo, but Kerry and I have got used to having the place to ourselves. Perhaps it would be a good idea if you started looking for a flat-share with some other girls? Don't get me wrong, we're not throwing you out or anything, take all the time you need. You'll have to get a job, I know. And I can easily lend you the first month's rent.'

The hot water pricked her skin. Squinting through the shower-curtain Zoe checked the time on the steam-resistant clock on the bathroom wall. She had another ninety seconds. It was the waiting that was worst, she thought. The not-knowing if Never Again was finished and not being able to talk about it to anyone; having to keep it all bottled up inside.

The heat was slowly relaxing her muscles. If only, she thought, someone could invent something to ease all the knots in her mind. But perhaps it was only by being tense, by keeping perpetually alert, that she could hold everything together.

She had very nearly lost control when she had first read about Bremen. Pieter had told her nothing; she had doubted if he had known anything himself. He had not allowed her to watch or listen to the news after her reaction to the car-bomb deaths, that poor man and his little girls. The following afternoon, Pieter had told her she was going home. He had driven her to the Schipol airport just in time to catch the plane. She had had no time to see a headline, providing of course she would have understood it.

It was not until she had landed at Heathrow and bought an evening paper that she had known. 'Terrorists killed in Shoot-out'. Three dead, a woman and two men. 'Anya, Dani and Xavier,' she had thought immediately.

She had frozen where she stood, by the Real Orange juice stall in Terminal Four, clutching the paper, unable to read on. Her stomach had lurched and sickened; she had swayed on her feet.

'You all right?' someone had asked her, but she had not answered. She had been thinking of Xavier, with the golden spiky hair, his body moving on hers that night; who had ordered her to kill, had screamed at her to do so, then had cared for her so tenderly and had protected her from harm. Dani, clever, stammering Dani with the smile of a child and Anya, whose bullet had masked her own failure . . . All dead, her comrades lying in blood. Dead faces, cold fingers. Zoe gulped; mingled with her grief and pity, she felt a great wave of selfish, intoxicating relief that she had escaped. She could so easily have been there when the police came in.

It had been only when she had forced herself to look again at the page that she seen it was not true. There were photographs to prove it; pictures taken from a wanted poster of a girl with dark hair and a man called Nico something. The third terrorist, the paper stated, had only been with 'the gang' a matter of weeks and the police had no pictures of him. There had been another photograph too, of a smiling man, a police inspector according to the caption. He was quoted: 'Those who live by the gun must expect to die by it.'

That phrase had made Zoe shudder then, and it did so again. 'Those who live by the gun.' Well, she was one of those, wasn't she? Sergio had taught her how to do it, and in Turin she had been part of the living and dying.

'You're not one of them,' she whispered out loud to herself. The water and the tiles caught the sound and sent it back to her. 'One of them, one of them.' She inhaled deeply. 'You haven't killed anyone. Remember that.'

No, but the next time? It was only by luck that no one had seen her alter her aim. It had been enough that the boy was dead; they had seen her fire and that was all that mattered. Zoe's secret was safe. But if she was to be activated now, she knew that she would be on her own. There would be nobody else to cover for her; she would have to kill. She was living, she knew, on borrowed time.

That was why, each day that passed, she prayed for a little more time, one more extension to her limbo, exhausting and terrible though the waiting was. She turned off the shower and stepped out onto the thick white mat. It was a wonderful bathroom; large and white with an old fashioned claw-footed tub at one end and a power shower at the other. Zoe picked up a fluffy white towel and began drying herself vigorously. 'No news is good news,' she told herself, and thought, 'One hour circuit-training. I'll be back in time for the Channel Four news at seven.' No one monitored the media closer than she.

A day later, the police forces of Turin and Madrid, acting independently of each other (although afterwards there were angry allegations of leaks), arrived at the same decision. It was a strange, not to say illogical one, but both forces had suffered agonising public humiliation for almost three weeks; neither having been able to produce the culprits responsible for their respective terrorist outrages.

Turin was two hours quicker in putting out its press release:

'The Commander of Police refuses to comment on reports [at ten o'clock that morning three journalists – one radio, one print, one TV – had received 'anonymous' tip-offs from the press office] that the Never Again terrorists killed in Germany nearly three weeks ago were responsible for the murders of two *Noi da Soli* members in Turin earlier this month.

'The Commander will only confirm that officers investigating the Turin murders are in close contact with their German anti-terrorist colleagues. Fresh teams of Italian forensic scientists have been sent to the north German city of Bremen today to examine evidence found at the safe-house that may link the dead terrorists with the Turin killings.'

The timing of the statement was all-important. If such a flimsy piece of speculation and no-news had been issued within the first week of Bremen, journalists would have seen straight through it, and probably said so. But coming as it did, when Italian news-editors were nearly as desperate as the police to find a new lead, the statement was a godsend. The Turin Commissioner was besieged with demands for interviews. The press office telephone lines were jammed, and within the hour calls had started to come in from Spanish and German journalists.

In Madrid, the police were furious. They felt their failure more acutely than the Italians; the deaths of the children had sickened the nation. It was generally agreed that if something did not break soon in tracking down the killers, there would have to be resignations.

What really goaded the Spanish was that the suggestion of blaming the Bremen cell had been mooted the day after the raid, but had been ruled out as too obviously improbable. Only abject despair had persuaded their police chief to dredge up the theory for public consumption. In the light of the Italian statement though, they scrapped their own and, amidst as much publicity as they could muster, despatched a team of detectives and forensics people to Bremen.

The sudden influx at that town of all those foreign experts and suspicious, anxious policemen produced a media stir. Matt heard about it while he was on the Liberal Democrat Campaign Tour bus in Devon, and Zoe caught it on the PM programme. Matt moaned and wished he had the guts to go freelance. Zoe, of course, knew that it could not be true, but for a fleeting moment had allowed herself the luxury of hope.

Anyone with a map and a watch could have worked it out, but for these few hours there was a conspiracy between German journalists and their visiting Spanish and Italian colleagues to maintain the myth. By that evening, front-page articles had been prepared, with maps on inside pages showing the route that the Bremen Three, as they had become known, had taken: dots across Europe linking Turin (marked in one paper with a sub-machine gun), Madrid (bomb) and Bremen (policeman, sub-machine gun, coffins).

The glaring problem of how the terrorists had managed to get from Madrid to the German safe-house in time to have been shot was glossed over by unstated mutual consent. Some of the articles stated that the Three had flown; others that they had taken express trains, adding rather limply, 'and taxis'. 'Exclusive' evidence, given anonymously to one newspaper, revealed that the terrorists had survived by taking huge amounts of cocaine which had rendered them incapable of sleep, and would have killed them – if they had not been shot – within a few more days.

At first the German police took it good-humouredly. There was a feeling that they had been pretty lucky with their raid and could afford to be generous. But when, later in the evening, German politicians started asking why money and precious police resources were being wasted on a group that no longer existed, irritation set in.

Perhaps the policeman most irritated by it all was Horst Gemmer. The past three weeks had taken their toll on him, too. What had started off looking like a gift from the Almighty had become, as the days passed, a weight around his neck. He shut his eyes: how much longer would he have to wait?

That was what the Interior Minister, the same man who had promised him 'one hundred per cent support' less than three weeks ago, had asked him that afternoon. 'This situation can't go on indefinitely, you know,' he had said tetchily. 'Can't you do something to speed things up?'

Gemmer glared across the room at the TV screen where a

journalist was telling him that the head of the Anti-Terrorist Intelligence Unit at Wiesbaden was having close consultations with his Italian and Spanish counterparts 'right now'.

'Am I indeed?' Gemmer stabbed the 'Off' button of the remote control and contemplated kicking something hard. He needed to speak to someone whose ideas and opinion he valued; someone who knew the game. He was not meant to discuss the situation with anyone outside the tiny handful of people directly involved, but there were times when rules needed to be broken. He took a deep breath and stood up, his decision made. He would act on it first thing in the morning.

Chapter Thirteen

At nine o'clock the following morning, the phone purred on Barney Turl's desk. He had switched it down to its lowest level and covered it with papers so it was a little time before he heard it, and another few seconds before he found it.

'Turl!' he barked.

'Barney? It's Gemmer. How are you?'

'Horst? I thought you weren't talking to me.'

'I'm sorry.' There was an awkward pause. 'You know how things can be sometimes. Delicate.'

'Yeah, well.' Barney tried not to sound sullen, but did not wholly succeed; in his opinion, Gemmer had been acting very strangely of late, and much to his own detriment.

With a General Election fast approaching, Hargreaves' demands on his department had been increasing daily, as had her sarcasm. But his most urgent task, to put together a full dossier on Never Again, still remained uncompleted. And that, Barney felt, was largely due to the sudden withdrawal of support from Horst Gemmer.

He could not understand what had happened. He and Gemmer went back a long way, over twenty years, ever since their individual dealings with Baader-Meinhof, when they had met, liked each other and joined forces to their mutual benefit. Their friendship had cut out a lot of bureaucratic red-tape; it had saved time and, on numerous occasions, had reaped excellent results. There was an unspoken agreement between them that they shared all that they had – at least, there had been until a couple of weeks ago, until the day after the Bremen raid.

A week before it, Gemmer had been his usual helpful self, when Barney had called asking to go to Wiesbaden for a chat on Never Again. 'Sure. We don't have that much – some stuff on the data-base, a few profiles – but you're welcome to it.

Come for a couple of days, we'll have a good time.' A date had been set.

Then, the day after Bremen, Gemmer had done a sudden volte-face. He was truly sorry, he had told Barney, but he could not make that meeting later in the week.

'Well, how about next week?'

'Aaah, that also could prove a problem for me.'

'Horst, I've got the Director breathing down my neck. You've got the most on these little bastards, and I could do with anything fresh that came out of the Bremen house.'

'Yes. I, uh, I'm in a difficult position right now. I'll let you know.'

But he had not. He had even, Barney suspected, not been returning his calls, leaving him to hash together something second-rate on Never Again and hope that Hargreaves would be in a good mood when she saw it.

Now here was Gemmer sounding friendly and asking how he was. Barney suddenly remembered the news of the previous day.

'I've had my hands full since we last spoke,' he said. 'But I was going to call you yesterday and thank you.'

'Thank me?'

'Yeah. At least I can write off Never Again, eh?'

'Don't, Barney. Don't joke about them.'

'Not finished, then?'

'This morning I come to work to find Italian and Spanish policemen wanting to kill me. They're downstairs now, sitting in a row. Some of them are crying. I tell you, Barney, I don't know how to cope with crying policemen.'

In spite of himself, Barney grinned at the picture. 'So to what do I owe the pleasure of your call?'

'I want you to visit me.'

'Do you indeed?'

'Barney, I'm truly sorry for the last two weeks. It was not of my making. I promise you, come and see me and you won't be disappointed.'

'No?'

'No.'

'Are we talking Never Again?'

'Hole in one.'

Barney smiled again: Gemmer's mastery of the English language always struck him as little short of miraculous, especially when his own knowledge of German was limited to: 'I have two sisters but no brothers.'

'I don't know, Horst. Joking aside, I really am pretty busy right now. When did you have in mind?'

'This afternoon. Say, four o'clock?'

'You are joking!'

'No. I'm very serious. Unless I speak to somebody sane soon, I'm in danger of committing murder.'

'I'd have thought there were more than enough people at Wiesbaden for you to talk to.'

'Barney, don't make me beg. It's you I want to talk to.'

'I'm flattered.'

'So you'll come?'

Barney jammed his glasses back into his hair and surveyed the chaos upon his desk. He had seven different reports to finish by Monday, as well as checking the data produced by his department. He had to see Hargreaves on the following afternoon to update her on overseas security threats to the suddenly highly mobile electioneering politicians. There were just not enough hours in the day. Yesterday, when he had heard about the Bremen business, he had found himself really hoping, however ridiculous he knew it was, that it might be true. One less security threat to deal with; one less report to write. It was hardly the time to go gallivanting off to Germany. On the other hand, if Gemmer came up with the goods on Never Again and he could produce a really stunning report on them . . .

'All right, I'll come. Any idea how long?'

'A day.'

'Can't do that. I've got to be back here first thing in the morning.'

'OK. It'll be worth it. For both our sakes.'

There was nothing worse, Matt thought, than being forced to cover a story when your heart was elsewhere. His heart was in Germany; in Wiesbaden, to be precise, at the German

Anti-Terrorist headquarters that had issued the statement he had just heard on the One O'Clock news.

But instead of being there, able to ask questions not just of the Germans but the Italian and Spanish too, he was stuck in a Barnstaple Forte hotel, eating lunch with a load of political hacks, campaign aides and local party hangers-on.

The star of the show, the Liberal Democrat leader, known to the Press Corps as 'Bomber' (having had an unfortunate tendency, earlier in his career, to produce obtuse one-liners), was at a Photo-Opportunity in Bristol. He was scheduled to arrive in Barnstaple by helicopter at 2.15 p.m., in time for a general media facility at the local maternity hospital. An ideal place, Matt thought bitterly, for kissing babies.

'How many babies can a grown man slobber over?' He muttered and stabbed angrily at his apple-dumpling.

Gloria, a bubbly young woman with red hair, always immaculately dressed and one of the Party's brightest aides, smiled at him. 'What was that, Matt?'

'Oh, nothing.'

'We don't seem very happy today. Not enough beauty sleep, is it? Too much drinking with the other boys, I expect. Never mind,' she patted his hand, not appearing to notice him flinch, and consulted her timetable, 'it's quite a relaxed afternoon. After the hospital he's going on a little walkabout in the shopping precinct and then we're all off to Exeter for his speech to the Student Union. You can have a nice long zizz on the coach. How does that sound?'

Matt was not listening to her. He was thinking instead about the German police statement that he had just heard on the lunchtime television news. It had been a short item and only Matt had been interested in it. The other journalists, all crowded together in the hotel's lounge, had set off in search of the dining room as soon as the political news of the day had been covered. Matt had stayed glued to the screen, as first film of the safe-house appeared, then old footage of Turin and Madrid, and finally a still-shot of a series of low-built brick buildings on a hill, Wiesbaden.

According to the voice-over, the German Interior Minister

had issued a statement repudiating suggestions that the Bremen Three had been responsible for the Madrid Atrocities and the two Neo-Nazi assassinations in Turin.

Matt had not been surprised to hear it. What had interested him had been some of the language used in the statement. The newsreader had read briefly from it: 'It is the opinion of the German Interior Ministry, and senior police officers, that it would be unwise in the extreme, indeed dangerous, to assume that Never Again has ceased its campaign of terrorist violence.'

The statement had ended with the usual warning for the public, both in Germany and abroad, to continue to be vigilant and report anything suspicious to their local police.

Matt frowned down at his dumpling. Beside him, Gloria gave up and turned her attention to the more receptive ear of the *Daily Star*'s Women's Editor.

The Germans sounded so very sure of themselves, he thought. 'Unwise in the extreme,' and 'dangerous' to write off Never Again – those were strong words, almost amounting to a warning. He wondered what the Germans knew. When he got back to the office he would try calling Wiesbaden, but he did not anticipate much help from the press office there. He resolved to go ahead with the decision he had made last night.

At six o'clock that evening, German time, Barney Turl was being frisked by an unsmiling, well-armed policeman inside the entrance-hall of The Bundeskriminalamt (Federal Criminal Police Office) at Wiesbaden. A plainclothes man sitting behind bullet-proofed glass took his passport and Security ID and showed them to his colleague. They passed them between themselves, their eyes narrowed and considering, whispering together, glancing up at Barney's face.

'I have an appointment with Herr Horst Gemmer,' he said loudly. Security at Wiesbaden was always very tight; the building had been the target of too many terrorist attacks, including, most spectacularly, the gunning down of the deputy Justice Minister on the outside steps by the Red Army Faction. Barney understood the need for such thorough security measures, but they always made him nervous. Ridiculous, he knew, given his line of work, but there it was.

He coughed slightly. 'Not long now till Christmas,' he said for something to say.

The two men ignored him. One of the uniformed officers indicated by a nod of the head that he should enter the Bomb Detection unit that two of his colleagues were monitoring. Once through it, his way still barred by steel security gates, Barney saw Gemmer coming down a flight of stairs towards him. 'God, he looks knackered,' was his first thought.

Gemmer's eyes were darkly bagged and his complexion was greyish. He seemed to have lost weight and something of the bounce that Barney remembered, but his smile was genuine and full of relief.

'Barney! So good to see you.' He seized his hand in a strong shake. 'Thanks so much for coming. Come on through.'

He punched a code into the security panel on the wall; there was a buzzing sound and the gate swung open. He steered Barney along a windowless corridor.

'Did you have any trouble persuading your director?'

'I didn't tell her. Not precisely, anyway. I said I was following an interesting lead, I am, aren't I?'

'Absolutely. I guarantee, at the very least, that you'll have a very full report on Never Again by the time you leave.'

'At the very least?'

Gemmer smiled. 'Yes. Wait until we get to my office.'

Wiesbaden was a truly labyrinthine building, made up of seemingly endless, identical corridors, offices and staircases. It seemed to Barney that its layout alone would have been enough to deter any but the most determined and well-oriented of terrorists. Even people who had worked there for years occasionally got lost.

They climbed a staircase and Gemmer led him through a door to an enclosed walkway between two buildings. Along either side ran large picture windows, painted with the black silhouettes of swallows to prevent real birds from flying into the glass.

Gemmer's office was at the back of a modern block, with

a view of Wiesbaden below, although little of it could be seen at that time of night. Gemmer's secretary had already gone home. He offered Barney the more comfortable of two black leather armchairs, and poured them both coffee. He swallowed his own in a single gulp and followed it with another. Only then did he sit down.

'Ah, that was good. The last couple of weeks have been hell.'

Barney raised an eyebrow.

'Something happened as a result of Bremen . . .'

'I gathered that.'

'And I was told that under the circumstances it would be unwise for our meeting to go ahead.'

'So what's changed your mind?'

'Oh, the passage of time and the realisation that, by my age, and in my position, I should be allowed to speak to who I like.'

'Perhaps we should've met somewhere more neutral?'

'No. I decided last night. I'm fed up playing games. If anyone asks, I'll tell them I talked to you.'

He set his coffee cup down on the carpet and went over to his desk. He picked up a file. 'This much I can certainly show you. Who's to say where you got it from? I've had it translated.'

He handed it to Barney. Inside were half a dozen typed sheets of A4 paper. Across the top of the first page in block capitals, ran the words: 'RUSSIAN INTELLIGENCE SERVICE', the organisation that had replaced the KGB, although some believed only its name was new.

Barney put his glasses on. In slightly smaller letters underneath he read: 'Intelligence Investigation Bureau'. The document was marked 'Security Starred Three. STRICTLY CONFIDENTIAL. For Addressee Only' and then Gemmer's name. Barney looked up.

'They won't mind?'

'Who'll tell them? Read it.'

Barney's eyes flickered swiftly over the rather formal greetings and hopes for continued and mutually-beneficial exchanges of information. Halfway down the first page, someone had drawn an arrow in orange marker pen. Barney slowed down.

Four days before, he read, a man had entered a police station in an outer district of St Petersburg and disclosed that he had information about a German national. The man, who spoke old-fashioned, schoolbook Russian had requested an immediate interview with the 'Head of the KGB'. On being informed that no such organisation existed, he had become abusive and had been arrested.

Under interrogation by two officers, one affiliated to the Russian Security Police, the man had claimed to be a former member of the East German Secret Police, the Stasi. He said that he had fled to Russia to seek political asylum before he was arrested or killed in the West. He had told the officers that he had not come 'empty-handed', but that he wished to do a deal to secure his safety and gain employment within the security service of 'Mother Russia'.

When asked what the deal was, he had repeated his earlier claim that it was about a German citizen, about whom he would say nothing more until he was satisfied that he was speaking to senior intelligence people.

At that juncture a doctor had been summoned to ascertain whether the man was insane. In the course of the examination, the doctor had discovered needle marks on both the subject's arms. When questioned, the man admitted that he had been a drug-user but claimed that he no longer injected himself, having had access for several months to high-quality cocaine. He had added that his supply had dried up a week earlier when his funds had run out.

The two officers had been on the point of having him committed to the nearest asylum, when he had begun to reveal details of certain interrogation methods that were formerly used both by the KGB and the Stasi. The officer affiliated to the Intelligence Services then escorted the man to a top security cell within the police compound where he questioned him further and became convinced that he was in fact ex-Stasi. He had him transferred immediately to Intelligence Headquarters in Moscow.

Barney took a sip of coffee before reading on: 'The man,

who for the purposes of this briefing document shall now be referred to as "Janke", has since been interrogated on numerous occasions by officers from the Intelligence Investigation Bureau. In spite of initial reluctance and odd discrepancies brought about by nervousness and lack of sleep, Janke has maintained the same version of the following account for most of that time.

'He is a forty-three-year-old German national, born in Potsdam, son of a policeman and nurse. He was recruited into the Stasi at the age of eighteen and was an intelligence officer specialising in youth dissidents until the age of twenty-three. During this time, he received a commendation for informing against his older brother for indulging in Anti-Communist black-marketeering.'

Barney looked up. 'Lovely chap, isn't he?'

Gemmer shrugged. 'It was the way the system made them over there,' he said.

The report went on, describing how in 1978 Janke had been assigned to Special Duties (Political) within the Stasi. He had became one of a select group of minders for ex-revolutionaries fleeing from Western police and Security Forces. Former members of the Baader-Meinhof group, Action Directe, and the Italian Red Brigade, had been helped to escape from the West via East Germany, Romania, Hungary etc. and had been hidden in friendly Arab countries such as Iraq or Syria. Their escapes had been funded by the USSR which viewed them as political revolutionary heroes. The Soviets had granted them covert political asylum, while openly denying to the West any knowledge of their whereabouts.

'These alleged heroes needed new identities and protection,' the report continued. 'For three years Janke minded a number of them and was apparently highly regarded. In 1981 he was given a minding job of supreme importance.

'It was to care for the Revolutionary, Beatrix Andrea Kessler . . .'

'Kessler! My God!'

'Ssh!' Gemmer's head shot round, checking that his door was closed. Then he turned and smiled at Barney. 'I'm glad you're pleased.'

'Pleased? My God, Horst, Kessler being minded by a Stasi coke addict! How have the mighty fallen!'

'Yes, poor Beatrix.'

'Poor Beatrix, nothing! Seems like she got what she deserved in the end.'

He continued eagerly. For ten years, Janke had been Kessler's constant companion. Unlike many of her former comrades, she had been 'active' throughout, performing a variety of missions for countries friendly to the Socialist ideal, including the USSR itself. Janke had provided a fairly extensive list of dates and places.

Barney gave a low whistle. 'If all this is true . . .'

'Yes, it's quite a card our Russian friends have, isn't it?'

'Are they willing to share?'

'Mmm. They're willing to do deals, I think.'

Barney dwelt briefly on the possibilities of such information. As soon as he returned to London, he would have to make contact with the Russians himself. He wondered what he had to trade. Not a lot, he thought; nothing that immediately sprang to mind; he would have to get one of his team digging through old files.

Gemmer cleared his throat gently.

'Sorry, Horst!'

He gazed down at the report once more. Four years before, it seemed that Kessler had expressed the wish to retire. Her request had been accepted, albeit reluctantly, and she had undergone a number of facial surgery operations. She had then been placed wholly in the care of Janke who had been instructed to ensure her safety and well-being for the rest of her life. Barney looked up; his voice was a little hoarse.

'You know where Kessler is, Horst?'

Gemmer shook his head. 'Finish it,' he said.

Barney bowed his head. Kessler and Janke had lived in a variety of Eastern Bloc countries but, when the Bloc began to disintegrate, Janke complained to his superiors that his job was becoming impossible; it was too dangerous for him to have to keep negotiating with the Security Services in states which were suddenly no longer secured for Communism. In order to silence him, the Stasi agreed to pay, into a numbered Swiss bank account, a lump sum payment of three million dollars. Janke was by then a frequent drug-user; he tried to gain sole access to the money on the grounds of security, but failed. Kessler, however, was aware of his habit, and not unsympathetic. She agreed to authorise payments so that he had sufficient funds to keep himself regularly 'fixed'.

From the middle of 1991 Kessler and Janke became independent of any control and extremely wealthy. Janke wanted to go to the United States, but Kessler insisted on remaining in Europe. They posed frequently as man and wife although according to Janke, never had sexual relations.

Then, in June of the previous year, Kessler declared that she wanted to return to the West. She gave no clear reason beyond saying that she wished to see her father before it was too late. Janke tried to dissuade her but his pleadings were in vain. And as he needed her signature for money, he had to agree.

'A really delightful couple they must have made,' Barney muttered.

'Ja. A very unholy alliance.'

They had taken up residence in Frankfurt. Janke had been extremely nervous because what he had feared was true: her picture was on the Wanted Posters, and it was one that Janke had recognised. It had been taken when she had first arrived in East Germany from the West; a photograph that had been in the Stasi archives. Janke suspected that the German police authorities had an informant within the Stasi – maybe someone who was willing to do a deal in order to escape arrest – and it would only be a matter of time before newer photographs were found of Kessler.

When he warned her, he was further concerned to realise that she did not seem to care. 'It was like she had a deathwish,' Janke had said.

Barney paused. 'Is it true about the Stasi informant?'

Gemmer grinned at him. 'Barney, we have so many Stasi informants that we have to catalogue them!'

Barney tried to imagine such a situation and failed. He returned to his reading.

According to Janke, all that Kessler wanted to do was

watch her father. Three times a week she had him drive her to the suburb of Frankfurt where the old man lived with a housekeeper. They went at different times of the day, for ten or twenty minutes only, and most of the time they had seen nothing. Once or twice, Janke said, the old man would come out, walk very slowly down the road towards the local shops. Once he went into the church where he had once been a priest.

In Janke's opinion, Kessler was preparing to surrender herself to the police. Twice she had told him that she wanted to meet and speak with her father 'just once' and then she would no longer care what became of her. She seemed very depressed and Janke grew increasingly concerned for his own welfare.

Without her knowledge, he had begun to make contact with various underground connections in Frankfurt and, through these people, to a wider network. He had let it be known that Kessler was for sale, dead or alive.

Barney looked up. 'I wonder why our Stasi friend didn't sell Kessler to you.'

What? For 100,000 Deutschmarks? He was looking for offers closer to a million dollars. The Federal Republic just doesn't hand out that sort of cash, Barney.'

Barney turned the page. The previous August Janke had been informed that two men were interested in meeting him with a view to buying Kessler.

Janke had been very excited; it was his first firm offer – Kessler was no longer the hot property she had once been. In the four years since her retirement, others had filled her shoes. He had met the two men twice, in Frankfurt.

Barney's eyes scanned the next paragraph, and stopped. 'One was a big chap, dark-haired, I think he was English . . .'

'Oh my God, no,' Barney whispered. He looked up at Gemmer. 'When did you get this?'

'Yesterday. It was that that made me decide I had to call you.'

Barney groaned and closed his eyes. Never Again was no longer someone else's problem; it was his. He did not want to read on, but he forced himself.

Janke had not been very fulsome with his descriptions. 'The man's German was pretty good, not much of an accent. He wore a very tailored suit, clean-looking. He was mid-forties. The other man was much younger, about thirty, small and thin. Very jumpy, nervous type. He kept getting up and walking round the room. He was American, looked Jewish. I'm not sure about the other one; he might have been American too.

'The first one was definitely the boss, very cool. He said they knew Kessler was right for them; they'd heard everything about her. I don't know who they'd been talking to, but whoever it was had sold them a dud. Anyway, that wasn't my problem.

'They had me tell them a couple of stories about the kind of thing Kessler had done in the past. You know, how she'd killed people. They seemed to get off on it.

'When we got down to business, they came across with the offer upfront. One million dollars. I should've got more but I was surprised, so I accepted. I asked what sort of thing they wanted her for, and they went on about a new Resistance. Anti-Fascist, they said, and that I, as a good Communist, would approve of the group . . .'

Barney took his glasses off. He gazed at Gemmer. 'I don't need to read any more.'

'No.'

'Kessler's with Never Again.' Barney closed his eyes again briefly. 'That explains a lot about them.'

'Yes. They've been professional from the first, haven't they? Not like a new group with its baby troubles and growing pains. They hit us fully-formed, with all their connections in place.'

Barney nodded. 'Yup. Safe-houses; arms-caches; cell network, the works. Even the propaganda was word-perfect, wasn't it?'

'Mmm. I remember thinking, after the second or third attack, that whoever had done it had a lot of experience and patience.'

'But you never guessed Kessler might be involved?'

Gemmer shook his head. 'No. Now it all fits. You remember I thought we had her last year in Frankfurt, then she disappeared? The information we got about where she was living and the recent photograph – either Janke or these two men must have sent it. They must have been blackmailing her.'

Barney nodded. An Englishman, he was thinking, who may or may not be Jewish, mid-forties, dark. It was not much to go on. To Gemmer, he said: 'What d'you reckon the chances of us of us getting a face-to-face with our friend Janke?'

'I've already tried it. Not at the moment. Later, if we catch Kessler, they would do a deal; they'd want her as a witness against a lot of the Stasi hierarchy. You know how murky that whole game is.'

'Poachers turned gamekeepers.'

'And we, of course, want Janke to testify against Kessler if we catch her. So you can see, everybody's playing games.'

He hesitated, but Barney did not notice. In his mind, he was already drafting the new Never Again report. It would be a lot of work to get it ready for the meeting with Hargreaves, but he had time, just. It was only seven-thirty, another hour perhaps at Wiesbaden and he could still make the last flight from Frankfurt to Heathrow. He smiled over at his host: 'Well, you were dead right, it was worth my coming. Kessler plus a Brit at the helm. That'll give Hargreaves something to chew over.'

He paused, hearing the sound of heavy male footsteps in the corridor outside. They stopped at Gemmer's outer office door; there was the static crackle of a radio; the sound of a man's voice and then the footsteps moved off again.

'As I'm here,' Barney went on, 'would it be OK if I had a look at your computer profile of Kessler? Ours'll be out of date, or there'll be some hitch in letting me use it tomorrow.'

Gemmer came out of his reverie. 'Sure. We've got quite a lot on her.'

'Anything recent?'

'No, not for over a year, not since she vanished. We had hundreds of calls, of course, after we put her latest picture on the Wanted posters, but nothing's come of any of them.'

'Mm. She's being well looked after then.'

'Yes. I'll take you downstairs, show you what we've got.' He stood up. The telephone rang on his desk and he picked it up. 'Ja?' There was no sound in the room, not a trace of the other voice on the line. Barney got up and stretched; it had been a long day.

'Ja?' Gemmer's voice had risen noticeably and, glancing over, Barney saw that his hand had tightened on the receiver. News, by the looks of it, he thought, and, judging by Gemmer's expression, good news.

Gemmer started speaking fast, a short flurry of questions, it sounded like, followed by impatient pauses and then the issuing of instructions. He put the phone down, looking rather stunned. Then he grinned. 'My God,' he said slowly.

'What? What's happened?'

Gemmer kept grinning. 'Come on, let's go,' he said, moving towards the door.

'To the computer?'

'The computer?' Gemmer stopped and looked blankly at him, then he seemed to remember. 'Good God no, Barney! Forget the computer.' He clapped his guest on the back. 'You've brought me luck, my friend. There was I wondering what to tell you, how much to say, and now this!'

'Now what?' Gemmer's smile was infectious, but Barney felt a twinge of apprehension: he needed that Kessler update badly.

Gemmer held the door open for him. 'That was the call I've been waiting for for the past two and a half weeks! That's why I haven't been able to talk to you or anyone else about it, except my bloody Minister, in case I gave something away.'

'Horst, what're you talking about?'

'We've got an informant, a bird, yes? And the bird's just started to sing. Let's go and listen.'

'It's OK if I come?'

'Oh you're coming. This is my game now. I decide who can play.'

Chapter Fourteen

Zoe kept her eyes on the digital display of the running machine. It told her that she had already completed five miles running uphill at 10.4 miles per hour. She tried to work out that distance in kilometres and failed. Instead, to keep her mind occupied, she counted to one thousand.

As she did so, she watched herself dispassionately in the floor-to-ceiling mirror that faced her on the wall. She was wearing her gym-kit of white shorts and T-shirt, one of five sets. It was only after she had bought them that she realised they were nearly identical to the uniform Sergio had given her. Old habits, she thought grimly . . .

In the last couple of days she had stopped wondering about Never Again's future. She had exhausted herself with hope and, although she continued to monitor the news, it was no longer with the same degree of intensity. What will be, will be, she told herself. She started to go to the gym every evening, both to fill in time and to make her fall asleep quickly.

Looking in the mirror she saw that she was scarcely sweating; her legs and arms were still slightly tanned from the Corsican sun, pumping away efficiently, their muscles well-developed. She remembered a phrase from the pep-talk that the Leadership, the large man, had given her: 'Be prepared.' 'Just like a girl guide,' she added wryly to herself and frowned a little at her reflection. 'I hope I don't get to look like a female body-builder. I'd hate that.'

She let her eyes wander over the other gym-users; expanding their chests, tightening their tummies, toning their thighs on the shining, sleek machines. Over the following six weeks, the gym's management was holding a 'COMMIT TO GET FIT!' contest. Prize: ten sun-bed treatments; people were clearly going for gold.

It was the usual early Thursday night crowd, she saw.

Mainly men, but a handful of women too, a couple of them horribly thin like famine-victims in Africa. Zoe could eat anything and remain at a constant weight of one hundred and three pounds. She knew she drew envious looks from other women in the changing rooms. It was, she supposed, one of the few plus points of her current existence. Becoming a Body Beautiful was hardly what she had had in mind when she had told Pieter – so long ago it now seemed – that she wanted to fight the Neo-Nazis; that she was prepared to give up her studies, everything, to stop another Holocaust.

She gave herself a mental shrug: it was pointless to go back over what she had meant nearly a year before. Back then she had known nothing; she had been as innocent as a newborn babe, unbloodied and unblooded . . .

She shied away from her memories and concentrated on her surroundings.

Out of the corner of her eye she saw Adrian Pyett watching her. He was about twenty-four, nice-looking, seemed intelligent and clearly fancied her. On Tuesday night, the last time he had been here, he had been using the rowing machine. She had stood to one side, waiting for him to finish.

'Hi, you're pretty fit, aren't you?' His blue eyes had danced admiringly over her body and then he had looked into her face and smiled, open and warm.

Her tummy had flipped a little and a voice inside her had cried out like a child starved of affection. To be flirted with, or just to have a normal conversation; not to have to guard every utterance and treat each stranger with suspicion. Zoe had felt herself melt: it would not hurt to talk, she had thought . . .

Then, as clearly as if he had been standing beside her, she had heard the large man's voice: 'Let no one get too near.' What right, she had thought, suddenly angry, did they have to impinge on every part of her? Nevertheless, she had heeded the warning: it was dangerous for her to be too normal. She had choked back the cry and extinguished the brightness in her face.

'Yes, I'm fit,' she had said coldly. 'If it's anything to do with you.'

His smile had wavered but lingered. 'Ouch! A prickly

Scottish lass, eh? Love the accent. How about a drink in the bar?'

'No thanks.'

He had looked surprised, unused to being turned down. He was, she had seen, really very cute. He had grinned widely again, his antennae sensing her approval. 'Is it something I said? Or just everything about me?'

She had bitten her lip. 'If you're finished, can I have the machine?'

He had ceded it to her in mock fear but had remained standing behind her, keeping up the line of chat. She had frozen him completely, refusing even to look at him, and in the end he had shrugged and left her.

She had thought that was an end of it, but by the way he was looking at her tonight, she could see he was going to make another approach. She fixed her eyes straight ahead, blocking him out of her vision.

'It's not fair,' she said to herself and then almost laughed at the inadequacy of the expression. 'It's cruel. I look good; I look like a normal person. And I've got much more confidence than I used to have; I know I could get on with people now. I'm not afraid any more.'

She blinked down at the read-out and saw she had nearly run her ten miles. Again, anger flared suddenly. 'But it doesn't matter how I feel or what I want, does it? The only thing that matters is keeping my body in excellent condition and my mind free of any emotional entanglements. Holding myself in readiness for the call.'

She looked up again and caught Adrian's eye. 'I might as well be a bloody nun,' she said to herself.

Sitting with a fixed smile on a hard wooden-slatted chair, Matt was remembering why he disliked going 'undercover' so much. It was the duplicity involved; the using and abusing of other people's trust.

He had forgotten how much he hated that aspect of undercover work when he had had his brainwave about Never Again. He had cursed Lomax to hell and back for not letting him off-rota, before realising that night in Barnstaple that of course he could do it. It would just have to be in his own time.

When he had returned to London the previous night, he had bought a copy of a listings magazine and turned to the Political/Fringe section. He had calculated it would not take him long to trawl through the anti-fascist scene. He was sure that there would be someone with a Never Again connection, at least someone who knew someone else, or had heard something on the grapevine.

That was the way to crack the story. Infiltration, merging into the background and keeping his ears open. He could easily do a day's work and then slip off in the evenings. And there were always the weekends.

'It's not as if you've got anyone waiting at home for you,' he told himself. 'Give you something to do, keep you off the streets.'

But the reality of it was what he was now enduring: sitting amongst trusting, decent people and lying to them.

They had been so delighted to see him: a new member, a young(ish) man, and apparently very keen.

'Just moved in to the area, Matthew?'

'Yes . . . well, I'm staying with my brother. He's got a flat down the road.'

'Oh yes? Which road's that? Not being nosy, you understand. Just that I pride myself on knowing just about everywhere in Catford. Been here all my life.'

Matt gave the name of a long road of large houses split into bedsits. His listener, a man in his sixties, in a jumper that was too small for him, rubbed at his chin: 'What number did you say? Aah, mmm. And your brother's called what? Umm, Steve Riley. No, can't say it rings a bell. Been here long has he? Oh, that explains it. There's a lot of coming and going in that road.'

A smiling old lady, a tiny figure with pretty, faded blue eyes, had touched his arm. 'Oh it's good to see a new face, Matthew. You'll liven us old fuddy-duddies up. You're just what we need.'

There were only eight of them: six females, two males and not one under fifty. The Anti-Fascist Society (South London

Branch). Their weekly meeting on a Thursday night, seven o'clock onwards in the upstairs room of the British Legion hall in Catford.

There had been nothing in the Listings entry to indicate the type of membership or the group's views on militancy. How could there have been? One could hardly expect to see: 'We welcome those seeking to join a terrorist organisation. Please come along.'

At the front of the room, standing behind a formica table, a determinedly dauntless woman who had introduced herself nervously as Alice and who must have been seventy, was reading out a lengthy article on 'The threat to democracy in Europe as posed by the forces of nationalism'. It was very dull, but everyone sat attentively on their hard wooden chairs and clapped loudly at the end.

A large woman sitting on Matt's left stood up. 'That was so interesting, my dear, thank you. Well, it's nearly time for our break.' She smiled at Matt. 'We have ten minutes now for tea and biscuits. We each put in twenty pence a week and take it in turns. We've got a rota system, if you'd like to put your name down.'

'I've got to get out of here,' thought Matt, smiling back. 'What a good idea,' he said heartily.

Chapter Fifteen

When Gemmer had said they were going to see an informant, Barney had expected that they would be taking a lift down into the bowels of Wiesbaden. He had said as much.

'No, no.' Gemmer had laughed. 'We don't keep these people here, not such precious cargo as this one is. He has a special place to himself. You'd better bring your things. It might be a long night.'

The 'special place' turned out to be over an hour's drive from Wiesbaden. They travelled in the back of Gemmer's Mercedes; in the front, beside the chauffeur, sat a silent, heavily-built man wearing a dark blue suit who kept a constant watch on the car's mirrors.

'My bodyguard,' Gemmer had introduced him. 'Surreal, don't you think? And feel safe: this car is bullet-proofed.'

Barney said nothing. He knew about the threats to Gemmer's life; knew also that Gemmer coped best by making light of them.

He peered out of the window but could see little. They had left the major roads some time before and were going fast through the dark countryside. Barney trusted that he was not being ungrateful but he hoped Gemmer's informant was going to be worth the journey.

'So, Horst, tell me about your man. He's a member?'

'Yes. Well, he was.'

Barney glanced over. Gemmer was smiling.

'Talk about the cat that's swallowed the cream.'

'Sorry, Barney? One of your English idioms?'

'You look damn pleased with yourself.'

'It's just the relief of him talking after all this time. His silence was becoming exclusively my fault. Very heavy pressure.'

'He might be talking rubbish.'

'No, they said on the phone he was making a lot of sense. Wanted to make a full confession. Can't do enough to help us.'

'So what's changed his mind?'

'That bloody Bremen nonsense.'

'Sorry? You've lost me.'

'It seems he thought the German government might decide he was an embarrassment to a neat solution.'

Barney blinked. 'You'll have to run that past me again.'

'You remember Bremen?'

'Of course I remember Bremen!'

'The boys went in, all guns blazing.'

'Yes, and killed the lot of them. Not too clever, in my opinion, but these things happen. So?'

Gemmer smiled at him. 'Not all of them were killed. One survived.'

Barney stared. 'Your informant?'

'Exactly.'

Barney gave a low whistle. 'I see. You've been very clever. How've you kept it so quiet?'

'Not really very difficult. It was luck. You know what it's like in such situations. Guns and screams, bits of bodies and blood, people panicking, confusion. The GSG-9 commander thought they'd got them all. He'd just called ceasefire when this one came out crying: "Shoot me, shoot me!"'

Barney raised his eyebrows. 'How unusual. Remorse or deathwish?'

'Bit of both. He's not a very, uh, strong person. In fact, I'm surprised if Beatrix had any say in his recruitment.'

'He's not . . .?' Barney fished for the tactful phrase.

'Tip-top quality? No, very definitely not. There's been times over the last two weeks when I've wanted to get him by his skinny throat and strangle him. But that's when he wasn't talking, when he was playing the hard man. You know all he's said until now? "God will judge me. God will forgive me. I'll never betray my brethren."'

'Religious, huh?'

'Like a bloody hermit. But now it appears he's been listening to the news, or to certain bits of it.'

'Which bits?' Barney paused. 'Aaah, that the Bremen Three were responsible for the lot?'

Gemmer grinned again. 'Unfortunately for him, he didn't hear the subsequent denials. No, he started to worry that we might find it useful to accept the theory, and that we might even consider him a barrier to our plan. An easily removable barrier.'

'Suddenly not so keen to meet his Maker then?'

'No. Now he wants to be helpful.'

'Your idea?'

'No. I must be truthful. One of the interrogators'.'

They were driving down a small road, scarcely wide enough for two cars to pass. On either side were high banks, topped with the shadows of trees. A sliver of moon shone weakly. The car swung off suddenly to the right down a concealed lane. A passer-by, if he had seen it, would have taken it for a forester's track – one in bad condition, overgrown and rutted – scarcely worth the effort of exploration. Despite the car's superior suspension, its occupants were jounced and tossed from side to side.

'Bloody hell,' Barney muttered as his shoulder contacted painfully with his passenger door.

'German roads, I know,' said Gemmer. It went on for a mile, then the car swung right again and onto a gravel track that widened after a few minutes onto a manmade road.

Outside, Barney could see nothing but the shapes of trees and the occasional glint of barbed wire, holding them at bay. Ahead, on his left, was a series of low red-brick buildings surrounded by two sets of high-wired fencing. It looked like an aerodrome or a military establishment. There were arc-lights spaced at regular intervals and, through the fencing, Barney could see roads and watching-posts manned with guards.

The car slowed and stopped before steel gates. A guard in a uniform Barney did not recognise, and with a grey sub-machine gun slung over one shoulder, stepped up to them and took the ID the chauffeur proffered. He examined it minutely, then saluted. A second later, the gates opened and their car crept forward to the next barrier.

'Where and what is this place?' Barney asked.

'It's Germany's most secure disinfection unit. Officially, of course, it doesn't exist. It's not on any map. It's like your safe houses, but all together in one big estate. It makes an interesting mixture sometimes: lethal enemies within a few metres of each other. We've had political asylum-seekers; hostages; spies; terrorists. You have to be quite important to get in. My Minister had to fight to get my boy a place.'

A thought struck Barney. 'He won't be here too?' he asked. 'Your Minister? I'm just thinking about protocol and such.'

'No.' Gemmer smiled widely. 'It couldn't be better. He's at a very hush-hush conference in Geneva tonight. Something to do with the exchange of information on terrorists between EC and non-EC member countries. He'll know about this, but he won't be able to get away. Perfect.'

A tall man in a heavy overcoat was standing by the driver's window. He bent down, looked at Gemmer, muttered into his mobile and the barriers swung up.

The car crawled inside the compound, and stopped.

'Time to stretch our legs, Barney. It's not far.'

He led the way across a strip of grass to a single-storey prefabricated bungalow, built up on bricks. It was like a child's drawing of a house: two windows with four square panes of glass, and a door in the middle. There were six wooden steps up to it, and an armed guard on duty. He checked their papers, saluted and rapped twice on the door.

It opened at once and Gemmer ushered Barney inside, his bodyguard following unaided. Barney saw that the bungalow was no more than four rooms divided in half by a hallway. Gemmer was talking in a low voice to a middle-aged man in jeans and a bright multi-coloured jumper. He nodded at Barney and showed them all into a room on his left.

The air was thick with cigarette smoke and Barney looked around for the other occupants, but it was empty. Their four selves filled it at once. Barney, trying to make room, stepped heavily on the bodyguard's foot.

'So sorry.'

The big man said nothing.

'Take a seat,' said Horst. 'I'm just catching up. Eduard here is one of the interrogators. The other one's a woman,

Astrid. It was her idea to let our boy see bits of the
Bremen news.'

Barney sat facing a two-way mirror that took up most of one
wall. It showed another similar-sized room on the other side,
also empty except for a rectangular table, two microphones
and four upright chairs. Below the mirror on his side, he saw
a bank of formidable-looking high-tech recording equipment
and TV monitoring screens, at the moment blank.

The briefing completed, Eduard excused himself and shut
the door. Gemmer took a seat beside Barney. 'Our informant
has just finished supper; he'll be along in a moment.'

Barney waved a hand at the switches and dials before him.
'It's quite a set-up you've got here.'

'Yes, purpose-built spy chambers. State of the art.'

His eyes flickered up to the glass partition. The door in
the other room had opened and a woman in her early thirties
with dark hair in a ponytail, presumably Astrid, had entered.
She was followed by a youth and Eduard. They all appeared
to know their places and went silently to them: Astrid sitting
down with her back to the glass; the men taking the two chairs
facing her.

'That's him,' said Gemmer. 'That's our boy.'

Barney stared. He saw a boy of sixteen, perhaps seventeen
years old, wearing a white T-shirt that was too big for him
and emphasised his puny arms. He was sitting hunched at
the table, his eyes darting nervously, now at the glass, now
at the ceiling, now at the woman opposite him. Barney could
see she was trying to engage him in conversation, trying to
calm him. He had a thin anxious face and a smattering of
angry-looking spots across his forehead. He did not look as
if he shaved, Barney thought.

'Um,' he said.

Gemmer laughed. 'You're not impressed, I can tell. I admit
he doesn't have a very macho appearance. But if he's talking,
who cares? And from what Eduard's just told me, he's been a
very talkative boy now that he's decided to co-operate. A boy
with a troubled conscience.

'You're looking at Christoph Sandsdalen, aged eighteen
and three months, from Mayen, a small town near Koblenz.

Only child of elderly parents. Father a retired shop-manager; mother who stayed at home and doted on him. Very quiet, respectable upbringing. Always a good boy at school.'

Gemmer sighed. Barney knew instinctively why: it was the old tragedy of how nice, normal children from decent homes became killers, men and women – or in this case, boys – who were prepared to take others' lives for an ideal. Barney was suddenly glad, for once, that his own job shielded him from this: the flesh and blood behind the propaganda and the police reports.

'Do his parents know?' he asked.

'Oh yes. We informed them within twenty-four hours that their son was alive! That he had walked out of that bloodbath without a mark!

'D'you know what they said?' Gemmer's voice was bitter. 'They said, "It would have been better if he had died. Tell him we wish he had." Ah well.'

He fell silent, staring at the boy, and Barney followed his gaze. Astrid was talking hard to him and he was nodding mechanically, clearly still nervous. Eduard sat quietly, occasionally glancing at the boy, his face impassive.

Suddenly Christoph smiled at something that the woman had said and, in looking directly at her, seemed to be smiling at his hidden watchers. The smile transformed his appearance, making him look alert, happy and very young. Barney and Gemmer both looked away.

Gemmer shrugged. 'We haven't told him. We can't have him breaking down on us, not yet. He's got years to do all that.

'Right,' he squared his shoulders. 'You'd have thought I'd have learned by now. Primary rule: don't get involved.

'If it's OK by you, Barney, we'll let Astrid and Eduard run the show, take him through everything from the start.'

'Of course it's OK by me!'

'I can ask Astrid questions through my headset, but I'd rather not do it too often. It's important the boy thinks he's just talking to them; they're the ones who've got his confidence. We don't want him getting confused.'

'Does he know we're here?'

'He'll know someone's watching, but he's got used to that over the weeks. I'll translate for you, and Eduard says they're going to try to go slow for us, and have breaks. If I miss anything the whole thing's being taped. OK?'

'Great.'

Gemmer put on a headset. 'They're just getting him warmed up now; asking him to go over what he said earlier. He's moaning about being tired and getting bored. Getting cocky, the little bastard. He knows we're not going to shoot him now. Right, here goes.'

His brow furrowed in concentration and the room fell silent. Glancing behind, Barney saw the bodyguard sitting massively in the shadows, staring ahead; they could all have been part of a theatre audience.

Through the glass he could see Astrid's dark ponytail nodding in time as she spoke; Christoph's eyes were fixed on her, drinking in everything she said. Probably in love with her, Barney judged, and anxious to show off in front of Eduard.

'Right.' Gemmer stopped scribbling notes and took off his head-set. 'He's getting a bit boring now about his feelings on Neo-Nazis.

'Christoph is, as I told you, a religious boy. Through his church youth-group he became involved in the anti-fascist fringes: protest marches, demos, meetings. He was very keen. You can see he's not a very tough specimen. The victim-type who identifies with other victims – you know the kind of thing.

'At a rally three months ago he met a Never Again recruiting officer. A Dutchman, apparently, called Pieter.'

'Real name? Surname?'

'No idea. He said he'd been impressed by Christoph's enthusiasm. Wanted to know if he was prepared to fight the battle, or just sit back and listen. He was good, most professional, by the sound of it. He got Christoph's wavelength very quickly, fired him up, telling him about righteous indignation; meeting violence with violence, defending the weak, all the martyr stuff. It went down very well with our boy, of course, appealing to his religious side.'

'Mm. St Christoph.'

'Exactly. I really think that's what he thought, Barney. Pieter was God's messenger, sent to tell him his mission in the world. He was flattered, naturally. Being selected for The Cause. He even used the words, "One of the chosen few".'

Gemmer coughed and they both studied Christoph in silence. He was still talking away, sitting on his hands, rocking himself gently back and forwards. Gemmmer went on: 'As soon as he showed interest Pieter handed him on down the line.'

'So Pieter was just the fisherman?'

'Ja. Other people did the knocking into shape.'

Barney nodded. 'As you say, professional. Of course, only what you'd expect from Kessler.' He frowned. 'Where's their money coming from?'

'Don't know.' Gemmer consulted his notes. 'Christoph was handed over to a trainer, a Spaniard, no name. This man ran what sounds like a very basic training centre on a farm on the north Spanish coast, somewhere outside Bilbao. He says he can't give any more details because he was taken there in the back of a van. He was there a week. There were three others, two Germans and, he thinks, an English boy.'

Barney groaned. 'There had to be, hadn't there? Any descriptions?'

'The Germans were called Max and Werner; the English boy was Simon. No surnames; they were told not to use them. Boys about his age or a bit older. Simon was fair, the other two dark. That's it for now. They'll go over it again and he might remember more, but I wouldn't be very hopeful about it.'

'Descriptions not his long suit, then?'

'I don't think so.'

'I mightn't bother Hargreaves with Simon's existence just yet then.'

'They all got a little combat training, the basics of shooting and a lot of indoctrination. "Foot-soldiers in the glorious war against the evils of Fascism" but their real training took place "on the job". At the end of the week they were each des-patched to their "cells". Unfortunately for our young friend here, he was sent to join the team of Inge von Buelen.'

'She's the girl who was killed at Bremen?'

'Ja. Quite a formidable young woman.' He pulled a file from his briefcase, and opened it, but he barely glanced at the typewritten material. 'She was shot first; they had to take her out; she was firing like a crazy person, completely out of her head.'

'Drugs?'

'No, no trace. Just killing-mad. She must have been one of their earliest recruits. Her parents reported her missing last December after she'd gone to an anti-Fascist demonstration in Munich.'

'Similar thing that happened to Christoph, then?'

'Precisely. Impeccable background. No history of any aggressive or anti-social behaviour. In fact, the opposite. She was a trained nursery nurse.'

'Good God!'

'Yes. Her teachers described her as a pleasant girl and excellent with kids. So whatever went wrong with her happened during her time with the group.' He put the ear-piece back on. 'Aah, this sounds better . . .'

Christoph was looking much more animated, sitting forward and gesturing with his hands. Barney imagined his voice, thin and reedy. He glanced at his watch, nearly ten o'clock, German-time. At this rate, he doubted that he would get back to London before tomorrow afternoon. He imagined himself rushing into the office to find Hargreaves drumming her fingers on his desk. Not that that mattered, he reassured himself, this was far more important. He glanced over at his friend, deep in concentration; he had a lot to thank him for.

It was ten minutes before Gemmer turned to him again. 'He's talking about von Buelen. About how mad she was, and bitter.'

'Why bitter?'

'He said something about her being passed over, not promoted. The interrogators have called a break, for our benefit and theirs; they want to keep him keen to talk. But they'll go back to it in a minute.

'OK. Von Buelen made our boy's life a living hell. He calls her the Devil and not without reason. D'you remember about three months ago there was a series of very nasty Never Again attacks? You might not, they were all inside Germany and no one was murdered in them. But they were vicious.

'One involved a man and his wife who ran a right-wing youth camp. Kidnapped and hooded, stuck down a drain and left for two days. Then a week later two little skinhead kids were knee-capped; they'll never be able to walk again. And up in Dortmund a man who'd spoken out against an Anti-Nazi rally in the town-square was paralysed in a beating.'

'Ugly stuff. He did them?'

'Ja.'

They both looked through the glass. Christoph stretched and yawned. Eduard offered him a sweet, and he took it, smiling.

'Little shit,' Barney murmured.

Gemmer shrugged. 'He was obeying von Buelen's specific instructions. He was frightened out of his wits. She was standing behind him all the time, screaming that she'd kill him if he didn't do it.'

'Or so he says.'

'I believe him. It fits in with the police report.'

'What about the Never Again hierarchy? Or were these cells totally autonomous?'

'It looks that way, doesn't it? The cells will have a contact for emergencies, access to arms caches etcetera, but apart from that, they're on their own. So much safer for security.'

'Right.' Barney saw Eduard give a slight nod. 'I think they're starting again.'

'All right. Let's hear it from the boy.'

Chapter Sixteen

Zoe kept her guns at the club.

In theory, she could have had them at the flat but it would have meant getting a firearms certificate, and being investigated by the police to ensure she knew how to handle them and keep them securely locked away. They would want to check that she was not insane; that she was not the sort of person likely to start shooting her neighbours. 'Or the kind to be a terrorist,' she thought, shuddering at that image of herself and immediately dismissing it from her mind.

She had returned from the gym an hour before; heated herself a chicken dinner and eaten it in front of a bland TV show. Now she checked the time and stood up; it was a twenty minute drive to the gun-club.

At first she had not been at all sure that she would be able to hold a gun in her hand again. Not after Turin, not after seeing what weapons could do, really do, to the human body. But the image of Sergio and the orders of the Leadership were fresh in her mind and if she disobeyed them, she feared that she might fall apart. That fear had driven her to the gun-club in Tooting, had made her go through the motions of joining and booking out a weapon, a small one, the Beretta.

And as soon as she had picked it up, feeling its coldness in her hand, and levelled it at the paper targets, the face of Emilio had vanished. In its place were the concentric circles only. She felt herself to be back in Corsica; could almost feel Sergio's breathing in the shadows behind her, and she had fired.

It was just as it had been before. The adrenalin surging through her, the exhilaration as the bullets punctured the circles, reassuring her that that was her purpose; that was what she excelled at. In the whole of her life as it now was, shooting was the thing she loved most, the bright spot in the enforced drudgery of her existence.

She simply ignored what she was practising for.

She picked up her car keys. She had a few minutes to spare but she liked to be sure to get to the club a little before 9.30 so that she had a full hour's practice before it closed.

She had chosen the time deliberately to avoid the 'macho' men. Their antics made it impossible for her to practise properly.

Although there were other women members, none of them, and very few of the men, shot as well as she. Naturally, therefore, she had quickly become something of a curiosity, especially when she refused to participate in any of the club's competitions.

'Why not?' Mark, the club coach had asked her in some exasperation. 'You're bloody good, you know, and we could do with winning a few trophies. You'd get free membership; picture in the paper . . .'

When she had stubbornly refused, she had been left strictly on her own, and at the mercies of the 'macho' men. There were five of them, middle-aged men in poor careers who claimed to have been in the SAS. When they arrived at the club they changed into New York Police Department shirts and bragged loudly about missions they had undertaken in the 'Service'. After word got round the club about Zoe's shooting ability, they began to pester her.

At first she had tried to ignore the sexual innuendo; the mocking of her stance and method of firing, the barely veiled threats, but in the end found it easier to avoid the times that she knew they would be there.

She zipped up her bomber jacket, wound a scarf around her neck and grabbed her keys. She was outside and about to slam the front door behind her when the telephone rang. She considered ignoring it. Five seconds later and she would not have heard it. She hesitated, cursed the caller, then ran back inside to answer it.

It was Alasdair. 'Hi, kid! Got you at last. How you doing?'

'Fine! How're you?'

'Pretty good. How's the job?'

It's as boring as hell, Zoe wanted to say. 'Oh, quite interesting really. I'm learning a lot.'

'Good. Must say I never saw you as a bookshop manageress in Clapham Junction. Still, the pay must be pretty good ... For your flat, I mean. Not that I've seen it of course!' He laughed, but Zoe reddened. She did not want Alasdair there; she did not want him contaminated by her life, and nor did she want him to start wondering how she could afford such a wonderful place on the pittance she would get as a salary.

'Zoe, are you there?'

'Yes. Sorry, I was day-dreaming.' She tried to change the subject. 'How's Kerry?'

'Fine. Working hard as usual. She says how are you and when're we going to see you. So do I, I mean about seeing you. You're not mad at me, are you? About asking you to move out?'

'No! No, of course not! It was about time I got my own place.'

'That's what I told Kerry. Good. Look Zo, have you worked out what you're doing for Christmas?'

'Um, I don't know. I hadn't thought.'

'Well, we're going to go up to the parents and I was wondering, would you be going too? I'd drive so it wouldn't cost you anything. Think of all that lovely food, healthy air and all that.'

'Al, you're sounding like a salesman!'

'Am I? Well I'd like you to come. Unless you've got something better to do of course. Exciting times with your lover ...'

'What lover!'

'So you haven't got one? I didn't think so but ...'

Zoe grinned in spite of herself. 'Kerry again?'

'Yes,' he sounded sheepish. 'Anyway, you'd be doing me a great favour if you'd come up with us.'

'I would? How?'

'It'll be the first time Kerry'll have met mum and dad, and you know what they can be like. I'm sure she can hold her own, but you'd be a buffer just in case.'

'Gee thanks!' Alasdair was always so transparent; she felt a warm rush of affection for him that for the moment blocked out other things. 'Seeing as you put it so nicely, I'll come.'

'Good. Thanks a lot. I really mean it. There's going to be a Hogmanay Ball at Kingussie. You never know, you might have some fun.'

'Mmm.' She looked at her watch. 'Al, I've really got to go now.'

'OK. But Kerry says to come to dinner.'

'Great, I'll do that.'

'Tomorrow?'

'Tomorrow?'

'Unless you've got other plans?'

'Uh, no. That'd be fine. Wonderful I mean. I'll see you tomorrow.'

''bout eightish? See you then.'

In the monitoring room, Barney watched Christoph attempting to twist a button off his shirt cuff. It was a nervous, fidgety action and the boy was probably not even aware that he was doing it, but Barney found it quite mesmerising. Gemmer's voice startled him.

'He's saying Inge used to beat him up for nothing. She'd say everyone had wronged her; no one was innocent. Sometimes she'd just sit in a trance, other times she'd start telling secrets.'

'Secrets?' asked Barney. 'Like what?'

'He's just coming to it, wait . . .'

Christoph seemed to be struggling with himself. He was rocking his body back and forth in the chair, and chewing at his fingers.

'Come on, boy,' Gemmer urged him.

As if hearing him, Christoph suddenly tilted his chair forward again and took his hand out of his mouth; his lips moving fast. 'He's saying she started talking about the Elite, that she'd been promised she'd be a member of the Elite . . . "But all she'd got was a sweaty Italian and a pansy boy."'

'Elite?' Barney said urgently. 'What sort of Elite?'

'. . . The top category of fighters in the movement . . . That her selector had told her she would be chosen because she possessed special qualities . . . One minute, Barney . . .'

Gemmer flicked a switch on the consul in front of him and

muttered something low through his mouthpiece. Then he turned back: 'I've just asked Astrid to try to slow it down so I can translate verbatim, OK?'

'Great.'

'"She said she hadn't just been given a two-day course in a garage like me and Nico ... She'd been taken to see the Leadership."'

Barney felt his heart-rate quicken.

'"She said that her recruiter – not Pieter but a Spanish man called ... Lorenzo – had taken her to a house near Stuttgart. Two men and a woman ... They wore hoods ... They asked questions ... Stupid things, she said, about the way she lived her life ... why she wanted to join ... If she wanted to be famous.

'"She said the men had English or American accents. That they fancied her ... but the old witch was jealous. Inge knew it was the woman who'd refused to let her join the Elite.

'"Lorenzo told her that they'd felt she didn't have the ... right temperament for the Elite. That she'd be more useful on the ... front-line. At least for a few months."'

Gemmer stopped; Christoph had leaned forward and said something to the woman. 'He just asked if she was getting his statement down properly.' Gemmer shook his head. 'Completely on our side now, isn't he? Oh, he's started again ...

'"Inge was very angry but Lorenzo said she had to obey the Leadership. Everyone did. He said ... they'd been very angry with him for telling her about the special category ... That he'd broken an important rule ...

'"Once she got got really mad. We were in a very expensive apartment, a safe house ... beautiful things. She started to scream and break things. She screamed that she'd done everything they'd wanted, more than they could have expected ... She said she'd done better than any man. She'd been tougher and done things men wouldn't do ..."'

Christoph came to a sudden halt, bowing his head. After a few seconds the woman leaned over and touched his hand. He looked up; his face was shining with tears and he sobbed as he spoke.

Gemmer caught Barney's eye. 'He's talking about what she made him do . . . about what God thinks . . .'

'What he's saying ties in with Janke's statement, doesn't it?'

'Yes, absolutely.' Through the mirror, Barney saw the door open in the other room and a uniformed guard came in with a jug of coffee and mugs.

'Gets good service, doesn't he?'

'Oh yes. Nothing but the best. For us there's a vending machine outside if you'd like a cup.'

'I'll pass. So how long'll he be kept here?'

'I'm not sure. Another few weeks at least. Until we're sure he's completely unburdened himself.

'Now he's started being a good boy he'll find life's quite pleasant. He'll get what he wants, within reason. Clothes, CDs, videos. You can imagine what people would say if they knew this was how a terrorist was kept.'

'Only too well.'

'And afterwards?' Barney thought but did not say out loud. Afterwards there would be a new name and identity; perhaps a new country, some cash, but not much more. None of the cossetting, the attention he was getting now that would make him think the interrogators were his friends for life.

He would not have had time yet to think about the future, a future where he would be forever looking over his shoulder, waiting for a knock on the door, for someone to recognise him on a street. Even if Never Again was destroyed, he would not be able to return to his old life. Not after this level of deception. Too much had gone into Christoph's death to allow him to live again.

Barney looked through the glass at Eduard's stony face; it had not been so foolish for the boy to believe that he might be killed for a theory.

Barney shook himself. He must not get involved; he would do much better to attend to what Gemmer was saying.

'"Inge said it wasn't fair. After everything she'd done, she'd been left to rot. Lorenzo had said he'd be in contact with her again after six months, but he hadn't. She'd tried to go directly to the Leadership, but no one would help her . . . They were all too scared.

'"She talked a lot about what Lorenzo had said about the Elite. She would have been set up somewhere in an expensive apartment . . . given lots of money . . . and she might never have to do anything. If she did, it would be something really· big . . . Everyone would be in awe of her . . ."'

Gemmer's voice trailed off even though Christoph was still talking. 'A Sleeper,' he said quietly.

'Sounds like it.' Barney was surprised that they both sounded so calm. Gemmer spoke softly into his mouthpiece. 'I've just said we're taking a break. If he says anything we can listen to the tape later.' He took his headset off and sighed wearily.

'We don't know that they actually went ahead and set up a Sleeper, do we?' said Barney.

'No, but the likelihood is . . .'

'The likelihood is that they did, I know.'

He stared at the other side. They, too, had decided to take a break. Christoph was pouring coffee; the woman adding milk, even Eduard was joining in, adding sugar. He said something and Christoph laughed: friends enjoying a joke.

Barney rubbed his tired eyes. 'A Sleeper,' he thought, 'wonderful.' He tried to think of strategy and risk assessments but his mind was a blank.

'So, somewhere out there we have a little time-bomb ticking?' Gemmer sounded strained. 'No idea who or where. Somewhere out there, there's someone who's never attracted the attention of the security forces; whose life looks blameless.'

'That's right. No ripples at all. A dull type that no one notices.'

'Ja. And then tomorrow morning, or next month or next year, he'll walk out into the street and commit some awful bloody atrocity, and it'll be you and me to blame. Why didn't we know? Why didn't we find him?'

Gemmer's voice had acquired an angry, accusatory tone and then he slumped forward and groaned. 'The Minister's going to love this.'

'So's my Director.' Barney imagined Hargreaves going nuclear and then realised there was no need; he would be seeing her very soon.

He shut his eyes. Sleepers were a nightmare; he had only dealt with one once before. A Czech who had been living in Bloomsbury for eighteen years and had a job as a security consultant for a computer company. A small, innocuous-looking man with wispy strands of hair and thick glasses whose mission, when finally 'activated', had been the assassination of a junior press attache in the South African Embassy. Barney's team had got to the Czech an hour too late: he had killed himself. Perhaps unable after all those years of living amiably, of clothing himself in the garb of normality, to strangle another human being on the orders of a far-off master whose ideals he no longer shared. Perhaps, Barney suddenly wished fervently, the same might happen again: disillusion might set in before the order came to strike.

'Barney?'

'Sorry, I was miles away.'

Gemmer gestured towards the glass. 'Astrid's just asked him what else Inge said about the Elite; if she mentioned knowing anyone who'd been chosen, but he knows nothing.'

'So we're totally in the dark.'

'Yes.' Gemmer sighed heavily again. 'And we mustn't assume that it's only one Sleeper out there.'

'No,' Barney swallowed hard. 'There might be one in every country of the European Community. There might be one in every city.'

'Ja. Where to begin, huh?'

'Well, there's your excellent profile system, isn't there? That looks for types, doesn't it?'

'Yes, but you've got to give it something to go on! You can't just say, "Find me the ten most likely people in Europe to become Sleepers!"' He hunched forward, his knuckles whitening on the narrow consul ledge. 'Sorry, Barney, I'm shouting at you as if it's your fault.'

'That's OK. I know how you feel. We'll have to put our heads together and come up with something.'

'Ja,' Gemmer smiled wanly. 'That's why I invited you over.

So we could try to figure out what to do. But that was before we knew about this. The ticking outsider.'

'Yeah, I must say my mind's a blank right now. The only thing I can think is that we've got to get to the Leadership fast and get them talking. Kessler would spill the beans if only we could find her. How about that Dutchman, what's his name, the recruiter?'

'Pieter? Yes, he's our best bet. We'll try and get the boy to give us a better description and get the Dutch working on it.'

'Right.' Barney looked into the other room and saw Eduard staring ahead, rubbing at his left ear. 'I think he wants us to hear this, Horst.'

'What? Oh, OK . . . Astrid's just asked him about Bremen. Does he know why there's been nothing since then?'

'Look at him,' said Barney.

Christoph was grinning and nodding his head like a clever child anxious to stun his classmates. He answered quickly, and Gemmer stumbled to keep up:

'"It was a . . . an important rule . . . the most important . . . after any disaster, for example . . . the taking of comrades or supporters . . . or a safe-house being discovered, or an arms cache . . . that for twenty-one days afterwards no further actions shall take place."'

'Aah,' breathed Barney.

Gemmer nodded, and went on translating. '"It was so that every group should have time to move . . . That was another order: If disaster strikes, move and resite."' To Barney, he said: 'Astrid's asking what happens after twenty-one days.' He's saying . . . "Within twenty-four hours there would be a big action . . . spectacular . . . to remind the world that we have not abandoned the struggle . . . to prove our renewed strength."'

'Marvellous!' said Barney.

'Ja, we've something big to look forward to as well as Sleepers. Super. Ah, there's more. He doesn't know why the time was set at twenty-one days. It was just the rule. ". . . That number of days must pass to ensure maximum security and survival of remaining cells and members." Is that it?'

Christoph was frowning hard, then a light seemed to dawn in his face and he hurried to pass it on. '"It was in case vital information . . . had been left behind at a safe-house. Any documents or weapons, or . . ."'

Watching, Barney saw the boy's grin suddenly replaced by a look of horror. It remained – stuck on like a mask – as Gemmer translated his last words: 'Or in case a comrade turns traitor and seeks to betray us all.'

In a splendid Viennese apartment with sweeping plum velvet drapes at the high windows, another meeting was in progess.

Three men and one woman sat around the large mahogany dining table. Above their heads hung an ornate crystal chandelier that sparkled in the light. It was the sort of room that should have been filled with tinkling laughter and elegant conversation, but its beauty was entirely lost on its present occupants.

The woman wore a dark, voluminous jumper and her grey hair hung limply upon her shoulders. Her large eyes looked dull and weary of seeing. She sat on her own, facing the men.

Body language spoke volumes, thought one of them. He would have liked to have sat next to her, if only to lend moral support, but when he had arrived, the others had already been seated and there had been just one place left for him.

Pieter van Hoeffen looked down at the pile of newspapers on the table. Articles had been ringed in red ink, but the Dutchman did not bother to read them; he knew what they contained. They were examples to boost Axel's argument.

The Englishman was speaking now, in the oily way he had when he wanted to appear reasonable. Beyond him, Pieter caught a glimpse of Leon nodding like one of those plastic dogs his father used to stick in the back window of the car.

'My dear Ms Kessler, I do take your point. Of course we appreciate your valuable opinion. You have, after all, so much more experience than the rest of us put together.' He smiled with profound contempt.

Pieter saw that Kessler had caught his meaning perfectly: her body stiffened in response. What had happened to her?

The woman whose very name had once signified terror to millions of people. Why did she not tear the carping Axel limb from limb? She seemed to be as toothless as a newborn kitten.

Pieter frowned down at the sumptuous Chinese carpet. He remembered his own trepidition the first time that he had met Kessler, the stories he had heard about her: the slaying in her bed of a lover suspected of turning informant; the brutal knee-capping of a journalist; the shooting-down of a woman prison wardress as she waved her children off to school . . . As well as all the countless atrocities that her group had been responsible for.

Now she sat, absorbing the body-blows and insults of a man she must despise, and did nothing. It did not make sense, he thought. She might not have a weapon; she might be guarded night and day by minders, but surely she could find the means to strike back?

He looked up. Kessler seemed to be studying the polish on the table. Axel's voice was rolling on: 'We understand that rules are necessary to the smooth running of any organisation. However, we,' he inclined his head each way, thus implicating Pieter as well as Leon, 'feel that it's crucial that the group must show strength as soon as possible. That's our opinion.'

Bastard, thought Pieter. Two hours ago, when Axel had summoned him here, he had said that an important decision had to be made. In fact it was clear that he had already made the decision. Pieter was here only to bolster the appearance of democracy. Three against one was the sort of ratio that Axel liked, and preferably three men against one woman: there was a lot of the playground bully in Axel.

Kessler still said nothing. Her eyes had become veiled and secretive. Pieter willed her not to give up, but he feared it was already too late. She seemed to be retreating into her own world, withdrawing from the intolerable situation she found herself in.

Axel resumed: 'We have all read these scurrilous newspaper reports which claim we are finished. "Never Again No More"; "Professor Henry Wilkins on the rise and fall of Never Again". Here's another one. An alleged expert on "Why this band of do-gooders-turned-bad could never succeed."'

He sniffed delicately. 'We have endured these attacks, knowing that our time will come. But then today, in this rag of a journal,' he held up a copy of an Austrian paper, 'we have the personal view of this politician, this Herr Blinen, a Jew-hating Fascist . . . Listen to it!'

His voice changed suddenly, losing its urbanity, and his hands trembled: '"Whatever crazed Jewish conspiracy, whatever longing to show their might, to show their equality with the rest of humanity . . ."'

Emotion seemed to overtake him completely, robbing him momentarily of speech. His face flushed a purply-red and his eyes were bulging. But he wet his lips, placed a finger on a line of newsprint, like a child having difficulty with the words, and stumbled on:

'"These futile . . . ill-starred and cowardly Semitic inspired attacks on the . . . the noble shock-youth brigades of Fascism . . ."'

He slammed his fist hard down on the table and stood up. Sweat was pouring from his face and his whole body was shaking; his voice threatening to go out of control. 'I will not have it!' he shrieked. 'They will not mock me! Hitler is laughing at us, I tell you!

'And you,' he glared wildly down at Kessler, 'sit there and say, "Two more days!" Two more days! How many more innocent children will die in two more days? Tell me that!'

He thrust his face across the table so that it was within a foot of hers but she did not move, not even when the man's spit landed on her cheek. Pieter flinched for her.

'We will not wait!' screamed Axel. 'We will not sit and take this! Have this, this . . .' he stabbed at the paper, 'garbage! This, this shit says these things about us . . . We . . .' His voice gave out suddenly, he stood heaving for breath, his eyes glassy, then he slumped down into his chair.

Heart attack, Pieter thought, beside the man in a moment and loosening his tie. He felt for the pulse; it was racing, and erratic; his face was grey. Leon plucked uselessly at his sleeve.

'Does he need a doctor?' he asked, terrified.

Axel moaned and opened his eyes.

'I think he's coming out of it,' Pieter said. Axel's breathing was easing and his eyes were no longer fixed in that unseeing stare. He blinked and sat up slowly.

Opposite, Pieter saw that Kessler had not moved a muscle. She was sitting as impassive as ever; her eyes looked brighter, though.

'Are you sure you're OK?' Leon was all anxiety. 'Sure you don't want to go to the hospital? Just for a check-up.'

'No, I'm fine. Stop fussing over me.' The voice was a little weak but growing stronger; the crisis had passed. He sat forward and tightened his tie. 'Thank you,' he said stiffly to Pieter. 'I'm perfectly all right now.'

He cleared his throat. 'My emotions,' he said hoarsely, 'sometimes carry me away.'

'You should be careful of that,' Kessler's voice was neutral.

'What?' croaked Axel and the flush started again at his neck.

'It would be foolish in the extreme to let one's emotions interfere with operational procedure.' She bestowed a smile on him: a long, slow, pleasurable smile that matched that glint in her eyes. It was the first smile that Pieter remembered her giving.

Beside him he heard Axel's breathing start to quicken once more. 'Foolish?' he repeated, snorting.

God, she's going to kill him, Pieter thought. Not with a gun or a knife, or by strangling him with her own two hands; she means to give him a heart attack.

'I reiterate what I've already said.' She held her eyes steady. 'There's little point in making rules if one is then going to break them . . .' She paused, deliberating. 'In a fit of childish temper.'

Suddenly Pieter could not hear Axel breathing at all. He shot him a glance. The man's shoulders were rising and falling rapidly, his mouth was open, but in profile at least his colour looked good.

She kept on: 'Twenty-one days is the time we agreed. It's

an absolute; one of the very few that the commandos have. I think it would be foolish, as well as extremely dangerous, to ask any of them to rush their preparations.' She hesitated again: 'Simply to satisfy a personal vendetta.'

There was silence. On the ridiculously ornate gold-leafed occasional table by the window, the lovely Louis XIV clock chimed the quarter hour.

Axel leaned forward and bowed his head. It was a submissive, contemplative gesture. My God, she's done it, Pieter thought in shock. She's won without lifting her little finger . . . stunning!

Axel turned suddenly, almost catching his expression.

'Which group will carry out the action?'

Pieter swallowed. 'The . . . uh . . . the ones in France.'

'Tell them to bring their operation forward. They're to go as soon as possible. That's an order.'

Pieter hesitated. Decisions were supposed to be unanimous.

'That's an order, I said!'

'I agree,' said Leon.

The woman said nothing. She lowered her gaze.

'It's a majority decision,' said Axel, suddenly grinning. 'Two against one. So get on with it, will you?'

At the same time, a young man, about twenty-four years old and rather well-dressed for his surroundings, was making his way to a Tapas bar in the old quarter of Bilbao. He walked quickly; his hand-made leather shoes getting scuffed on the rough cobble-stones; the knowledge that he should not be here adding to the echoing urgency of his footsteps.

It was loneliness that had brought him.

Antonio Valente lived far away now, in a splendid apartment in Madrid, the sort of apartment that his mother had always dreamed of. It had a balcony and a roof terrace and glorious high windows overlooking a private piazza where a fountain played. He had a maid to cook and do his laundry for him – he, Antonio Valente, son of Enrique the hotel-porter and Cristina, the chambermaid, lived the life of the idle rich. But he had no friends; no one to confide in; no one who knew his past or where he had come from.

He was cold. It was nearly November after all, and the weather up here on the Northern coast was always harsher than further south. He should have brought something warmer, but the thin denim jacket he was wearing was the only garment he possessed that did not look too expensive. He pulled its collar up as far as it would go and huddled down into it. He had been stupid, he realised now, to have thrown away everything from his past life. Stupid, too, to have bought such expensive items; to be living in such a luxurious apartment; to have such a rich boy's car. And it was against orders. But it had been asking too much, after a life with no money, to have turned his back on all the cash that he had found sitting in his bank account.

No one, as far as he knew, was monitoring him. He was a free agent, entitled, he told himself, to a spending spree before settling for a more frugal existence. He promised himself, in that first week of mad buying, that in six months' time he would settle for less showy things. Now he wanted to have fun.

But it had not been fun. He had no one to talk to; no one to show off to and he did not fit in to his surroundings.

He blew on his hands in an attempt to warm them. In thowing away his past, he had nothing to remind him of who he once had been.

In Madrid, people called him Antonio or Senor Valente; they respected him only because of his wealth. No one called him Anton. Sometimes the loneliness was so bad that he felt it as a physical pain. It was the reason that he was back here tonight, trying to find a bit of everything he had lost.

Bilbao was his birthplace and where he had spent the first eighteen years of his life. His parents still lived in the mean little house on the outskirts of the city where he had grown up – or at least he supposed they did. He had not been home for six years. It hurt just thinking about the reason for the rift.

Until that day, six years ago, Anton had adored his parents, and been proud of them: the way they had worked so hard and uncomplainingly through all the difficult years of raising him and his two sisters. He had taken the close relationship for granted, something unchangeable that was the bedrock of his life.

Then, during his first term at university where he was studying to be an architect, he had brought home his girl-friend, Marianella. He had loved her so much that he had been blind to his parents' hostility. On the second day, his father had taken him aside: 'Anton, you aren't serious about this girl?'

'Yes, Papa. Does it show so much? Isn't she the most beautiful creature?' The words had spilled out, he had been so happy. Marianella was training to be a doctor, but as soon as they had both qualified, they intended to get married.

'Marry! Are you mad? Why would you do such a thing to your mother and me?'

Anton had stared, unable to comprehend. 'What d'you mean? What's wrong?'

'She's an Arab, isn't she? A dirty, scheming little Moroccan whore who's only after you for your nationality and a passport! We forbid it.'

From that day, Anton had cut himself off completely from his parents. He had gone back to university and buried himself in his work and his love for Marianella. He had rejected all attempts on his mother's part – his father was too proud – to re-establish contact: he had returned her letters unopened and, when she had called on him at his student digs, he had refused to see her. His older sister had telephoned, pleading tearfully for a reconciliation. If only Anton would show a little understanding, ditch the Arab and ask for forgiveness . . .

Anton had spent the vacations with Marianella in their tiny studio flat. When the relationship had ended six months later, he had been bereft and blamed his parents for it: it was their racism that had destroyed his love.

On his own, all he had felt was a hollow inside, an emptiness that had at times threatened to swallow him whole. He had hated to be alone and tried to fill every moment with being seen to have a good time; he had become known as a wild boy; his work had suffered but he had become popular with a rich crowd. Anton who would do anything; who did not care.

When university finished he had found himself with a

mediocre degree and no job prospects. It was then that he had met the people who were to change his life.

'Watch where you're going!'

Two young men walked into him. Anton automatically felt for his wallet in the back pocket of his jeans: still there.

'Sorry,' he called after their backs. 'Wait!' He wanted to call, 'I might know you.' But they were already gone; their footsteps receding on the stone.

Anton remembered these narrow streets so well. As a teenager they had spelt 'Life' to him; a warren of little bars and cafes where he and his friends used to hang around at weekends. The tapas bar where he was headed had once been his particular haunt. It was a vast place on several floors, spartan and draughty like an old barn and the meeting place in Bilbao for everyone under the age of twenty-five.

He remembered how he and his friends would stand shouting at each other – normal conversation being impossible against such a din – eyeing up the girls, and smoking each other's cigarettes.

He turned the corner of the street leading to the bar. He could hear the noise as he got nearer; it was past midnight and everyone would be warmed up by now. 'You shouldn't be here,' he said to himself. 'What if you see someone you know?' He had no cover story that would survive two minutes with one of his old friends.

Still, he took a few paces onwards. He saw the bar up ahead: a tall building of crumbling stone, bursting at the seams, its warmth and light spilling out into the street. Life. He stopped, took one great shuddering breath of it, turned and walked away, getting faster and faster. He was sweating hard; he must get back to his car and away from here, back to Madrid.

He saw a group of young people approaching; their voices ringing out loudly in the frosty night. He hunched himself forward, keeping his head well down. He had been wrong to come; to risk everything for one evening among old friends.

His life was not his any longer, he knew that. It belonged to the Cause that had given him so much; something to fight for, a focus for his terrible anger, a way to eradicate the cancer of racism once and forever. He cursed himself as he quickened his pace: he had not only been wrong to come, he had been selfish and ungrateful. The Leadership trusted him and they had given him so much: all his training, his apartment, his car, his clothes. All he had to do in return was keep himself in good condition and remain concealed until the time came when he was needed.

'You're going to have to learn some discipline, boy,' he told himself, then shuddered at the memory of the man who had first said those words to him. The big, good-looking man who had instilled the fear of death in him and then had made death seem not so terrible – at least it would come as a release to the hours of tortuous training. Sergio, his trainer, his tormentor. Anton prayed fervently that it would be a long time before he was summoned back to Corsica. He shivered: God knows what Sergio would do to him if he could see him now.

He came to his car: a low black convertible parked beside the river. It was the kind of car he and his friends had once dreamed of having and now it was his. Sometimes he thought he must be dreaming everything. He smiled a little bitterly to himself: well, he was a Sleeper, wasn't he?

Barney and Gemmer sat facing each other in the spartan room that Christoph and his interrogators had just vacated. Eduard had done his best to persuade them to go to the staff-hut – real food, decent coffee, comfortable chairs – but they had reluctantly declined; they needed to stay awake, to concentrate, and the interrogation room provided the right atmosphere for that.

Barney took a bite out of the prawn and mayonnaise sandwich that the vending machine had provided. The bread tasted slightly stale. He wondered about salmonella – how long it took, how painful it was, did it always kill you – and went on eating.

Gemmer took a swig of black coffee.

'We can reissue Kessler's photograph, saying she's behind Never Again. We can have them up in a day or so.'

'Yes. And flash all the agencies; put out a full alert for airports, ports, government buildings, etcetera, etcetera.'

'I'll get onto the Dutch first thing. I've got a mate at headquarters in Amsterdam. He owes me a favour.'

'The Dutch? Oh, for Pieter.' Barney sighed and scratched his head. 'I can't see there's any point in me asking anyone at home to look for a middle-aged, dark haired man who might be Jewish. But I'll see someone gives Special Branch a call.'

'I'll see what our Profile system comes up with for potential Sleeper types.' Gemmer sighed as well. 'We haven't got a lot to go on, have we?'

'No. How many days since Bremen?'

'Eighteen.'

'So we've got three days. Hopeless. We'll never find them in time.'

'No, it's impossible. We need a miracle.'

They both lapsed into a heavy silence. Then Gemmer said tentatively: 'Maybe we can't stop them, but maybe we could spoil it . . .'

'How?'

'Christoph said that the action would be a spectacular, didn't he? Something to wake us all up, take us by surprise. Suppose news of this plan was leaked to the media?'

Barney stared. 'What, you think a leak might really screw them?'

'Don't you? Think! They'll have been plotting for weeks! Imagine if suddenly it's announced that the security forces of Europe are onto them!'

'You could be right. Especially if whatever we leaked implied that we knew what their target was . . .'

'Brilliant!' Gemmer grinned. 'I knew I was right asking you to come over. What a team, huh?'

'Well, we don't know it'll stop them, but it's worth a try.' Barney frowned. 'I don't think we should have it generally leaked though,' he said slowly.

'No?'

'No. Not if we want it presented as if we know more than we do. We'll need some control over our leak, not the scatter-gun approach.' He looked up. 'We want a journalist eating only what we give him and being so grateful he wouldn't ask too many questions. I think a newspaper, ideally. And the rest would pick up on it and run the same story. I think that's the way to do it. Maximum coverage, and as accurate as we can hope to get it . . . Horst?'

Gemmer was leafing through the file that he had brought from Wiesbaden. He took out a few sheets of paper. 'There's a British newspaper journalist who's already done work on Never Again. He wrote about a conference in Hamburg last year . . .'

'I know that article. It's from *The Clarion*, isn't it? Said the conference was a front for a recruiting drive?'

'Ja, that's it.'

'I was going to use bits of that article for my report and hope Hargreaves hadn't read it too closely at the time. But I didn't know you lot monitored the British press so closely.'

'I confess I didn't read it at the time. It was only this evening, when I was waiting for you to arrive, that I went through everything we'd put together on the subject.' He flicked over a page. 'The journalist spoke to one of my people at the time.'

'He did?'

'The day after the conference. He was trying to get information but we honestly didn't know anything. He knew more than we did, and he wasn't saying too much. Didn't want to spoil things for his own story, I suppose.' Gemmer scanned the page. 'The officer he spoke to made a report of the call, just for our records. The journalist had asked about an American, who'd been one of the guest speakers, Ernst Zimmerman . . .'

'He wrote about him too, didn't he?'

'Ja. We ran a check on Zimmerman at the time.'

'Yeah, we did too. Nothing much, as I remember. A rabblerouser as the article said.'

'We had a couple of men go to the conference hall but it had been swept clean. Too late. He did a good job, your journalist. Very thorough and he's been interested in the subject longer than we have.'

'He has?'

Gemmer turned the page. 'We ran a check on him as well, of course, and his name first appeared on our files over a year ago. He'd been making enquiries about a series of attacks on Neo-Nazis inside Germany; asking about the possibility of a organised anti-Fascist resistance.'

Barney raised an eyebrow. 'He was ahead of us, wasn't he? You think he could be our man?'

'I think so. He's the expert on the subject.'

'You don't think he's too inquisitive, too independent-minded?'

'He's not going to have time to find out anything much, is he? It's Friday morning now. If you arrange to give him the leak tonight . . .'

'*The Clarion*'s a Sunday paper. Isn't it cutting it a bit fine?'

'Christoph said twenty-four hours after. That's Sunday night onwards. So the story coming out Sunday morning is perfect. It'll upset their plans at the very last moment.'

'All right. You don't want to give this to a German journalist?'

'Why? None of them has done as much as your man. Also, I'm quite keen for somebody else's intelligence agency to have some media attention. We've had plenty.'

'OK. I'll get things moving as soon as I get back.'

Chapter Seventeen

That evening Matt descended the stone steps to The Sorry Lettuce wine-bar in Floral Street, Covent Garden, and looked around for Steve Carrington. Not seeing him, he ordered himself a glass of Cloudy Bay Sauvignon Blanc and carried it to an empty booth at the far end of the room.

The Lettuce was a converted cellar, with sawdust on its floor, a real log fire and wooden stalls separating its tables. It was a place well-suited to dark winter nights which was presumably why, he thought glumly, the management had gone overboard with the Halloween decorations. Witches were suspended from the ceiling on broomsticks; bats and ghosts jostled on cobweb strings across the walls. On his table a turnip lantern winked at him. He had nothing against Halloween except that it reminded him that Christmas was not far off.

The Lettuce was only half-full – not a good sign at nine-thirty on a Friday night – but perfect as far as Matt was concerned. Neither too noisy nor too quiet for a nervous contact.

He took a mouthful of wine and closed his eyes to savour it. Not that Steve had sounded nervous, exactly, on the telephone. More . . . jumpy, and very keen to see him, quite insistent in fact, which was unusual. Generally speaking it was the other way round: Matt the supplicant, the beggar at the table, the one prepared to drives miles out to the pub near Heathrow and sit waiting, sometimes for up to an hour before the Special Branch man arrived.

On the phone three hours earlier, Steve had asked for a meeting the following afternoon.

'Sorry. Election duties call. I'm following the Leader of the Opposition on a tour of the capital's teaching hospitals.'

'Shit! How about tomorrow evening then? Uh, early?'

'No can do. Can't really leave the office till about nineish. But I'm going to be through quite early tonight.'

'Tonight? I, uh, don't know . . . Tomorrow's really out?'

'Yeah, I just told you. I can't guarantee any spare time tomorrow. Not unless it's really important? If you could give me a clue?'

'. . . Uh . . . I . . . OK let's do this evening. Name somewhere.'

The original 1950's juke-box began playing 'Old Devil Moon'. Matt took another gulp of wine and let the music flow over him. Cagey as hell, that's what Steve had been and verging on the desperate. Was he in some kind of trouble? About to spill the beans on police-corruption? A hush-up, a miscarriage of justice? Was he going to produce internal memos, altered statements, evidence of wrong-doing going all the way up to the top of the Met?

Matt reined in his imagination with difficulty. It had been a dull week. Apart from getting nowhere on the Never Again front, he hated being on rota and he hated politicians.

That morning he had had to interview Mrs Helen Taylor, Tory MP for the constituency of Milton Keynes West, one of the safest seats in the country, or it had been until the last twelve months. If the Opinion Polls were to be believed the Tories stood a very good chance of losing the Election in two weeks' time and Mrs Taylor was not taking the prospect well. In crisis she had seized on a scapegoat.

He could hear her voice: 'There are too many immigrants in this country, Matt. I may call you Matt?' Not waiting for his reply, she had leant forward confidentially – they had been having tea in the Commons tearoom – and put her hand on his. Close up, she had smelled of rose talcum-powder.

'Do you know there are areas in London where English is not the first language of the streets? Yes, I'm telling you the truth!' Out of the corner of his eye, Matt had seen another Tory MP, drinking orange squash at an nearby table, give them a worried look. He had felt a twinge of sympathy for the man: having Mrs Taylor on your side must be pretty nerve-racking.

'Or the classroom?' she had hissed. 'Do you know that there

are whole families of Asians working together to gain control of newsagents' shops, and little street supermarkets. You know, those dear little corner-shops? And where will they go from there, may we ask? Control of schools, education . . . It's a terrifying prospect, Matt, terrifying.'

She had only just stopped short of advocating forcible repatriation ('Financial incentives would get most of them to go home on their own. The more intransigent ones, well . . .').

She had rendered him monosyllabic. However, the piece he had written for Sunday's paper had been eloquent. He grinned; she would be furious.

'Bloody awful place to find.' Steve's voice made him jump. The policeman sat down opposite. 'I'll have a beer,' he said. 'Becks.'

Matt grinned. 'And nice to see you, too.' When he returned with the drinks, Steve swallowed half of his in one gulp. Then he eyed the journalist quizzically.

'You're a lucky bugger,' he said.

'I am?'

'Yeh. Wish I earned the money you do for sitting on my backside in a bar having your work handed to you on a plate.'

Matt's curiosity sharpened. 'OK, Steve, the suspense is killing me. What is it?'

Steve took another swallow, more slowly. 'That bloke you wrote about at that conference in Germany last year . . .'

'Zimmerman? What about him?' He sat forward. 'You've got something about Never Again? They're not finished are they? I was right!'

'Calm down. One thing at a time. Been in touch with Zimmerman have you? Lately I mean?'

'I might have been. Why?'

'I'm just interested.'

Matt set his glass down carefully on the table. It was important not to lose his temper. 'What is this, Steve? It's you who wanted to see me, remember?'

'Yeh, I've just got a couple of questions first. You been doing anything else on Never Again since we last spoke?'

'I've been keeping an eye on things.'

'And?'

'Nothing to report.'

The policeman smiled, not unpleasantly. 'But you're still interested in writing about them, I take it?'

'Naturally. If it's good enough.'

'Oh, it is. But I've got to have a few guarantees first. What I'm about to tell you, you never got from me. OK?'

'Sure.'

'It's totally unattributable.' He finished his beer. 'You're not even to tell your editor who told you. Right?'

'Right. You've made your point. I'll just say an "impeccable source close to the Security Services".'

'I'm not even sure about that.'

'Oh come on! That could mean anything.'

'I'll think about it. The other thing is, we want it to go in your last edition, and only your last edition.'

'We? Is this just Special Branch or is it a step higher? MI5 for instance?'

Steve gave him a mean look. 'You want the story or don't you?'

'All right, all right but . . .'

'These seats free?' A young woman in a black and red polka-dot dress, with a witch's pointed hat perched on top of her head, sat down next to him. 'White Christmas' started playing on the juke-box. She smiled at him.

'No,' Matt told her rudely. 'We're expecting friends.'

'Charming!' She flounced off.

He took a deep breath. 'OK, what else?'

'You're not to tell anyone about the story until tomorrow night, say an hour before your last edition goes.'

'But that's crazy! I'll have to tell the night-editor and the back-bench! They'll have to know what's coming so they can find a space.'

'You can tell them you've got something really special; you can say you can't confirm it until the last moment. I know you, Matt, you'll think of something.'

'It is good, is it? I mean, we can't change much at that time of night unless it's really worth it.'

'Have no doubts on that score.'

Matt drained his glass. 'OK, I'll play by your rules. I don't have much choice, do I?'

'No. I'll have another beer.'

In a ground floor apartment in a fashionably seedy street near Place de la Republique in Paris, a young man with blond, crew-cut hair was running through a final check-list before setting out on his journey.

'Dani, once I've parked the car, how many minutes have we got?'

'Oh, fuck it!'

Anya, always the peace-maker, tried to intervene. 'We've been through this a dozen times, Xav. You know how much time you've got.'

Xavier swung around on her. 'And we'll go through it another dozen times if I want. It's my neck out there tonight.' He turned back to Dani.

'Tell me again.' The bearded man glared. They had all been on a knife-edge since hearing that morning that the operation was to be rescheduled. Tonight instead of Sunday night. God knows why, Xavier had said. Orders were orders. End of discussion.

But Dani felt he had born the brunt of the rush. He needed peace and as much time as he wanted to perfect his work. That day there had been too little of either and far too much pressure. Dani knew that corners had been cut, risks were going to be taken. He snapped out his answer:

'You've got fourteen, maybe seventeen minutes, but fourteen to be on the safe side.'

'And I should get to you, walking at a moderate pace, by what time?'

'Eight minutes past midnight,' Dani said sulkily.

'When do we get back here?'

'Thirty-nine minutes past midnight.'

He anticipated Xavier's next question: 'Driving at normal speed and allowing for two delays on the lights.'

'How long d'you give me if I fail to show?'

'An extra four minutes past the allotted time.'

'Unless?' Xavier's voice was inexorable.

Dani shot him a looked of pure hatred. 'Unless I hear a big fucking bang . . . unless the thing goes off prematurely. Which it won't. I don't make fucking duds, even when I've been working around the clock.'

Xavier said nothing. He turned to Anya, sitting at the table beside him. She had her exercise book open before her, like a child doing her homework. He saw that she had bitten her nails down to the quicks and remembered how much she hated being on her own during an operation. Now, however, was not the time for pity.

'When d'you call Agence-Presse?' he demanded.

Anya slowly tucked a piece of her dark hair behind her ear before answering. Xavier knew it was to give herself sufficient time to control her voice, but it still quavered slightly. 'Fifteen minutes after you both leave, I go to the telephone booth at Père Lachaise to phone the warning.'

'And if it's occupied?'

Anya stared at him.

He ground his voice down a notch. 'If it's occupied, I said?'

'There's a bank of six booths, five of which were working this evening at seven o'clock. If all are in use, there are four more within half a kilometre.'

'How long will the warning take to deliver?'

'Twenty-six seconds.'

Xavier stared down at the table. It had a blue-and-white checked cloth on it and a small glass vase of white flowers. Pretty, he thought, momentarily distracted.

Whoever owned this apartment cared for it, or had such touches been done for their benefit, for the Cause?

Behind him, the fridge rattled and for a moment he was back in another kitchen, in another city not so long ago, watching Anya try to comfort the blonde British girl who looked like she'd lost her mind.

He pushed himself to his feet, checked the pocket of his denim jacket for the Peugeot's keys and said: 'Right, let's get going.'

Zoe had spent the evening watching Alasdair and Kerry

being in love, not in an exclusive or embarrassing way but unobtrusively, as if they were hardly aware of it themselves. When they smiled at each other they seemed to be having a secret conversation; they finished each other's sentences and when they touched there was an element of making sure the other one was real.

Zoe glanced over at them, sitting together on the sofa, watching TV, looking supremely comfortable and relaxed. 'They fit,' she thought, 'without even trying. I wonder if I'll ever have that.'

They had prepared the most wonderful supper for her, not even pretending to have cooked it themselves, but proudly displaying the white cardboard boxes Kerry had bought from Soho delicatessens during her lunchtime. Carpacchio to start with, fresh pasta with a spicy seafood sauce, and a mouth-watering French apple tart.

Zoe, who had arrived tense, expecting questions, relaxed and began to enjoy herself. Happiness, she remembered hearing, was contagious and certainly she had never seen Alasdair so happy.

'Every scrap's got to be eaten,' he warned, ladling out the fresh tagliarini from the pan of boiling water. 'Or else Kerry sleepwalks in the night and I find her with her head in the fridge.'

'Al, don't be mean! Just because you've got a tapeworm in your intestines! I think thinness must be a family trait. Look at you, Zoe, you're tiny. How d'you do it?'

After eating, they had all moved into the sitting room to watch the Friday evening movie, *The Godfather Part II*.

Zoe watched the screen, the violence that so quickly became acceptable, and let her mind roam. This flat was no longer her home; no longer the haven that it had once been. She was an impostor here, as she was everywhere.

She caught Alasdair's eye and returned his smile, but she was thinking: 'If he knew what you were, what you've done . . . he wouldn't believe it. He'd never feel the same about you again . . . His kid sister, part of a killing team. Little Zoe, the Sleeper, waiting for her orders . . . whatever they might be.' She shuddered.

'Are you cold?' Alasdair asked. 'I can turn up the central heating.'

'No, no, I'm fine.' I joined Never Again, she continued to herself, to stop the Nazis. Remember what they're like; remember what they did to the Jews; remember those poor people in the hostel. I'm lucky to be part of the Resistance . . . She saw the room in Turin, but shut her mind to it . . . It's an honour to have been chosen. It's what I wanted, to belong to people who felt the same way.

'But I'm more of an outsider now,' she thought, 'than ever before. I can't belong to anyone, not even my brother. I can't even tell the truth. Everything is one lie after another and I'm getting further and further away from everyone.'

When the film finished at ten-thirty, Alasdair yawned and stretched, dislodging Kerry from his shoulder. 'I'd better be taking you home Zo, unless you've changed your mind about staying. You're more than welcome to.'

Kerry uncurled herself from the cushions and smiled. 'Do, Zoe. We could go shopping in the High Street and have lunch at that Greasy Spoon we told you about.'

Zoe was suddenly tempted by the prospect. To go to sleep in her old room; to hear other people's voices in the morning and sit around in the kitchen at breakfast, rather than facing the clocks and news bulletins at home.

That evening, as she had dressed to come here, she had watched the seven o'clock news on Channel Four and, counting back, realised it was nineteen days since the last attack. Surely after all this time, with no attacks, no statements, it must mean . . .

Kerry and Alasdair were both looking at her, waiting for her answer. Staying with them would be just a pretence, she thought. The sort of thing that normal people did. For her, at best, it would be a few hours relief, at worst an awful reminder of everything she had lost.

She smiled. 'No honestly, I've got to get back tonight.'

Xavier indicated right onto the Boulevard St Martin and checked his rear-view mirror; Dani was still behind him in the white Fiat. In one minute's time they would be parting company: Dani to drive to the little side-street by the choir-school and Xavier to continue to his destination outside the offices of the Government Immigration Department.

He felt coldly calm. He was quite well aware of the impact that the explosives stuck to the chassis of the car would make on his body. There would be nothing left of him, bits and pieces of flesh and clothing, that was all. They would have to use dental records to identify him. It made him a cautious driver, but even as he carefully changed up a gear on the nearly empty road, he thought that it would not be too bad a way to go. He would know nothing about it, for sure.

He thanked God he was always like this during a mission: clear-headed and methodical. Afterwards, he could let rip. He remembered the last time, in Turin, with Zoe . . .

His eyes flickered to the digital clock above the radio. Fifteen minutes and ten seconds since he and Dani had left the apartment. Anya should be on her way to the phone booths by now.

The road up ahead was getting busier with people and cars, and there were shops with Christmas window displays on either side: reindeers and plastic Santas. 'Gross,' Xavier said to himself. He knew the route by heart. After the Elf service station on his left, there were two more turnings before the one-way street. The second was coming up now. He checked his mirror again and it was then that he saw the police car slip out from the side of the road and tuck in behind him . . .

Matt was driving home, with the radio tuned to a London station that he was not really listening to. In his head, he was writing the story that Steve had given him and, as always with a really good story, the words were tumbling over each other in their rush to make it on to the page.

European intelligence agencies convinced that Never Again would commit a major terrorist attack on a soft target within twenty-four hours of Sunday night.

Absolutely perfect bloody timing for a Sunday paper.

Matt grinned. He could see Lomax's face; even clearer, he could see the story on the front page, with a big 'Exclusive' on it. It might be the splash, it depended on the Election

news, but if not it would most definitely be second lead.
Brilliant.

Steve had been cocky, difficult to take at times, but in the
end most forthcoming.

All ports and airports on maximum security, with extra
armed police to be drafted in and the possibility of army patrols
around the perimeters. The security status at government
buildings to be upped from Special Black to Amber ('and
that hasn't happened,' Steve had told him, 'for the past
three years'). The alert to be Europe-wide; delays should
be expected at all border crossings and points of entry.

He had asked to take notes and Steve had said: 'You'd
better had. We want you to get it right.'

That 'we' again, Matt had thought. Everyone knew that
Special Branch were used as MI5's messenger boys.

He was aware that he was being used, too, but so what, he
thought, if he got fed stuff like this? Besides, he had always
wanted an MI5 contact; perhaps if he played this one correctly,
they would feed him more.

'It's important to use the word "Spectacular", got that?'
Steve had said.

'Why? It's one of their codewords, isn't it?'

'No comment.'

Which meant it was.

Matt wound down his window slightly to give himself a little
air. Cold hard spikes of rain hurt his face and he shut it again
quickly. He had not noticed it had started raining; he switched
on the car's wipers.

'What d'you mean "soft target"? Shopping centre? Political
headquarters? Or what?'

'Just "soft target" will do.'

'But you know more than that, don't you?'

Steve had shrugged and drank his beer.

It was clear that the information had come from an insider.
A mole; someone who had turned or been offered a deal
against prosecution. He could check at the office in the
morning but he was fairly certain there had been no recent
arrests. Maybe the tip had come from an undercover cop?

Matt stopped at the lights leading out onto the A3 from

Wandsworth. The rain was increasing, drumming on his roof and making visibility difficult. He switched his windscreen wipers up a notch.

He was meant to be going undercover himself again on Monday night – a group up in Camden. But if Never Again did make their comeback, he would be too busy following it up. He wondered where the hit would take place – Steve had not told him – but one of the European capitals seemed most likely for maximum attention.

On the radio, the music had been replaced by a phone-in. A man with a grating voice said he had a question for the legal expert.

'I'm calling from my front room at 35 Albemarle Street, Hendon, North London. For the third time this year my West Indian brethren in the dark-brown chocolate house opposite are having a "Gathering" . . . I expect you can hear them. All that chanting and banging tambourines!

'What I want to know is, what can we, as white British citizens who want to watch the telly of a Friday night, do about it? The police won't do anything . . .'

Matt pressed another button. Sometimes it seemed that racism was everywhere; first that awful Taylor woman, now this. No wonder people got frustrated; no wonder Never Again had come into existence.

The A3 opened up in front of him. It was virtually empty and with a brief glance in his rear-view mirror, he put his foot down. He already had six points on his licence, but he knew where the speed-cameras were and he was feeling lucky that night.

Xavier felt the blood pounding in his head. He fought with the desire to slam his foot hard down on the gas and get out of here, away from the trailing police car.

It had been there for a minute, just cruising. He could discern two shadows in the front seats, one of them talking into a radio. He kept driving at the same speed, his hands clammy on the little steering wheel. It had started to rain; he fumbled for the lever for the front windscreen wiper but turned off his lights instead. He moaned out loud: Why didn't they pull him over? Why this torture? The rational part of his brain said, 'They can't know. If they did they'd have you. And there'd be more of them – van-loads of shooters. But maybe this is the only marked car?'

In fear he gazed at the other vehicles on the road: a grey Citroen pulled out of a street ahead and there was a van a couple of car-lengths ahead of him. A van! He was going to be boxed in, made to sit in this time-bomb until the last moment came ...

Sweat trickled down into his eyes. 'No, no,' he calmed himself. 'They wouldn't take the risk. Not if they know what this baby's got strapped to her.'

He checked his mirror again and in that second the police light came on, throwing out its beam lazily, it seemed, as if mocking him. He pulled into the side of the road. In his wing mirror he saw one man get out, slowly, zip up his jacket a bit higher, and begin to walk towards him.

Xavier ran his tongue over his dry lips. He had his gun in the glove compartment; shoot a cop, why not? But there were two of them and the other one would get him.

'Excusez-moi, monsieur?' The cop's face was beside his own; only the window separated them.

He stared at the policeman: a big face with big features, mouth, teeth and eyes. One of those busy dark moustaches that had a lot of white hairs in it. Bored-looking eyes, not eyes that knew they were a few centimetres away from death.

'Monsieur,' the cop tapped again. He was getting wet out there in the rain. A car passed, soaking him. 'Merde,' he said in mild disgust.

Xavier rolled down his window, putting on his best smile.

'Officer?' He saw that the man had one hand on his holster, but it looked as if it was more a gesture of habit – what one did when talking to the public – than intended threat. 'Papers,' the policeman demanded.

They were perfect. They gave his name as Jules Baudelot, aged twenty-six, an aeroplane engineer from Toulouse. Xavier handed the documents over. The policeman flicked through them, taking his time. 'This your vehicle?' he asked, looking at Xavier, then the bonnet of the car, back to Xavier.

'Yes, officer.' Bought cash, three days before from a pretty housewife in Reims. The car was registered under Xavier's false name.

'You're driving slowly,' the man said. 'Something wrong?'

Christ, no. Just leave me alone. There's no time for this. 'No, officer. I haven't driven the car before at night. I'm not used to it, that's all. Keep using the wrong levers, as you saw!'

'So you're just being careful?'

'That's right. It cost me a lot of money.'

The policeman eyed him consideringly. Xavier saw that he was wondering whether to believe him or not; and, even if he did, whether he was worth playing with a little more.

Whole seconds passed. The rain got heavier. Xavier hung on to his helpful expression, but his mind was screaming: 'This is taking too long. Much too long! There's only four minutes leeway!' From a church nearby he thought he heard a bell start to toll the hour.

The policeman's radio crackled into life. Xavier stopped breathing. He heard a garble and then 'Assistance required' quite clearly. The officer grunted in annoyance.

'Here.' He thrust Xavier's papers back at him. 'Count yourself lucky tonight.'

After Steve Carrington had left the wine bar he had caught a taxi to the address he had been given, a dismal looking place beside Vauxhall railway station.

As he paid the driver, he wondered briefly why the M15 man he was going to meet did not have an office in the fancy yellow building opposite – the place that had taken how many millions of pounds of public money to build? – then made a face. 'Mine is not to reason why,' he thought moodily.

He had not enjoyed the evening. He did not like to be used as a errand boy – not so obviously, not to the press. He liked Matt Anderson well enough; they had traded information over the years, but he had always been the one in control, quite well aware of how much he told the journalist. Anderson had been his contact, his property, but no longer.

That afternoon his boss had called him into his office, told him the script and how he was to play it with Anderson, and no more. No explanation, no background briefing, just do as he was told and make a good job of it.

Now, at eleven o'clock on a Friday night, he had to report in, like a bloody schoolboy.

The building was worse inside. Linoleum peeling back from the floor; dirty yellow walls and the fusty smell of a building never properly aired.

An old man, dressed in a dark blue uniform, appeared slowly from behind the reception desk and raised his eyebrows for his ID. He had a deep bronchial cough and an unhealthy pallor to his skin.

He sniffed over Steve's pass and dialled a number on his mobile phone. The gadget looked far too good for its surroundings.

'You can go up. Third floor. Someone'll be waiting for you.'

He was greeted by a curly-haired, cheerful young man with a genuine smile. 'Hi, I'm Martin Gregson. One of Mr Turl's team. We're just along here in the Director's office. Filthy night, isn't it?'.

He steered Steve left and along a corridor. On either side were walls of dirty green cloth-board and ribbed glass. It was vast, Steve realised, and all open-plan. He had imagined the Secret Service working in dark cubby-holes. In spite of the hour, lights were on everywhere. At the end of one partition a grey-haired man stood by a photocopier, slapping down sheets of paper on the platen glass, and thumping at buttons. He yawned with deliberate disinterest as they passed.

'It's in here.'

The room he was shown into was wood-panelled with a dark green carpet. It was dominated by a large mahogany desk over which hung a dusty chandelier. Behind it sat a woman, with a portrait of the Queen behind her head.

A man who had been sitting three quarters turned to the door, stood up.

'Carrington? I'm Turl. How'd it go?'

There was a rumble from the woman. 'Lavinia Hargreaves, our director,' Gregson said hastily.

The woman inclined her head and the light from the chandelier caught her glasses. Steve could not easily judge her age, around the mid-forties he guessed. 'Do sit down,' she said wearily as if he was cluttering up the place.

Turl tried again. 'He liked the exclusive did he?'

'Oh yes, sir. He lapped it up.' Turl, he saw, looked absolutely exhausted, his face drained of colour and great dark bags under his eyes.

'He didn't ask anything awkward? Too many questions?'

'Hardly at all, sir.'

'I don't suppose he gave anything away himself?'

'No, he was acting cagey, but I don't think he's got anything new.'

The woman cleared her throat again. 'He's to be trusted, I presume? He won't try selling the story to another paper?'

Steve turned to her. It was impossible to look her in the eyes and she appeared to be staring at the door behind his head. She had a hair-do, he thought, rather than a style: carefully folded brown waves leading back from a high forehead. 'No, uh, ma'am. I really don't think so. I've known him for a good while . . .'

'If anyone can be said to ever really know a reporter.' She parted her lips in a thin smile.

'I do think he can be trusted.' Steve was surprised at how firm he sounded; he had not expected to be defending Anderson. 'He's a staff-man on the *Clarion*. He's not going to sell it to anyone. It wouldn't be in his interest to; he wants the story for himself. He wants his name on it.'

She raised her chin and looked at the door. 'It's such a shame that he had to be told tonight,' she murmured.

Steve heard Turl's intake of breath. 'It was unavoidable,' he said briskly, 'as we know.' To Steve he added: 'There was no problem about not using it till the last edition?'

'No, he didn't comment on it.'

'But you're sure he got that message? Loud and clear?'

'Very. Besides, when I've dealt with him before on a big story, he's always held it back till the last edition.'

'Oh?'

'Yes, sir. To make sure the rival papers don't steal it. Seems they do, sir, with the earlier editions. The ones that come out at nine on Saturday nights; the papers all try to steal each other's exclusives.'

'Oh. They do?' Turl looked a little confused. 'Good. Well, that's an extra safeguard for us, isn't it? So by Sunday afternoon at the latest, whichever little commando's about to pull the trigger, will be tearing itself to shreds. Wondering who's spilled the beans, who's been talking to the cops. Thinking maybe they're going to be walking into a trap.'

'As long as they're still active, of course,' said Hargreaves. 'As long as we're not all sitting here at . . .' she peered at her wrist-watch, 'five minutes past eleven on a Friday night, wasting our time.'

There was a tense pause, then Turl said quietly: 'I truly don't believe that to be the case.'

'Yes, but you have been wrong before, haven't you?'

The temperature in the room seemed to drop several degrees. Turl stood up again. 'Anyway, Carrington, thanks for doing this little job for us. Very useful, you knowing Anderson.'

'Not at all, sir.' Steve got up to go, forgetting all hopes of finding out exactly what was going on.

'Just to let you know, matter of courtesy, seeing as he's your contact, Anderson's home and work phones are being tapped as from tonight.'

'Turl! I hardly think Carrington needs to know that!' Hargreaves looked furious.

'No, maybe not,' Turl half-turned towards her. 'But as I said, a matter of courtesy. Thanks again. Gregson will show you out.'

All the way home, Alasdair talked about Kerry. How pretty she was, how clever, how kind. Zoe's fears that, away from Kerry, he would start to ask difficult questions evaporated; all she had to do was nod and smile.

They turned into Prince of Wales Drive and passed her car. She wondered if she had been over-cautious in leaving it behind that night, thinking that even her brother, vague as he was, would be curious as to how a part-time shop assistant could afford a nearly new Golf. In Alasdair's current frame of mind, she doubted if he would have noticed.

They pulled into a space near the front door of her block.

'So this is where you live?' He craned his neck upwards.

'Yes, way up on the top floor.'

'What, the penthouse!'

'No, no,' she laughed. Her voice sounded unnatural to her and she felt her face grow hot. She fumbled with the door handle. 'I'd ask you in, but . . .'

'You'll get a good view of the Park. And these are big flats. I'd have thought they'd be pretty expensive, but you said it was cheap? You must have charmed the landlord, eh kiddo?'

He grinned at her. Unsuspicious, trusting Al. She felt terrible. She should have asked him to drop her at the end of the road but, in all this rain, that would have seemed too peculiar.

'I'd better be going. Thanks for the lift, and the meal and everything . . .'

'Oh that's OK. It was great to see you. Zo,' he darted a look at her, 'Kerry says I should . . . uh, I mean, I just wanted to know . . . What I'm trying to say is, you're all right, aren't you? You're not in any sort of trouble?'

She was sure he must be able to hear her heart thumping.

'Like . . .' She heard him gulp. 'Like . . . drugs, or . . . well, anything?'

She almost laughed out loud in relief. 'Drugs?' she echoed and saw him flinch at what he took to be mockery. She laid a hand gently on his arm. 'No, Al, I promise you. It's sweet of you to be concerned, you and Kerry, but no.'

He smiled shakily. 'Thank God. You're not annoyed at me for asking, are you? It was Kerry who said you seemed so quiet, and so difficult to get hold of, and when I thought about it, I think she's right. It's nothing I've done, is it?'

'No,' she whispered.

'I said it was probably you just growing up, becoming independent. And I know Kerry and I have been a bit exclusive. But if there's anything you'd like to tell me, you know I'm always there for you?'

She could not trust herself to speak.

'Or,' he fiddled with his gear-stick, 'if you'd be happier talking to a girl, Kerry says she'd be glad to listen.'

'No, Al, honestly. Thanks, but I'm OK.'

'She said maybe you've met someone you think I wouldn't approve of . . .?'

She gave a tiny shake of the head.

'Cos, you know I'm pretty open-minded. So long as you're happy?'

'I . . .' She gulped and opened the door, keeping her head turned away so that he could not see her face.

'I've got to go now,' she mumbled. 'Don't worry. Thanks. Bye.'

She did not cry properly until she had got inside her flat and locked all the locks on the front door, every one of them. The Banham, the chain and the sliding bolt. She needed to lock everyone out, especially anyone who loved her.

She leant against the door and let the sobs rack her, sending her sliding, inch by inch down onto the floor. She felt too wretched to move. She had left one of the windows slightly open in the sitting-room and now she lay in the darkness, listening to the sound of the wind and the rain. Above the storm came the sounds of the city: people hurrying on wet pavements, their voices carrying clearly up to her; doors slamming, cutting off welcomes; cars swishing down the road, the far-off wail of a police car or an ambulance on its way to an emergency.

Xavier indicated right. Through the rain he saw the name of the street and allowed himself a tiny smile. The Immigration office was less than a minute away now, just to the end of this road, left, and there it was.

He gave a sudden sob, startling himself. His knuckles were white on the steering wheel. If he just kept his head and kept going. That fucking cop had taken four and a half minutes and they had only allowed for four minutes leeway ('For emergencies,' Dani had said. 'In case you get a flat,' and they had both laughed) but supposing they had got it wrong, supposing it had only been three minutes, thirty seconds . . .

Xavier bit down hard on his lip to stop the tears. They had

started to threaten as soon as the cop had let him go. They were tears of relief, but inexcusable. He had lost his cool and hated himself for it: the proximity of death making a coward of him. Thank God he was on his own.

At the end of the road now and turning left. Tick, tock, tick, tock went the indicator, a reassuring, solid sound. The car was only two years old, in good working order, had to be, could not have it breaking down on the way to a job.

His breath came in short, painful pants. There it was, a small, three storied office block, quite stylish; built in the early eighties when there was still money around; enough money to build a government office in old brick to fit in with the church next door.

The road was empty except for two cars parked further up by the church. Xavier pulled over by the overhead street-light that shone its light onto the wet pavement. He was well within the radius that Dani had said was essential if the explosive was to take out the building and perhaps a sizeable bit of those either side. It was essential that it was a big blast, for the 'Spectacular'.

He resisted the urge to get out and run – just leave the car here, lights and wipers on. Who was going to notice? There was no one around; this was a business district and it was after midnight. Even if someone should come by and think it was odd – a car sitting there, engine running – and went to investigate, or even call the cops . . . In a few minutes, what would it matter?

He got out of the car, locked it and stepped back. It was white with red go-fast stripes. It looked so innocent, somehow, still shiny with polish from its recent sale. He started walking away, past the immigration office, increasing his pace, going past the church now. Although he always said it was madness to run, to show any behaviour out of the ordinary during operations, he thought now that he would start to trot – not too fast so that it could appear he was simply jogging – once he got clear of the church.

He heard a car pull up behind him and park. From the end of the street, the end where he was headed, another vehicle approached, a coach, and stopped opposite him. Standing in the shadow of the church, Xavier thought he was going to wet himself. He looked over his shoulder at the car behind him. A woman sat in the driver's seat, waiting.

'Good night, Father!' A child's high, treble voice.

Xavier's head slewed round in the direction of the church. A small boy stood on the steps, well wrapped up against the weather in a waterproof jerkin and a woolly pompom hat pulled down about his ears. Behind him the church door opened, throwing out light. The child started to run down the steps towards the parked car.

'Wait, Michel!' Xavier saw the figure of a priest emerge from the church. 'Is your mother here yet? Ah yes, all right, off you go!'

Xavier stood transfixed. Michel got into the car. Xavier saw him bouncing on the passenger seat. 'Go, go,' he whispered to the boy's mother but she seemed to be in no hurry. In despair, Xavier watched her run a tissue over the front windscreen, wiping away the mist of human breath.

He turned his head back to the church entrance. There were children spilling out everywhere, darting from behind the priest, racing each other down the steps.

Choir-practice, a service, at this time of night! Xavier jammed his fist into his mouth then turned and started to move fast along the outside of the buildings, up to the top, left into the little side-street where Dani would be waiting by the school.

He turned the corner and started to run, not caring how it looked. The threatened tears pricked at his eyes. 'Oh God forgive me, God forgive me,' he prayed as he ran.

Anya dialled the number she had memorised. Her hand was shaking but she told herself that did not matter, there was no one around to see her. She was grateful for the rain; it seemed to have kept everyone off the streets, even the gang of youths she had seen on both 'reccying' occasions. Suppose, she had thought in panic as she rode here on the Metro, they started messing around? Trying to chat her up? Flinging open the door while she was reading out the message . . .

But there was no one outside; no one even using one of the

other telephones. It was just her on her own, standing wetly in her blue reefer coat, spotlit under the booth-light.

'Agence Presse Newsdesk,' said a man's voice.

Anya shoved in the coin. She read from the script:

'This is Never Again. Code word, Battle-cry, I repeat, Battle-cry. A bomb is due to . . .'

'Shit!'

It shook her. She had not allowed for comment. It was not in the script. She paused, panicked at the loss of a second and started again, reading too quickly: 'Within the next twelve minutes, a bomb is due to detonate outside the offices of a Government Immigration building in the centre of the city. Please pass on the warning to the relevant . . .'

'Which building? There's more than one isn't there?'

She gulped. 'This isn't meant to happen,' she thought desperately. 'They're just meant to take it down, aren't they?' She started sweating; it was a trick.

'Pass on the warning to the relevant authorities!'

She slammed the phone down, pushed open the door and ran across the road to the Metro station. If a car had been coming it would have hit her but none came. She plunged down the steps.

At the bottom, a tramp swayed to his feet. 'Spare some change?'

Her brain would not work. She stopped dead.

'A bit of cash, love? It's a bad night to be outside.' The man made a lurch towards her. The touch of his hand on her sleeve galvanised her.

'No, get away from me!' She flung him off and ran for the station door.

'Bitch!' howled the tramp behind her. 'May you rot in hell!'

Dani had been listening to the car-radio. It was a rock station, specialising in his favourite Seventies music, so at first he did not realise that Xavier was late, nearly four minutes late. He checked his watch and came to with a start.

Xavier was never late; his punctuality infuriated Dani. He stared again at his watch. It was eleven minutes, forty seconds past midnight. Xavier should have been here at zero, zero, eight. It took a further three seconds for Dani's mind to accept the obvious: something had gone wrong.

'Mother of God,' he muttered. He switched off the music, felt naked in the sudden silence and switched it on again. Fear hit him in the stomach and crawled out over his skin. He wanted to retch.

If Xavier did not show in the next ten seconds, Dani had to go. He had to get back to the apartment, get Anya and run. They would not be able to take this car, or if they did they would have to dump it soon and steal another. They had to assume that if Xavier was caught, he would talk: the authorities would soon know everything: the address of the Paris apartment, their descriptions, where they came from, what they had done, car registration numbers . . .

Dani moaned. It was all over.

He knew he would never survive prison: they buggered you in there, didn't they? And the confinement, the jailers' eyes watching you, hating you; day after day of bars and locks, all those wasted years.

How long before Xavier talked?

Dani's hands gripped the steering wheel. Maybe he did not have time to go back and get Anya. They treated women better in prison, he was sure that he had read that somewhere. He glanced at his watch again and saw that his whole body was shaking. Thirteen minutes ten seconds past midnight. No question now. He started the engine and checked the rear-view mirror.

A man was running towards him. It looked like Xavier, ran like him and was wearing the same clothes, but could hardly be him. Xavier was always so fussy about looking as if you were just out for a stroll, acting normally. Who was it, then? Terror gripped Dani. He whimpered: who was running towards him out of this dark night? He slammed the car into gear but it was already too late. The man had reached him and was wrenching open the passenger door. A body landed with a thump beside him.

'Get the fuck out of here!' Xavier's voice, high-pitched. He never sounded like that, like he was afraid.

Dani stared, motionless, unable to obey. Xavier's face was wet and all twisted up. His body, even, looked knotted.

Xavier shoved his face into Dani's. 'You stupid fucker!' he screamed. 'Get us out of here!'

Zoe woke up on the floor of her flat. Her neck felt stiff and her eyes were puffy. Groggily, she sat up. Something had woken her but in the fuzz of sleep she could not remember what it had been. She felt a little better; the brief sleep had done her good, had at least made her realise that she should go to bed. Sleeping on the floor was a pointless exercise, the kind of thing that only someone like Sergio would get a kick out of.

Zoe got slowly to her feet. There was a sudden bang outside, loud and cracking, like a gunshot. It was the same sound that had woken her. She froze and felt her heart thundering, then she gave herself a mental shake: it was a car back-firing, that was all. She shoved back some of the hair that had fallen into her eyes and moved towards the bedroom.

Matt had fallen asleep in front of his coal-effect gas fire. The heavy-bottomed glass tumbler that had been balancing on his leg for over an hour, woke him as he moved in his sleep, sending it shattering onto the marble-tiled surround.

He was instantly awake but disoriented. He blinked up at the mantelpiece to the brass carriage clock – a Christmas present from his mother – and saw that it was twenty minutes past one. He groaned and stretched; he was stiff, his head felt groggy and he had an early start in the morning.

It had been fatal to sit down and pour himself a whisky, but his mind had been buzzing when he had got in. Zimmerman, he had thought. Why had Steve asked him about Zimmerman? And why hadn't he picked him up on it at the time? What had Zimmerman been up to that had made the British security services suddenly interested in him? Did he have something to do with this 'Spectacular'; was he in fact much closer to the nub of the group than Matt had realised?

Perhaps, after this, Lomax would let him go to New York and get that interview. He got up to fetch a brush and pan for the broken glass and the telephone rang.

At one twenty-five in the morning? It could only be an emergency. He snatched up the receiver.

'Anderson? It's Lomax. Did I wake you?' He sounded hopeful.

'No, I was just going to bed.'

'Burning the midnight oil, eh? You've heard the news, I s'pose?'

'No, what news?'

'Oh come on. You're the one in the know, the one who'd told me they'd be back!'

'Told you who . . .' He felt suddenly sick. Someone's leaked the story, he thought. Someone else in Special Branch with a press contact. He closed his eyes: 'Fuck it,' he said softly.

'What? What did you say? Oh, never mind, I was just calling to say go straight to the airport in the morning. First flight's about seven I think. But be there early, everyone'll be going.'

'Going where?'

'Paris, where else?'

Matt ran his fingers through his hair. He felt wild and lost as if he had woken up in the wrong place. 'Chris, what're you talking about?'

'You're telling me you really don't know? I thought you were just pissing me about.' Lomax sounded really pleased; it was not often that he held the upper hand. 'Your Never Again chums have only gone and blown up a church full of kids, that's all.'

'What!'

'Happened about an hour ago. They phoned a warning to Agence-Presse, too late of course. Latest is there's seven dead, including two Brits, but they're still counting.'

'A church?' Matt was dazed. 'Soft target,' he heard Steve saying the words. But not tonight, it was two nights too early . . .

'Yeah, real bastards eh? I'd have thought you'd have already heard. One of your famous contacts not tip you off?'

Matt was not really listening. What had Steve been up to; had he been setting him up? No, that was too ludicrous. MI5 had got it wrong, badly wrong, which meant their informant was no informant at all. What a godalmighty mess, and actually, he thought, not a bad story in itself. He opened his mouth to tell Lomax then hesitated; if he did he would be kissing goodbye to any future contact with Steve or MI5. He bit his lip; he would think about how much to say in the morning.

'You still there? Not sulking are you? I know you said they'd be back but it was only a hunch, wasn't it? And you were right. Back with a real bang, aren't they ... Oh just a minute ...'

Lomax's muffled voice conferred with the Picture Desk: 'How many snappers have we got over there? Is that all? Can we get some others fast? What d'you think, one of them at the hospital; the other at the scene? I don't think the church is as important as getting to the injured tonight. We can always get pics of the church in the morning, can't we?'

He came back to Matt. 'There's a bit more just come in. Blah, blah, aah ... "the dead children were members of English and French choirs who were making a record to raise funds for Bosnian child refugees."'

'At this time of night?'

'Yeah, weird. Oh, it explains it here. Seems it was the only time when they'd be guaranteed no traffic noise. The church was in a very busy area ... It's called the Church of the Holy Innocents by the way. What a name, eh? The death counts gone up to eight now, plus thirty-six injured.'

'Oh no,' whispered Matt, the human tragedy touching him for the first time.

'Yep. They're real charmers, your friends, aren't they? Hang on, more's just come. Aaah, according to the bomb warning, the target wasn't the church at all, but the immigration building next door ...'

'At least that makes more sense.'

'Yeah. But according to the French police, the warning was deliberately vague, as well as too late. "The despicable work of cowards" said a police spokesman. OK, so you're up for it tomorrow then?'

'Sure.' His exclusive had gone down the drain; best to salvage what he could.

'Right, off to bed for your beauty sleep then. I'll let you know if there's any other developments.'

Chapter Eighteen

Later that morning, as the first Paris shuttle of the day taxied to the end of the runway at Heathrow, Barney Turl laid his arms down on his desk, put his head on top of them and closed his eyes.

He was so tired. He had not slept for – he tried to work it out – over thirty-six hours, apart from one hour, so long ago it now seemed, when he had fallen asleep in that interrogation room in Germany. For a man his age, it was not good to do without sleep.

One of his telephones chirped and he opened an eye. It stopped after the first ring. He contemplated taking both the receivers off their hooks; they seemed to have been ringing incessantly, one after the other, sometimes both at the same time, ever since he had got back to the office at two-thirty that morning. Number Ten, the Ministry of Defence, Special Branch, Interpol, a host of counterparts across Europe who less than twenty-four hours before had been singing the praises of himself and Gemmer, were now either curt or incredulous, a few insulting.

But worse was to come, he knew. The Deputy Director General would be calling him as soon as he had been tracked down at his weekend residence.

Barney had only been home for forty-five minutes the previous night, had been chatting to Alice who had waited up for him, when the Duty Officer had called. He had scarcely replaced the receiver, had still been trying to absorb the awful news, when the phone had gone again. Hargreaves.

'I simply fail to see,' she had said towards the end of the conversation, 'how you and your German ... comrade ... were so entirely taken in by the words of a terrorist. How you could have swallowed this twenty-one day nonsense, without further interrogation, without questioning ...'

Barney had said nothing; it was easier that way. And she had paused long enough to let him know that that was an end to it. Then:

'I mean, Turl, I need hardly remind you that this is very much the Wrong Time for mistakes, need I? The Election is a mere two weeks away. If a new Government wants to be seen demonstrating its muscles, what could be better than sweeping the Service clean? We're rather handing ourselves to them on a plate, don't you think?'

Her voice had suddenly become silky and caring, making him immediately suspicious.

'You are sure, Turl, are you, that you don't want anyone else to handle this, er, little potato? A younger person whose sensibilities have not been dulled by time?'

He sighed and arranged his arms more comfortably. He could only ride out the storm.

The other phone shrilled. He opened one eye, then the other and glared at it. Then he picked it up.

'Barney? It's me. Gemmer. I can't apologise enough.'

'Apologise? What for? I was there too, remember.' Although at around four o'clock that morning, when he had been dealing with the supercilious bastard from the MOD, he had cursed Gemmer to hell and back for ever inviting him to Wiesbaden, for taking him to that bloody security compound to hear that wretched boy.

'Oh come. You don't have to be polite. No one else has. My director got to me an hour ago.'

'From his conference?'

'No, no. He's at home now. He's talking about the pride of the German people being destroyed. Being made a laughing stock. He's worried about losing his job. He hasn't thought about mine yet.' Gemmer sighed mightily. 'I've spoken to Astrid and Eduard. They got Sandsdalen out of bed and Eduard had a go at him ... Nothing too much, just a little reminder of who's boss. In case he was playing with us.'

'And?'

'They're convinced he was telling the truth, as he knew it. Absolutely convinced. When they told him about Paris he cracked up. He's under sedation. Don't know how much use he's going to be again. Probably burnt-out.'

'Oh. So it means Kessler and the men changed the ground-rules.'

'Ja. For whatever reason.'

Gemmer sounded so despondent that Barney tried to rally him. 'We shouldn't forget that feeding the story to the media was a last-ditch attempt. Paris could very well still have happened on Sunday night.'

'I know, but we were so near! And it was such a fucking massacre!' He lapsed into silence for several seconds. 'You'd already primed your journalist?'

'Oh yes.'

'Will he write an article saying British intelligence got its timing wrong?'

'I hope not.'

'Tell him it was the Germans. Give him my number.'

Barney smiled wearily. 'We're not the ones to blame, remember? Once this has blown over, they'll all be looking to us for the answers again. How're your new posters of Kessler getting along?'

'They're ready; they'll be going up today. At least after last night it'll be pretty difficult for her and her friends for a bit.'

'Yep, who knows? A good old-fashioned member of the public might save our bacon. Any news yet on that Dutchman?'

'No. I spoke to them yesterday evening and they were bad-tempered. They asked me how many Pieters I thought there were in The Netherlands. God knows what they'd say today.'

'But we're only interested in the missing ones, aren't we?'

'Are we? I've been thinking. Maybe he isn't listed missing. If he's as professional as he seems to be, he might have the kind of lifestyle that takes him out of the country a lot, gives him good camouflage.'

'Yeah, you're right.' Barney rubbed at his eyes. In front of him were the notes that he and Gemmer had made in that interrogation room, so long ago it now seemed. 'Briton, middle-aged, possibly Jewish', he read. By ten o'clock that morning he had to produce a report of some kind for

Hargreaves so that she could have something to take with her for an encounter at Number Ten. He closed his eyes: all he wanted to do was sleep.

'Horst, I'd better go. If you hear anything, let me know.'

'OK. You do the same.'

Barney shuffled through his notes. 'Sleeper', he had written in capital letters, and underlined it, then on the next line, 'Or Sleepers???'. He laid his arms on his desk, rested his head on them and closed his eyes. Just a few minutes, he promised himself, a few minutes to think . . .

The telephone rang.

'Turl,' he said groggily.

A woman's voice. 'Mr Turl, I've got the Deputy Director General on the line for you. Putting him through.'

Normally Zoe would have seen or heard the news before she set out on her Saturday morning run but she had woken up feeling shattered. Quite suddenly the effort of sitting through the litany of news items was more than she could bear.

She decided to give herself a break. Drawing back the curtains, she felt her heart lift at the sight of the clear blue sky and bright sunshine. Last night's heavy rain had gone with her mood; today everything looked different.

Quickly, she pulled on a black tracksuit and trainers, shoved her hair up into a bobble-hat and unlocked her front door. The cold hit as soon as she stepped outside, hurting her lungs. She gasped, sending out a puff of white air, and began jogging along the pavement, pausing briefly to check for traffic and then over the road, along the railings to the gate and into the park.

At this time, nine o'clock on a Saturday morning, the only other people about were dog walkers and other joggers. Zoe loped easily past two of them and felt warmer as her blood started to circulate properly.

She had always loved winter days like this: frost on the hard ground and the bare trees stark against the sky. It was the sort of day that promised good things. A boy on a bicycle went by and grinned at her. 'Morning!' he called, and she found herself grinning back. A normal thing to do, she thought and told herself, 'Well, you're a normal girl.'

'I might even,' she continued, as her feet took their usual path along by the boating-lake, 'go shopping in the King's Road.' For weeks she had bought nothing for herself except necessities. A shopping spree seemed suddenly a glorious act of rebellion against the confines of her existence. 'Buy a whole wardrobe,' said the voice inside her head. 'Winter boots and a new coat . . .'

She stopped and frowned slightly, remembering the source of her wealth. 'No,' she told herself firmly. 'I'm not going to let them spoil it. I'll only spend the money that's mine, that was in my account before . . . Or that I've earned at the bookshop.' She reached the turn and began the long run that bordered the park. 'Today's mine. They can keep out.'

Zoe did two laps of the Park, and then headed up to the newsagents on Albert Bridge Road. Not to look at the news, she told herself resolutely, but for the weekend TV. She was going to spend two days indulging herself.

There was only one other customer in the shop, an old lady in a long brown puffa-jacket and headscarf who was engaged in conversation with the newsagent.

'Dreadful, isn't it?' she was saying.

'Yes,' said the man, looking over her head and smiling encouragingly at Zoe who smiled sympathetically back.

She pulled off one red wool mitten to get her five pound note.

'Little choirboys like that,' the woman tutted. 'What were they? Nine and ten years old? Think of their poor mums and dads! And that young priest that was killed too. Shocking. Just coming out of church too.'

'Yes,' said the man again. 'Can I help you, love?' he asked Zoe.

She picked up her usual broadsheet from one pile, and then, in a fit of daring, picked up a tabloid too. 'I'll just have these,' she said.

'Ought to be strung up, they ought,' the old woman insisted. 'Murdering savages.' She sniffed loudly and picked up her own paper. 'Outrage is right,' she said, preparing finally to withdraw. She noticed Zoe and stopped. 'It's outrageous. Don't you think?'

Zoe smiled at her. 'I'm sorry?'

The woman stabbed a gnarled finger at her own paper. 'This bomb in Paris. Haven't you heard about it? It's all over the telly and everything. Two little British boys blown to bits. And some Froggies too.' She squinted sideways at the papers in Zoe's hands. 'It's there on the front page. Look!'

Zoe looked. The bombing had happened too late for it to be the lead story, but it ran, nevertheless, on the far panel of the front page. The story's headline made up for the lack of column inches: 'BRITISH CHILDREN SLAUGHTERED IN "NEVER AGAIN" OUTRAGE'.

The colour drained from Zoe's face. She stood staring and staring at the page. The day had not prepared her for this. It was a terrible trick.

The old woman looked triumphant. She clicked her tongue against her teeth: 'Yeah, it's shocking, isn't it? Makes your blood run cold just at the thought of it. Nothing left of the poor little mites . . .'

In the fine Viennese apartment that had been her 'home' for three weeks, Beatrix Kessler was sitting with her head slightly bowed. It gave her the appearance of listening – even of submitting to the whiplash of the man's words – while allowing her to continue her assessment of the situation.

It could not, she thought calmly, be much worse.

Axel Shiner, now ranting at her, was insane, she was convinced of it. In the course of the previous four meetings, she had watched him deteriorate from a driven man to one who craved power above all else. His moods had become increasingly erratic and his behaviour more despotic; there was no longer even the pretence of democracy amongst them.

Now it appeared he was unable to tell fact from fantasy: he genuinely seemed to have forgotten that it was he who had ordered the Paris bombing be brought forward.

'You stupid German bitch,' he hissed, passing her once more. His shoes were beginning to make a groove in the beautiful carpet; he had been pacing, on and off for hours, ever since they had heard the news.

'Don't you realise what you've done? The damage something like this will do to us?' He stopped by the marble chimney breast, staring at the carved figures of cherubs.

From under her lashes, she watched him. She was not unduly surprised at his degeneration; she had seen it before. Some people simply could not take the stress of undercover warfare: the planning, the secrecy, the constant moving, the fear of discovery, of capture or death. Andreas Baader, for instance, had displayed the same trait of blaming others for his mistakes. He too had started to believe he was someone special, rather better than the people he was supposed to be fighting for. She frowned, but at least Baader had got his hands dirty, whereas this man only played at war, letting kids die for it.

He swung round suddenly in her direction, his face contorted with rage.

'Your record, Madame Operations Commander, is fucking diabolical. Don't you think? Nine children killed. Nine little children who were singing for their brothers and sisters in Bosnia . . .' His voice broke, he let out a sob. 'Children whose lives have been snatched away because of you and your evil, twisted mind!'

She kept her head down. She was powerless, that was the worst of it. Minded day and night by professionals who never let their guard down for a minute, never stopped watching her and who never engaged in casual conversation. If she made a superhuman effort, she suspected that she could still escape. She might get to Frankfurt; she might get to her father's house, even talk to him, but her freedom, she knew, would be short-lived. Even if she disguised herself so that she did not look like her 'wanted' picture, she had no doubt that Axel would ensure the police were not far behind her.

She saw herself in her father's house, imagined him not recognising her at first and then the joy in his eyes, spreading across his face, the embrace, the return of his only much-loved child. Then the police helicopters circling; the shoot-out; the terror and bewilderment in her father's old face . . .

No, if she was to see her father again, it must not be like that. There must be no shadow at her shoulder; no fear of embroiling him in her arrest; no crazed Axel tipping off the authorities. Better that she should wait, that she should endure until she could step from the chains of her confinement and move freely once more.

Thus, bored and trapped, with only the visits of the men to break the monotony of her existence, it was no wonder, she told herself, that she was finding it so pleasant to daydream. With practice she had discovered that she could remove herself entirely from her surroundings into a dream-world.

Axel's voice rose, interrupting her. 'They'll call us murdering scum! D'you appreciate that? They'll say we planned it that way! That's what the newspapers'll say!'

There was a crash as he stumbled against a small table. She wondered why he cared so much about what newspapers said. He was like a movie-star hooked on his ratings.

'But it's not us! It's you, you murdering German bitch! You're nothing but a dried-up, barren old whore, are you? Never had kids. Too busy killing them. Gives you a kick, doesn't it?'

She entered her favourite daydream, the one where she was six years old sitting in a sunny field, making a daisy-chain. She was wearing a blue-and-white checked dress with smocking on the yoke, a beautiful dress that her mother had made her. Her mother was there too, young and happy, running towards her, arms outstretched . . .

Axel intruded again: 'Coming so soon after your last notable success, those two little girls, those babies in Madrid – you must be feeling pretty pleased with yourself, eh?'

She sighed; her dream had gone and in its place, at the back of her head, a dull ache had begun. She had not slept last night, none of them had. They had heard the news on the radio, the flash at one o'clock, the fuller details half an hour later.

The voice of the reporter at the scene had been cracking with emotion: 'Teams of rescuers are at this moment attempting to lift heavy masonry with their bare hands. The air is filled with sirens . . . the cries of the injured . . . the screams of children . . .'

She had left the room, knowing it was not good to dwell on such things. One had to keep going.

Axel's response had been disbelief, then fury and the apportioning of blame. He had followed her into the kitchen, roaring at her, as she had made herself a drink.

Leon, whom she scarcely noticed these days except as Axel's occasional echo, had run to the bathroom and thrown up.

Some time later – she had slightly lost track of time – Pieter had arrived, white-faced and exhausted. He had been in contact with the commando, he had said. There was an important matter that required the Leadership's immediate attention.

'Later,' Axel had snarled. 'I've a few things to get clear first.'

That had been some while ago. It was eleven o'clock in the morning now. Remembering Pieter, she looked around for him. He was sitting on a chair near the window, his elbows on his knees, his face in his hands. His eyes were glazed; he looked exhausted, almost beaten. She frowned: Pieter truly believed in the Cause, or had done when she had first met him the year before. He was an intelligent man, a psychiatrist – how had he got mixed up with those two?

'We paid a lot of money for you, bitch,' Axel said softly, suddenly close to her ear. 'For all your so-called "experience" in the field. We didn't expect to get shoddy goods. We'd send you back but we don't know anyone who'd take you.'

From the sofa behind her came a titter: Leon, Axel's squeaky toy.

Pieter suddenly rose to his feet. 'I really must ask that you listen to me,' he said loudly. Standing, he made Axel look small.

'I told you to wait!'

'There isn't any more time to wait.'

'All right! What is it?'

There was a blue tinge around Pieter's eyes and mouth, and he swayed very slightly on his feet. Beatrix realised that he must have driven several hours to reach them. 'The commando's cracked up.'

'That's all we need,' said Axel.

Beatrix ignored the interruption. 'All of them?' she asked fearfully. She could identify with the commandos far more easily than with their victims.

Pieter turned to her, gratefully she thought. 'Well, pretty much. The French boy who delivered the bomb is the worst. He's not making any sense. The girl was calmer by the time I left, but her boyfriend's quite a wreck.'

'They came to you?' she exclaimed.

'No, not exactly. They started running. They took their spare car and thought they'd try to get over the border into Switzerland. Then they hit a roadblock. I don't know if it was one, or only roadworks, but it freaked them out. They called their link-man and he got through to me. I wasn't that far away . . . I went to meet them.'

'That's against the rules isn't it?' Axel asked nastily. 'No contact whatsoever between yourself and operational commandos.'

Again she disregarded the interruption. 'Could you get them to a safe house?'

The Dutchman swallowed. 'There weren't any nearby, not that I could just take them to without warning. I took them back to the place I've been using and told them to stay away from the windows, not to put any lights on. But I don't know how long I can keep them there. I'm not meant to be there myself beyond today. I need to know what you want me to do. Where I should send them next.'

He appealed to her, but it was Axel who answered.

'Yes of course.' He had his back to them both, standing by the windows, hands clasped behind him. 'It is of course understandable that the Ninth Commando is feeling a little . . . what shall we say, distraught? In need of some time to themselves, to recuperate. Perhaps some expert counselling, Pieter?'

He turned round, smiling.

Pieter, taken unawares, faltered: 'I don't really feel I'm the . . . appropriate person. I'm too involved . . .'

'No, no. I didn't mean you.' Axel was shaking his head at the very idea. 'I think perhaps,' he continued slowly, 'they could do with a complete break and a completely new person to talk to . . .' He paused, then: 'Corsica, I thought.'

Beatrix stared, understanding at once. 'You mean to have them killed?'

Beside her, she heard Pieter gasp.

Axel studied the nails of his right hand, buffing them on the sleeve of his jacket. 'Oh, I think so. Yes.' He looked up: 'They're a security risk, aren't they?'

Pieter found his voice. 'Christ, they're only in shock from last night! Give them a chance.'

'What chance did they give those choirboys?'

'What?' Pieter repeated, unbelieving.

'You heard me. I hardly think those murderous little bastards deserve our pity, do you? If their bodies were to be left in a prominent place, perhaps with a message attached to them in some way, it might help restore our image. Show the world what we think of the killers of innocents. How we wash our hands of them.'

'Brilliant!' Leon sprang to his feet and came over to stand proudly by him. 'Wonderful solution!'

'I won't do it,' Beatrix said quietly.

'I beg your pardon?'

'You heard me. I won't pass the order on.' She looked Axel in the eye, and he held her gaze for a moment, then his lips twitched and he sniggered. 'She still thinks she's the only one who can get to Sergio Brunelli,' he said in a stage whisper to Leon.

The younger man giggled.

Beatrix flinched: she had never told them Sergio's last name.

'You really are becoming a bit of a liability yourself, have you thought of that?' Axel went on quietly. 'Fucking up operations. Disagreeing with Leon and me. Giving us bad advice. Bringing our organisation into disrepute. You ought to be more careful. More agreeable towards us.'

He shifted his gaze to Pieter and his voice hardened. 'If you're too squeamish to hand them over yourself, we can have someone else collect them.' He yawned widely. 'How very convenient for us that they ran to you like frightened rabbits, don't you think? Now, I really must get some sleep.'

Chapter Nineteen

Matt had voted first thing in the morning, before going to work. At the office there had been a holiday atmosphere, with all the television sets on loud and sweepstakes being held in each department.

Lomax had been impossible, demanding instant analysis of results before they had come in and insisting that everyone should stay until they had. At six, the newsroom had decamped to the local pub, leaving him still worrying away at the political team. At seven, Matt had left for home.

He took a Chinese dinner for one out of the fridge and heated it up in the microwave. In doing so, he chastised himself for acting like a slob, but that was how he felt. Settling himself in his old velvet armchair, feet up on his mother's antique chest, TV on, he thought that it had been one hell of a fortnight.

Paris had been terrible. The world's press had been there: Japanese, American of course, Russian, every European country represented. Everyone doing the same thing: interviews with shocked, unbelieving parents, too numb to notice the intrusion of the microphone or the TV camera; brief 'condition' statements from red-eyed doctors and medical teams; the scramble to get to the various press conferences on time; to think of a question that had not already been asked, an angle that had not already been taken.

He and the rest of the British press corps had stuck with the British parents, twelve sets of them, two of whom, quite inexplicably it seemed to Matt, had brought their other children. Kids ran up and down hospital corridors while parents leant on walls and wept.

There had been six choirs – four French and two English – in the process of leaving the church when the bomb went off. Apparently parents of the youngest children had expressed

concern at the lateness of the hour and the record company
had had to promise that the session would end as soon after
midnight as possible. It had been frustrating – they had
needed at least another hour which would have had to be
found another day – but they had kept their word and let the
children go on time.

The youngest of the dead had been a nine-year-old boy
from Newcastle-upon-Tyne, Mikey Fry. He had wanted to
make sure of getting the back seat on the coach. His small,
rushing body had taken the whole impact of the bomb.

Of the eight others killed, five had been under fourteen
and the last three had been waiting French parents, including
a woman whose son had also perished.

Three of the British Sunday tabloids had competed volubly,
in the hospital corridor, over the 'buy-up' of the parents of the
dead children.

One father, still waiting to hear if his son would lose his
left leg, had punched a photographer in the face.

Matt had been speaking to one couple from Leeds when
two doctors, a man and a woman, approached. Matt knew at
once by their faces. 'We're so sorry,' the female doctor said
in pretty, broken English, and burst into tears. The mother,
a young woman with soft brown hair, had started to scream
where she sat, her mouth wide open, screaming her son's
name: 'Mikey! Mikey! Mikey!'

Then Matt had gone to the church, or what remained of it,
to do a 'colour' piece. The explosion had wrecked its intended
target completely: what remained of the government building
would have to be demolished. But no one was interested in
that: it was the church that drew the crowds.

The blast had taken off the front of the old building, leaving
much of the interior intact, like a doll's house laid bare. From
behind the police lines, Matt had stood staring. Just inside
the church he could see a golden angel blowing on a trumpet,
suspended from a wire above a crib. The record company had
put it there for publicity shots for the album. The church steps
had been demolished and people had thrown flowers down on
the rubble. They made a great growing pile, along with the
other detritus: sheets of music and a child's bobble-hat.

It had been a day straight from hell. In the late afternoon, after Matt had filed everything he had, he had telephoned Steve at home. The policeman had been monosyllabic.

No, he could not explain why Never Again had acted prematurely.

No, he had nothing to say about MI5's involvement. Not that he had ever admitted they had been involved.

If Matt wanted any further information, he suggested that he call the Press Bureau.

That had been too much.

'Steve, it's me you're talking to, remember! That information you gave me must have come from an informant . . .'

'I've told you, I've got nothing more to say.'

'I could still do the story, you know. How the tip-off came too late, what a cock-up by the Security Services. It's a terrific story.'

Steve had said nothing.

'I mean, I don't want to do it,' Matt had tried again, urgently. 'I don't want to burn you, but if you won't give me any explanation . . .'

He had found himself speaking to the dialling tone.

Now he put the last forkful of chow-mein into his mouth and chewed. The prawns, he found, tasted much the same as the chicken had done, and the noodles were over-cooked. He stared at the TV screen which showed a map of Britain split up into constituencies, like a jigsaw puzzle. The presenter made a sweeping movement with his hand, like a magician, and lots of pieces went blue. Another wave, and they went red.

Maybe he should have carried out his threat and written the story. It would have been another great exclusive and it would have been a cause of major embarrassment to the government. He had been sorely tempted, but pragmatism had won out in the end.

Special Branch contacts were hard to come by and he had grown used to the little favours Steve did for him: the occasional access to the Police National Computer, ex-directory telephone numbers, the 'nudges' about a person or organisation that sometimes led to great stories . . . Better to keep Steve sweet, he had reasoned, and to have a go at him once he had returned to London.

But Steve had continued to keep himself at a distance. He was not as curt, more agreeable to the idea of a meeting, but always unable to make it that night, or tomorrow. It was difficult right now, he was so busy ... 'Let me call you,' he kept saying but of course he had not, and Matt had been left frustrated and dangling.

He had tried looking for another angle to the story for the following Sunday's paper. But as the days had gone by, the dailies seemed to have mopped everything up: the denial by the French police of incompetence over handling the warning; the dismissal by the French government that its immigration policies were racist. The sensational announcement on Sunday afternoon that the notorious terrorist Beatrix Kessler was believed to be behind Never Again was well-covered in Monday's papers. Matt had read those stories greedily. Kessler was a name he seemed always to have known. He remembered as a child watching TV footage of the aftermath of one of her bombs in Rome and hearing her described by a priest as 'Something unnatural; a she-devil'.

That she was behind Never Again; what a story!

On Tuesday, one more of the injured choirboys died and the papers were full of interviews with his parents and teachers.

By Thursday, there seemed little else to say.

Matt had called everyone he could think of – Clive Fisher, the original policeman he had spoken to in Lubeck, the newer one at Wiesbaden – but had got nowhere. If anyone knew anything they were not talking, but actually he doubted that any of them did. He had gone to another anti-fascist meeting without reading the advertisement properly and had found himself in the company of a dozen under-seventeens.

On Friday night, he had been about to admit defeat and give in to Lomax's demands that he join in the Election Special planned for that week, when the news had come in about the deaths of the Paris terrorists. Three bodies, two men and a woman, had been found on a beach near Nice by French police. They had been mutilated; their injuries carried out before they had each been shot twice in the back of the head.

Tied around their necks had been macabre notices, stating their names, ages and nationalities, along with each one's alleged role in the bombing. 'I was the evil bomb-maker'; 'I was the cold-hearted delivery-man'; 'I callously telephoned the warning too late'. Each notice added: 'No mercy was shown to them, as they showed no mercy to the innocents they slaughtered', and was signed 'Never Again'.

Never Again torturing and killing their own: it had made a good story, a page-lead. But the killings had puzzled Matt: everyone had accepted that the church had been a horrible mistake, even the French police. What would it do, he wondered, to the morale of the others in the group. Would it not make them all too scared to lift a finger in future?

He sighed and looked at the screen again. The first results were coming in, Sunderland South and Torbay, one Labour win, one Tory. The presenter seemed to be prematurely excited: there were at least another six hours to go. He supposed it was start of the countdown to the big moment.

He got up and took his plate with him into the small kitchen. The hot water tap ran cold for several minutes and he stood waiting for it to heat up.

This week, there had been no question of Matt doing anything other than the Election. He wondered if, this time, the Polls would be any more accurate than the last: they gave the Tories the victory but by a very small majority.

He finally saw steam coming from the water, rinsed his knife and fork and threw out the microwavable tray that had contained his dinner. He smiled, imagining what Louise's reaction would be if she could see him now.

Then he felt his heart lift. The one bright spot in the whole of this, and he had nearly forgotten it. Last night Louise had rung to invite him skiing for New Year.

It was the first time they had spoken since she had walked out three months before, and she had sounded nervous. She and a group of friends were renting a log cabin in the Scottish Highlands, near Aviemore. Snow was guaranteed, she had said with a high laugh. And there was a Highland Ball at

Hogmanay which she had thought might be fun to go to. Matt need not be afraid, she had added in a silence, the log cabin had lots of bedrooms, and there were plenty of other people for him to talk to . . .

'I'd love to come,' he had said and meant it. A week's skiing at New Year might even make Christmas bearable. He grinned to himself, remembering how pleased he had been to hear from Louise.

It had been an acrimonious parting, with bitterness on both sides: she accusing him as always of caring more about his job than her, of not being capable of holding a conversation that did not relate to work. He had called her spoiled and spiteful, empty-headed and a whole lot more.

But they had lived together for two years and he missed having her around. He remembered how pretty she was, and how funny she could be. Maybe she had been right; he was selfish about his work and had expected too much of her. He grinned, remembering the first time they had met, when she had been so impressed by his job.

'A journalist! How glamorous!'

He suspected that she still thought that. She had certainly taken his occasional forays into the darker side of life as sheer exhibitionism.

'I don't see why you have to talk to Crack addicts,' she would complain. 'They got themselves into the mess they're in, didn't they? Why don't you do nice stories? Interviews with famous people who've done some good?'

He smiled, forgetting the endless rows they had had; the mutual knowledge that their relationship would never work. He was certainly willing to give it another try if she was.

Since the Paris bombing, Zoe had stopped hoping. Never Again's terrible reappearance had shattered all her fragile imaginings and now she was like the mouse in the apple barrel: round and round, round and round; no way out, no way out.

Had she really joined an organisation that killed choirboys? For two days it seemed she had done nothing but read, and watch news items about the children's deaths and injuries. By

Sunday lunchtime she had had enough; her mind could not take any more and she had gone first to the gym, then to the gun-club.

Taking aim, she had remembered Sergio teaching her to shoot, drawing the swastika on the target's helmet. That was what she had to remember, she had told herself. She was fighting the Nazis, a noble underground war; Paris was just a mistake. The children, she had gulped, were as Pieter had said of the little Spanish girls, the tragic casualties of war. Innocent people always got caught up in war. She repeated the phrase so often that it became like playing a tape.

To give herself a rest from the horror, she had stopped news-watching for the rest of the week. When she had resumed, everything had been about the Election; Never Again seemed to have faded into the background.

On the TV screen now, she watched the cardboard swing-ometer inch shakily towards the Tories. It was half past midnight and a lot of the results were beginning to come in. The commentator kept interrupting the politicians in the studio with the latest result from Mid-Staffordshire or Renfrew West and Inverclyde. Zoe gave a little cheer when her parents' constituency voted again for the Liberal Democrats. It might not mean anything in the great picture of things, she thought, but at least it was a poke in the eye for the Tories.

She was finding the Election quite gripping. She had got home from the gun-club at ten, switched on the TV, and been hooked to it ever since. It was such a welcome change for her to be engrossed in something that she had not noticed the time pass.

Since Paris, she had determined to take each day as it came. She had increased her daily exercise routine still further, doubling the length of her morning run; spending twice as long at the gym and the gun-club. This last had elicited tart comment from the coach that she must be in secret training for something, a competition perhaps? 'Or maybe you're planning an armed robbery, or a revolution, is that it, Zoe? You're going to lead the uprising, huh?'

He had been standing behind her when he had said it so he had not seen the terror cross her face. By the time she had turned around, she had managed to banish it, assuming an exasperated look instead. 'Damn, and I thought I hid it so well.'

She had become quite an adept liar. At work on Monday a new boy had started, a part-timer like herself, a student trying to earn cash on the side. Edwin was studying Russian and Economics at one of the south London universities that had once been a polytechnic. It had not taken him long to reveal his political views: extreme right-wing.

'Take the Russians. They've had the Communists, they know it doesn't work. They think right and they're going to be the biggest consumer market in Europe in the next five years. That's why I'm doing the language. It's going to pay to speak Russian, you'll see.'

He and Zoe had been stacking stock in the back of the shop. 'Oh yes,' she had said in a bored voice but it had been enough to keep Edwin talking:

'Yeah, my family's lived in Poplar for years. But d'you know my sister and her kid's been told they can't have a council flat 'cos the Asians need it? The Asians get everything round our way. They're taking over.' He had paused to wipe his nose on his sleeve. 'They don't smell like me and you, you know. It's all the muck they eat. Makes them stink.'

It had come as no surprise when Edwin had told her that his whole family, himself included, had voted for the successful UK Nationalist candidate at the last by-election. 'We're on the way now,' he told her. 'You see what happens Thursday. Once we're in power, we'll get these niggers out.'

She had kept her expression neutral, maybe too neutral for Edwin had suddenly gripped her arm. 'You feel the same way, don't you, love? I can tell. Wanna come to one of our meetings? Quite a lot of girls come. I can take you.' He had misread her stunned look. 'It's nothing grand, don't worry. Just ordinary people who feel the same way we do. Tell you what, think it over and let me know.'

Zoe dipped her hand into a large bag of New York Cheddar crisps. Edwin's why you're in Never Again, she thought; Edwin and all the people out there like him.

'We have four results coming in now,' said the presenter

sounding a trifle panicked. 'I'll read them out and we'll go back to the counts later. They are as follows: Esher, a Conservative win; Stoke on Trent North, Labour; Blaby, a Liberal Democrat victory and Deptford in Lewisham, UK Nationalist party . . .'

Zoe stared at the screen. The presenter stared at the auto-cue but it gave him no further information. 'My goodness,' he extemporised desperately. 'That's the first seat that the UKN has won. This is history in the making . . .' He halted, clearly unsure of how to proceed. Someone fed him a few lines. 'The UKN have, as we said earlier, eleven candidates across the country, but so far none of them has got more than nine per cent of the vote . . .

'But in Deptford tonight they have a narrow majority of forty-six votes over Labour. To discuss, briefly, what this means to the country as a whole, let's ask one of our guests here with us tonight . . . ah, the former Home Secretary, first I think . . .'

Zoe went on staring at the screen, watching the politician's mouth move. Edwin and his ilk were right: the Fascist nightmare was going to come to Britain. They would hound and terrorise people from their homes and jobs; drive them out into the streets; put them in lorries and drive them away into a forest and no one would ever see them again. No one would ask any questions so long as the problem was solved . . .

Zoe had a feeling her time was running out. She wondered when her wake-up call would come.

The following morning, two hours into his shift, Kevin Monk saw the red light flashing on the telephone beside the consul. He took off his headphones and picked it up.

'What's the latest on your subject?' a brisk voice asked.

'Not a lot,' said Kevin. He was the son of a postman from Doncaster and he had never imagined that working for MI5 could be so boring.

'He had a call from his mum first thing about Christmas. "Firming it up," she said. He's not very enthusiastic about going. He's had one call on his answerphone about five minutes ago from someone on the list. Clive Fisher. Wanted to get together for a drink when the subject could spare the time. "Drown our sorrows about last night", he said. He meant the Election, I think.'

'Oh? I'd never have guessed, Monk. Keep at it.'

Personally, Barney had no politics. He had seen too much of too many politicians' private lives to have any respect for them. But even he had to admit that last night's Election had produced a very interesting result.

It was very nearly a hung Parliament. The Tories had lost a staggering amount of seats, giving them their slenderest ever hold upon the country: 327 to 323, a working majority of just four.

The other sensation, of far more immediate concern to him, was the success of the UK Nationalist Party. They had won four seats: two in London, one in Birmingham and one in Sheffield. Everyone was talking about it: even Alice had said at breakfast this morning: 'It's like the Nazis getting in, isn't it?', and there had been more of the same from the commuters on the train.

There had already been disturbances in Hackney and Poplar. Minority groups were frightened and angry and the new Government needed to act swiftly to calm fears and forestall further unrest. That meant that there needed to be instant, accurate information on all extremists, both at home and abroad; anyone or any group that might seize upon the uncertainty and seek to use it for their own ends.

Barney's department, like all others in the Service that day, was working flat out. He had allocated a group to each of his six staff – Gregson had Never Again – while he himself got on with the task of incorporating all the information into a report that had to be completed by that evening.

He was also looking at the detailed security reports on the four new UKN MPs that had been sent to him from across the road. Two of them had links with the Far Right in France and Italy and the campaign of a third had been at least partly funded by a group of white supremacists in the States.

'Lovely bunch,' Barney muttered, then, remembering that the dictating machine was on, added: 'Delete that, please.'

Never Again would have a field-day with this lot, he thought. The run-up to the Election had temporarily halted his progress on that front and he had to admit it had come as something of a relief – chiefly because there had been so little progress.

He and Gemmer had been in contact every two or three days since Paris, but their efforts had brought little reward. The Dutch had forwarded a list and photographs of missing 'Pieters' to Wiesbaden; Gemmer had in turn shown them to Christoph, but the boy had not recovered from Paris or Eduard's beating. He had stared dumbly at photographs and started to shake; when pushed he had become hysterical and had had to be sedated again.

Since Kessler's picture had gone up, along with a reward of 100,000 deutschmarks, there had been hundreds of alleged sightings across Europe. None of them so far had amounted to anything.

Regarding Zimmerman, Barney had had a Special Branch man contact an opposite number in the New York Police department. He himself had called a friend in the Criminal Intelligence Bureau in New York and the result of both calls had been a 'friendly' visit to Zimmerman. The man had been hostile in the extreme and very unhelpful. When pressed about his Never Again connections, he had pleaded the Fifth Amendment.

Barney sighed and stretched. His shoulders hurt from sitting all morning hunched over the dictating machine, but he had a sense of achievement that had been singularly lacking since Paris. He had tried to point out to Hargreaves that the Sleeper information should not be overlooked but she, perhaps understandably had been dismissive.

'And this "tip off" comes from the same source as the twenty-one day delay, does it?' she had said with a smile.

'Yes, but . . .'

'Thank you, Turl. File it or whatever you do with such, ah . . . hot tips. Now, we're all busy people . . .'

It was just after three-thirty. He finished giving his opinion on the American supremacist organisation, stopped the machine and took the tape through into his outer office where his secretary sat. 'Any messages for me?'

'Nothing urgent.' Mrs Harris had been with Barney for fifteen years. She did not look up; her fingers kept flying over the keyboard. 'The Director's office has called about six times to change the time of the meeting this afternoon. They've just put it back again to five-thirty, so you've got time to get yourself something to eat.'

She did glance up then and saw Barney standing in his doorway with the tape. 'Chuck it over,' she said, and caught it deftly. She checked her memo pad. 'Oh, Martin Gregson called about half an hour ago. Said he'd like a quick chat when you've got a moment.'

'Oh? I'll give him a call.'

Gregson was eager for what he called a 'face to facer'. He arrived, slightly out of breath, within a couple of minutes and sank gratefully into a chair.

'Thanks, Chief. Didn't want to say anything over the phone. Just in case.'

Gregson was still young enough to enjoy the cloak-and-dagger aspects of the Service. Barney smiled encouragingly.

'It's about?'

'Matt.'

'Mat?'

'Anderson, the journalist.'

'Oh him. I'd forgotten about him. What's he been up to?'

'The listener gave me a call just before three. I don't know how important it is, but Anderson's got lucky-ish with Zimmerman.'

Barney sat up. 'He has? He spoke to him?'

'Yep, he did.' Gregson looked down at the note-pad he had brought. 'Anderson called Zimmerman's secretary and said he was doing an article – which he is, by the way – on how the UKN victories are going to affect Anti-Fascist Extremists in the UK and Europe. Asked if Zimmerman would like to relay a message through *The Clarion* to the British anti-fascists.

'That got Zimmerman on the line pretty quickly. He ranted a lot about Britain showing its true colours at last, anti-semitic and racist, etcetera. Then he said, and I wrote this down word for word, "At least there's one of you lousy Limeys on our side."'

Barney came upright with a jerk. 'What else?' he demanded.

'Anderson just said "Yes?" and Zimmerman said: "Yeah, he's rich. He's a financier and he's got powerful friends. *Real* powerful."'

'Powerful friends,' Barney repeated, savouring the phrase like a sweet. 'Any more?'

'No, 'fraid not. Zimmerman suddenly seemed to remember who he was talking to and put the phone down.' Gregson looked up. 'They're transcribing it now and sending it over, but that was all there was of real interest.'

Barney frowned into space. 'Rich, powerful financier,' he lingered over each word, then sighed deeply. 'But where does it get us? What would you say, Gregson, if I told you to run a security check on every rich financier with powerful friends?'

Gregson looked suddenly wary.

'It's all right. I'm not about to. Thanks for telling me about it anyway. We'll add it to the file.'

Matt was enjoying himself. He had been given a thousand-word slot to fill for Sunday's paper and Zimmerman's quotes had been wonderful: 'Perfidious Albion!'; 'May your rivers run red with the blood of your treacherous politicians'; 'Act now! All across Europe your brothers and sisters are waiting for you to light the flame, the flame of the purifying fire!'

Matt paused, considering this last one. Perhaps it was a bit strong? Might it not be said that it was inciting racial violence? He decided to leave it in anyway. The lawyers could always take it out.

He had had the idea of calling Zimmerman that morning on the way to work; of torturing him with the Election results, just to see what he might let slip . . . and it had worked like a charm.

Matt came to what he thought was the juiciest morsel of all: Zimmerman's tantalising reference to a British 'financier'. What a story! Never Again given financial backing by a British . . . Matt stopped again, staring at his screen.

By a British what? A British man who was rich and had powerful friends. It was not that much to go on. Had

Zimmerman meant to say that this financier was a Never Again backer or merely that he sympathised with the cause?

Matt checked his shorthand again, but it afforded nothing more. He decided to run a speculative story under a separate heading: 'British backer for Never Again?'

'This'll set the cat among the pigeons,' he said to himself as he started typing away.

Chapter Twenty

Twelve days later, in a discreetly luxurious New York hotel close to Central Park, 'Dreams of America' was holding an emergency meeting.

At first sight the term 'Emergency' might seem too melodramatic: none of those present in the fifth floor conference suite looked distraught. Over the previous year, in the course of three meetings, the seven financiers of Never Again had come to know each other a little. Likings had sprung up, mutual respect, and a certain amount of trust. They exchanged pleasantries about health, courteously poured out coffee and tea for each other and passed the little plates of biscuits down the length of the polished table.

However, the fact that they were there at all, on the very day before Thanksgiving, was proof enough of the crisis. The financiers were feeling extremely nervous.

The eighth person present, who should have been feeling the most nervous of all, was enjoying himself immensely.

Axel Shiner smirked as the old Englishman in his three-piece suit, with the pink, surprisingly boyish face and tuft of white hair, stumbled through his apology.

'I assure you all that yesterday was really the first time I could get away without arousing suspicion. After a General Election, someone in my position is expected to attend the first meeting of the new Parliament to see the new faces . . .'

'Yes, yes, it's tradition, of course. We understand,' smiled the Spanish landowner whose father and grandfather had been executed by Franco's blackshirts.

'May we congratulate you on retaining your position?' put in the Frenchman of gypsy descent whose software package had made him a fortune.

The English politician blushed. 'Thank you, most kind. And, ah, because of my, ah, special relationship with a certain member of the Cabinet, who also fortunately retained his seat . . .'

'By some bloody miracle,' Axel interposed.

The Member of Parliament looked discomfited. 'Yes, well, um, I was called upon by him to be present, to give advice in a number of matters, over a number of days. Some policies, new directives . . . and I really could not absent myself without arousing certainly his concern, if not suspicion.' He swallowed and glanced around the table. 'I should not want anyone to think that I was not keen to attend this meeting. My concerns are, I know, the same as yours. And there is another matter that I'd like to bring to your attention . . .'

The chairman, a German industrialist of Asian descent, intercepted with utmost civility.

'My dear sir, if we may first turn to the matters which touch us all?'

The politician nodded most fervently. 'Of course, of course.'

The chairman smiled and turned to the rest of the table. 'Dear ladies and gentlemen. We know why we are here. The terrible loss of life in Paris is most unfortunately the price we pay for our covert warfare. A tragic mistake that we have to live with.

'But the killings, the executions, if that is what they were . . . of the three persons responsible for that bomb, that is what troubles us all.'

There was a ripple of assent from six people around the table. Axel looked blank.

'We are all busy people,' the chairman continued, 'with Thanksgiving, I know, pressing down upon two of us, so perhaps if we ask immediately for a report from our man in the field?'

Axel nodded his head graciously. He would rather have been referred to as the 'Leader' of the men in the field, but he decided not to press the point, he was feeling big-hearted. He smiled at them all. 'Thank you. I will also be brief.

'I gave the orders for the executions.'

A gasp ran around the room.

The chairman cleared his throat. 'Aah, indeed? Various of

us had thought perhaps it was the work of a dissenter. Or a quarrel . . .?'

'No,' Axel replied, still smiling.

'Why did you order the deaths, and in such a brutal fashion, of these three young people?' An American woman fired the question from the other end of the table. 'Young people who, it must be remembered, were recruited by yourselves?'

'They were not recruited by me, madam. I, personally, had never met them.'

'They were recruited in our name,' the woman insisted. 'In Paris, they acted in our name. Why did you order them killed?'

Axel looked up, straight into her eyes. The little smile that had played around his lips had gone. 'When you appointed me and Leon Kleineman as your representatives in the field, you gave us absolute authority over all operational matters, did you not?'

The woman glanced down at the table. 'I . . . I believe that we indicated to you and your colleague that we had faith in your abilities to take responsibility for the day-to-day running of the group. We agreed that you would not have to refer everyday decision-making to ourselves . . .'

'Precisely,' interrupted Axel smoothly.

'We do not call murdering your operatives everyday matters. We think you have overstepped the mark.' The woman paused, returning his stare. 'Quite considerably. Those disgusting placards around their necks . . .'

There was a general murmur of agreement.

'My idea, yes,' said Axel blandly.

The woman drew breath sharply 'So?' She stared at him. 'We think that perhaps power has gone to your head,' she said quietly.

For several seconds he said nothing but his body rocked very gently back and forth in his chair. When he spoke, his voice was low but rose quickly.

'Power has gone to my head? Am I hearing this? Do you,' he stabbed a finger at her, 'who sits in her fancy office in Seattle and has nothing to do all day but dream up fashions for next year's catwalk in Rome, have any idea what it's like to be out there on the front line, day after day, week after week, making life and death decisions? Do you?'

The MP leaned forward. 'I hardly think it's necessary to yell. Especially at a lady. We are all aware that you and the other two members of the Leadership must be under a great deal of strain. You are, however, still ultimately responsible to us.'

Axel turned on him, glaring. 'Responsible to you? If it was left up to you, Never Again would still be a pipe-dream. Something else to amuse you while you drove between your stately homes! It's me and Leon that've put what you wanted into action!'

He glowered around at them all. 'We're responsible to you for results, yes! But results only! How we get them is our business. I gave the orders for the executions, yes, and I got the results I wanted!'

'You did?' asked the politician, raising one white eyebrow.

'Yes I did! Have you been reading the papers in Britain or have you been too busy working out how your Tory friends want to crawl up the arses of the Fascists?'

The elderly man reddened. 'There's no need for rudeness,' he said.

Axel smiled at his embarrassment. 'There's a need to do things the way we're doing them. Since the executions we've had some good press coverage. I've brought some of them with me. Here's one: "Cleaning up its act: Never Again kills the killers" and "Harsh Justice Never Again style" . . .'

'Excuse me, but there have also been articles saying "Good, a step on the right path. Let's hope they all kill each other!"' The speaker was the black television station owner from Houston. He took a sip of coffee and looked around the table. 'I do hope,' he murmured, 'that our Man in the Field is not solely concerned with improving his media image . . .'

Axel shot him a look of pure hatred. 'You arrogant, jumped-up . . .'

'Gentlemen, gentlemen!' The chairman looked distressed. 'Let us not waste time insulting each other. Mr Shiner, please do not think we are criticising you. We are full of admiration for what you have thus far achieved. But perhaps in future you will consult with us before carrying out such drastic measures?' He finished with a smile; he was a nice man.

Axel appeared engrossed in an examination of his fingernails. He did not look up as he spoke. 'I can give no absolute guarantees. Emergency, or if you will, "drastic" measures are sometimes the only measures to be taken and it would hardly be practical for me to seek your advice before action. You must learn to leave operational matters to the professionals.' He paused and rubbed speculatively at his chin, aware that everyone was watching him. 'However, I take on board what you say..'

'Excellent, excellent!' interrupted the chairman. 'And now to our other matter of concern. These posters of your, er, comrade, Miss Kessler?'

'Yes? What about them?'

The chairman cleared his throat. 'We wonder how the police found out she's part of the organisation?'

'So do I.' Axel let his gaze move slowly around the room.

There was an awkward silence. 'Are you suggesting someone's been talking?' the Frenchman asked eventually.

'Someone must have been. The police aren't known for telepathic inspiration. Anyway,' he took a sip of water, 'there's no need to worry about it. She's well hidden and well-guarded. And, just to make certain, for the forseeable future myself and Mr Kleinman will be in constant attendance upon her.'

'Good, good,' said the chairman hurriedly. 'We feel reassured then. And now, my dear sir,' he turned to the MP, 'you have a particular matter you wished to bring to our attention?'

The politician shifted in his chair and cleared his throat. 'Ah, I'm sure it's nothing. Just wanted to let everyone know. It's another newspaper article, actually, from *The Clarion*, a British Sunday paper. It's, ah, two weeks old, but it's given me some cause for concern. It's only brief: "Ernst Zimmerman, a New Yorker notorious for inciting young Jews to attack anyone he considers anti-Semitic, and who is thought to have close connections with Never Again, has told *The Clarion* that the group has a British financier: a rich man with powerful friends."'

The Seattle fashion designer made a growling noise.

'That bloody Zimmerman again. Why doesn't someone shut him up?'

'Is that an order?' Axel asked.

The woman blushed furiously. 'Of course not! But Zimmerman's a liability. Whoever it was amongst us who thought that he could be trusted has been proved wrong, haven't they?'

There was a brief silence. The MP, red in the face, broke it: 'I'm sure that's all Zimmerman said and obviously there's nothing to identify me, but, er, nevertheless and just in case he has said more to someone else, I wondered if there were any particular precautions I should be taking . . .'

His voice trailed off and he looked down unhappily at the article in front of him.

Axel closed his eyes and frowned, as if deep in thought. 'Continue to behave perfectly normally,' he said. 'I trust you've been doing nothing to attract attention?'

'Nothing!'

'No comments about the UK Nationalist Party winning those seats?'

'No! Certainly not.'

Axel opened his eyes wide. 'Oh? That might attract more attention, mightn't it? Surely it's the gossip in the Corridors of Power? And with your Cabinet friend?'

The politician flushed. 'I . . . I may have joined in with the odd comment. "Who'd have thought it?" "Frightful little fascists!" You know the sort of thing?'

He looked for support around the table but everyone averted their gaze.

Axel straightened his tie. 'If you're sure that's all . . .'

'Yes, oh yes! Absolutely.'

'. . . Then I'm sure you've got nothing to fear. Just go on keeping your head down. And of course letting us know if you feel you're being watched.' He paused and ran his tongue tenderly along his bottom lip. 'You do have, as we're all aware, including Mr Zimmerman, powerful friends. I'm sure you're one of the first to hear things on grapevines?'

'I, uh . . . I do have certain privileges in my position, yes.'

Axel nodded and placed his fingers together in a sepulchral steeple. The focus of the meeting was again upon himself; he smiled. 'Tell us then, do you think that these four fascist MPs indicate that Britain is becoming more racist?'

The politician visibly relaxed. 'No, no, I don't think so. It's a terrible indictment of my nation, of course, that the electorate, however misguided, however impoverished and desperate for a scapegoat, should begin to believe the foul mouthings of the Far Right, of those who advocate repatriation, segreg . . .'

'All right, all right save us the speech,' interrupted Axel. 'You'd agree, then, would you, that it's time that Britain – my nation, you will remember, as well as yours – attracted the attention of our combatants?'

The man paled. In one with such a healthy, outdoorsy look, the change was most noticeable. Everyone stared. 'I . . .' he coughed. 'I, aah, wonder if that is wholly necessary at this current juncture?'

The Frenchman made a low noise in his throat. 'On that score, I wonder if Paris was wholly necessary.'

'What? Oh, yes. Sorry.' The MP's colour returned with a vengeance.

Axel rubbed his fingers together. 'I, for one, think the British Election results are quite shocking,' he said. 'I don't see why Britain should escape simply because we number amongst ourselves one who is part of the Establishment . . .'

'I say! That's not what I meant at all! It's just that . . .'

'You'd rather not know the details, is that right?' Axel interrupted. 'That's all right. Leave the details up to me. It's an operational matter.'

Everyone understood his meaning perfectly. He watched them seethe; it gave him such a feeling of power! He continued speaking slowly, meditatively. 'I think perhaps it's time to bring in the cavalry. Give the foot-soldiers a rest. Ye-ess, why not? Wake up a Sleeper. They've had it pretty easy up till now.

'And a specific target this time, not a bomb. Bombs do tend to be a teensy-weensy bit messy. A marksman's bullet. A neat little job. A one-to-one.'

After the meeting had ended and Axel, anxious, as he put it, 'to get back to the Front Line', had departed for

La Guardia airport, the financiers felt freer to express themselves.

'The man's a monster,' breathed one.

'A monster of our own creation,' agreed the black media mogul. 'Y'know it surprises me. I thought he was the sane one. The other man, the young guy, Leon, he seemed the nut.'

'He might have gone completely ga-ga of course,' said the lady from Seattle. 'We haven't seen him all year, have we?'

'So the group's in the hands of at least one or maybe two madmen and that awful woman terrorist.' The Spaniard shuddered. 'What a mess.' He glanced over at the politician. 'You're an influential man, sir. Can't you do anything?'

'I really don't see what. If we had him arrested, he would implicate all of us.'

Silence fell in the room.

The chairman spoke up at last: 'How about cutting off the funds?'

'It wouldn't stop him.' The Frenchman shook his head. 'He's got enough cash to keep going for another six months.'

'No,' sighed the MP. 'We're in it up to our necks.'

Zoe had always loved Christmas, which was why, on the first Sunday afternoon in December, she was lying full-length in front of the TV screen watching *It's a Wonderful Life* and trying to do her Christmas list.

She had already bought presents for her mother – a small Dresden figure that she had seen in a local antique shop – and her father – a new deerstalker – but Alasdair was proving more difficult.

'A gilt-framed picture of Kerry,' she thought wryly, 'that should do the trick.'

As for Kerry . . .? Zoe chewed the top of her pen. What to get a successful, confident, cherished young woman who had great taste and ample resources? On the screen the old guardian angel was telling James Stewart: 'Every time that you hear a bell ring, it means that some angel's just got his wings.' She found herself smiling at the sentiment and grinned. Christmas was the best time of year, she considered, for conjuring up pictures of idealised happiness: ice-skaters in white fur-hats, horses dragging sledges through the snow, families gathered in front of roaring fires, singing carols. Thinking of her own family thus engaged, she giggled, but quickly sobered. She was going to be with them all in less than three weeks, and the expectation of Christmas generally surpassed the reality.

Perhaps matching baggy jumpers for her brother and Kerry? She wrote it down. But what colour?

She jotted down the rest of names for her list: her grandmother, Agnes her old nanny, her aunt and uncle, cousins and her godparents. How many of them could she get away with giving books to, she wondered.

Her arms were beginning to cramp and she stretched them out in front of her, one at a time. They were strong now, she noticed with a twinge of pride, not muscular in the least, but taut and well-conditioned, in excellent shape for holding a weapon . . .

She frowned and dismissed that train of thought.

Her grandmother loved cookery books, so she was easy. And Agnes would love the latest Jilly Cooper. Zoe crossed both names off and felt remarkably pleased with herself.

The phone rang and she got up, still watching the film and hoping whoever it was would not want to talk for long.

'Hello,' she said, not turning the volume down so that her caller would take the hint.

'Hello.' It was a girl's voice, not someone she recognised. James Stewart was running through the snow-covered streets of his town calling his wife's name.

'Hello,' Zoe said again. 'Who is it?'

'Oh, Zoe,' the voice was suddenly breathless and girlish and now becoming familiar. 'It's me, Alicia here. Your friend from university. I've got the Almanac you lent me . . .'

Zoe held the phone away. Her hand was shaking. It was Junie's voice and she had just used the codeword . . .

Chapter Twenty-One

It had been agreed that Zoe would spend the night before Christmas Eve at Alasdair's flat, so that they could start at dawn for the long drive north.

Kerry had packed efficiently and their one case stood ready in the hall. Beside it was a Fortnum and Mason hamper – their contribution to the Christmas feast – and two carrier bags of brightly wrapped parcels. It was nine o'clock and Zoe was due at any moment.

'She's really gone into her shell these last couple of weeks,' Kerry said. She was trying to make mulled wine with sachets she had bought from the supermarket. 'The last time we saw her she hardly said a word and she didn't look as if she'd slept for a month.'

Alasdair looked up from the latest Dick Francis. For him, Christmas had already started. He smiled lazily. 'Zo's always been quiet. She keeps things to herself, that's the way she is. Anyway, if there is a problem, she doesn't want to talk about it. I've already tried.'

'You have?'

'Yeah. I asked if it was drugs.'

'For God's sake! I'm surprised she still talks to you!'

'Why? I was only showing concern. She knows that.' He grinned at Kerry's exasperated look. 'Don't worry. She's been through moody phases before. She'll snap out of it.'

'She's not fourteen!'

The doorbell rang. 'That'll be her now.' Alasdair got up. 'Maybe all that good Highland air will sort her out.' He kissed Kerry's neck on the way out to the hall. 'That stuff you're making smells foul,' he added conversationally.

On Boxing Day morning, Matt opened his eyes and, for a dreadful moment, thought he was a child again at home with his mother. It was his old bedroom. The wallpaper was exactly the same: green trains and red planes forever stuck in motion against a blue background. At nine, Matt had loved it, at sixteen it had become a cause of hideous embarrassment. He had begged his mother to let him paint over it but she had refused. It was the last thing your father did, she said, before he went away and left us.

For Sheila from the office, Matt remembered. She had been the first of a string of young women whom his father had lived with after leaving. A glamorous figure he had been to young Matt, a freelance photographer who had indulged him wildly on his infrequent access visits and who now lived in the States with a string of slightly older young women.

Thinking of his father, Matt smiled. He loved him, for all his irresponsbility and lack of concern over material things, but he had made his mother's life wretched. Or was it her fault, her expectations that had wrecked the marriage? Matt sighed and turned over; he was not going to start trying to figure that one out again.

He only ever came home now once a year, at Christmas, and that had been yesterday. Not too bad – well, the same as ever. Mum and the aunties and himself, being polite over presents, eating too much and becoming cranky as the day went on. As the sole 'child' present, he had taken the brunt of it; he was too thin; his shirt was creased; he needed to get married and settle down, only bear in mind what had happened to them; maybe he was wise after all to be single. It was extraordinary, Matt thought, how the three sisters were each divorced – Auntie Vi twice. If it did run in families, he had no chance.

Tomorrow he would be escaping. He was catching a morning flight up to Inverness where Louise and her friends would be meeting him. The log cabin was forty miles south, only about an hour's drive so long as the roads were clear. From Louise's description, the place sounded wonderful: set in its own few acres, backing onto a glen. It had an open fire and a vast, beamed ceiling. Matt wished he could have gone for Christmas but he knew what his mother's reaction would have been, and it hadn't seemed worth it.

He sat up and swung his feet down onto the carpet. His

new ski-boots stood beside his case. He grinned, thinking of the week ahead, the white slopes of the Cairngorms by day and the hot toddies around the fireplace by night. And maybe, just maybe, a reconciliation with Louise. Whistling, he got out of bed.

After breakfast, Zoe followed her father into the vast room that he called his 'snug'. There was nothing snug about it. It had a stone floor and was as high-ceilinged and draughty as the rest of the house, or maybe more so. A large picture window that overlooked the glen had never closed properly and the wind howled down the chimney of the cleanly swept fireplace.

The furniture was old dark wood, heavy and most uninviting. Nevertheless, her father liked to sit there in the mornings and read his paper. That was what he was doing now.

'Dad, could I have a word?'

Her father looked up in surprise. He had not seen her come in. He put his paper down and smiled at her. She noticed how much older he looked wearing his glasses, older and vulnerable. 'Of course, darling. Take a seat.'

What she was about to do, Zoe considered, was tantamount to betrayal of the worst kind. Using her own father, taking advantage of his trust. She looked at him and saw suddenly how grey his hair was looking. He doesn't deserve this from me, she thought.

He seemed to be in a mellow mood. Indeed, for her father, he was almost garrulous. 'Did you enjoy Christmas?' he asked.

'Yes, it was lovely.'

'Nice girl that Kerry, isn't she?'

'Yes. Yes, she is.' Zoe bit her lip.

Her father waited a few seconds. She saw that he wanted to get back to his paper but she still could not frame the words.

'What did you want to talk to me about?' he asked pleasantly.

Zoe remembered the telephone call three weeks ago at the flat. Hearing the codeword, feeling as if she had just swallowed ice, she had tried to reassure herself that it might not mean what she feared. All that the word signified, she had told herself as she had caught the train to Victoria twenty minutes later, was that there was an order for her, or a message.

It had kept her fairly calm; calm enough to get off the train, take the escalator up to the cafe above the railway station, see Junie sitting at the back and walk over to her, with a little wave as if to a friend.

Junie had delivered the order, bending so low over her cup of milky coffee that Zoe had had to strain to hear the words. It had not been her wake-up call. The initial sense of relief had been so overwhelming that she had felt giggly and light-headed. Junie had glared, and repeated the order.

On the surface it did not seem a terrible thing to do. Junie had not explained further; she probably had not known any more and Zoe had not asked; she had not wanted to.

But the unknown had plucked away at her ever since, depriving her of sleep, making her jumpy and nervous. She had avoided people as much as she could, certainly any close contact in case anyone asked her what was wrong. Christmas, she thought with a shudder, would never be the same again. She had forgotten to buy the rest of her presents until Christmas Eve: everyone, bar her parents, had got books.

It had been a strain to look happy yesterday; to enthuse over presents and sit at the table pulling crackers and eating turkey, as if nothing was wrong. She had been sure that someone would notice, but no one had.

'I can't do it,' she thought suddenly.

'Zoe, darling? What is it?' Her father's voice sounded concerned but also held a hint of impatience. The pale sun, catching his glasses, gave him a harder look.

'I betrayed him three months ago,' she rationalised to herself quickly. 'When I spoke to Pieter. I betrayed my father and my mother, and Alasdair and everyone I know. Everyone who trusts me.' As she had betrayed them, so now Pieter had betrayed her. What more did she expect, she thought dully. She remembered Beatrix's words: 'This is not a game for children,' and asked herself, 'What does one more lie matter?'

'Dad, I was wondering ... are you still friendly with Magnus?'

'Magnus? Old Tufty? That's a funny question! 'Course I'm still friendly with him. Been friends since we were at prep school together. You know that!'

'Yes. Of course. I saw he kept his seat at the Election.'

'Wouldn't have expected otherwise,' her father said loyally. 'He's a good MP. Cares about his constituents. Not like some of these types you hear about, never listening to the folk that've elected them. No, always takes his own surgeries, always has. And he spends a goodish bit of time up here. Oh, I know he's got a flat in London and a place on the south coast, but that's only what you'd expect from a man who's always on the move and who's got a lot of family money.'

Talking about his friend had animated him. Zoe could not remember her father making such a long speech before, certainly not to her.

'Why're you asking about Magnus?'

'Oh, it's just . . .' she stopped. Suddenly what she was about to say sounded so false.

'Come along, dear, what is it?' Her father rustled his newspaper meaningfully.

She took a deep breath and it all came out in a rush. 'A couple of friends in London, new friends, work in the House of Commons. For MPs. They keep telling me what fun it is, how glamorous, and how you meet so many interesting important people. I wondered if . . .' she had been addressing herself to the fireplace but now she looked directly at her father, 'if you think Magnus might be able to find me a job like that. Somewhere in the Commons.'

She felt herself flush and thought that her father must see it, but he made no comment.

'Well, you do surprise me! I thought you were all set up in your, uh, um, your mother did tell me . . . library is it?'

'Bookshop, Dad. I work in a bookshop.'

'Oh! Yes, well, bookshop. Big one is it, Foyles? Management trainee?'

'No, Dad.' She had to get him back on the subject.

'What about the Commons?' she asked abruptly. 'D'you think Magnus would help?'

Her father looked a little startled. 'I'm sure he would. If you're certain that's what you want. The bookshop's not working out then?'

She shook her head.

'What sort of job did you have in mind in the Commons? An MP's assistant, that kind of thing?'

'Yes! Well, anything really.'

'Anything so long as you're working in the Palace, eh? Keeping up with your friends, meeting important people?' Her father looked at her, quizzically, head on one side. 'Sometimes I feel I don't really know you terribly well, Zoe. I wouldn't have thought you'd have been interested in glamour.'

He paused again, and smiled. 'But it's good to hear you've got some friends your own age. That you're mingling. I know your mother's been worried sometimes that you're not sociable enough. Too shy for your own good. But you're obviously coming out of yourself.'

Suddenly he got up, came over to her and kissed the top of her head, something he had never done before. 'You leave old Tufty to me,' he said. 'He might not have a vacancy himself but I'm sure he'll know people who have. All right darling? Run away now and let me get on with my paper.'

At a little after dawn on New Year's Eve in Madrid, a travelling alarm clock woke Anton Valente with a start. It was still dark in the room, but light was beginning to seep in through the wooden shutters. Checking the time, Anton saw he had twenty minutes to wash, dress and get out of the apartment. His flight left in two hours' time.

His wake-up order had arrived four days before, a message of twelve words that to the casual eye would have signified nothing more than a New Year's greeting from a friend. He had gone to the pre-arranged meeting-place, a tapas bar, and been informed of his mission. He had felt nothing except numbness through which he had moved like a sleepwalker, marvelling at the actions he was performing. How had he been able to carry on sitting at that little table after his contact had gone, order tapas, drink a glass of wine, even joke with the barman?

He had spent Christmas on his own in the apartment. He had watched television a lot, and listened to the church bells ringing out all over the city. He called no one and no one called him. He had eaten when he was hungry: twice in four days. His last meal had been twenty-four hours ago.

Now he got up and went into the shower, letting the hot water fully wake him. He had already memorised every detail of his orders until he was no longer aware of remembering them. They were part of him.

By ten o'clock, at the outside, he would be in Malaga. He was to hire a car under his false name and then he was to drive. There would not be much traffic about. It was estimated that he would arrive at his destination by two o'clock in the afternoon. He was to collect the equipment from the address he had been given and then he was to get into position. He would have ample time, at least an hour, to find the best place.

Matt had realised almost immediately that his coming to Scotland had been a mistake. As soon as he had seen Louise waiting for him at the airport, he had known: he no longer felt anything for her beyond mild affection. Louise clearly felt otherwise. The result had been bitter recriminations, accusations of never having loved her, of playing with her affections and then storms of weeping.

And the open-plan nature of the cabin meant that everyone had a good view when, on that first evening, he had moved his things out of Louise's room and into the icy boxroom next to the verandah.

The rest of the party, whom Matt had imagined to be a mixture of singles, turned out to be three very married couples, who sided entirely with Louise. Hardly surprising, he told himself; they were her friends after all. He had not been totally ostracised; he was still set a place at mealtimes and he was thrown the odd morsel of conversation, but generally the atmosphere was frosty. Louise had hardly helped matters by pointedly ignoring him and being chattily over-bright to everyone else.

He had taken to going to bed early, leaving the others to their hot toddies around the open fire.

At least the skiing had been wonderful. Up on the slopes, he had been able to forget everything except the thrill of the sport, the hiss of his skis on the snow, and the exhilaration he always found in throwing himself against nature. Today, however, the runs were closed. Rather than accompany the others on a drive to Blair Atholl, Matt had decided to explore the glen on foot and no one had attempted to dissuade him.

The scenery was glorious. Once over the cattle-grid, there was mile upon mile of rolling purple and black hillsides with the mountains as a backdrop, and sheep and the cry of curlews for company. Far away in the distance, Matt could see the dark clouds of the bad weather but here the sky was blue and the sunlight bright and sharp. Squinting against it, he thought he saw an eagle hovering over one hillside but his knowledge of birds was too scanty for him to be sure.

He walked for miles without seeing another human being, or even, apart from one large grey stone house just at the mouth of the glen, any sign of human habitation. The wildness of the landscape might have daunted him in another mood, but today he loved it. He bent himself into the cutting wind and enjoyed the sensation of pitting himself against nature.

It had been a strange, frustrating year, he mused, where he had nibbled at the edges of things without properly getting his teeth into anything. The whole business with Never Again had taken up so much of his time and energy and yet had produced no definite result. The week before Christmas, he had finished his tour of all the Anti-Fascist groups in London, but he was still no closer to finding anyone with a way in to Never Again. He sighed: either his acting was lousy, his instincts had dulled or Never Again were just too smart at covering their tracks. Steve, he thought gloomily, was being as awkward as ever. He kicked at a stone, and sent it spinning ahead of him. He should have burned the bastard; what was the point of holding back if the policeman never talked to him?

Most frustrating of all to Matt was the knowledge that the story could be cracked. He knew that if he could get to Zimmerman he might make the man talk, but Lomax would never send him to New York without a promise, preferably in blood, that he would deliver the story. And that he could not guarantee.

He checked the time, surprised to see that it was nearly three o'clock and that he had been walking for two hours. By the time he got back, it would be growing dark and the others might have returned. He had hoped, just for once, to be able to enjoy the luxury of a hot bath without worrying that someone else needed the only bathroom.

He turned round and started back. He thought about tonight: everyone else was going to the Hogmanay Ball in the next village three miles away.

The alternative, sitting on his own with a bottle of whisky, no matter how good the whisky or how roaring the log fire, seemed too miserable. He decided to go and enjoy himself; New Year in Scotland had to be celebrated in style. He would forget about the past five days and offer to squire Louise. She would need a partner as much as he did.

Anton shivered with cold, not because of the weather, a mild thirteen degrees centigrade, but because he had been lying unmoving for so long and, after over thirty hours without food, his blood sugar levels were very low. Now, trying only to move his eyes, he looked at his watch: 16.15.

He had been in position for seventy minutes. He lowered his head a fraction and looked down his sights. The front door was still closed. He flicked his eyes once to the left, once to the right. No one was coming.

He flexed his numbed fingers. They looked to him like little antennae; they moved so slowly and seemed to be no part of him. He was terrified that, when the time came, they would not obey his brain. He was going to kill a man he had never seen before, who had done him no wrong; a man who was not prepared for death. He shivered again. He had to do it; he had to carry out his mission perfectly. It was, and must be, the only thing that mattered.

He was lying sprawled out on the flat roof of a modern building four storeys high. Because he was skinny and not very tall, he could easily have been mistaken for a child. But he would have had to have been unlucky to be spotted: his building was two storeys higher than all the others around him for half a mile. To further improve his chances, he lay in the lengthening shadow of the ventilation shaft. Propped up beside him, on its spindly tripod mount, sat the long-nosed sniper's rifle, pointing downwards at an almost perfect forty-five degree angle, to the dark yellow front door of the white-stuccoed house opposite.

In the latter half of the afternoon, the Governor of Gibraltar would be going through that doorway for afternoon tea. It was a quaint tradition, the intelligence operative had told Anton: on every New Year's Eve the British Governor had tea and sandwiches with the Chief Justice. The venue alternated yearly but the occasion was fixed like the sea coming home to the beach.

Anton tried to keep calm, but he had thought that four o'clock was the British teatime. If it got much later, if it got dark, what was he supposed to do? How long was he meant to stay here?

His legs inside his jeans felt clammy and the muscles were starting to cramp. Very gently he moved them, one at a time, sideways in a scissor action and then up a couple of inches into the air and down again. Everything he did was in slow, considered motion, just in case someone was watching, training a pair of binoculars on him, or by chance, looking up, should catch the flicker of a movement. Not that there was anyone to watch.

The absolute lack of security had shocked him. Surely a man as important as the Chief Justice should be better protected? True, there was a uniformed man on the four steps leading up to the front door, but only one and, from his vantage point, Anton was fairly sure that the man was not armed. It was disgraceful, he thought indignantly. Why, anyone could get through the door of the building on which he lay, climb the stairs and break the lock on the wooden screen leading to the roof. Anyone with a grudge, any one of the hundreds of criminals that the Chief Justice must have sent to prison, any madman, any terrorist.

From the road below, Anton heard a car approaching, then

another, their tyres shushing on the tarmac. His information
had been that the Governor would be in the second car. The
first would contain the police and security men – just in case.
No one would be expecting anything untoward: this was a very
low-key affair, more of a private visit. There might be another
security man in the back of the second car with the Governor,
but probably not. It was much more likely the Governor would
be accompanied only by his assistant.

Anton heard the cars slowing down, the first one stopping,
doors opening, the sound of men's footsteps. A heaviness
seemed to invade his limbs like sleep. He lifted his arm
and dropped it into position, his right eye hard against the
telescopic sight. He swallowed; he saw three men moving
in the street. Two were climbing the steps of the Justice's
house and the policeman was coming to attention. The third
man remained in the street, looking all around, then walking
backwards to the rear of the Bentley. He stopped by the rear
passenger door and talked into a radio.

Anton felt rather than saw movement at the top of the
steps, the front door opening. He was concentrating hard,
saving everything for the second car, the sleek grey Bentley.
The driver's door opened – Anton had a brief flash of red
upholstery – and a grey uniformed chauffeur stepped out,
adjusting his cap. Two steps and he opened the back door, two
steps backwards with it in his hand. Anton was mesmerised:
it was like a dance.

The Governor emerged all at once: black shoes, grey suit,
a head of grey, wavy hair. The man straightened, pulling down
his jacket. In Anton's sights, he came into magnified focus;
the cross hairs in line with the bridge of the Governor's
nose. A hawk nose in a thin, white face. Perfect. Anton
began squeezing the trigger.

Zoe had been lying on top of her bed for the past hour, telling
herself that she must get up and join the others. Otherwise, her
absence would be noticed and someone would come looking
for her, maybe even her mother. Normally, that thought would
have galvanised her into action but the strain of the last two
days, on top of the last few weeks, had left her exhausted. She

knew exactly what the cause was, and she did not want to think about it. Not now; all she wanted now was to be able to sleep, but she knew she must not . . .

At lunchtime, her mother had been most adamant that 'the children' be present for this afternoon. 'After all, it's a tradition that dates back to . . . well, centuries probably. Doesn't it, Malcolm?'

'What? Oh, yes. Centuries.'

'So no sneaking out of it. And you two,' she directed a look at Kerry and Alasdair. 'I want you to be sociable. Talk to people. You're not to sit mooning at each other.'

'Mother! For goodness' sake, we're not kids.'

'No, well. As long as you remember not to let the side down. That goes for you too, Zoe.'

Zoe had been wondering if she could fit an extra run into the afternoon. Since Junie's message, she had found that hard physical exercise was one of the few things that relaxed her. But up here it was difficult to go on more than one run a day; her family would surely want to know why. At the sound of her mother's voice, she had jumped.

'Miss Daydream. I want you to do your bit too. Pass round the cake, talk to Miss Allen. She always asks after you. She was so pleased to hear you'd be home for the holiday.'

'That old battle-axe!' said Alasdair. 'I thought she'd be dead by now.' To Kerry he added: 'The headmistress of our old primary school. Made our lives a living hell.'

'Alasdair! That's not true at all. Miss Allen's always been so fond of you and Zoe . . .'

Zoe yawned widely. It was such a stuffy, patronising tradition; the villagers calling on the Laird and his family on New Year's Eve afternoon. Drinking sherry, eating fruitcake and no one staying more than forty minutes. Remembering previous New Year's Eve afternoons. Zoe was surprised anyone stayed that long. No one could possibly enjoy it. She opened one eye and looked at the time: 3.22. The first guests would not arrive before half past. She could have two more minutes. She began drifting towards sleep . . .

A knock at the door woke her.

'Zoe!' It was Kerry's voice. 'Can I come in?'

'Sure!' Zoe jumped out of bed, blinking her eyes wide open. 'I was just coming.'

Kerry entered shyly. 'I didn't wake you, did I?' She stopped, staring out of the window. 'What a fantastic view! You're so lucky to have grown up here!'

'Mmm.' Zoe looked over her shoulder, trying to see it with Kerry's eyes, but it was impossible. To her, the purple hills, the heather and the sheep was just the glen, same as it always was, miles upon miles of it, and beyond, way off in the distance, would be the snowy peaks of the Monadhliath Mountains, only they were hidden in cloud today.

'Zoe, what're you going to wear for this thing?'

'Um. I hadn't thought really.' Zoe looked down at herself. Jeans and her chunky brown jumper were probably not appropriate. 'I s'pose my awful tweed skirt and a blouse. Something boring.'

Kerry was looking at her as if she had lost her mind. 'A tweed skirt? Zoe, don't you think . . .?'

Words seemed to fail her, then she suddenly blushed and slapped her hand over her mouth.

'Aaah! Sorry, sorry. My mistake! I meant tonight for the Ball! Is it very grand? I've only got one outfit that's anywhere near dressy enough.'

Zoe smiled. She genuinely liked Kerry. And she was so glad that she had not come to question her about whether she was happy.

'So've I. The same one I had when I first went, when I was sixteen. It's like putting on an old friend. I wouldn't worry about it. Anything goes really. Well, p'rhaps not tweed skirts.'

Anton's bullet flew through the air, totally missing its target. He gasped, not believing it. It had been a perfect shot. But through the sights, he could see the Governor was standing, quite intact, with that little frown still between his eyes. The bullet hit the car, driving into the metal. A split second later, the time it took Anton to reload, it was already too late. One bodyguard had thrown the Governor to the ground and was covering him with his own body.

Anton stared as if he was watching a film. Everyone had fallen down. The chauffeur in his uniform on the road. The policeman at the top of the stairs, sprawled across the threshold like some great watchdog. He was mouthing into a radio. The two security men were flat on their faces, but moving, shimmying like snakes down the steps, bump, bump bump and onto the pavement. Anton saw they both had guns out. He heard one yell, 'Cover!' and then got to his feet and ran behind the Bentley. The other man, the one covering, was waving his gun around in the air like a wild thing.

Something, some movement, brought Anton's attention back to the target. The bodyguard was trying to shove the Governor under the car, not an easy task when he was still on top of him, like an eagle on its prey.

Anton heard the static crackle of many radios. He did not have much time.

He applied his eye to the cross-hairs again, but it was not so easy now. The target was moving, and he was wearing the same colour as the bodyguard. Anton could not tell them apart; they were merging into each other and getting away from him. He had set the rifle for a static, or near-static target, but the target was not static any longer. He released the weapon from the mount and at once felt better, more in control, holding it in his arms. Now, as the target moved, he could move too, inching himself forward, following the Governor in his sights. There was a sudden flash of white, a thin leg above a sock. Tempting, but Anton held off, his finger aching, the flesh cutting into the metal trigger. He knew the bodyguard would have to rise to let the Governor roll under the car.

. The man lifted himself. In slow motion, the governor seemed to roll sideways, he was getting away, moment by moment. Anton fired. He saw the torso buck but he could not see if it moved again.

'On the roof!'

'Arnold's hit! Arnold's hit!'

The second shout cancelled the first. Anton gave the grin of a delighted child; he had achieved his mission. He failed to see that he had edged too far forward. That his rifle was now showing a clear two inches of glinting steel barrel over

the parapet. That his own fair head was now peeping out
behind it.

A bullet cutting through the air by his ear, so close that his
skin felt singed by it, pointed out the danger of his current
position.

'Up there! On the roof!'

Instinct took over. He started crawling backwards, fast,
feet first, hand-over-hand on the roof, the palms of his hands
hitting the rough surface and hurting like crabs on hot sand.
They were shooting at him! The thought shocked him. For
some crazy reason he had not expected it. He had not thought
beyond hitting the target.

Bullets were flying everywhere. Bouncing like rain on the
roof, pinging against the metal ventilation shaft. They were
hoping to hit him by chance. From way down below, in
the street, he heard a pounding, metal on metal, then more
gun-fire, volleys of it. They were shooting through the door.
It was a heavy security door, but not impregnable.

Anton's trainers touched the frame of the doorway leading
to the fourth floor. In less than a second he was through it,
flinging himself down the short flight of steps. He was in the
corridor now and running for the fire exit at the end, his
breathing coming in great noisy gulps, his heart bursting in his
chest. From down below he heard a crash. They were in the
building, their footsteps thundering on the stairs. They were
coming to get him. Another sound, a distant wailing coming
nearer, ambulance or police sirens, impossible to tell.

He threw himself at the fire door. He was out on the metal
fire escape, jumping down the stairs, twisting his body round
the bends. He looked down. Two more flights to go, and then
the courtyard and the side door leading onto the back street
where the car was waiting.

He landed badly on the final platform, turning his ankle.
The pain made him cry out, its sudden intensity blinding him
for a moment to everything else. He did not see the small
door open just below him, nor the muzzle of the weapon nose
through it.

'Halt!'

Anton spun on his heels, looking wildly round for the voice.

A man in dark clothing stood in a door under the fire escape. He was pointing a gun levelly at Anton's heart.

Anton felt it beating so hard that the sound drowned out all others. His eyes flickered to the door on the other side of the yard, the green door that led to the street. He calculated the distance. His body tensed for the run.

On the periphery of his vision, the man with the gun came a step closer out of the shadows. 'Don't even think about it, matey.' The words were English, soft and menacing. Anton understood their meaning. He let his arms drop down by his sides.

The Ball had started at ten o'clock, with most of the guests arriving within the first hour. It was quite an affair, Matt thought. Judging by the turnout – about five hundred he guessed – it was probably the event of the year.

It was being held in a huge country house hotel. The whole of the downstairs had been given over to the night's proceedings and a sizeable proportion of the grounds outside.

In the main hallway games and tombola stalls had been set up and a great fire was burning in the stone fireplace.

To one side, a doorway led to the ballroom; to another, pleated wooden doors folded back into the vast reception room. At the back, just beyond the majestic staircase, a few steps led down to the conservatory which ran the full length of the house. There, the disco was going on, its lights flashing out into the gardens.

Outside were several marquees, their white and yellow stripes spotlit by arc-lights, and wooden walkways led between them. In one, there was a display of sword-dancing; in another the gaming tables were set out and in a third was a shooting range.

Food and drink was everywhere, on tables and on trays borne by passing waiters. Everyone was having a terrific time.

'My Lords, Ladies and Gentlemen!' The voice of the Master of Ceremonies boomed out of a speaker above Matt's head. 'The hour approaches! If you will all make your way to the Great Hall, we shall welcome in the New Year together!'

People began surging past: women and girls of all ages, in gowns and dresses, sashes and bows and lots of black velvet. Very little tartan, Matt noticed, except amongst some of the older ladies. Perhaps if one was truly a Scot, one did not wear tartan. The men made up for that. With no hint of embarrassment, the kilts were out in full splendour. Plus all the trappings that went with them: sporrans and skean dhus and velvet jackets adorned with lacy jabots.

Matt stood back in the shadows of the sweeping staircase and let them all flow past him. His own dinner suit looked dull in comparison. But it was not only the clothes that marked him out, he thought gloomily, it was that everyone else seemed to be having such great fun.

A girl with short dark hair, beautifully cut and wearing the most clingy of soft, short dresses, brushed past him, her arm on that of her partner, a medium-sized man with a bump on his nose. The girl was laughing up at him, her eyes dancing, but her partner . . . Why, the man was not even looking at her, Matt thought indignantly.

'Not fair,' he told himself.

Within twenty minutes of their arrival together, he and Louise had parted company. Earlier in the evening, she had greeted his suggestion that they should partner each other at the Ball with a moody shrug of her shoulders and an 'All right, then.' In the mini-cab bringing them, she had not addressed one word to him, but had kept up a girlish flow of chatter with the other couple, and as soon as they had entered the hallway, she had made a beeline for the disco. Matt hated discos and she knew that. He told her so.

'D'you think I care what you like?' she had hissed at him, her face flushing an angry red and thrust alarmingly close to his own. 'I'm going to have some fun tonight. Why don't you stay here?' And then she had gone.

Matt started moving with the crowd down towards the fireplace where the Master of Ceremonies was standing on a firebox to give him extra height and counting out the last seconds of the old year on his wristwatch.

Matt picked up a glass of champagne from a passing waiter. There was nothing so lonely, he thought, as being on your own at a party, especially a huge one like this. Out of the corner of his eye, he caught a glimpse of the pretty blue dress that Louise had been wearing. She was about thirty feet away on the other side of the hall. He did not see any of the others near her. Matt hesitated, wondering whether to join her, whether she would toast the New Year with him or throw her champagne in his face. While he wondered, he saw her turn to a man on her right, a tall man in a kilt who was looking down at her and smiling, who encircled her bare shoulders with his arm and kissed her.

Matt looked away.

'Ten, nine, eight . . .'

The room took up the chant. The vast, baronial-style front doors were flung open, letting in the chilly night air and the distant chimes of a town-hall bell.

In front of him, Matt saw a fair-haired man, quite tall, not particularly broad or special-looking, with his arms around the shoulders of two girls, one dark-haired and one as fair as himself. The three of them were bouncing up and down in time to the count: 'Five, four . . .'

On the last chime of midnight, the room exploded. Everyone, was kissing and laughing, and toasting each other. The man in front of Matt turned to the girl on his left, the dark one and kissed her long and slowly on the lips. The other girl watched them and smiled. She was small and she wore her fair hair in a loose plait over one shoulder. She had grey eyes with long dark fringes and a small straight nose. There was something about her that struck him as sad. Something in her expression that said she did not belong, but wanted to. And he had the oddest feeling that he had seen her somewhere before.

She turned suddenly, aware that someone was watching her.

'Hello,' said Matt.

'Hello,' said Zoe.

Barney Turl had always resolutely refused to carry a pager, or a portable phone, maintaining that he was not 'a damn doctor' and that no message could possibly be that urgent that it could not wait until he either got to work or home.

He did, however, have an answerphone. At ten minutes past two on New Year's Day, just after he and Alice had returned from the Dinner and Dance at the Golf Club (where they were social members only), Barney saw that the red light was flashing madly. He blinked at it, aware that he was not entirely sober. The machine, sitting on a marble shelf beside the fridge, flashed back.

'Are you bringing the ice, then?' Alice called impatiently from the front room.

'Jussa minute.'

A thought struck him: it might only be his brother, calling from Huddersfield to wish him Happy New Year. He was still thinking this when the telephone rang a second later.

'Hello!' he called cheerfully into the receiver.

'It's the duty officer, sir,' said an anxious voice. 'I've got a priority message for you. I've been calling every ten minutes since it came in at 23.08.'

'Who is it?' called out Alice.

Barney put down the ice bucket with a thump. His head had cleared miraculously. 'Have you reached anyone else yet?

'No sir. I've been unable to contact the Director. Being New Year and everything . . .'

'Yes, yes.' Thank God, Barney thought. He remembered that Hargreaves always went north of the border for New Year. 'Anyone else?'

'No, sir. It's marked for your and her eyes only. Shall I send it through the scrambler, sir?'

'Do that.'

Five minutes later, he was sitting at his desk in the spare room that had become his study, staring at the words he had scribbled down. Anton's bullet had not killed the Governor but it had lodged dangerously close to his spine. He had been operated on earlier in the evening and the doctors were waiting to see if he was sufficiently stable to be flown back to the UK for further emergency treatment in the morning. That would mean today, he realised, wishing that his brain would work faster.

'I got my own ice!' Alice stood in the doorway holding a glass that contained, so far as Barney could see, only ice-cubes.

She was swaying slightly. She was still a very pretty woman he thought, smiling at her.

'Anything wrong? she asked carefully.

Barney loosened his bow-tie and got to his feet.

'Depends how you look at it,' he said. 'I've got to do a bit of work now and then get up at five. Going on a little trip.'

'Oh,' her mouth drooped. They were supposed to be going to the Sales together.

'It's nowhere nice, honestly love,' he sighed and adjusted the anglepoise. 'You go to bed. I've got to send a message.'

It was Pieter who finally took the decision.

It was true, he agreed, that something could have gone wrong with the communications system; it had happened before, but this time there were crucial differences. Firstly, there had been nothing on the radio or TV about the shooting; secondly, it was over twelve hours since Anton had left the Storemaster but they had heard nothing to say how the mission had gone. Thirdly, Anton was the first Sleeper ever to be activated. If something had gone wrong, if he had been captured, he could give a lot away. Corsica, for example; Sergio Brunelli; his list of contacts. He could endanger the whole network. People needed to be warned, just in case.

'And he could identify you,' Pieter added.

Axel and Leon had exchanged a look. In spite of claims to the contrary, both men had become increasingly nervous over the last six weeks. Neither had taken well to their self-imposed exile with Kessler, a decision allegedly taken to make her feel more 'secure' although it was clear to see that it was really to allay their own fears.

Axel had lost some of his arrogance and had fits of depression; Leon had become whiney and clingy like a child. Only Beatrix seemed untouched by it all, although it was she whose face seemed to be everywhere on the new Wanted posters.

He watched her now, sitting over by the fire, staring into the empty fireplace as if the discussion did not concern her.

Axel was definitely not as smooth-looking as usual after a sleepless, anxious night. His hair was mussed up from running his hands through it and there was a tic in his cheek. When he spoke, his voice was high and querulous. 'He might not talk.'

'Everyone talks,' Beatrix said quietly, still not taking her eyes from the fire. 'Everyone knows that.'

Axel ignored her. He addressed Pieter: 'You know the boy best. You're the psychiatrist. Will he talk?'

'I've no way of knowing, but probably. We must assume so.'

Leon shifted in his chair. 'But he doesn't know where we are! I don't see why we have to move. We've got used to it here.'

Pieter knew how foolish this remark was. He waited for Beatrix to say it: that in their position they could never afford to settle anywhere, never think they were safe. But she gave no sign of even having heard the words.

Axel nodded. 'Yes. But so what if he describes us? We're not wanted and nobody's reported us missing. We won't be on any police computer.' He stopped glaring over at the woman. 'Not like her. Her bloody face is all over the place.'

Beatrix turned. 'I'm sure they know quite a lot about us already.'

'What d'you mean?' Axel demanded. Pieter saw that the veins on the side of his head were standing up. 'D'you know someone's talked?'

'For sure? No. But after all this time, it's likely, don't you think?' She paused and smiled at the two men. 'Someone must have told the police about my involvement, mustn't they? And now this boy. If he started talking immediately . . .' She shrugged. 'And how do we know that someone here in Vienna has not seen my face at the window?'

Leon gave a little whimper and Axel laid a hand on his sleeve. 'Don't,' he commanded. 'She's just trying to spook us.' He chewed at his lower lip, another new habit he had developed.

'What's the time now?' he demanded.

Pieter pushed back his sleeve. 'Half past three.'

'How long did you say it'll take to get to the new place?'

'At this time of night, three, maybe four hours.'

Axel rubbed at his mouth with one hand. Pieter saw him glance down at Leon and then over at Beatrix's profile. Fleetingly, he felt sorry for the man.

'What d'you think we should do?' Axel finally asked. Pieter did not hesitate. 'You've got to move. At once.'

Obediently, Zoe held her plate out and let Matt spoon on the kedgeree from the copper tureen. She watched him, thinking there was something velvety about him, and trying to analyse what it was.

There was his colouring of course. He had brown floppy hair that she had the urge to push back out of his eyes, very dark bright eyes that lit up when he laughed. An open, square shaped face, a nice creamy-coloured complexion, but nothing remarkable in it. His mouth was maybe a little too wide, but he had such nice-looking soft pink lips . . .

It was not simply his appearance, she told herself, frowning; it was his whole manner. The way he talked and looked and listened; a certain gentleness in him that made her feel warm and relaxed and cherished. Enveloped in velvet.

He was grinning at her. A nice grin, she noticed, cheeky and fun. 'I said, d'you want any more? I mean, after you've finished counting my freckles?'

She blushed. 'Sorry, it's very rude of me. And no thanks, you've already given me loads. I'll never get through it.'

'You do eat, don't you?' He looked suddenly alarmed. 'You're not one of those girls that nibble on a carrot once a week?'

'I eat like a horse. I promise.'

'Good. Glad to hear it.'

They had reached the end of the breakfast line and were causing an obstruction to the three old ladies behind them.

'If we could get a little food . . .' one of them said loudly.

Matt smiled. 'Shall we go?' he said and touched her gently on her shoulder. Something like an electric current ran through her. Tony had never had such an effect, but she remembered the touch of Xavier's hand on her breast and reddened.

'You do that a lot, don't you?' He looked amused, one corner of his mouth turned up.

'What?'

'Blush. I expect it's very rude of me to mention it. Forgive me. But it's very appealing.' He grinned again and she had to laugh.

'Champagne?' asked a waiter standing at the foot of the staircase.

They each took a glass and looked around for somewhere to sit. Most of the chairs were already taken. 'How about up here?' Matt climbed a few stairs and sat down, looking immediately very comfortable. Zoe stepped passed the waiter and joined him. He had been right: the red stair carpet was thick and soft. Side by side, they forked kedgeree in an easy silence.

Zoe could not quite believe that they had only met three hours ago. It was as if she had known Matt for a long, long time. At midnight, when she had turned round and found him smiling at her, she had thought that she recognised him from somewhere, but could not remember where. 'Maybe I dreamed you,' she said softly and giggled.

'What?' he asked.

'Nothing.'

He ran the tip of his forefinger gently down her bare arm. The magic worked again; she felt that thrilling charge. 'You're so lovely,' he said.

She felt stunned by him, someone who could make her feel so sexy and relaxed both at once. It was as if there was a spell on her, she thought, or a wand had been waved to make this an enchanted night. The bubble would surely break but just now, being inside it was the loveliest feeling in the world.

He had already asked her all the basics – name, age, career, boyfriends – in fact he had asked her all these things in the first half hour of their meeting.

'What is this?' she had protested at last. 'A census?'

'Sorry. It's my job,' He looked sheepish. It had passed through Zoe's mind, briefly but with the effect of an express train, that maybe he was a policeman. Her heart had pounded.

'I'm a reporter. I'm trained to be nosey.'

'Oh! Is that all? I mean, gosh, how exciting!'

'You think so?' He looked delighted. 'Some people think it's one up, or maybe down, from being a Traffic Warden.'

She had asked him about his work, partly to detract any further questioning about herself, but also because she was genuinely interested. He had told her funny stories about his early days on a local paper, being sent to cover Marrow Contests and the sort of things he apparently did now – doorstepping Captains of Industry at two in the morning, sitting in his freezing car listening to photographers drone on about exciting assignments in the Middle East.

'I'm sure you do serious things, too,' she had said, laughing.

'Oh I do, but they're too boring to talk about.'

She could never imagine him being boring; he made everything sound so interesting and vibrant – perhaps that was part of his skill, she wondered. When he had told her where he worked, she had been most impressed. 'But I like that paper!'

'You read it?'

'Sometimes.'

'You do? May I shake your hand? Is there anything, short of human sacrifice, that I can do for you?'

He had picked up on her accent, of course. Just about the first thing he had asked was whether she lived round here. When she had explained, he had looked so pleased that she had laughed. 'Why, we're practically neighbours in London,' he had said.

The huge amount of kedgeree finally defeated her. She put her plate down on the stair beside her and he immediately picked up her hand. He put it to his lips and kissed it. Their first kiss. She giggled like a schoolgirl.

'Here's to us,' he said.

Anton had been in police custody for fifteen hours. Considering everything, he had to admit they had not treated him too badly. They had slapped him around a bit at first, the bodyguards especially, and there had been a few punches and kicks on the floor of the police van, but once they had brought him into the station all that had stopped.

He had been taken into a small interrogation room and pushed down into a seat. It was a gloomy place: brick walls painted white and a single lightbulb covered by a plastic shade. It looked the kind of place where they tore out your fingernails, he had thought, swallowing hard.

But all they had done was question him. Two policemen in civilian clothes repeating the same questions over and over again. In a way, he would have preferred it if they had carried on the beating. At least if he had been dealing with pain, he would have had something concrete to deal with. But the slow drip, drip, drip of questioning might eventually wear away his resolve . . .

One of the interrogators had adopted a paternal, concerned air – asking him if he was cold or needed coffee, something to eat – the other had played the hard man. Yelling in his face, banging on the table, coming up softly behind him and roaring in his ear.

Good guy, bad guy, the classic technique. Anton could handle it, no problem.

But it had gone on. Hour after hour, the same words, the same routine, and it had started to become difficult. They had taken away his watch and there was no clock in the room. In the end, he did not know how long he had held out before it had suddenly become unbearable: he had to speak or go mad, say anything to stop those questions.

'Never Again!' His own voice had sounded strange to him. 'I am a commando serving with Never Again. I claim the rights of a political prisoner. I demand the protection of the Geneva Convention!'

'What rights did you give the Governor, you little bastard?' the hard man yelled. 'Shooting a man in the back?'

'Luis! That's enough! What's your name, son?'

Anton had given it, and his date of birth. It was such a relief to be communicating again, to have the good man smiling at him, hanging onto his every word! So he had gone on talking, until he realised that the room had fallen silent, all except for the sounds of a pen flying over paper and his own voice.

He had stopped mid-sentence. 'I'm not saying any more.'

'Oh, come on, Anton. You're doing so well.'

'No, no. Nothing. That's it.' They had tried to get him going again, but he had stuck to his new silence, cloaking himself with it in shame and blocking out their words. In the end, they had stopped and gone away. A uniformed policeman had brought him a plastic cup of coffee and a sandwich, and a mattress and blanket had been laid on the floor for him.

That had been several hours ago, or so it seemed. He had completely lost track of time. He had not moved from his chair, had sat upright, arms folded, trying to remember exactly how much he had said. He had not revealed anything essential, he was pretty sure about that. Only how he had been recruited by the Dutchman and sent for training in Corsica. He had told them quite a bit about training – he bit his lip – but the good policeman had seemed so interested.

'Sounds tough going,' he had said, looking impressed.

Anton had described Sergio. Then they had shown him pictures and there had been Sergio staring up at him. Remembering that, he began to tremble until he realised it did not matter. At least now he was out of Sergio's reach. He smiled unpleasantly to himself. Sergio had better watch out: they would be coming to get him soon.

In the adjoining room, Barney was being briefed. It was just before ten o'clock in the morning and he had been in Gibraltar for forty-five minutes, flown directly onto the Rock, courtesy of a military jet from Brize Norton.

At the last moment there had been some doubt over whether he should come at all. Hargreaves had called shortly before the car had arrived to take him to the airfield. Did he think it was entirely necessary? Weren't the Gibraltarians capable of interrogating the gunman themselves?

Barney, short of sleep and with a hangover that he knew would last all day, had been curt with her.

'I think this boy is what we've all been waiting for. That's me and half the security forces in Europe. I think he's a Sleeper, and I think he's the first one they've activated. We've been unlucky enough to have him shoot the British

Governor – but it gives us first call on interrogating him, doesn't it?

'And I want to get over there fast before the Gib police start inviting all their friends to come and look at what they've caught. All right?'

Hargreaves had given in surprisingly easily. He suspected it had a lot to do with being unavailable the previous night. He grinned: and maybe she was suffering a hangover herself.

Sitting opposite him now was Inspector Douglas Eriz, one of Anton's interrogators. The man looked Spanish and spoke English with a heavy accent. Barney, never having been to Gibraltar before, had expected everyone to be British. This mixture of races threw him a bit.

'We've already notified the French police in Corsica. They thought from the description they knew the area where Sergio Brunelli might be.'

'Brunelli?' Barney repeated slowly. 'Red Brigades?'

'Yes.'

'Ah, the Kessler connection again.'

'Excuse me?'

'Sorry, thinking aloud. When'll we know if they've got Brunelli?'

'Soon. The French Legion are sending in their anti-terrorist unit.'

'Wise precaution. So, Valente's talked about Pieter and his training. Is that it?'

'Yes.' Inspector Eriz stood up. 'We'd have kept at him but we got your message. I'll take you into him now.'

Every New Year's Eve, Gerda Boellard had a telephone call from her brother. They had never been exactly close – their divorced parents had chosen to rear one of them each at opposite ends of The Netherlands – but that call was a tradition, one that Pieter had always observed.

He might forget Christmas and birthdays, but never New Year.

Mrs Boellard had three children under the age of ten and it was not until New Year's Day that she realised Pieter had not called. It was really too bad of him, she said to her husband.

He was the children's only uncle; he had sent them nothing for Christmas, not even the usual cheques; the very least he could have done was to have called her yesterday. You would think he would want to know how they were all getting on.

'Maybe he's busy,' her husband suggested. 'Or on holiday.'

'But he should have called!'

Gerda went to sit in the kitchen. She plucked angrily at the browning leaves of her table-top geranium, imagining her brother sunning himself on a Caribbean island, forgetting what day it was. But slowly her feelings of petulance and being hard-done-by began to be replaced by unease.

Now she came to think of it, she could not remember exactly when it had been that she had last heard from Pieter. It must have been four or five months ago, she realised with a start, when he had called to say that he had a new job and was doing quite a bit of travelling outside the Netherlands.

She frowned, trying to remember what he had said the job was, but she had been only half-listening to him and had not taken it in. But whatever it was, he should have made contact since then . . .

She flushed guiltily; she ought to have noticed how long it had been since they had last spoken; she ought to have called him. He could be ill or in trouble. She would call him right now.

After a few minutes' rummage in her bedroom bureau, she found the card with his address and telephone number. She dialled it. 'This is Pieter Van Hoeffen,' his voice said. 'I am unable to come to the telephone right now.'

She left a message. As she put the phone down, she expected her fears to evaporate, but they did not. She stood indecisively in her bedroom, looking out over the back garden of her neighbour's house. Then she ran downstairs and picked the car keys off their hook in the hall.

'I'm going to drive up to Amsterdam,' she told her husband. He was watching football; the two boys were playing with a new game on the floor.

'What?'

'I'm going to see if Pieter's all right. I called but I only got his message machine.'

'It'll be a wasted journey then, won't it?'

'I don't care. It'll only take me an hour. Elsi will be back from her party at five.'

Her husband looked alarmed. 'But what about food?'

'We have a fridge full of food. Give them whatever you like,' she said, impatiently.

It took her a little over an hour to drive to the outskirts of the city where Pieter had his neat little house, modern brick, not too much paintwork, with a long front garden and a double garage. It was on a development of identical properties, popular with young families, and Pieter seemed out of place there. She had said as much on her first and only visit there with the children six years ago, just after he had bought it. 'Are you planning to marry then?' she had asked, trying to show interest. But all he had said was something about not fitting in anywhere so it hardly mattered where he lived.

She frowned into her rear-view mirror as she turned into Pieter's road. Her brother might be very clever; he might have four degrees and earn lots of money as a psychiatrist, but he had never seemed to be very happy. As far as she knew he had not had a girlfriend since the doctor he had been living with had left him eight years ago. She wondered, with a stab of guilt, whether he had been very lonely and she, his only relative now that their mother was senile and their father dead, had neglected him.

She pulled up outside the house. The lawn was not overgrown; the windows looked fairly clean and the curtains were drawn. She got out of the car and walked up the driveway, beginning to feel foolish. Her brother was most likely away on a holiday, probably skiing. She reached the front-door. Now that she was here she might as well find out . . .

'Hello there!'

She stepped back in the direction of the voice. In the garden next door stood a young man, holding a toddler by the hand. 'Are you looking for Pieter?' he called.

'Yes. I'm his sister.'

The man stepped carefully over the low stone wall that divided the gardens, bringing the child with him.

'Pleased to meet you. You'll have come to check on the house and pick up his post then?'

'His post?'

'Well, he hasn't been here for so long, it must be a mountain by now. We've been keeping an eye on the place, just in case, but it's a pretty safe neighbourhood.' He paused. 'Pieter's off on a long trip, then? Great job he's got, whatever it is. All that travelling! He never will say what he does exactly . . .' He ended on a hopeful note.

'I, uh,' Gerda cleared her throat. 'When did you last see him, did you say?'

'I didn't. But it was some time ago. My wife and I were only saying last night we can't remember when we last did see him! A good three months it must be.'

'But what about the house? And the garden?'

The man looked at her curiously. 'Well, his company arranges it, I suppose, or else he does. The gardener comes once a week, keeps the place looking trim. And an empty house doesn't need much looking after, does it?'

Zoe rolled over in bed and opened her eyes. The amount of daylight filtering through her curtains told her that it must be very late, approaching noon. She listened, but could hear nothing from the rest of the house. Maybe everyone had gone out. She ought to get up, she knew, but she was so warm and comfortable where she was. She yawned extravagantly and snuggled back under the duvet. She would have just a few more minutes.

Matt had not wanted to let her go. When Alasdair and Kerry had come looking for her and found them together on the stairs – Zoe lying stretched out with her head in Matt's lap, and both of them gazing at each other and laughing at themselves for doing so – he had not let her move.

Alasdair had been a little drunk, a little belligerent. 'Hey, that's my sister you've got there!'

'Have I?' Matt had grinned down at her. 'I was wondering whose she was.'

'Who're you, more's the point?'

'It's OK, Al,' she had called, trying to sit up.

'I'm Matt Anderson. Pleased to meet you, Al. I would get up to shake hands but I'm afraid your sister'll run away.' He blew her a kiss and she giggled.

Alasdair started to climb the stairs, but Kerry dragged him back. 'Al, come on.' She smiled up at them. 'Nice to meet you, Matt Anderson. You'll bring her home, will you?'

'I promise.'

'See you later in the day, Zoe. Happy New Year.'

Matt had spent forty minutes on the telephone before he could find a mini-cab that would take them home. He had kissed the tip of her nose and said, 'See, the gods have brought us together,' when they realised that his skiing lodge was under a mile's walk from Zoe's home and that he had passed her house during his walk in the glen.

When she had shivered slightly as they emerged from the hotel into the frosty night, he had taken off his greatcoat and wrapped it round her. In the back of the cab he had made his arm a pillow for her head and held her closely to him.

It was such little acts of caring that made her love him. 'I will see you again?' he had asked urgently when the car stopped in front of the house. 'Won't I?'

'Oh yes! Yes please!'

'Promise?' He had kissed her full upon the mouth. The warm rush had gone right through her and she had opened her eyes wide. 'Yes, I promise.'

She let herself drift off towards sleep again. She was aware that she was smiling and that everything seemed to be a golden colour. 'Just like in the movies,' she murmured and giggled.

She slept. She was back at the Ball with Matt and they were dancing, floating over the ballroom floor, the only couple there. Matt's hands were gentle on her flesh and he was smiling down at her, telling her that they would be together for always. She was feeling so happy and full of hope but she wanted to show him something that was important, although she did not know what it was. She led him to a mirror at the far end of the room, a huge mirror that took up the whole wall, and she gave it a little push, then took his hand and went through it. The room behind was very cold and dark.

'I can't see anything,' he said.

'Wait, you'll see it soon,' she told him.

And it was getting lighter. Looking up they saw stars, hundreds of brilliant lights very far away but between them and the stars were the struts of a blackened building with a vaulted ceiling.

'It's a ruined church,' Matt said, puzzled, and she was frowning, trying to remember why she had brought him here. On the floor near them were bundles of clothing, blue and white, strewn all over. Suddenly one of them moved, and a child's face emerged, twisted in agony. Something was terribly wrong with him, something was happening to his face; the flesh was disintegrating, leaving only his skull but the jaws were wide open and from them came a terrible scream that tore at her heart. Then he lifted up his right hand – it was untouched – and he extended his child's finger at her. Matt turned to look at her and there was a look of horror and disgust on his face. He stepped backwards through the mirror, running from her. She wanted to stop him and explain but her legs would not obey her and she knew she was stuck forever in that other place.

She woke up. Her heart was pounding so loudly that the sound filled the room. She felt giddy and closed her eyes. Immediately she saw Matt's face again, the terror in his eyes as he saw her for what she truly was.

She gave a little sob; of course she could never have him! She had been a fool to think that she could, to let herself believe that the Ball was anything other than a few hours' reprieve from her life.

How could she, after all she had done, ever have thought otherwise? She, who had only to close her eyes to see the face of the begging boy in Turin, or remember that less than twenty-four hours before she had used her own father to obey her orders . . .

A hot tear trickled down her face and she brushed it angrily away. Self-pity was the last thing she needed. She ought to remember the reason she was fighting and be proud that she had been chosen: be proud that she could never belong to just one person.

She lay back down and tried to think calmly. But if anything the thumping of her heart seemed to get louder. She realised that someone was knocking on her door.

'Come in,' she cried, glad of any diversion.

It was Kerry, grinning and bursting with news. 'Sorry to wake you, but I thought you'd like to know at once.'

Zoe blinked. 'Know what?'

Kerry laughed. 'Feeling a bit the worse for wear? Never mind, this'll cheer you up. Guess who's downstairs in the kitchen?'

Zoe shook her head. She was too drained to play games.

'Matt Anderson, that's who! He's very nice, Zoe, and I'd say,' Kerry looked arch, 'that he's rather taken with you. I said I'd come and see if you were awake. There, I thought that might put some colour back in your cheeks!'

Barney peered at Anton Valente through the spyhole of the cell door. The boy knew he was being watched. A little smirk played around the corners of his mouth, as he let his gaze wander self-consciously about the room. Barney clenched his fists. The desire to go in there and hit him hard was considerable.

It was a temptation that Barney had been resisting for three hours. At first, when Inspector Eriz had ushered him into the room to start his interrogation, Barney had been reminded of Chrisoph. Valente had the same skinny form and youthful face.

But very quickly he had realised Valente was entirely different from the German boy. Valente was smug – and proud of himself, enjoying his role as the fearless revolutionary.

All morning he had sat opposite Barney and the inspector, staring at a point behind Barney's left ear and saying ... nothing except for his name and the fact that he was 'a political prisoner taken hostage in the battle against fascism'. Barney had tried flattery, threats, promises, even insulting the boy's mother. All to no avail. Valente had remained mute.

Through the spyhole, Barney saw him give a great, exaggerated yawn. His own jaw clenched: to think that that piece of scum had blown away a man's right to live as a fully functioning human being!

He took a deep breath. The news that he and the police officer had just been given and the strategy that they had devised might well prove Valente's undoing.

A minute later, when he, Eriz and the interpreter re-entered the cell, Anton watched them coolly, jerking his head as if in time to music.

Barney leant across the interpreter and said to Eriz: 'I don't fancy the lad's chances, do you?'

Eriz inhaled in a whistle and shook his head from side to side. 'Not at all.'

For a moment, Barney thought that he saw a look of interest cross the boy's face.

'D'you speak English, Anton?'

The boy blanked him.

'Well, it doesn't matter either way. If you do, you'll hear what I'm about to tell you twice. Awfully boring for you, I'd have imagined – but then, you've got time on your hands.

'Right,' he took a sheet of paper from a cardboard file he was carrying and placed it in front of him on the table, 'Inspector Eriz and I were, as you saw, called away half an hour ago to receive some news.

'It concerned Sergio Brunelli. You remember, Anton, don't you, how you very helpfully supplied Sergio's name, description and whereabouts to Inspector Eriz and his colleague earlier on? When you were being a nice, co-operative lad.'

Anton flinched at the memory of his betrayal, and Barney saw him. So he does understand English, he thought.

He continued at a friendly pace: 'Now, I'm sure you're as keen as we were to find out what's happened to Senor Brunelli. Because of your absolutely excellent description of the farmhouse and its location the Corsican authorities were able to pinpoint it. At first light this morning, the French Foreign Legion's Anti-Terrorist unit descended on that little farmhouse. You can imagine it, can't you? Helicopters, men abseiling onto the roof, glass smashing, stun-grenades going in. The firepower these guys have got!'

Barney studied the document in front of him and chuckled. 'Yes, there wasn't much left of that farmhouse or the barn after five minutes, I can tell you. And as for Brunelli . . .'

He glanced up. Valente swallowed several times and wetted his lips.

'What d'you think was left of him?'

The boy looked directly at him. He had understood that perfectly; there was a breathless, gleeful look about him.

'Not a lot, huh?'

A couple of tiny nods. Valente was right there with him.

Barney dropped his eyes to the table. 'Well, if only he'd been there, I'm sure there would have been nothing left of him.'

He had spoken too quickly. He had to wait for the translator before he saw the truth hit home and the boy gasp.

'Yup, seems that Brunelli doesn't live there except when he's training one of you lot. Kind of his office. He lives in Corte, in the mountains, did you know that?'

Anton was hooked. He was frowning in the effort to understand every word. He gave a couple of shakes of the head; he was starting to look worried.

'No? No, I don't suppose you did. It was an old woman who told the police. An old peasant woman who lived in one of the cottages on the main road at the start of Brunelli's track. Seems she used to do the laundry for you. She had to be leaned on a bit, but her son's in prison for blowing up a French official in a nationalist attack and she didn't like the idea of not seeing him again, so she eventually remembered Sergio's address in the town. Of course, the Legion went straight there.'

Anton sat forward again. The hopeful look had returned.

Barney studied his document. 'Yup. Senor Brunelli lived in some style. Big house, lots of expensive furniture, swimming pool. He got pretty well paid to put you through all that torture, didn't he? Oh, and he had a very angry girlfriend.

'It wasn't just that she objected to a couple of dozen commandos somersaulting in through her windows and chucking gas canisters about at seven o'clock in the morning. She was already absolutely furious before her visitors arrived. It seems she'd been woken up by a telephone call for Sergio at three o'clock this morning. As soon as he put the phone down, he grabbed the money from the safe – all of it – took some documents and a few guns he kept at the place, and left. No mention of where he was going; when he'd be back; no forwarding address. And he didn't leave her a sou. No wonder she was angry, eh?'

Barney paused again, giving all his attention to the document, although the single sheet of paper ran only to fifteen lines. He waited a further minute after the translator had stopped to ensure that he had Anton's full attention.

'They're pretty good, these Corsican police. After the French Legion had climbed back into their helicopters and buzzed off back to Calvi, the police began visiting some of their contacts. It didn't take them long to find a young chap who'd been paid a great deal of money at four-thirty this morning to sell a very expensive motor-launch. Of course, it wasn't his to sell – he's supposed to maintain it for the owner during the winter months – but the Italian who bought it was in such a hurry to leave Corsica, and so very generous with his cash. We can guess who that man was, can't we, Anton?'

He did not bother to check whether Valente was with him; he knew he was. 'It was a big boat, equipped with lights and plenty of fuel,' he continued conversationally. 'A man like Brunelli could be many places by now. Italy, France, Sardinia, Sicily, Tunisia even. Of course, Interpol have issued warnings but I don't think either of us believe that Brunelli'd be silly enough to risk going through a Customs' check, do we? No, he's gone, Anton. He's out there, somewhere.'

There was raw fear in Anton's eyes now. As soon as he saw Barney watching him, he dropped his head.

'I imagine he's a vengeful sort of chap, don't you, Anton? He's not someone who's likely to pat you on the shoulder and say, 'Never mind, son. I can understand the pressure you were under.' But of course, you know him so much better than any one of us. I'll let you imagine what Senor Brunelli might say to you if you two should ever meet again . . .'

Barney leaned back in his chair and considered the badly cracked ceiling for a few moments. 'Inspector Eriz, I think

Brunelli and Pieter and Ms Kessler would be proud of our young friend here, don't you?'

Eriz cleared his throat. 'Absolutely.'

'Yes, here he sits in the Lion's Den itself, facing God knows what from your men out there – they're lining up in the corridor, you know, Anton, and once the Inspector and I have left, well, they'll be paying a visit – but Inspector, we know how brave Anton is, so that wouldn't worry him. He isn't showing the slightest sign of cracking, is he?'

'No, none.'

'Not a word has passed his lips . . .'

Eriz coughed. The translator was working furiously; just in case Valente was not getting everything, Barney gave him a few moments to catch up. 'Well, Inspector, let's be fair. I think we can pass over that earlier stuff. He was still in shock. But since then, he's been extremely uncooperative. Sitting there like the noble warrior Brunelli would have expected.'

'Si, the model commando.'

'Unfortunately, although his bosses would doubtless be delighted to witness his present behaviour, we are very fed up with it aren't we?'

'Very,' said Eriz. 'We are very pissed off.'

Anton frowned and edged back in his chair. Maybe he thought the beating was imminent, Barney thought. He turned to Eriz: 'In fact, Inspector, I think we've had enough?'

The policeman nodded slowly. 'Yes, why should we sit through the shit that this kid's giving us any longer?'

Barney frowned across at Anton. 'You're right. I mean, what's in it for us? Over the last few years we've both seen too many guilty men walk free, haven't we?'

'We're really pissed off with British justice,' said the Inspector.

'Too right! We break our balls to catch the villains and then some judge gives them a year or probation. I mean, what d'you reckon Anton'll get for shooting the Governor in the back?'

The policeman gave a magnificent heave of his shoulders. 'Should be life, but if he gets a clever lawyer, and a stupid jury, five years, six?'

'And with remission, that could go down to three or four. Pathetic isn't it?'

Valente looked both suspicious and bewildered. Good, Barney thought. He spoke across the table to Eriz. 'So shall we do what we said?'

'Yes. I'm very tired.' The policeman leaned back in his chair and closed his eyes.

'Anton, I'll tell you what we're going to do.' Barney spoke directly to the boy; he had his full attention. 'We're going to set you free.'

Valente stared at him.

'You don't think we mean it, do you, son? But we do.'

Tentatively, a smile spread along the boy's mouth.

'Of course,' Barney continued, glancing once more in Eriz's direction, 'it'll be a special kind of freedom, won't it?'

The man kept his eyes closed. 'Short-lived.' He repeated the phrase in Spanish.

The boy's smile trembled.

'Oh, we'll let you go, Anton!' Barney assured him. 'In fact we'll take you to the mainland and fling you out onto the streets. But at the same time, we'll let be alerting certain people known to us in the revolutionary underworld that you bought your freedom. D'you understand what I mean?

'We'll tell them how you grassed up Sergio, and Pieter and Beatrix Kessler and her two companions. How you sold everyone to save your own rotten little hide.'

He stopped until there was silence in the room, then he said softly: 'I don't think you'd see another twenty-four hours.'

Valente twisted in his chair. There was a look of real terror in his face.

Eriz opened his eyes. 'If he was lucky, they might kill him quick. If not . . .' He smiled sadistically

Anton gave a bleat of distress. He leaned forward across the desk. 'I talk to you!' he cried in English. 'I tell you more things! Please, sir!'

Forty-five minutes later Barney was speaking to Gregson in London.

'Once he got talking, there was no stopping him. I've made notes and I'll get a transcript of everything to bring back with me, but I wanted to get this out on Priority right away. You'll have to get Hargreaves' say-so, but she won't give you any problem, not on something like this.

'All right. We've got a British sleeper. A girl, about twenty years old – say twenty to twenty-five at the outside.

'Blonde, slim, about one metre sixty-three, whatever that is in English. She was in Corsica at the same time as the boy, that's late August last year. If she got the same treatment as he did, she'd have been booked into a tourist hotel in the north of the island and there can't have been that many blondes staying in Corsica on their own last summer, can there?

'What's more relevant is that Valente heard something the girl said, and it has to be identifiable. He was skulking behind a rock, but he saw her pointing up at the sky, at a big bird. And she called out to Brunelli: "Isn't that a Golden Eagle?" Then she said something about having one near her home.

'We've been over and over it with him, and he's adamant that she said "Golden Eagle". He says he remembers it, because when he heard the words he looked up at the bird and could see nothing gold about it, just a huge wing span.

'I think this could well be the clincher! Our little girl comes from a place where eagles swoop.

'Narrows it down quite a bit, don't you think? Put it together with the other stuff and it can't be too long before we get her. Which is just as well.

'I don't know for sure, of course, but I think it's highly likely that Never Again's about to let rip in the UK. I think Gibraltar was the first shot – pardon the pun – and our girl may be activated at any moment.

'What? No, we've got to assume she'll still be around. The damage done by Anton isn't enough to stop them. The Leaders'll run and regroup, same as they did after Bremen. Brunelli, too. He'll be hiding out somewhere.

'OK? Can you get it sent out to everyone pronto? Did you manage to get hold of Gemmer? Good. Can you call him again, say I'll be back tomorrow and I'll talk to him first thing? I'd better get back in there and see what song Anton's singing.

'Oh, just a minute! Talking of birds, get onto the RSPB and find out where eagles fly in Britain, will you?'

Chapter Twenty-Two

Matt carried the drinks over to the table where Zoe was sitting. 'I got us crisps as well,' he said, producing them. 'Cheese and Onion or Roast Chicken flavour, take your pick.'

He sat down beside her. 'D'you realise I'm worn out, trying to keep up with you? I thought I was pretty fit, but compared to you!' He took a gulp of beer. 'What d'you do? Run a marathon every day? Or weight-training?'

Zoe looked into his eyes but said nothing.

'Did I say something wrong? I didn't mean to imply you'd huge muscles, honest. I think you're perfect.'

An elderly man sitting at the next table in the pub turned and gave Matt a long, searching look. Zoe, however, fixed her gaze on the table.

Matt felt a little flicker of panic.

Last night, or this morning rather, he had been so sure Zoe had felt the same way. Her eyes had danced when she looked at him and she had responded so openly to his caress; she had lain in his lap like a puppy while he had stroked her and she had smiled up at him as if he was the answer to everything she wanted. He had felt so lucky, as if he had entered a world designed just for him.

When he had first seen her, standing with her brother, he had thought she looked too cute to be interested in him.

When she had not cut him dead after that first 'hello', he had held his breath, and that curious sensation of knowing her from some other time or place had swept over him. Fleetingly he had remembered something about a Chinese proverb, that when the souls of two partners meet both shall know, but he had managed to pull himself together sufficiently to ask her if she wanted to dance. When she had agreed, he had been so happy he had wanted to laugh out loud; when she had seemed to want to stay with him, listening with that little smile on her lips to everything he said . . .

But now this. Matt frowned; the whole afternoon had been strange.

From the very first moment he had seen her that day, she had been different. She had looked incredibly pale and tense, as if she was afraid. When he had grinned at her like an idiot, unable to stop himself because he felt so happy, she had smiled nervously but had not met his eyes. Her mother, who had been sitting at the kitchen table, cross-questioning him about his job, had said: 'Zoe, darling, you look like a ghost! Why not put on some make-up?' but Zoe, he was glad to note, had ignored her.

Perhaps she had a bad time at home, he thought.

He had suggested a walk in the glen and she had agreed readily enough. But then she had been like a little robot throughout, marching ahead of him, pulling away when he tried to draw her to him. And yet . . . once or twice on that route-march she had turned to look at him and in her face had been such sorrow and longing that his heart had turned over. She had looked so defenceless, so small, standing there in the over-large donkey jacket, a tiny figure against the hills.

But when he had caught up with her and asked her what was wrong, she had not replied. She had tried to, opening and shutting her mouth, but the words got stuck. The only conversation they had had, if you could call it that, was about a bird he had seen hovering high above the hillside.

'What's that? A kestrel?' he had asked, more of himself than her. He had thought she was too far away to hear.

But her voice, with its lovely, lilting accent had come answering back: 'No, it's an eagle. There's two pairs here. They've got their nests higher up in the mountains but they hunt all over the glen.'

'Aah, an ornithologist! Tell me more.'

She had stopped, half way up the hill, turned and smiled at him, then gone plunging ahead again.

He took another gulp of beer. Maybe she was simply a very moody girl or perhaps she was just young. Twenty-three, she had said last night: he could not remember himself being so changeable at that age, but then she was a girl. Maybe she had psychological problems. He frowned into his pint then set it down on the table and gave her a sideways glance. He saw the outline of her pink lips and longed to kiss them. Or maybe, he told himself firmly, in the cold light of day she did not fancy him at all and was too nice to say so. He braced himself: nothing could be worse than not knowing.

'Zoe,' he said gently, 'was last night a mistake for you? You can tell me. I'm big and ugly enough. I can take it.'

She sat beside him, not moving, not saying anything.

She had taken off the swamping wool jacket, and the heavy blue sweater. Underneath she was wearing a soft pink jumper that hugged her body perfectly, rising and falling over the small mounds of her breasts.

'Zoe? You only have to say the word.'

She turned to him and he saw her eyes were brimming with tears. 'Please don't go, Matt,' she whispered.

He touched her shoulder and felt her tremor. Then he moved closer and encircled all of her in his arm. The old man at the next table turned for another look, gave an audible and prolonged sigh of disgust before pointedly turning away again.

Inside his arm, Zoe was shaking. The desire he felt for her was swallowed by pity and a longing to comfort her. 'What is it, darling?' he asked, and the endearment that he had never used before, had always indeed mocked, seemed suddenly natural to him.

'I can't explain,' her voice trembled. 'Please don't ask me. I'm sorry.'

He kissed the nearest bit of her, her hair. 'It's all right,' he said inadequately. 'You don't have to.'

'It wasn't a mistake last night . . . this morning. I've never been so happy in my life.'

He squeezed her. 'And now that's changed?'

'No.' She started mopping at her face with a hand-kerchief.

'You could've fooled me.' He looked down at her teary face and she smiled shakily. He felt her relax against him in the way she had at the Ball.

'I'm really sorry for this afternoon. I . . . there's something I can't tell you about that sometimes makes me sad.'

'In your past? Something bad happened to you in your past?'

'Yes,' she was hesitant. He could see that he was on dangerous ground.

'I really can't tell you. Please, don't ask.'

'I won't. I just want to tell you I'll never let anything bad happen to you again.'

She smiled at him so strangely: both happy and sad at once; longing and disbelieving.

'That would be nice, Matt,' she sighed, dropping her eyes.

'And we're going to carry on seeing each other? Here and in London?'

She peeped up. 'You really want to after how I've been today?'

'Hey,' he picked up her hand. 'I want to see you all the time. God, what am I saying? This is so uncool!'

She grinned and all the ghosts fled. 'But it's how I feel too!'

Three hours later Matt was battling up Glen Road, his head bent into the icy gusts of wind, his eyes streaming and his whole being suffused with warmth. He felt like a kid on his first date. No, he corrected himself, remembering the terror of that experience, he felt a whole lot better than that. He grinned: he felt like he had met the girl of his dreams. 'Aaargh, what a cliche!' he cried to the wind but he carried on grinning nonetheless.

He remembered her smile and the blue and gold specks in her eyes. The way she looked at him from under those great dark eyelashes; the feeling she gave him as she had cuddled in closer to his side as the evening progressed.

All the afternoon's tension had gone. Now the prospect of losing her seemed utterly remote, part of a horrible dream that no longer needed to be remembered.

They had talked. Matt pulled a face: he had talked, and Zoe had listened. He had probably bored her to tears, telling her about his childhood and then going on about his job again, as he had done at the Ball. He felt his face redden. 'Will you never learn?' he asked himself, suddenly angry. Had it not been exactly that, his obsession with his job, that had cost him his relationship with Louise?

Not, he hastened to reassure himself, that he was comparing the two: Zoe had none of the harshness or the selfishness of Louise; Zoe was soft and sweet, unspoilt. She seemed so happy sitting there, listening, a different prospect entirely to Louise. But Louise had not always been wrong, he did talk too much about work.

The next time he saw Zoe, he would shut up and let her speak. It was not simply to stop himself hogging the conversation; he wanted to hear more about her. Something beyond the bare rudiments that she had gone to boarding school, university and was now filling in time working in a bookshop. Oh, and she knew a lot about birds, he thought fondly, and she was shy.

But she should not be shy with him. Nothing she could tell him would put him off. She filled him with delight. A tiny doubt pricked at him, even as he thought that: what was the bad thing that had happened to her? What had made her run away from him? Rape? He shuddered. He had interviewed rape victims; he knew how deep the scarring could go. But Zoe had responded so eagerly and naturally to him . . .

He replayed the scene when they had said goodnight in the driveway of her home. She had buried her head in his chest and hugged him as if she never wanted to let him go. When he had kissed her, he had felt her whole being open up to him. He had wanted to pick her up in his arms and take her away, to be with him forever. He imagined Zoe at home, in his bed and himself slowly kissing her, exploring her with his hands, finding what she liked, lingering over her.

It was starting to snow again. His torch picked out the fresh white falling on grey. He turned into the track that led up to the log cabin, thinking how Christmas-cardy it looked, with its lights twinkling down on him. He stamped up the wooden stairs to the front door and heard the others laughing inside.

It was a shame, he thought wryly, to ruin their evening with his presence.

They were sitting around the fire; the three couples and Louise. But with her on the low sofa sat a tall, dark-haired man Matt remembered seeing at the Ball. He smiled, feeling genuinely glad for Louise.

She turned her head slowly in his direction. 'Oh it's you,' she said. 'The office phoned you about six hours ago.' She shot a loving look at the man beside her. 'They said it was urgent. You'll have to go back tomorrow . . . or something, can't really remember. I said we hadn't seen you in ages, you'd probably got lost in a snowdrift. The man was so frightfully rude I put the phone down.'

Matt cursed himself. He should have taken his bleeper; he imagined how Louise must have enjoyed winding up the office. Everyone would have gone home by now; he would have to call someone at home. 'Who was it? Lomax?'

Louise was playing with the man's fingers. From his surprised look, Matt saw he had not had so much attention all night. She looked up. 'How should I know? All these nasty little newspaper types sound the same to me.'

Sergio Brunelli should have been feeling tired, but danger always elated him and kept him alert. It was eleven o'clock at night; he been travelling for nearly twenty hours but he felt more awake than he had done for years. He guessed it was something to do with the animal instinct for survival. He smiled at himself in the bathroom mirror as he shaved for the second time that day. Another animal instinct was coming into play: the sharp desire for a woman. For Sergio, the two went hand in hand.

From outside the hotel window came the sounds of the city at night. Car horns blaring, people's feet on the sidewalk, sudden startling blasts of music and the more distant sound of klaxons from the river. Intoxicating! It had been a long time since he had been in a big city, and longer still since he had been in this city. But as always, even recovering from New Year, Paris was vibrant and full of life.

When he had left Corsica that morning he had given little

thought to his destination. The message had been to get out fast; that Valente had been taken. He remembered the boy and knew that he only had hours: Valente had been determined but not strong.

As he had raced his car out of Corte, screaming it down the mountain bends, he had at every moment been expecting police lights behind or helicopters overhead.

He had bought the boat, made it to the Italian coast by seven, stolen a car and driven to Turin. On the radio he had heard the news that the Governor of Gibraltar was in a critical condition and that police were still interviewing his attacker. Nothing more; no indication that the boy had spilled his guts yet.

At Turin airport he had caught a flight to Milan and then, hopefully, vanished. With each passing hour, it looked more likely. The police would be able to trace him there but no further.

He had come from Milan and he still had many contacts in the city; his blood brothers, he called them. One of them had fixed him up with false papers while another had arranged his transport and change of clothes. Five hours later, unrecognisable in a dark blue Armani suit, close-cropped hair white shirt, dark tie and glasses, Sergio had been the sole passenger in a private six-seater jet that landed at Charles de Gaulle airport. As a private passenger, he had bypassed the public terminal, going instead to a small Customs' shed. The bored-looking official had barcly glanced at his papers before waving him through.

He had taken a taxi straight to the Georges V hotel. In the mood that was upon him, nowhere else would have done. He had booked into a suite and ordered a bottle of champagne and steak-frites. If this should be his last night of freedom, or even his last night on earth, he intended to enjoy himself.

In the late afternoon, he had left the hotel to find a telephone booth. After making two calls, he had waited, then made another. Five minutes later the telephone had rung and he had spoken to Kessler.

'No news here. And you?'

'Quiet.'

'You'll be looking to move on soon. I'd stay in the country, if I was you, but north, near the borders. Beautiful scenery up there. Remote, not too far from the seaside.'

Sergio patted his face dry with a white fluffy towel and applied the Gianni Versace aftershave he had bought from an exclusive shop opposite the hotel.

Tomorrow, he told himself, if he was still at liberty, he would start the serious business of relocation. He did not know northern France particularly well but he had little doubt he would find somewhere suitable. He wondered why Kessler wanted him up there, what was in her mind. But as long as the money kept coming in, he would do as he was told. Whether it was Kessler herself giving the orders or the man, the one who had described himself as her 'superior', Axel, who had called upon his services two months before, to 'deal with' the kids who had planted the Paris bomb.

The money had been very good indeed for that job, more than enough to pay the two men who had carried it out, and still keep a part back for himself. In the mirror, Sergio grimaced, remembering the orders he had been given; that they were to be 'ugly killings'. It was not something that he could have done himself: to kill cleanly or to wound for a purpose, yes; to carve people up and then kill them, never. That was torture, not something he liked to think about.

He stepped out of the bathroom into the glitz of the room. There was an enormous bed, with an intricately carved gold painted headboard showing nymphs cavorting and playing the lyre. The sheets had been turned down earlier in the evening by the maid who had also left chocolates on the pillows. But Sergio had no intention of sleeping in that bed tonight.

Smiling in anticipation at what lay before him, he put on his suit-jacket, wound a cashmere muffler around his neck and left the room.

Zoe was on her own in the kitchen the next morning when the telephone rang. It was only quarter to eight and the rest of the house was still asleep. She grabbed at the phone, smearing it with marmalade.

'Hello!'

'Zoe? Hi darling! Am I glad I got you! It's Matt.'

She grinned down the phone then realised he could not see her. 'Hi, how're you?'

'Fine. Look, something's come up. I've had to ...' His words were drowned out by a tannoy-announcement that Zoe could not understand.

'Damn thing! Can you hear me?'

'Yes.'

'I've been called back to work. I'm at the airport now, at Inverness. When're you coming back?'

'Monday.' Alasdair was planning to leave before day-break.

'I've got three days off from Sunday. Why not fly down first thing Sunday morning? I'll pay for your ticket and I'll meet you at the airport. We'll spend the whole day together. Do anything you like. I'll even show you my boat. Zoe? Say yes!'

She gripped the receiver until her hand hurt. She ought to end this now, slam down the phone and cut the connection. He did not know her address in London; she had told him the name of the bookshop but she was not going back there. He might try her parents if he was desperate enough, but she could tell them an awful story about him, make something up.

Put the phone down now, said a voice inside her head. Before it's too late.

'Zoe? Darling, are you there? I'm really sorry about this. Please say you'll come down on Sunday. Zoe?'

'Yes, Matt.' Once she had said it, she knew that it was the only answer she could have given. However crazy it was, however many rules she was breaking, she just wanted to be with him.

'Oh that's wonderful. That's terrific. I'll call you this evening, OK? You look after yourself, you hear? And Zoe, I love you.'

'And I love you too.' She put the phone down, hearing in her mind the echo of his voice, and smiling at his happiness. Her own happiness was so immense that it seemed to swallow her whole.

She sat down at the kitchen table and wrapped both hands around her mug of tea. Outside she could see that it was beginning to thaw. Great dollops of snow were dropping off the branches of the fir tree in the garden.

'We don't expect you to be a nun,' she heard the smooth voice of the Leadership man. 'But be circumspect.' It had seemed easy then. There had been no one in her life like Matt and, judging by her romantic experience up to that point, little likelihood of one.

But now . . . with Matt she could imagine everything being different. He cared for her as she was, without demanding that she change into someone she was not. He thought she was perfect; he would never harm her or make her afraid. Already she could feel that she had grown stronger.

She brought the cup up to her lips and drank the liquid slowly. Sunday morning seemed suddenly too long to wait; all that happiness was within her reach and she wanted it now. She closed her eyes and saw herself walking hand-in-hand with Matt along the bank of the Thames. The sun was shining, making the water sparkle and everything looked fresh and bright. They were as one, laughing and talking like two people in love . . .

The kitchen clock chimed eight and she flinched as if she had been slapped. 'What're you doing?' she asked herself. 'You know what the Leadership said. And it makes sense. You can see that. You'll never be able to talk to Matt properly. You'll always be lying to him. You can't afford to have a close relationship with anyone. It's like . . . it's like you're already married.'

She stared down at the table, seeing the tiny rings around a knot in the pine. Married to the Cause, not free to love. It was not fair, she thought angrily. How could she have pledged herself to something that demanded all of her, her unquestioning allegiance, love and hopes, leaving nothing for herself?

She shut her eyes and let her mind drift. She saw herself walking through the forest again, and all the dread and terror that her newfound happiness had made her forget, came rushing back. All those people then and all the people now who were looking to her, beseeching her to help, not to turn her back . . .

That was why she owed everything to the Cause. That was why she should not be allowing herself to dream of any other commitment, any other love. She would be tearing herself apart.

She bit her lip, remembering her dream of the night before. She had been back in Corsica, doing shooting practice with Sergio. His dark presence was behind her. They were outside with the blue and purple mountains in the distance.

She was aiming at a bolster that he had hung from an olive tree. He had tied a string around the top to give the target a head, and to make it look more realistically like a body. It was spinning around and around and as it span its face kept changing. Sometimes it was the face of her father, sometimes her brother, sometimes the boy in Turin.

'Hit the target!' Sergio's voice, roaring at her.

She held the gun steady, pulling the trigger towards her as the bolster swung again to face her.

'Just hit the target!'

She squeezed. Matt's face had come into focus too late . . .

Barney had gone straight into the office from Heathrow. It was Friday morning, January the second; he had had precious little sleep since the night before New Year's Eve, but he was buzzing.

He took a gulp of his third coffee in less than an hour and checked the time. He had fifteen minutes before the meeting began; time to try to gather his thoughts.

He checked the list of those who would be attending the conference in the room next door: the Deputy Director General of MI5; someone from Number Ten; Hargreaves, of course; a representative from the Home Office and another from Immigration and a medley of police officers. One of the Met's Deputy Assistant Commissioners, two intelligence-liaison people, a Special Branch co-ordinator, the head of the Association of Chief Constables and one Interpol man. Plus Gregson and himself.

Barney leaned all the way back in his armchair and surveyed the ceiling. He was not, he assured himself, a vain man, but he would have to have been super-human not to have been feeling rather pleased with himself at that moment.

By ten o'clock the previous night when he had left the Rock, he was convinced that Valente had told everything he knew. Indeed, the boy was treating him like his long-lost father, spilling out his soul.

Valente had met Kessler, face to face. She had looked worn out and had hardly spoken; the older of the two men had done most of the talking. A very impressive figure, Valente had said, definitely English; he had been pleased that Valente knew his language, had said that it might come in useful one day. Valente had given a very rough description of the man: fortyish, dark, big-built and quite fleshy in the face. Very much the leader, the boy had added. No, he thought the woman was not important. She had only asked one question.

'She asked me if I would kill my dad!' Valente had exclaimed. 'When I said she must be mad, no way, she said that it proved I was not committed to anti-racism as I claimed to be. I thought I had failed, but the Englishman said not to worry. I think that woman . . .' Valente had smirked.

'What?' Barney had asked.

'I think, you know . . .' he had tapped his head. 'A bit mad.'

A police artist from the Yard was being sent over that morning to see if Valente could be any more explicit in his description of the Englishman. The Americans, too, having been notified, wanted to send their own people to interview Valente, for any clues on the American in the Leadership.

Barney smiled. Good stuff that might soon yield much more, but the prize unquestionably had been Valente's revelation of the English girl Sleeper. Her existence had now been corroborated by the Corsican woman who had divulged Brunelli's address: yes, she had told the police the previous night, there had been a girl staying at the old farm at the end of the summer. She had laundered her clothes.

If they could find the girl, make her talk, get her to take them to the Leadership . . .

He tried not to imagine too much, but it was hard. Grateful as he had been to Gemmer for letting him see the Russian report, for letting him share Christoph – no matter that that had gone sour – he had been acutely aware that he had been feeding off the German's plate; that he had contributed nothing to the tracking down of Never Again himself. He remembered thinking, in the aftermath of the Paris bombing, that at least Gemmer had lines of inquiry to pursue while he sat twiddling his thumbs in London, bleating that there still might be a Sleeper out there and there was still the fact that Christoph had mentioned an Englishman in the Leadership.

Hargreaves had been so dismissive, so scornful. Barney smiled again, slowly. She had been proved wrong on both counts. Now he was finally on the field, playing the game. And if he was right, his game could be the one that finished Never Again for good.

He heard a noise in the adjoining conference room. The secretaries were laying out the files and glasses of water. He glanced down at his own file, open in front of him. It listed the very brief known facts about the girl, but he was convinced that they presented an excellent chance of trapping her.

On his desk, a phone rang. It was Gemmer.

'Horst! How can I help?' He had already spoken to Gemmer that morning, telling him in full about Valente's admissions.

'Glad I caught you before you went into your meeting. I've just heard, the Dutch have identified Pieter.'

'What!'

'Ja, his sister reported him missing yesterday evening. And guess, Barney, he's a psychiatrist.'

'A what!'

'Yes, a psychiatrist. One presumes to help with the psycho-logical problems of killing children.'

'My God!' Barney felt his head reel. All this information, all at once. He picked up a pen. 'What's his name?'

'Pieter Van Hoeffen, aged thirty-six from Amsterdam. Unmarried. No criminal record, no interest to Dutch intelli-gence. Left his job at a major teaching hospital in Amsterdam eighteen months ago. Lots of money in his bank account . . .'

'Shit! It's all coming together isn't it?'

'Let's hope! And Barney, there's something else.'

'Good God, what? Tell me gently. You've arrested Kessler?'

Gemmer laughed. 'No, no. Never Again carried out another attack this morning. Just something small, they burned down the meeting hall of a right-wing group in Munich. But it's the fact that they've done anything so soon after Valente's arrest . . .'

'Yeah, I see what you mean. Not even a gap in their operations now, never mind the twenty-one day rule.' Barney paused, considering. 'So, a psychiatrist as their recruiter and they're trying to show they're undeterred by Gibraltar. That'll give my lot plenty to chew over. Thanks a lot for letting me know; they'll think I've really got my finger on the pulse. When's the stuff on Pieter coming over from Amsterdam?'

'At least another couple of hours. I only got a tip-off from that Dutch friend of mine twenty minutes ago.'

'Great. And nothing new on Sergio?'

'Nothing since they found the boat drifting near Genoa.'

'Yeah, he's gone hasn't he? False papers, new identity, he's done it a hundred times before.'

'Another bloody professional. OK, I'm off. Good luck with your people.'

Thirty minutes into the meeting, Barney started to relax. He had delivered the Dutch and German news to satisfactory expressions of surprise, then gone on with his own briefing on the Valente material which had earned him more approving nods. He felt that at least for the moment he had done all he could. It was up to the others now.

One of the Yard people gave a very short report on the Governor. His condition had stablised slightly; he had been flown back to the UK the previous night and was due to be operated on that morning. It was still not certain that he would survive.

Everyone made suitable murmurings of regret and hope for recovery before turning to the business in hand.

One of the Special Branch men said that his officers, working with the Home Office and Immigration departments, were already checking records for the girl's trip to Corsica.

'There are only six holiday companies which do packages to Corsica,' he said.

'But we don't know for sure it was a package, do we?' asked one of the intelligence-laison men.

'No. We're also checking all flights-only and independent villas.'

'How about ferries?' put in someone else. Barney looked up but did not recognise the speaker. He glanced down at his sheet of paper: it was the Number Ten spokeswoman, a pleasant-looking young woman whose presence there, he knew, had caused a few ruffled feathers. There were still many in the Service who thought the Prime Minister should keep his nose out of their affairs.

Hargreaves glared at her. 'Ferries? I hardly think we need concern ourselves with ferries! Most unreliable means of transport, I'd have thought. Amateurish. I can't imagine a slick organisation like this sending out ferry tickets!'

The Deputy Director General gave a gentle cough. Barney liked the man – late fifties, nicely spoken; even when he had been bollocking him over Paris, he had not sounded as if he meant it. 'I think we're all agreed on the importance of working together. It's essential in such a delicate matter as this.'

He nodded at Hargreaves. 'I think we should start off by assuming that the girl flew directly to the island from these shores. It would certainly be the easiest option. She could hardly get lost on an aeroplane.

'So, all flights from the UK to be checked first. Then other connecting flights. Then,' he smiled down at the Number Ten girl, 'we might cross that ferry bridge later.

'Mr Turl?'

Barney jumped. 'Sir?'

'You said in your excellent report that you suspected that this Sleeper may be activated quite soon. Can you be more precise in your reasons for that judgement?'

'It's more trying to second-guess them, sir. I think the UKN success may have sparked a campaign here. Especially with an Englishman at their helm.'

'Yes, and the Munich arson attack this morning. You think it's significant?'

'Only inasmuch as it shows they don't intend a ceasefire, even to regroup, after Valente's capture.'

'Quite. So you think this girl's activation may be imminent?'

'It could well be, sir.'

'The possibility being strong enough, in your opinion, to devote a great deal of manpower to finding her, even though all of us are so stretched at the moment?'

'I believe so, sir.'

Hargreaves grunted quite audibly but was ignored.

The Deputy Director looked at his notes. 'This other "clue" that you mentioned, the matter of eagles . . .'

'Yes sir?'

The Met's Deputy Commissioner leant forward. 'You're not suggesting sending a policeman to every eagle's nest in the British Isles are you?' he asked drily.

'How many of them are there, anyway?'

'According to the RSPB, four hundred and twenty-five pairs, of which all but one are to be found in Scotland.'

'So she's Scottish, then!'

'Well, sir, not definitely. She might only have lived in Scotland for a short while – recently or as a child. So she could be English, or Welsh for that matter. Or I suppose Irish.' Barney heard another rumble from Hargreaves and hurried on: 'All I'm saying, sir is that we can't assume she's Scots, but it does suggest that she might be.'

'Where's the other area outside Scotland?'

'The Lake District. There's something else we must bear in mind too . . .' Barney looked directly at the Deputy Director General for the most sympathetic hearing. 'Valente said that the girl said something about there being golden eagles near her home, though we have to remember his English isn't perfect.'

'I do hope we're not dealing with another of your dodgy informants,' interjected Hargreaves nastily.

Barney looked past her; best to put everything on the table: 'And we're presuming that the girl knew what she was talking about.' He paused. 'I mean, she might have meant to say kestrel.'

There were quite a few sighs from around the table but the Deputy Director answered civilly. 'Quite. So perhaps we'll leave the eagle matter until we have a list of possible candidates from flight checks.

'I suggest we devote maximum manpower to this for, shall we say, one week? D'you think that'll give us enough time, Mr Turl?'

'It should do, sir.'

'Good, excellent. Now, what else can we do? Phone taps on all the usual people.'

'Obviously Missing Persons'll be checked for her,' put in the Special Branch co-ordinator. 'Just in case her parents or a boyfriend have reported her missing.'

'Unlikely isn't it?' asked one of the intelligence-liaison men. 'But I suppose its best to cover all possibilities.'

'Aaah, now talking of covering possibilities,' interjected the Deputy Director, 'I think we'd better go up from Special Black to Amber on all government buildings. What'd be the PM's view on that?' he asked the Number Ten girl.

'I don't know, I'll ask him. But I'm sure he'll go along with anything you suggest in this matter.'

'The press'll pick that up at once,' the Home Office representative warned.

'Can't be helped,' said the Deputy Director stoutly. 'We'll have someone feed them some gumph about the IRA. We can't have any of this getting out so there must be an absolute moratorium on the press.'

Matt had spent a day and a half on the phone, trying to get sufficient new material for a whole page three on the events in Gibraltar and their aftermath. Thank God, he thought, that the Spanish stringer had come up with something: an eyewitness account of the shooting by a young woman who lived in the block of flats that Valente had used.

Normally Matt would have demanded that Lomax send him to the scene, but he was desperate to see Zoe, desperate enough, he had realised with some astonishment, to miss a foreign trip.

Lomax, who had been prepared for battle, had been astounded too. 'What's got into you?' he asked.

'Nothing. I'll concentrate on the repercussions and the

reasons why. I've got some intelligence contacts on this and I can milk them better from here.'

'Oh.' Lomax stared at him. 'What kind of intelligence contacts? Your Special Branch man or someone else?'

'That'd be telling.'

It would indeed, Matt thought now. It was ten o'clock on Saturday morning; he had twelve hundred words to write by two o'clock and very little to say. He glanced in Lomax's direction and saw that he was locked in conversation with the chief sub. 'Probably arguing for more space,' Matt groaned.

Why had he bragged about intelligence contacts when he knew how Steve had been acting of late? What had got into him?

'You all right, Matt?' asked Pete Trollope, the education correspondent, passing by. 'You look like you're in pain.'

'No, no, I'm fine. Just thinking.'

'Oh, the creative juices, huh?'

'Yeah, that sort of thing.'

He chewed at his thumb nail. He had been so sure that he would have been able to persuade Steve to help him. The two of them went back a long way but, most importantly, Matt considered Steve owed him a favour for not writing the story about MI5 and the Paris bomb. Steve, however, apparently felt otherwise.

He had called the policeman's work number several times yesterday without success. A bland male voice had assured him that his messages were being passed on, but Steve had not called back.

At eight, Matt had tried his home number.

'He's not here,' said the woman who answered. She had sounded very fed-up. 'God knows when he'll be back. Yes, I'll tell him you called.'

Matt had waited up for the call until one o'clock. At eight that morning he had tried the number again; it had rung out, seeming to mock him.

'How's it going, chief?' Lomax had come up soundlessly behind him. He was being nice, Matt knew, in anticipation of the piece.

'Fine, just fine.' He grabbed the phone. 'I've just got one more call to make.'

He found he was praying when he dialled the number. After six rings, it was answered with a gruff 'Hullo?'.

'Hullo, Steve? It's Matt.'

There was a brief silence, then: 'Yeah, hi Matt. You calling from work?'

'Yep. I've been trying to reach you. Didn't you get any of my messages?'

'I've been really busy.'

No apology, no explanation; in fact he sounded snappy. Matt felt his stomach lurch. 'Steve, I'm doing an article on the Gibraltar shooting. Implications for national security. I thought maybe you'd heard something. From those people you said were so keen on, Never Again, and . . .'

'Can't help you. Sorry.'

'I can meet you anywhere you like.'

'No, it's no good.'

'Steve, please. It's my neck on the line here.'

A fractional pause, then: 'Try someone else. I've got nothing to say.'

Panic spurred him on: 'Well, how about confirming that Special Branch and the security services have put out an all-ports alert for suspected Never Again terrorists? And that the membership files of all anti-fascist groups are being trawled by dozens of police officers working with their European counterparts to come up with identities of any home-grown Never Again members?'

'How d'you know that?' Steve sounded almost frightened.

'For God's sake, I'm a journalist! I'm only using my head.' He paused. 'And what you've just said has confirmed it. You've been working on this thing, haven't you?'

'I'm hanging up.'

'Steve, just tell me . . .'

Matt replaced the receiver and stared at it. 'Well, thanks a lot, old pal. If you ever want a favour, don't hesitate to ask.'

He flicked through his notebook: it was all dull stuff; everyone had stone-walled him.

Scotland Yard had taken twelve hours to respond to his

queries and the wait had not been worth while. They were unable to comment, the Press Bureau spokeswoman had said, on whether the terrorist Antonio Valente would be brought to London to stand trial. Nor were they in a position to respond to 'speculation' that the Gibraltar shooting was the start of a Never Again campaign in Britain.

'How about security around VIPs? I understand that's been stepped up?' he had asked.

'I am unable to confirm that that is the case.'

Direct calls to the police in Gibraltar had also yielded little. The inspector who had been detailed to deal with the press only read out statements that had been faxed to him from Scotland Yard. The man had become irritated when he realised that Matt was from *The Clarion*. 'We already spoke to the Spaniard who works for you. Goodbye.'

Matt had tried the Home Office and the spokesman there had acted dumb. No, he could not really comment on the Amber security alert. 'But just between you and me,' he had added in a quieter voice, 'I think it's got something to do with a remnant of the IRA.'

The only person who had spoken to him had been a Professor at Newcastle University, who was a self-acclaimed 'Terrorist' expert. He had talked at length about the Japanese Red Army and the Shining Path organisation in Peru. But what about Never Again? Matt had finally interrupted.

'Ah, not too knowledgeable on that front, yet. Still I'm sure we'll find there are parrallels between them and the Revoltionary Cells in the Low Countries . . .'

Matt suppressed a moan. Twelve hundred words in a key position in the paper, and he was going to fill it with this!

From the newsdesk, Lomax called: 'Copy by two please, Matt! And can we have three hundred words for the front, on the latest about the Governor?'

'Sure!' Matt allowed himself a tiny whimper. He stared at his screen where the cursor blinked, waiting for him. All he had was denials and speculation. Lomax was going to crucify him.

He squeezed his eyes shut and imagined Zoe's sweet face and the way her mouth faltered before she smiled. He was going to be there, waiting for her at Heathrow in the morning; that was all that mattered.

With his eyes still shut he began typing: 'Angus Delton may never walk again, according to doctors who operated on him yesterday for the second time in twenty-four hours. The sixty-four year old Governor, who has not yet regained consciousness after the shooting . . .'

Barney had retreated upstairs to his study with a tumbler of whisky. Downstairs, Alice was furiously watching television. Not only, she had informed him in a sandpaper voice, had his job wrecked her New Year plans, but when he had finally come home that night, it had only been to say that he was on twenty-four hour call.

'But we're meant to be playing Bridge with the Foleys!'

'I'm sorry, love. There's nothing I can do about it.'

Barney flicked through the security file that he had brought home. The information on Never Again was growing: to Valente's statement had now been added that of Dieter's sister. And who knows, he thought with a flip of excitement, what the next few days might bring? Even at a conservative estimate, he thought that by the start of the week there was a good chance he would know the identity of the Sleeper.

There were about two hundred people working around the clock on this operation, 'Operation Beauty' as it was now known, having been christened by the Special Branch co-ordinator. 'As in Sleeping . . .' he had added helpfully.

Barney took a mouthful of whisky and closed his eyes. He tried to imagine what life must be like for the young girl he was hunting; living a double-life, lying to her family and friends. Would she fool a boyfriend, though, he thought suddenly, presuming of course that she had one.

Surely such a secretive existence would be impossible to maintain? 'Serving God and mammon,' Barney muttered. He knew that Anton had done it, but with a girl, it seemed different, much harder. Girls were more emotional; they had girlfriends they told everything to; they poured their hearts out to their mothers. They needed more affection; more reassurance.

So what kind of girl could she be? A wounded creature who had been cruelly led astray? Someone with no family or friends, a social misfit? Or a psychopath?

No, he crossed the last one off the list. Never Again was too professional. No serious armed group had any room for psychiatric cases: they needed to know that the person would deliver the bomb to the right place at the right time and not crack up in the process.

He took another sip. He knew he was being sexist but there was no one to hear his thoughts. He hoped, for the girl's sake, that his side would get to her before her own did.

The red telephone interrupted his thoughts and he snatched it up. It was Gregson: 'Just thought you'd like to know, sir. The final total for the number of young British girls who visited Corsica during the month of August last year is six hundred and eighty-three.'

'Right. Passport checks?'

'They're being done as we speak, sir.'

'Good, good. Let me know if there's anything. Anything at all.'

Chapter Twenty-Three

Sergio Brunelli drove, as he always did, with one hand on the wheel. He used to tell anyone who asked that he liked to keep the other hand free for his gun. Just now, he had no gun, but that was a situation he intended to rectify in the morning.

The last of the Paris suburbs began to peter out. He checked the fuel-gauge on the dashboard and started looking out for a petrol station. There was a fairish journey ahead of him tonight – most of it on small roads – and he had no wish to be stuck in the middle of the French countryside, a sitting target for any curious gendarme.

He was heading for Picardie. A cursory glance at the map that morning had shown it looked promising: lots of countryside to lose himself in, an hour's drive from the Belgian border; two hours, he guessed, from Brussels' airport which should satisfy Kessler's orders that he be within striking distance of a major airport.

He was to find a suitable place and be in regular contact, Kessler had said.

'You want me to do the same as before?'

He had waited a long time for an answer, and when it had come, she had sounded remote and dreamy.

'Perhaps, yes. Or maybe not for a bit. It depends . . . on various things, how things work out. Ideas are being discussed. We'll have to see.'

Up ahead, he saw the faint blink of a small neon sign advertising petrol. He moved into the slower lane and indicated right.

What was wrong with Kessler, he wondered? She had sounded spaced out and nervous, repeating the same things, telling him three times to be in touch. Had someone been listening; had she been scared? 'Ideas are being discussed'? He echoed the words in his mind. That had not sounded like Kessler. To his recollection, Kessler had never listened much to anyone's ideas and no one had ever stood in her way for long.

He pulled onto the forecourt. It was a service garage. An undersized man in an orange uniform appeared at his window.

'Monsieur?'

'Fill her up.'

He lit a cigarette and watched the man struggling to get the pump's nozzle into his tank.

Had Axel, the one who liked things to be 'ugly', somehow got a hold on her; was that why she was losing her grip? He felt a moment's pity and the image of himself as Kessler's rescuer flashed through his mind. He shook his head: the old days were gone and he was not going to endanger himself for mere sentimentality. Her problems were none of his affair; she knew how to look after herself, always had done.

He drew hard on his cigarette and saw the little garage man frown and jerk his head at the 'Défense de fumer' sign. He rolled down his window and blew smoke out into the night.

'Monsieur! It's dangerous to smoke!'

Sergio looked at the man.

'The risk, monsieur,' he muttered, taking a step back.

Sergio paid him in cash using crumpled notes. He added a fifty centime coin, 'a tip for you,' and watched the man's face purple with rage as he drove off.

He glanced in his rear view mirror and saw his eyes, staring back, looked slightly weary. He wondered what might become of himself. He would chose a bullet in the back of the head or long life beside the sea. He grinned: with a young woman, of course, or maybe several of them, fighting for his pleasures. Life should never be too quiet.

He glanced over his shoulder at the nylon hold-all on the back seat. He had spent an hour that morning in a department store kitting himself out as a struggling artist. The clothing was all of the poorest quality and he had exchanged his Gucci loafers for a pair of canvas sneakers. The rest of his finery – the handmade shirts, the Hermes tie, the Armani suit – he had left behind at the hotel.

He had kept only one thing: the dark-blue cashmere scarf. It was around his neck now. Oddly for him he had grown attached to it. It was not impossible, he thought, that the struggling artist could have made a sale.

He was on the open road now, with very few cars in either direction and his headlights showing a dull, flat countryside. He leaned down to turn on the radio before remembering that this eight year old Renault had come with nothing; its windscreen wipers barely worked. There was a hole where the radio should have been.

To amuse himself as he drove, he tried to imagine what the police forces across Europe would be doing right now to find him. Carla, the woman he had left behind in Còrte, would not be able to help them, though recalling her rage when he had left, she would probably want to. He had never told her anything about himself. Of course, they would put a picture of him on the Wanted Posters but the most recent photograph was fifteen years old.

He smiled, remembering himself as a young man on the run, standing in front of one of those posters, staring at himself and saying to anyone nearby, 'Aie! He doesn't look like a crazy terrorist, does he? To think he's killed all those people!' No one had ever recognised him and it had given him such a kick to do it.

He squinted up as a road sign approached but it was only a warning of bends ahead. He put his foot down hard on the gas and wondered what price they would put on his head now. Half a million dollars maybe? The prospect was pleasing. He began whistling as he approached the first bend.

Zoe felt a child's pleasure in being given a window-seat on the plane. It was ten minutes past eight on a cold, clear Sunday morning and she was on her way to see the man she loved.

For the past twenty-four hours she had resolutely pushed all thoughts of Never Again from her mind. In their place she had seen herself with Matt, laughing as she ran to meet him, imagining his arms wrapped around her tight.

'Newspaper, madam?'

She had not listened to the radio, watched the TV news or

read a newspaper since New Year's Eve. It was, she realised, a true indicator of how deeply she felt for Matt. She simply did not want to know if Never Again had done anything else horrible. No more bombings or killings; she just wanted to be happy. On the other hand, Matt was a journalist working on a Sunday newspaper . . .

'Madam?' demanded the British Airways stewardess.

'Sorry! Have you got *The Clarion?*'

'No, we're out of it. You can have the *Sunday Telegraph, Mail on Sunday* or *News of the World.*'

'Oh, no thanks.' She would ask Matt for a copy.

She settled back into her seat as the plane began moving backwards from its stand. The last time you flew, said a voice inside her head, was back from Amsterdam, after you'd seen the Leadership, after that poor boy in . . . She cut the connection.

Maybe there would be no Day of Reckoning, she thought dreamily. Since she had met Matt all things seemed possible. She felt so strong, so complete; no longer on the outside of things, longing to be accepted. She was just a normal girl going out with a wonderful man.

She stared out at the sky. Even though it had only been four days since she had met Matt, she felt that she belonged to him, like two jigsaw pieces fitting together. And the strength of her feeling was making her question other things.

Had she really joined Never Again purely because she wanted to stop the Nazis? Had she not also longed to be part of the group because they wanted her, because they had made her feel important? She remembered how proud she had been that day when Pieter had told her she had been selected for special training. Then she remembered his words, and that strange, pitying look on his face when he had told her she did belong to the Cause. How strange, she had thought at the time: how he had made it sound like a prison sentence, as if she was chained to them against her will!

But now . . . now she was beginning to see what he had meant. She gulped; the very thought was treacherous, a betrayal of the Cause, and of the people she had dedicated herself to. But was she still willing, the little voice continued in her head, to do anything they asked of her? After the horror of Paris; knowing as she did what it was like to see men die ... knowing that there was another way to belong, and that was being with Matt?

She bit her lip. She ought to stop thinking about it; it was so confusing. She was sure that was why she kept having terrible dreams. She would concentrate on the here and now, on being the girl that Matt loved.

She selected a scene from her small store of memories, and leaned back in her seat.

'You're really smitten, aren't you?' Kerry had asked her last night as the two of them did the washing-up.

'Yes, I think I am.'

'Good! It's the best thing that could have happened to you. Or to anyone, come to that!' Kerry had given her a hug. 'I'm really pleased for you.'

'Does Al like him?'

'Oh I think so, yes. I think it's come as a bit of a shock to him, though. He still thinks of you as his baby sister who needs protecting from wolves!'

Zoe smiled. The only person she wanted to protect her would be waiting for her at Heathrow in – she glanced at her watch – forty-five minutes.

Matt stood in the domestic arrivals lounge, staring up at the escalator on which Zoe should soon be descending. He felt sweaty and nervous. He had not felt like this since ... he frowned. He could not remember when he had ever felt like this.

He had arrived twenty minutes before the flight was due to land. He had set two alarm clocks and placed one on the bedside cabinet, close to his head. In the event, he was up and making coffee when they both went off.

He had never given much thought to what he wore, but that morning, at six-twenty, he had been standing in front of his wardrobe, moaning out loud at its contents. He had work clothes or sailing clothes and nothing in between and, added to that, he had no idea what Zoe liked! If he wore the grey Paul Smith jumper, it might look as if he had not tried, but a shirt with something over it might look too formal. In the end, he had put on the same sweater he had worn in Scotland. At least she had not said that she did not like it.

He had made the bed with care, telling himself that it was only important in case he showed Zoe round the whole flat.

It had taken him three hours last night to clean and vacuum the place. He could imagine what Louise would have said if she could have seen him, duster in one hand and Mr Sheen in the other, but he had quite enjoyed himself. At least boring housework had taken his mind off Lomax's rage.

'What's this crap?' he had demanded, shaking a copy of the story under Matt's nose.

Matt had determined not to argue with him. 'You don't like it?'

'You're dead right I don't like it! Is this your idea of a joke? What happened to your precious security sources, Anderson? Your very own Mr Deep Throat? Unavailable for comment, was he?'

Matt had said nothing.

Lomax had lowered his voice a fraction. 'What's with you? Never Again's one of your areas, one of your best! I argue to get you more space and you cock it up like this!'

'Sorry, Chris.'

'Why? What went wrong?'

'I, er ... hoped someone would talk to me. And he wouldn't.'

'That's it? That's all the explanation I get? What the fuck am I going to fill page three with now? It's too late to get anything new now, isn't it? We'll just have to use pictures and the stringer's story.' He moved away in the direction of the newsdesk, then obviously thinking he had let Matt off too lightly, came back. He put his face close to Matt's and spoke menacingly:

'Don't ever tell me again that you've got the goods on these fuckers and you've got to have it in the paper. Don't ever ask for time off-rota, or beg me for a foreign trip, or speak to me about them again. Got that?'

Matt had nodded.

'Fucking chief reporter!'

Matt had never had a bollocking like it. He grinned, still sore at the memory: he guessed it was what came from letting your heart rule your head. Not that he would have exchanged being here, knowing that in a few minutes he would be with Zoe, for an Exclusive tag or a pat on the head from Lomax.

After yesterday he would cheerfully have consigned every scrap of information he had on Never Again to the shredder. And he would have liked to have got hold of Steve and done him some serious damage.

It had been the thought of what he would do and say to Steve, if he ever saw him again that was, that had produced the shiniest bath taps in town.

Not that he was expecting Zoe to have a bath, of course.

He checked the time again. She had landed five minutes ago; she only had an overnight bag with her, she should be here any moment. He looked up at the moving stair, watching the people glide down so effortlessly. Several families, a few couples, an older woman on her own; no one like Zoe.

There was no way that he was going to pressurise her into anything. He was going to let her take the lead on the sexual front. If she had been assaulted in the past, he was aware that it might take her some time before she felt she could trust him enough to be intimate. He clenched his fists: just the thought of what a stranger might have done to her made him angry. How anyone could have harmed such a delicate, sweet, beautiful girl . . .

Outside, the sun broke through the clouds and a burst of light hurt his eyes. He squinted up and saw her. She was wearing a dark coat that nipped in tightly to her waist and flared out down to her ankles. Against the sun, her hair looked white blonde. She was coming closer; he could see her eyes and nose and lips.

'Matt!' She called when she was still three steps away. 'Matt!'

She seemed to fly into his arms. He circled her waist and lifted her up to kiss her; she was as he remembered, as light as gossamer.

He set her down and took her hand. He knew that he was

wearing a silly smile but he did not care: 'You look like an angel descending from heaven.'

She giggled and her grey eyes danced. 'And I bring you good tidings of great joy!'

'What?'

'Me!'

Looking into her eyes, he remembered hearing that people in love could glow. He thought that he and Zoe must be standing out like Christmas tree lights.

'You're staring at me!' she said, blushing and laughing at the same time.

'Am I? I'm just so pleased to see you. Should I take your bag?'

'It's fine. It weighs nothing. Oh, Matt, before I forget, I've got a confession to make.'

'Shoot.' He took her hand and they began walking in the direction of the lift.

'I haven't read your paper today. I don't know what you've written about.'

'Believe me, angel, you don't want to read it.'

'Was it that bad?'

'Worse. It's not a subject for discussion. Today we're going to have fun.'

Chapter Twenty-Four

Pieter looked at his hands and saw they were shaking; his whole body was trembling. He tried taking deep, slow breaths as he walked swiftly away from the railway station, but it was hard to breathe at all. Surely someone had seen his reaction; the way he had stared, mouth open, eyes bulging at the picture of himself.

'Die Polizei bittet um Mithilfe' ran the black letters across the top of the pale blue poster. Then in much larger letters: 'TERRORISTEN' and the photograph of him. Beside it was the recent one of Beatrix that he had seen many times before. It was his own face that riveted his attention.

The picture was two-and-a-half years old. He remembered it being taken, at his house, by his sister. He had been sitting on the sofa, beside his two nephews, wondering why he felt nothing for them beyond annoyance that they were so noisy. He remembered that they had been fighting over possession of the TV remote control. 'Smile!' Gerda had cried, and the camera had flashed.

It showed him frowning and looking off into the distance. Not a good picture and very slightly out of focus. Odd that the police should have taken that one, he thought, and then realised it was probably the most recent of him. And it was not that bad: it was recognisably him.

It had been before any of this, Pieter thought as he turned up the collar of his jacket with one hand. Before he had begun attending the protest meetings or met any of the people who would eventually lead him to Axel Shiner.

Back then he had had a job, a house and a girlfriend. Life had been ordered, its future set. He had been in a good position, deputy leader of a team of psychiatrists at a prestigious Amsterdam teaching hospital. He had only just started treating the Bosnian refugees, trying to help them come to terms with their multitude of terrors; feeding them white, middle-class solutions for the terrors they had daily endured.

Back then he had not yet despaired. He had thought he was helping. It was only when they kept coming, telling of new horrors of ethnic cleansing, systematic torture, rape and killing, that he had realised he had to do more or go mad himself.

Now they were offering ninety thousand deutschmarks for him. He tried to work that out in guilders but his mind would not compute. He glanced back over his shoulder.

There was a man behind him, a slightly tubby, balding man wearing a raincoat. He had exactly the nondescript features that Pieter had heard the Security Forces used as trackers.

He crossed the road, heading for the car park. He thought he heard the man behind him step off the pavement and follow. The urge to run was nearly overwhelming but he forced himself to remain calm. If the worst should happen, he knew now that he would rather be arrested than die.

It was not cowardice, more a gradual realisation – recently considerably speeded up by the deterioration of the Leadership – that Never Again was not worth dying for. Not as it now was with Axel power-crazed, Leon a mere echo and Beatrix lost in her own world. It was not that he had ceased to believe in the Cause itself – how could he? Things were worse than ever, with the Neo-Nazis growing stronger, old Fascists being rehabilitated, new ones in power. No, it was being forced to witness the high ideals of Never Again's beginning brought low. All those kids he had recruited now being butchered and brutalised. Whenever he thought of the Paris bomb team, how they had ended, he felt sick with guilt; it was he who had chosen them, picking them out of their lives, putting them on the path that had led to their horrible deaths.

He had killed as well: two men, leaders of a Neo-Nazi movement in Germany. He had left a bomb for them in their car; all had been killed outright. Those deaths he did not mourn; they had deserved to die. Their followers had come after him, at the conference in Hamburg where he had recruited Zoe.

He remembered the young British girl well; her confusion and terror at the past repeating itself; her loneliness; how he had used it all for Never Again, to turn her into a soldier. He remembered making her talk that night in the Dutch safe-house, smiling as he scanned her conversation, looking for flags: financial, political, security connections, or anything that struck him as a crease in the landscape; anything that one day might be of use to the Cause.

It was not Never Again that had failed him, more that the people who ran it, himself included, had failed it.

Never Again had not stopped the Fascists, far from it. Their mistakes had been seized on with relish by the other side, and used by their politicians to bolster themselves in the opinion polls. By the same token, their own violence had weakened the Anti-Fascist's political stance. 'They're all as bad as each other,' Pieter had heard people say on the radio, on the TV news, in newspapers.

It had all gone so wrong.

He turned a corner and saw the bonnet of the cloud-blue BMW on the far side of the car park. He shifted the bag of newspapers and groceries from his right to left arm. Then he looked back again. There was no one in the street. It was Sunday morning in the centre of Frankfurt and very few people were about. He was going to be OK; all he had to do was get to the car, drive away and keep going until he found a safe place to hide.

So long as he could change his appearance.

He lifted one long leg after another over the low wall of the carpark. He knew enough people now that he could go to and ask for false documents. He would have to pay, but he had plenty of money sitting in his account; money that he had not touched for over a year. Then he remembered: the police knew who he was and they would be monitoring the account.

He got into the car and took out his wallet. He had a lot of money on him, but not enough to pay a forger – especially not a forger who knew the price on Pieter's head.

He rubbed his hands over his face, trying to think logically. There was no one he could trust or appeal to for help. Gerda had co-operated with the police or been tricked into helping them. Either way, he could not approach her; the house would be watched.

If he ran with no papers, the chances were that he would be caught within the day. It was the worst time to run: that poster was brand new and the police would be freshly acquainted with the pictures. Although he would rather be caught than killed, he would rather not be caught at all.

He started up the engine and took the car out of automatic for reverse. He had only one option: to persuade the Leadership to cut and run.

It was a twenty minute drive to the house. As soon as Pieter had pulled into the driveway he saw a face at one of the upstair's windows – just a brief glimpse. It would be either Axel or Leon. Beatrix would be on her own somewhere.

He let himself in through the back door and saw her sitting at the kitchen table. Open before her was a photograph album that she had found in an old trunk in one of the attic rooms. She seemed to be fascinated by it, poring over the old black-and-white pictures.

She looked up. Her face was grey but there was a softness in her eyes that Pieter had not seen before. 'Such a lovely family lived here,' she said. 'You see them? Mother, father and two little girls. This one was taken in 1947. In this room, they were all laughing.'

She pushed the album round so that he could see the picture. It was just an old grey and white photograph showing a very old-fashioned kitchen. Pieter barely glanced at it: he had to tell her before the men came down. Upstairs he heard a door slam. He dumped the bag of groceries and the newspapers on the table.

'They've got my picture up on the Wanted Posters.'

'You see the pinafore that the mother is wearing? It has tiny white flowers on the frill at the hem. My mother used to wear one just like it.'

He heard footsteps descending the stairs. He bent down to her level. 'Didn't you hear what I said? They know who I am!'

The door opened and Axel came in. 'Did you get the newspapers?'

Pieter straightened up. 'Yes.'

Leon, coming in behind, said: 'I told you, any main railway station has international newspapers.'

'What've they said about us?' asked Axel.

'I don't know. I haven't looked.'

Leon rummaged in the bag. 'Did you get the teabags and the soap?'

Pieter did not reply. Axel picked up one of the English Sunday newspapers and scanned the front page. 'Here we are. Not much, all about the Governor. But there's a page three as well; that's better.'

He could not let this go on. If he did, he would become like Beatrix, burying her head so far into the earth that she was no longer in touch with reality . . . 'We've got to get out of here. The police know who we are.'

'What?' Axel looked up. He had not heard the words properly. He had been too intent on reading the article: an eye-witness account of the shooting by a woman. A smile lingered on his lips.

Beatrix lifted her head. 'They've got his picture. It must mean Valente's talked. And if he's identified him, he'll have described you two.'

She paused. Axel was still holding his newspaper, but rigidly, as if he had been frozen in a spell. Leon gave a little moan and sank into a chair.

'Is it a recent picture of you?' Beatrix asked Pieter.

He swallowed and nodded. He felt enormous relief: she had heard him after all. If she engaged, she could get them all out of this mess.

'Ah,' she smiled. Then she went back to her album.

Axel swayed on his feet.

'Where did you see this?' he whispered.

'At the railway station, when I was getting the papers.'

Beatrix put in calmly: 'The posters'll be everywhere. Borders, airports, police stations. I expect they'll put up artists' impressions of you two. At least for now, until they know more.'

Axel stared at her, too shocked to retort. He put a hand on the back of the chair to steady himself. 'You think they've got our names too?' he asked Pieter softly. 'Mine and his?'

'I don't know . . . I shouldn't think so. Valente never knew them. He'd identify Beatrix of course, easily. And me.' He looked down at the table. 'My sister seems to have gone to the police.'

'The first betrayal,' put in Beatrix, turning over an album page.

Axel still did not respond. His reaction was surprising Pieter; he was much calmer than he had expected. He was staring into space now, deep in thought.

'What are we going to do?' Leon asked suddenly, his voice high with fear. He ran his tongue around his lips. 'We've got to do something! We can't just sit here!'

No one said anything. Pieter heard his watch ticking, very loudly it seemed. He took the plunge. 'I propose that we get out of here at once. Buy ourselves some new IDs – there's a man here in the city who'll do that, won't he – change our appearances, and split up. Certainly Beatrix and I shouldn't be seen together.'

'Yes! Let's do that!' Leon jumped up. He was still holding the box of English teabags. 'I'll just go and get a few things and then we can be on our wa . . .'

'Shut up and sit down.' Axel had come back to himself; his eyes were clear and focused. He drummed his fingers on the table. 'Nobody's going anywhere. We're all staying here.' He looked around at the room. 'Together.'

Pieter stared at him. The fear and shock of a few moments ago had been replaced by the dictator's voice, the voice of a man who does not listen. Nevertheless, Pieter tried:

'Axel, I'm pretty sure no one saw me at the station but if we stay here we're bound to attract attention sooner or later.'

'Why?' Axel glared at him. 'This house is cut off from everywhere isn't it? How much land is there here? Three or four acres, I think. The nearest house is half a mile away. And we've got a cover story, haven't we? So why should anyone notice us?'

Pieter felt as if he was falling. He clutched out to save himself: 'We . . . I have to go out to get food, and newspapers.'

'No.' Axel looked at him through narrowed eyes. 'It's not necessary any more.'

'What's not necessary?'

'There's a freezer full of food, isn't there? And tins. It'll keep us going for weeks.'

'And what then?'

Axel swung on him, his face suddenly charged with rage. 'Don't question me! Don't ever question me. Remember who works for who here.'

Pieter kept his own voice quiet. 'Your plan is to stay here. Never going out?'

Axel smiled. 'Correct. We're burying ourselves.'

The dictator in his bunker.

'How about security?'

'We've got a bloody armoury upstairs!'

Leon suddenly looked up. 'But Axel, we're the Leadership! We've got to be in contact with the front line! Pieter's got to be able to get out to pick up the messages and pass our orders on!'

The Englishman bestowed a smile upon him. 'The front line can run itself for a bit. We can always be in contact if necessary. And we have Brunelli calling us every day. We can relay our wishes through him.'

'And what are our wishes going to be?' Pieter asked.

Axel took a deep breath and stretched his neck upwards so that his chin was pointing at the ceiling. It was that that he addressed himself to.

'Our wishes are that the British Sleeper be fully activated. She was, as I think we all remember, a rather good candidate, with that interesting family connection. And she's already had her preliminary instructions . . .'

Pieter dropped his eyes. He saw Zoe sitting opposite him, all her confidences spilling out, entrusting him with her very soul.

Axel had launched into a speech: 'The appalling political situation in Britain merits our attention, a fact I think we have all agreed upon before. Our first salvo has not been wholly successful. Our second will be a glorious triumph for the Cause.'

Pieter tried again. 'Axel, you can't mean to carry on with that now.'

'Don't question my orders! It's my best ever plan! It's magnificent!' He was red-faced, furious, but not, Pieter saw, in danger of losing control, of bringing on an attack. Indeed he took a deep calming breath before continuing. 'It's only possible through my own planning, my own dedication, and the fortunate circumstances of the girl.

'Once this blow is struck, no one will ever deny our ability to hit at the very heart of evil. The Governments of Europe will be begging, yes begging, us to come to the negotiating table! We shall make our demands and they will give us all we want.'

Leon shifted in his seat.

'What is it?' Axel snapped irritably.

'Couldn't we discuss this further? Before taking any decision that's going to affect us all?'

'No discussion is necessary.'

Leon soldiered on: 'I think it might be better to do as Pieter says and clear out.'

Axel closed his eyes, a patient man sorely tried. Pieter saw that he was deep-breathing again. He spoke quite calmly: 'The time for discussion is past. I have taken the decision. We shall stay here and see it through. There will be no surrender.'

Beatrix shut the album with a loud snap and looked up. She was wearing the soft-eyed expression Pieter had noticed when he first came in. 'Many fools have died with those words on their lips,' she said sweetly.

Steve Carrington was spending Sunday afternoon in a small airless room on the ninth floor of a tower block in Croydon with a young civil servant called Terry Harding. Together they were sifting through the passport applications of young women.

'Here's one,' said Terry. 'Aged twenty-four, fair hair. Looks natural, though it's a bit tricky to tell, isn't it? She comes from Potter's Bar. That's near me! Quite a looker isn't she?'

'Um,' said Steve, not looking up. 'Potter's Bar hardly counts as one of the areas, does it? Was she born in Scotland or the Lake District?'

'Uh,' he consulted his computer screen. 'No. Wanstead.'

'Parents Scottish or from the Lake District?'

'No. Mother born in Tunbridge Wells, father from Northampton. God! Wonder how those two met up?'

Steve suppressed a sigh. Harding must be one of the most stupid young men he had ever encountered. He had been assigned to Steve allegedly to 'show him the ropes', but Steve could have done the work far quicker on his own. Harding was only there to stop the Home Office getting huffy about having to hand over its secrets.

'Have you checked her previous addresses?'

'Oh! No, not yet. I'll do it now. If people only knew what we'd got on them, eh? Never mind the Data Protection Act, eh, know what I mean?'

Steve said nothing.

'Ah, here we are! Oh, she's not what you'd call adventurous. Still, nothing wrong in that my mum says. Shows stability. Previous addresses, Wanstead. Only left home last year. I'll cross her out then, shall I?'

'Do.' Steve went back to work.

He and Terry had been closeted together since noon. The first passport checks of the possible Sleeper candidates had revealed three hundred and eighty-seven girls with light brown or blonde hair. This was the second stage of the enquiry: to check current and past addresses to see whether the girl had ever lived in the relevant areas.

It was a slow and painstaking task. In fours hours, Steve had set aside two possibilities. Both girls would be visited by local Special Branch officers as soon as possible. He squinted at the pile of papers beside him on the desk: at the current rate, he guessed that he might be there until eight tonight. His only consolation was the thought of all that overtime, and the chance that he might be the one who found the girl.

He picked up the next form. The face that looked out at him was very pretty: she had a fringe of light coloured hair that in the Mediterranean sun might have turned blonde. She lived in London; she was twenty-three years old and on her passport application she had listed her occupation as 'student'. Steve entered her details on the computer in front of him, pressed the return button and waited. When her parents' address appeared on the screen, he ran his finger down the single sheet of paper. Yes! He put her on top of his little pile.

'What's all this about then?' Terry asked suddenly.

'That's confidential, I'm afraid.'

'Oh come on! Give us a clue. I've signed the Official Secrets Act, you know.'

'I'm sorry, but I really can't tell you.'

'I know! She's a drug-dealer's girlfriend! That's it, isn't it? I expect your lot's working with the FBI on this!'

'Look,' Steve said, turning to him. 'I appreciate it must be very frustrating not knowing what you're working on. But that's the way it is. So why don't you get on with your pile, and I'll get on with mine, and that way we'll both be finished before midnight.'

Terry was offended. He hunched his shoulders over his pile of forms so that Steve could not see them. 'Play it your way, then,' he said. 'Suits me fine.'

Zoe lay peacefully on Matt's right arm. The weight of her head was crushing it but he did not mind; in fact, he scarcely noticed. He watched her eyelashes flutter and her lips move slightly and then break into a smile. She was smiling in her sleep! He would have kissed her and asked her what she was dreaming of, but it would have woken her.

It was Sunday evening and they had spent the whole day together. In the car that morning, just as they left the airport, Zoe had pronounced herself ravenous and he had taken her up to Covent Garden for brunch at Joe Allen's. Afterwards they had wandered through the covered market-place, pausing to watch the jugglers and then on through the back streets of Soho. It was a cold, wintry day that had threatened to snow, and her beautiful coat did not have pockets. In a little shop he had bought her a pair of red woollen mittens. The buying of the gift had delighted him; he wanted so much to do everything to make her happy.

She had seemed utterly happy all day, bubbling like a child on a treat. When he had asked her if she would like to come back to Hampton, she had hugged his arm in both her hands and given him a wicked grin. 'What, to see your etchings?'

'No, my boat! I thought we'd go for a walk down by the river and then, if you'd like to come back to the flat, we could have a drink?' He had held his breath.

'I'd love to,' she had responded easily. 'I don't mind what we do.'

The towpath had been busy with families and dogs out on Sunday walks. They had walked hand-in-hand; she had seemed to love the place as much as he had. 'Doesn't the river look angry?' she had said and it did: dark and choppy, slapping into the banks and sending little waves smacking against the bridge up ahead. She had admired his dinghy, saying that she had never sailed but would love to learn.

Two brothers, whom he had known for years and who were as crazy about boats as he was, had stopped to chat.

'Well, you're an improvement on the other one,' one had said.

'Thanks, Charlie.'

'What's a nice little girl like you doing with a hulk like him?' asked the other.

'Sorry about that,' he had told Zoe once they were past.

'I don't mind in the least,' she had smiled at him. 'And I'm not going to ask who the "other one" was, either.'

'No,' he had agreed fervently. 'Don't.'

There had been not a trace of the withdrawn, unhappy girl of New Year's day afternoon. Conversation had been easy; they had been playful and relaxed together. She had told him quite a lot about her childhood and he was beginning to get a picture of her. He understood that she lacked confidence, and he thought that that explained her tendency to down-play what she was doing now. Indeed, it did seem strange to him that such an intelligent girl was not already at the start of a glittering career, but then he reminded himself that she was young.

Zoe muttered in her sleep and he looked down at her. 'What is it?' he whispered, but she only smiled and slept on.

He pulled the duvet up around her shoulders, just in case she was feeling cold.

'So you stack shelves in Clapham Junction all day?' he had asked.

'Yes, and there's no need to sound so snooty about it. Anyway, I'm going for a job somewhere else.'

'Oh yes? What's that going to be?'

She had hesitated for a moment and a tiny frown mark had appeared between her eyes. Then, 'Oh, let's not talk about work. You said you weren't going to, and I don't want to either.'

'Agreed.' It was a resolve he intended to keep, and if she felt the same way, it would make it easier. He had paused and picked up a flat pebble from the path. 'Are you any good at skimming stones?'

'I'm ace. My brother taught me how.'

'You're pretty close to your brother, aren't you?'

'Yes. He used to be the only person who understood how I felt.'

'Used to be?'

'Yes. Now I've grown up a bit.'

'So who understands you best now?'

'That position's free. That was six jumps my stone made. Beat that!'

He wanted to be the person she would entrust everything to. He would never misuse her, or mock her; he wanted her to see herself as he saw her, utterly lovely, a girl with everything before her. He wondered what her new job was going to be. He wanted to help her in any way he could.

They had been so natural together all day that by the time they had got back to the flat at five, the sense of ease had flowed on. She had genuinely seemed to like everything: the stripped pine-flooring; the long low sofas in loose cream covers; the thick cotton curtains at the picture window, the same ones that Louise had dismissed as impractical and cheap-looking. He had drawn them, shutting out the dark sky, and lit the fire. Then he had poured them both brandies and they sat together, letting themselves be enchanted by the flames.

Forgetting his earlier decision that she had to be handled with kid gloves, Matt had put his arm around her shoulders and drawn her to him. She had responded willingly, and so he had kissed, and gone on kissing her. When he began to touch her, she had given little soft whimpers of enjoyment, wriggling in closer to him, her hands touching and exploring his body.

They had made love there on the sofa and for him it had been perfect: she had been so sensuous and yet tender and yielding.

Afterwards, they had tried to lie side by side on the sofa and he had fallen off, so he had picked her up and brought her to bed, and they had both slept. It pleased him enormously that he could carry her. He guessed that this was another example of his unreconstructed, caveman approach to women. But at the moment he did not care.

'What are you smiling about?' Zoe's voice was soft and amused.

'You've woken up!' He kissed the tip of her nose.

'What's the time? Have I been asleep for long?'

'Only an hour. You want to carry on? Or I can get up and make us some toast?'

'Matt, I don't want you to think . . .' She stopped, blushing.

'What?'

'I don't want you to think I'm the sort of girl who jumps into bed with someone on the first date.'

'And I don't want you to think I'm that sort of boy.' He smiled down at her. 'You're not regretting it are you?'

'Oh no! It was lovely.'

'Good.' He kissed her again. 'So how about that toast?'

'Sounds perfect.'

'OK. You lie there and look beautiful. I won't be long.'

In the kitchen he dropped four slices of white bread into the double-toaster his mother had sent him as a house-warming present. He had been wrong, he thought. Zoe could not have been raped. He tried to imagine what else in her past could have the power to have made her so wretched, but he was in too content a mood for such thoughts. He slapped enormous quantities of butter onto the toast and carried it through to Zoe.

In the library of a sixteenth century manor house in Oxfordshire that had belonged to the same family for five generations, one of Her Majesty's six hundred and fifty Members of Parliament was sitting with his head in his hands.

He was terribly afraid.

During the two minute telephone call half an hour before he had tried to say as little as possible, fearing that his voice might shake and alert his wife, or one of the weekend's houseguests. Thank God he had picked up the phone in the hall when everyone else was in the drawing-room. He would never have got away with it if the others had seen his face. Sarah had always said he was as easy to read as a book.

After he had put down the receiver he had stared into the mirror above the Jacobean trestle table and barely recognised himself, he had been so drained of colour. The white tuft of hair, sticking upright in the same fashion that it had done since his schooldays, had been necessary assurance that it was indeed himself.

He had had to wait until his breathing slowed down before he called around the drawing-room door:

'Spot of bother with one of the backbenchers! Photographed by one of the tabloids cruising for a girl in Shepherd's Market. I'll have to put my thinking-cap on a bit, p'rps make some calls. Won't take me long.'

'Oh darling, don't be dull,' Sarah had cried. 'Come in and give us all the gory details. Christopher's just told us the most sensational story about the Royals' doctor. You wouldn't believe it!'

'I'll hear it when I'm through with this thing.'

'But it's Sunday and it's your holidays, after all.'

'Sorry! Duty calls. Won't be long.'

He had been sitting like this for forty minutes, and he knew that he still could not face the social chatter of the others. He would have to say he had the 'flu coming on and go to bed. It might not be wholly a lie: his forehead felt hot and clammy.

That terrible man Axel Shiner had called him here, at home.

'I've had such a time trying to get hold of you,' he had complained in that strange voice that was a cross between hectoring schoolmaster and over-pushy sales assistant. 'I've called your London number, and your Scottish place; it was your housekeeper there who gave me this number. I must say, old chap, I don't think much of your security.'

The MP pushed himself backwards in his armchair and moaned out loud. Of course, he reminded himself, he had given permission – as had all the group's financiers – that he could be contacted in an emergency, but he had never envisioned such an emergency taking place. Moreover, at the meeting a year before, when he had written down his address and two of his numbers on the sheet of paper going round the table, everything had seemed so different.

Shiner himself had appeared to be a passionate, caring man, driven to violence as a last resort against the sickening enemy of fascism.

That man was now out of control, cruel and at best careless of human life, at worst a sadist given power over the lives of nearly fifty young people and, through them, potentially hundreds of innocent men, women and children.

To think that what had begun as a visionary and noble enterprise had come to this!

The MP stared into the empty inglenook fireplace. His life was falling apart around him. He could hardly believe the horrors that were unfolding before him, both in his work and in Never Again.

His involvement with the group made him little better than a murderer's accomplice. He shuddered when he thought of how those three young people who had planted the Paris bomb had been butchered on Shiner's orders, to improve the man's image of himself. There had been so many victims; so many senseless acts.

The MP looked at himself and saw only darkness: if he had not been so afraid for his own skin, he would have notified the police long ago. After each atrocity he had steeled himself to do it, but then his nerve would fail. And because it did, more people were maimed; more lives ruined.

He had known poor Angus Delton for twenty years. He did not know how he would ever be able to face the man again; to look him in the eyes and know that he was responsible, at least in part, for the bullet that had condemned him to a wheelchair for the rest of his life.

He could telephone the police right now. He looked over at the old-fashioned black telephone sitting on his desk. It was the same phone that Lloyd George had used when he had stayed here in 1916. The MP could almost see the ghost of the great statesman turning to look at him, urging him to act.

But no, he thought, filling himself afresh with self-loathing, he was too much of a coward, morally and physically, to inform the authorities . . .

'We'd like you to come over. We need your expertise,' Shiner had told him smoothly.

Where, he had asked, keeping it to that one word.

'Paris. Charles de Gaulle tomorrow at noon, or the soonest to noon that you can make it. Someone will meet you. We've done our best to describe you, but if you could be wearing a yellow rose in your buttonhole, it would make it that much easier.'

He had swallowed, then, keeping his voice low: 'You're in Paris?'

'I don't think you need to know that. All that you need to do is be there tomorrow, without attracting anyone's attention. Do you think you can do that?'

'Yes. I'll do that.' He had cleared his throat and added in a whisper: 'This is a full meeting?'

'No, just you.'

For the past half hour he had tried telling himself that the summons could signify anything. Shiner might want to talk to him about financial matters; logistics; perhaps he even wanted to use him as a sounding-board to see whether the financiers would welcome a cessation of violence.

The politician knew that he was deluding himself, even as he marshalled those ideas in his mind. He did not know if there were any Never Again units already in Britain, but he did know that there was an English Sleeper, a girl, the only girl selected by the Leadership for the dubious honour of that role.

Shiner wanted his 'expertise'. The MP knew what that meant. At the back of his head, the pain started that was the forerunner to one of his terrible headaches. What if he should do nothing? Not go to Paris. Slam the phone down when Shiner rang again . . .? It would never work. Shiner would not let him go; he knew too much. The MP's eyes rounded at the realisation of what that man would do: he would send a killer after him, the same butcher of those poor kids, to silence him for good.

He had no option. He stood up, walked over to the desk and flipped open his card-index file. He dialled the airport, releasing each number reluctantly with the long index finger of his left hand.

On Monday afternoon at two o'clock, the second full meeting regarding progress on 'Operation Beauty' took place. It had originally been scheduled for ten o'clock in the morning, but a quick review of the information so far received had alerted Barney to the fact that more time was needed.

Progress had been slightly slower than anticipated. He was not worried, he told himself, as he shuffled the papers in front of him on the table. Among them was a copy of the artist's impression of the Englishman in Never Again's hierarchy – as described by Valente. The poor artist had done his best, but the Spanish boy had been very vague: he had only seen the man once; he had been quite nervous; he had not really noticed the shape of the man's eyes, or his mouth. He thought it was fleshy, but then again, it had been months ago . . .

The portrait had been copied and circulated to every police force in the country. So far, nothing; no one had reported as missing a man in his early fifties with a long chin and small dark eyes. There had been talk of putting the picture on television, but not yet, not until they had tracked down the Sleeper. No one wanted her to panic and do something foolish.

Barney chewed his lip: there was still every chance that

within the next twenty-four hours the girl would be in custody.

He was relieved, nonetheless, that this meeting was lower key than the first. There were only seven of them present: one each from the Home Office, Special Branch and Scotland Yard; the pleasant young woman from Number Ten, Hargreaves, Gregson and himself. Unfortunately, the Deputy Director could not be present and Barney could see that Hargreaves was itching to take command.

He cleared his throat. 'There are at present eighteen individuals categorised as Grade A suspects who still remain to be interviewed.'

'How long will it take?' asked the Number Ten girl, smiling at him.

'If we're lucky, two days, maybe less.'

'And maybe more,' put in the Special Branch co-ordinator dolefully. 'There's no saying these girls live where they're meant to or go to work or college where they're meant to.'

'No, quite,' Barney agreed. 'But of course the girl may well be found at any moment.'

'But there's always a couple who aren't where they're supposed to be,' the man insisted.

'Well, surely the one we're after will be someone like that?' said the Home Office representative cheerfully. He was young, Barney noticed, the optimistic type. Time to put him right.

'It's much more likely to be one of the impeccable ones,' he said.

The Branch man raised an eyebrow. 'Are you suggesting that my officers aren't up to the job? That they'll miss her?'

'No, no, not at all. I only meant that if the Sleeper's any good, she's likely to give us a run for our money. She might well appear a perfectly normal girl. It's possible that she might be missed on the first sweep.'

'I think my officers are capable of finding a terrorist, sleeping or otherwise!'

Sod it, Barney thought, staring down at his report. He had enough on his plate without having to mollycoddle touchy policemen.

Hargreaves pitched in. 'So what're you suggesting, Turl? That we keep all of them under surveillance? That's how many girls, Gregson?'

'Uhh ... there were orginally twenty-seven Grade A suspects, ma'am.'

'Even if the personnel were available, how much would it cost to watch twenty-seven people around the clock?'

'A hell of a lot,' suggested the Special Branch man nastily. 'A waste of the taxpayer's money, if you ask me.'

'Thank you, I agree. I think, Turl, we'll allow our highly efficient and hard-working Special Branch colleagues to complete their enquiries before we go flinging limited and valuable resources about.'

Barney counted slowly to ten. Then he looked up in her direction. 'You're absolutely right. These sort of enquiries do take their time. I'm sure if she's out there, she'll be found.'

'How about enquiries overseas?' asked the Number Ten woman. 'What news of Sergio Brunelli or the Dutchman or the German terrorist woman?'

Barney smiled back at her. 'There've been several alleged sightings of Kessler and Van Hoeffen since the posters went up at the weekend. But it doesn't look as if there's anything concrete yet.'

Hargreaves glowered. 'Well, could we know a little more, Turl, or do you intend to keep all the information to yourself?'

There's no point, Barney thought, just play along. He looked down at his notes: 'There've been sightings all over Germany and also in Prague, Lisbon, the Hague, Athens, Paris and Copenhagen ... Police officers from all these cities are in the process of checking the alleged sightings, but as yet their enquiries have yielded nothing.'

'How about the photofit of the Englishman in the Leadership?' asked the intelligence laison man from the Yard. 'Any joy on that from whoever it was you were having it sent to?'

'The Russian Intelligence Service.'

Gemmer had organised that side of things. Kessler's minder, still in custody and likely to remain so, had been shown Valente's impressions of both the Englishman and the

American. He had apparently shrugged and shaken his head. He could remember neither man looking like that. What had he looked like then, he had been asked. Another shrug; the drugs, you know, he had forgotten so much.

'No joy from Moscow, I'm afraid,' Barney admitted. Or the States he could have added, but did not feel inclined to do so. Zimmerman had been visited, but had refused to co-operate; would not even look at the faces.

'Dear, dear. Nobody's doing frightfully well are they?' Hargreaves said, tapping her pen on the table top. 'I suggest that if that's all the information there is, we'd all better get back to our desks.'

'The next meeting's scheduled for Wednesday morning at ten,' Barney called as people began to leave. 'Unless, of course, we get any news before that.'

'I'm sure you'll let us know,' added Miss Hargreaves on a trill. 'You'll phone us up, day or night. It's one of the things you're good at, isn't it?'

Sergio had had an interesting afternoon. The way that people showed fear had always fascinated him. Some were a little too obvious about it – trembling from head to foot – but others thought they had hidden it well. They did not see how their eyes darted around in their pale faces, or how, standing, they shifted slightly from foot to foot, or sitting, were stiffly upright on the very edge of their chairs, knees together, both hands clasped before them as if in prayer.

The old man that Axel had sent to him that day had been deathly afraid. He had walked into the room with his shoulders up around his ears, his mouth slightly open, his fists clenched hard down by his sides. When his eyes had grown used to the darkness – Sergio scorned the wearing of masks, they made his face too hot – and he had seen Sergio watching him from the shadows, his whole body had jerked in a convulsion of terror.

When Sergio had told him, in his heavy English, to sit down, the man had gone on standing, waiting for the bullet or whatever other means of death was playing on his mind.

They had been together for over an hour but Sergio could

count on one hand the number of times that his guest had blinked. And he had seen how, at first, the man's mouth had been too dry to allow him to form words. Then, in a burst so fast that the words jumbled:

'Where's the Leadership? I thought I was being brought to see the Leadership. I must be taken to see them.'

'No. It is only necessary that you see me.'

His guest's brow had wrinkled up, making the tuft of hair move forwards on his bald head. 'And who're you?'

Sergio had said nothing. He had just gone on staring at the man, this old politician from England.

'Why can't we have some lights on? Why're you sitting in darkness? What d'you want?' With each question, the voice had risen higher.

Sergio waited until the last echo of it had died away. 'I am a *specialista*, specialist, *si*? I sit in the dark because I don't want you to see my face. Why is my affair. I tell you what I want, and what I don't want. I want you to tell me what I need to know. I don't want you to ask me questions. *Capiche*?'

Perspiration had broken out in a smudged line under the man's nose. 'What're you going to do with me?' A painful swallow: 'Afterwards.'

Sergio had shaken his head. Outside had come the sound of a motorbike being kick-started into life and then the revving of the throttle. The messenger boy, a monosyllabic seventeen-year-old whom he had found in the local town that morning, was doing as he had been ordered: making himself scarce.

They were quite alone now. Sergio stared at the yellow rose in the man's buttonhole. The sight of it, and the old-fashioned business suit in these shabby surroundings, amused him. 'You had a good journey, I hope? You did not have to wait too long for a taxi at the airport? And the boy found you quickly in the town?'

The politician moistened his lips. 'Let's just get this over with quickly, can we?'

He had watched the man flinch when he told him what Axel required. Then his shoulders had slumped and his complexion had changed from pink to red with the speed of the sun setting into the Mediterranean. He had hesitated, twisting in his chair like a creature crying out for mercy, and then he had started speaking fast, so fast that Sergio had told him to 'Slow it'.

'Now draw me the plan,' Sergio had ordered and the man had obeyed, his pen shaking but fairly flying over the page. 'Aah, an artist!' Sergio had commented, but this time it was his guest who had kept the silence between them. Looking sharply at him, Sergio had seen the fear replaced by self-hatred in his eyes and in that moment had known that it would not take much to kill this old man; he was as good as dead already.

Right at the end he had shown courage. He had stood up and said, 'All right. That's everything you need isn't it? Now I've co-operated with you and saved you the trouble of torturing it out of me, may I make a final request?'

Sergio had kept the amusement out of his own face. He shrugged: 'Si. As you wish.'

'Would you make it look like a car crash? My wife . . . I want my wife never to know.'

At the end his voice had shaken, but he had held himself upright. Sergio had let several seconds pass before speaking.

'A car crash?'

'Yes. Or something else that could have been an accident.'

Sergio had nodded his head consideringly. Far away, getting nearer, came the sound of the motorbike returning. His guest had heard it too. He turned his head to the window, and the firm resolve left his face. 'I don't understand.'

'Signore?'

'I thought . . . I thought this was it.'

Sergio had shrugged. 'I only obey my orders. I have now carried them out in full.'

'But . . . you bastard! I needn't have told you any of this! You let me believe . . .'

'How can I control what you believe?' Sergio had smiled. 'But many thankyous for your co-operation. The boy will take you back to the town where you may take a taxi to the airport.'

After the politician had gone, Sergio had poured himself a glass of red wine. He imagined the old pink-faced man with the clump of white hair clinging onto the pillion; his suit getting smeared with oil and mud from the country road.

Then he checked the time – five o'clock – and took his wine over to the table where the telephone sat. Last night Axel had wanted to have his number, had screamed at him when he had refused to give it, but he had been entirely unmoved. With the Leadership in its current peculiar state, he had no intention of divulging any information that could lead to his whereabouts. 'I'll call you,' he had said, and put down the phone, cutting off the ranting voice.

As he dialled the number, he wondered which one of them, Axel or Kessler, would answer. There was a third, he knew, another man, who had been referred to but to whom he had never spoken.

Sergio had asked no questions the day before when he had rung, expecting Kessler but getting Axel instead. The man had sounded tense, but at least he had been decisive – a far cry from Kessler of late.

'Hello?'

It was Axel. Sergio told him briefly of the afternoon's revelations.

'What! His party's going to do what? I can't believe it . . . but wait, yes I can! Those fucking bastards. Well, they're going to get their come-uppance now, aren't they?'

He broke into a laugh, oddly high-pitched.

'And the old fool told you the lot did he? Fantastic! What a choice I made selecting him! But I had no idea he'd be so forthcoming! You must have superb persuasion skills.'

Sergio said nothing.

'He told you exactly who'd be there?'

'Yes. He answered everything.'

'And you're sure you can make the . . . practical arrangements required?'

Yes, he was quite sure.

'When did he say this was going to happen?'

'Very soon. He was not sure of the exact day. He said he would know later this week. I arranged for him to contact me.'

'You?'

There was a hint of anger in the man's voice.

'Yes, me. It's best.'

A few moments' silence and then: 'Good, good. You're sure he'll go through with it?'

'Si. He knows he's in too deep. He's a man without hope.'

'Excellent. You've done well.'

'Grazie.' Sergio took a gulp of the wine. For cheap stuff, the kind that a poor artist could afford, it was not bad. 'My comrade – she is with you still?'

There was a split-second's silence at the end of the line, then Axel said smoothly: 'Ah yes, Miss Kessler. Poor Beatrix. She's here, but she's downstairs. I wonder, in that connection, if I could make a suggestion to you? There would be a considerable extra sum of cash involved . . .'

As soon as Zoe had unlocked the front door of her flat and stepped into the dark hallway, she wished that she had stayed down in Hampton with Matt. The place felt cold and musty; it had been empty for nearly two weeks. She felt the ghosts of her old loneliness and isolation crowding about her, making the darkness black.

Quickly she switched on the hall light and stooped for the pile of post at her feet. Circulars mainly, a telephone bill and a couple of late Christmas cards. Her sense of foreboding lifted fractionally: there was nothing from them.

She went through the flat, opening windows a couple of inches and drawing curtains. In the bedroom her eyes fell upon her gym-bag, sitting on the floor beside the wicker chair, waiting for her. She had not been for a run since New Year's Eve; she would be out of condition. She saw Sergio's face in her mind, his scorn as he looked at her . . . and she had not even thought about shooting practice which was odd, remembering how much it used to mean to her, to hold a gun in her hand.

She frowned and shoved her gym-kit under the chair, out of sight. She did not have to think about anything she did not want to, she reminded herself. Memories could be crushed.

In the kitchen she switched on the radio and tuned in to

the station that she and Matt had been listening to earlier in the day. She smiled when the track came on that Matt had sung to her in the bath.

'When I have you, oooh, oooh, oooh . . .'

A large chunk of her had wanted to stay with him, but a little bit had needed a few hours on her own to absorb everything that had happened in such a short space of time. 'I feel as if I'm floating,' she had told him. 'I just want to touch base and sort a few things out.'

'That's OK, that's fine.' He grinned at her as she sat on the edge of the bed, towel-drying her hair. 'I've swept you off your feet, haven't I? I've never done that to a girl before.'

'Well, don't make a habit of it.'

'I don't know. It's kind of fun. I could get used to it.'

It is extraordinary, she thought, how close two people could become in such a short space of time. They had made love again last night, and then again that morning. It had been, she shut her eyes remembering, quite lovely. Feeling him between her legs, inside her, had seemed the most natural thing in the world. As if they were two parts of a whole so that, of course, when they came together they fitted perfectly. They had gone out for breakfast to the transport cafe at the top of his road. Double egg and chips and steaming mugs of hot tea. And then he had taken her home to make love to her again.

'I'm sorry,' he had said as he pushed her backwards onto the bed. 'But I'm going to have to ravish you again.'

Afterwards, he had brought the television into the bedroom and they had watched black-and-white films all afternoon.

'I'll let you go on one condition,' he had said.

'And that is?'

'You come over here, or I'll come up to your place tomorrow night. Seven o'clock?'

She had crawled across the bed until she was an inch from his face. 'It's a deal,' she had promised seriously, kissing him.

She filled the kettle and began singing the song on the radio. The happiness that had been bubbling out of her for two days came back. She felt warm inside. She wrapped both arms around herself and grinned: loving Matt was making her love herself too. Nothing must stand in the way of it. Not guns, or the gym, or Sergio or the Leadership's voices; or even, she thought, taking a deep breath, people who had died over fifty years ago or those who were being hounded today. There must be other ways to help them, other than the gun and the bomb.

Not once in all the time that she had been with him had she let Never Again intrude more than a millimetre into her thoughts, and the process of blocking out the whole subject was becoming easier. Soon, she thought, feeling her stomach tighten, the whole thing might have become no more than a bad memory. All she had to do was think of Matt, and being with him, and he would protect her from harm. Just as he'd said he would.

She made herself a cup of instant coffee and wandered into the sitting-room. She looked around, as if seeing the room for the first time: the long, low, dark velvet sofa, the old trunk that doubled as a table, and the slatted wooden chairs with bright cushions. She had bought everything quickly and without much thought, but now she realised that they fitted in well. She smiled; everything was different because of Matt.

She sank back into the sofa and reached for the remote control. Maybe tomorrow she would go out and find Matt a present: something personal and precious, a tiny token of how much she felt for him.

The low bleat of the telephone interrupted her thoughts. Matt, she thought, and snatched it up, smiling.

'Zoe? Is that you?'

'Dad!' The smile faltered. Her father never called. 'Is something wrong?'

'No, nothing. Well, except I was starting to wonder where you were, then your mother reminded me you'd be with your young man.'

She felt herself blushing. This is stupid, she thought. I'm a grown woman, after all. 'I . . . I've been out.'

'Seemed like a nice chap. But he was a journalist, he said.'

'What's wrong with that?'

'Well, one hears so many stories about journalists, doesn't

one? Sticking their noses into people's private affairs; sneaking pictures of them in their baths, that kind of thing.'

'He's not that kind of journalist!'

'No, let's hope not. Right, I've done what you asked.'

Zoe had no idea what he meant. 'Oh, good,' she said cautiously.

'I got hold of him last night actually. Took me quite a while I can tell you. He wasn't up here for Christmas and there was no reply at his London flat.'

Sir Magnus, she thought, and felt her head spinning. She sat down suddenly on the floor. She had been so successful in blocking out everything that she had managed to forget what she had asked her father, so long ago it now seemed, in the time before she had even met Matt and knew what it was like to be loved and to belong with someone.

He was talking: 'It was your mother who remembered that he had another place, down in England. He said he'd be only too pleased to help you. He remembered you as just a little thing from a party we had here, must be a good ten years ago.'

Oh God, she prayed. Oh God, get me out of this.

'As it happens, he thinks he can use you himself at the moment. He's done some project on poor housing in one of the London boroughs. Showing how black people are discriminated against. He's already got one assistant but she's more his secretary. He'll need someone to put the facts together. So I told him you were a bright lass, got your degree in English and German.'

'French,' Zoe corrected him automatically.

'Yes, all right, French then, and he said he can see you either tomorrow afternoon when he'll be in London or else next Monday when the House re-opens.'

Zoe stared sightlessly at a small coffee stain on the carpet.

'Are you there?' her father asked impatiently.

'Yes, yes I'm here. I . . .' She shut her eyes. She saw Matt's face, his eyes alight with love. He deserved better; someone who would return all that love unreservedly, without keeping most of herself hidden; someone who would not always be lying to him. She had been wrong to think she could have him. She swallowed hard, locking him out. 'I'll see Sir Magnus tomorrow.' Her own voice surprised her; it sounded bright and in control. 'Thanks very much, Dad. Can you give me his address?' She picked up a pen and started writing.

Chapter Twenty-Five

Steve Carrington had been teamed up with a woman police constable. They stood together at seven o'clock on Tuesday morning on the top step of a flight of stairs that led up to the block of flats where the girl lived.

Steve glanced at the WPC and thought how wrong, and actually chauvinist, was the assumption that a woman would relate better to another woman. From his own experience, as a divorced man living with the girlfriend who had ended his marriage, women much preferred relating to men. Certainly, he thought uncharitably, a twenty-four-year-old girl would have little in common with Sarah Pearson, a WPC of at least forty-five, who was said to batter her husband.

'I'll speak to her first,' she told Steve gruffly. He could have pulled rank but he was not in the mood.

'As you wish,' he said.

She buzzed the bell, once, twice, no answer. The third time she left her finger on it, and after several seconds came a sleepy voice: 'Whoosit?'

A girl's voice.

'It's the police here, Miss . . .'

'What?' The girl came fully awake. 'The police? What for?'

Distantly, from six flights above them, Steve heard the sound of a male voice shouting something indistinct.

'Are you known as Susie Alice Thompson?' Pearson asked.

'Yeah. What d'ya mean known as?' said the girl, rather belligerently. 'What's this about? I haven't done anything. Have I been caught in one of those speed-traps?'

'If we could just come up and ask you some questions, Miss.'

'Is this some kind of joke?' A male voice, definitely belligerent.

'No, sir. This is important police business. It shouldn't take more than a few minutes.'

'You got a search warrant?'

Steve and Pearson, united against the enemy, exchanged a look. 'Why would we need a search warrant, sir?'

'Oh, let them in, Ben,' the girl's voice came back through the entryphone quite clearly. 'We can ask to see their IDs at the door.'

The words did not, Steve thought, sound like those of an underground killer confronted by the police. Much more like the words of a girl who worked a forty-hour week in a local bookies and passed her evenings watching too much television. However, she fitted the framework and Steve was well aware of the dangers of relying on first impressions.

Three minutes later the girl opened her front door.

The fair hair that in her passport photograph had hung to her shoulders had been cropped to a quarter inch. She was wearing leggings and a man's shirt, and she was very plump.

Surely not, Steve thought.

Six minutes later he was quite sure. He got up from the black vinyl settee where he had been uncomfortably wedged between Pearson and Ben, the still belligerent boyfriend.

'Thank you Miss Thompson. I think we've taken up quite enough of your valuable time. Don't bother to get up. We'll see ourselves out.'

Pearson glared. 'There are one or two other matters . . .'

'I think everything's been covered.'

'Here!' cried Susie after him. 'You never told me what this is all about!'

'Just routine enquiries, Miss.'

In the lift on the way down to the ground floor, Pearson said furiously: 'Why did you cut short the interview?'

He did not reply.

'She stayed in the Lake District as a child! Near one of the eagle areas!'

'She lived four miles away, in the town, in a flat above the fish and chip shop. She wouldn't know an eagle if it hit her in the face!'

They were outside walking towards the car.

'It might all be a perfect front!' Pearson hissed.

Steve unlocked the driver's side. 'Never Again would never have been that desperate.'

'I'm going to say in my report that I'd not finished my questions!'

'Say what you like. But if you want a ride back to the station, I suggest you get in the car.'

Zoe gave the appearance of having dressed conservatively for the interview. She was wearing a long black jersey skirt, a high-necked white blouse and low-heeled black granny-boots. In fact, it was the only smart outfit she possessed and it was very important to her that she looked the part. Like the amateur actress hiding behind her props, she told herself as she waited in Sir Magnus's homely drawing-room.

It might once have been grand; it was, she knew, a very 'good' address in Holland Park, but the furniture was wrong for the room. A modern leather sofa; an old mohair armchair that was balding and bursting at the seams; a new one in a rather startling shade of yellow and several occasional tables, all spilling over with photographs and books. In one corner was a battered, grey filing cabinet; in another a very large African tribal shield.

But it was a cheerful room: a real coal fire burned in the grate; the brass surround and rather fierce dogs were highly polished and on the wide mantelpiece stood two oval bowls of velvety purple winter pansies.

Mindful of her father's warning that Sir Magnus was a stickler for punctuality, Zoe had arrived half an hour early and had tried to keep warm by walking swiftly around a square a street away. It was a bitterly cold day, made worse by an easterly wind and by three twenty-five, she had felt quite numb.

Sir Magnus's housekeeper, a very tall, austere looking woman with kind brown eyes, had tut-tutted as she had shown her in.

'No gloves on a day like this! Your hands must be quite frozen!'

They were, but Zoe had not been able to put on the precious

red gloves that Matt had given her. Her hand had reached out for them as she was about to leave the flat, then stopped. She had no right to them. They belonged to something that she knew she had to give up and to wear them would have been too painful.

Now she stretched her fingers out to the flames. Slowly, the feeling in them began to come back.

'My dear young lady!'

He was quite a large man, somewhere in his early sixties with a very pink face as if it was he who had been sitting too near the fire. He was wearing the dark grey pin-striped trousers of a business suit and a very baggy green polo-necked jumper with a reindeer on it.

He seized her by the hand. 'Malcolm's daughter! My, my, how lovely to meet you! Yes indeed! You probably don't remember me, but I remember you sitting on your stairs at home and being too shy to come down and greet me.'

He laughed loudly and Zoe reddened. The memory of such events were acutely embarrassing. Then she looked into Sir Magnus' blue eyes and saw that he was a genuinely kind man. She smiled at him.

'It's very good of you to see me.'

'Not in the least. Not at all. May I say you've grown into a lovely young lady. Your mother's beauty and your father's colouring. Oh dear, I'm making you blush. I'm afraid I'm a dreadful old chauvinist. My wife says that one of these fine days, some girl is going to smack my face. But there we are, I'm too old to change.' He smiled at her again.

'Oh good, tea.' The housekeeper had entered with a tray. 'Put it down here, Hilda, I'll pour. Milk? There we are, my dear. May I call you Zoe? Please help yourself to sandwiches and cake. Now then,' he settled back into the deep mohair chair with a large slice of Dundee cake, 'I understand you'd like to join the poor worker bees that help to run this muddled old country of ours.'

'I . . .'

Zoe had her cup halfway to her lips but felt herself begin to tremble. She set it carefully back down in the saucer. 'I only thought of being an assistant, or a researcher.'

'Precisely! Precisely so. The very people that we ignoramuses depend on. How d'you think we get the facts for our speeches and who d'you think writes them for us, eh?' He took a noisy sip of tea and a great bite of cake.

'You'd be one of the backroom boys, sorry girls, that keep me – and the rest of the duffers in the House – afloat. You might have to work long hours and it isn't very well paid. Sure you want to do it?'

'Yes. Absolutely.'

'All right then. Has your father told you about this housing project I've had someone working on for me?'

She nodded.

'I don't know how interested you are in social affairs or immigration issues?'

'I . . .' she swallowed. The words would not come. He must think her an idiot.

'Perhaps you haven't given much thought to such things yet? No matter, you'll soon learn. Michael, that's the young fellow who's done the research, is very thorough but not too hot on the written word. I need someone to knock all his facts into shape, make it a readable report. Think you can do that?'

She found her voice. 'I'm quite sure I can.'

'Good! I want to use the material for a speech I'm making on Homelessness and Race in six weeks' time. There's some sterling stuff in it; it's quite shocking how black people are treated.' He frowned into the flames of the fire and some of the kindliness left his face.

'Families hounded out of their homes by organised teams of thugs then dumped in estates that have been condemned as unfit for human habitation and told it's either that or nothing. Ghettos, that's what's being created in this country. Black ghettos, where life-expectancy is up to twenty per cent lower and children are developing diseases that haven't been seen in this country for sixty years or more. Makes my blood boil. And most of us sit back and say, "Dear me, how dreadful"! Even when these appalling Fascists win seats, all we say is: "Tut, tut, the price of democracy". I tell you, if I was a young man . . .'

He trailed off. What, thought Zoe. What would you do if

you were a young man? Just demonstrate or go a step further? Hurl eggs at the Nazis or send them a letter bomb? Looking at Sir Magnus, lost in his angry dreams, she felt so much the elder of them; older and sadder and trapped.

He recalled Zoe's presence suddenly. 'I'm sorry, my dear. It's my hobby-horse at the moment and I'm the most awful bore on the subject. Nothing worse than some white middle-class meddler trying to stick his oar in. Objectivity's what's needed. And if you're coming to it fresh, you're just the person to provide some clear thinking.'

He picked up a daintily-cut egg sandwich and swallowed it whole. 'I think we'll suit each other perfectly. After you've done this report for me, I'll see what else has come in that wouldn't bore that pretty little head of yours too much, and then after that, maybe I'll have a word with a few people and see if we can get you something permanent.'

He twinkled at her. 'That is, of course, if you're still as starry-eyed about working in the House after you've been with me for a couple of months.'

He was so nice, Zoe thought. If only she had not been acting a part, she would have wanted to work for him. 'I know I'm going to enjoy it,' she said.

'Mmmph. We'll see. Are you working at the moment?'

'I've just left my last job.' She had not actually given her notice, but she guessed that her continuing absence from the shop would eventually be noticed.

'So you could start work this week? I don't mean to pressure you, but the new session starts next week and I'll be frantic. If you could come in, say . . .'

'I could start tomorrow,' Zoe put in. Better to be active than left sitting in that flat, thinking.

Sir Magnus beamed. 'That'd be tremendous! I could introduce you to my secretary and give you a tour of the place. How does that sound?'

'Fine. It sounds great.'

'Good. Now I know I've got some Union people coming to see me in the morning and I'll probably give them lunch in the cafeteria, so would two o'clock suit?'

She nodded.

'You'll need a security pass, a temporary one to begin with. I'll inform the Serjeant-at-Arms that you're going to be doing some work for me and I'll be waiting for you in the Central Lobby at two. I can take you to his office and introduce you, speed things up a bit. Not that there'll be any problems but it'll be a shortcut to have me there vouching for you. They'll just want to know a few details: name, address, education, but all very basic, and you'll have to have your photo taken.

'Then, m'dear, you'll be free to wander the corridors of power!'

She smiled back at him.

'Now, let's turn to the sticky subject of your pay.'

Barney had promised himself that he would wait until first thing on Wednesday morning before calling Stuart McGuillan, his direct line in Special Branch and someone he had worked with many times before. He held out until five-thirty on Tuesday night. Then, telling himself that McGuillan would, in all probability, have left for the night, he tapped in the number. It was answered immediately.

'Mr Turl! I was going to call you. There's quite an interesting one, just heard about her.'

Barney's hopes surged like a fever.

'Blonde, twenty three years old, family's from Scotland, she lives in London. Her flat was visited this afternoon, no one in. A neighbour told the officers where she worked and the manager there said she hadn't turned up for work today after the holidays. Said she's a very odd girl, no friends, keeps herself to herself.'

'You're right, she does sound interesting. When's she being seen?'

'First thing. If there's no joy again, I think we'll give the flat a closer look, eh?'

'Yep,' Barney felt suddenly buoyant. 'None of the others look any good?'

He heard McGuillan shuffling through papers. 'All the girls living in Scotland have been seen and eliminated. There was one who looked hopeful in Edinburgh. She was being very cagey about Corsica but the woman officer got it out of her: she was there with a married man.'

'Oh. And the ones outside Scotland?'

'Apart from the London girl, there are only two others remaining to be seen, both scheduled for tonight. One in Sheffield and one in Brighton. And that's it. No luck from abroad then?'

Barney had had a gloomy conversation with Gemmer an hour previously. 'No. Same as before. People keen to get their hands on the reward money, but that's about it.'

'So it's down to us then, is it?'

'Looks like it. Call me tonight if there's anything on the last two, will you?'

'Sure.'

'And let me know either way on the London one, OK?'

'You'll be the first, Mr Turl.'

Matt had been made very aware, that Tuesday, that he had a great deal of ground to make up after his great 'Non-Exclusive' as Lomax called it.

The man had been in Rottweiller mood at conference. 'I s'pose you've got another Security Special for us this week, have you, Anderson? One that's going to be too secret to share with the rest of us?'

Matt had kept judiciously quiet. As far as story ideas went, his mind was a blank. He had not even read a newspaper that morning. All he wanted to do was replay the glorious weekend and look forward to the evening when he would be with Zoe again.

Lomax slapped down a cutting on the table, making everyone present jump. Reading the headlines upside down, Matt saw with a sickening feeling, the words: 'Psychiatrist in Never Again Leadership.'

Oh shit, he thought.

'This,' Lomax told the room at large, 'is not an exclusive story, it's in all the papers this morning. But it's a good story and it deals with facts. Maybe, Anderson, if you'd got onto Interpol last week instead of faffing around with your secret squirrels, we could have had that in the paper instead of the garbage we did!'

After conference, Matt read the story himself. A psychiatrist who had got depressed and turned to violence; Lomax was right, it was a good story and he should have got it.

He would have to think of something really good for the forthcoming week – but tomorrow, he told himself. His mind was not on work today.

He spent most of it sorting out his pile of correspondence and trying to do his backlog of expenses. At quarter to six, just as he was about to call Zoe and tell her he was on his way, the telephone rang.

'Matt? It's Clive. I think I've got something for you.'

'I've seen the Dutch psychiatrist story.'

'Who hasn't? No, this is something much juicier than that.'

Matt's journalistic instinct resurfaced, gasping for air. 'Oh yes?'

'I've only just heard it and it's from a source that I can't contact, so neither can you. You'll have to do quite a bit of digging on your own.'

'That's what I'm here for. Don't keep me in suspense.'

'OK. The word is that the Government is in talks with the UK Nationalists about a Repatriation Bill.'

'What?' Matt was too stunned to even raise his voice. 'I don't believe it.'

'Oh they're dressing it up as a . . . just a minute, I wrote it down . . . a "Voluntary Aided Returning Programme". No one'll be forcibly driven from this country, but they might find it much less pleasant to live here in the future.'

Matt remembered the awful Tory woman he had interviewed before the Election. What Clive was saying sounded horribly similar. 'Go on,' he said.

'Various suggestions are being put forward, all under the banner of "Re-vitalising Britain" and re-establishing the national identity. Want to hear them?'

'Yes.'

'OK. Preliminary proposals: Education. The Union Jack to be flown outside every state school.'

'That doesn't sound too terrible. A bit jingoistic but it'd never work. Half the head-teachers would rather burn the flag than fly it.'

'But suppose it was law?'

'What're you talking about?'

'I told you, these are proposals that the Government's listening to. Very seriously. You want to hear more? Only Christianity to be taught in schools. There'll be an immediate "cessation of tolerance" towards other religions. Muslim girls won't be allowed to wear head coverings. Jewish and Muslim children won't be permitted to observe their religions' practices . . .'

'Clive, this is too . . .'

'Let me finish. Housing. White families will be given priority housing, followed by white singles. Non-whites or those from the minority religions will be assigned special areas "for their own protection" . . .'

'Oh come on! That could never happen!'

'I'm sure that's what lots of people thought in the mid-thirties in Germany.'

Matt took his point, 'but Clive, this is too fantastic.'

'Maybe, but there are apparently very high level talks going on right now between senior ministers and the five UK Nationalists. They've already met three times, once two weeks before the Election and twice after, the last time just before Christmas, so by now they should all be quite pally.'

'But why? What's in it for the Government?'

'Use your head, Matt. It was nearly a hung Parliament, wasn't it? The UKNs hold the four crucial votes. Now what piece of legislation is this government desperate to get through?'

Matt closed his eyes. 'The new house tax? But they wouldn't . . .'

'Wouldn't they? They've promised it, haven't they? It's their reputation that's at stake and, with their pathetic majority, even with a Whip on it, they're going to need those four votes.'

'But Clive— ' Matt stopped and swallowed hard. He could not be hearing this. 'These proposals'll never be put into practice. I know things are bad, but the public would never allow it. The media . . .'

'S'pose the media was censored?'

'You're talking fantasy! The Government might be going through the motions of listening to the UKNs but they'll never let this stuff become law. Imagine what the rest of Europe would say!'

'The rest of Europe's got its own problems, hasn't it? Neo-Fascists in power, or in waiting all over the place! But granted these proposals are too extreme; granted it's too early yet for the Repatriation Bill, the fact is that the UKNs are going to get something in return for their votes, aren't they?'

'Yes,' Matt said slowly. 'You're right. Maybe just the flag flying. Few people would object to that too strenuously.'

'And if they did, the tabloids and the Tories would tear them to shreds, wouldn't they?'

'Yes. They'd be loonie lefties and traitors. There'd be demands that headteachers who wouldn't fly the flag be sacked. I can see it all.' Matt screwed his eyes up tight. He had just walked into a nightmare. He continued, more to himself than to Clive:

'And after the initial outcry, when people are all wound up and feeling patriotic, the climate'll be just right for another slice of the UKN cake. If they're really clever, and they probably are, or certainly their advisers will be, perhaps they'll orchestrate a little press campaign: an exposé of cruelty to animals by Halal butchers.'

'That's it,' said Clive. 'Once the first barrier is down, all hell could break loose. Racism and Anti-Semitism will no longer be taboo. We're talking about the thin end of the wedge. So you're interested?'

'That's like asking if the Pope wears funny hats. How good's your source?'

'Extremely good and very shy.'

'D'you know which ministers are involved in the talks?'

'No, not for sure. Just very senior. Might even be the Home Secretary.'

'I interviewed one of his right hand men last year, what's his name, that old MP . . . Sir Hugh Leigh. He was all right in a wishy-washy way. I'd have thought he'd have known about these talks.'

'I don't know. They're very secretive. But you're the journalist, you find out.'

'No one else knows about this? I mean in the press?'

'No one. Well, not as far as I know. But I'm pretty sure the source won't go blabbing to anyone else. And I won't, not until you've had a crack at it at least.'

After Clive had gone, Matt glanced over at Lomax. The temptation to tell him about the tip-off was considerable, but, on consideration, remembering the pain of that morning, inadvisable. He would make sure the story was copper-bottomed before he opened his mouth about it.

He reached for the phone and called Zoe's number. As he did, he resolutely put all thoughts of work from his mind; not one word about it would pass his lips.

Zoe heard Matt's buzz on the intercom on the steps outside but she did not move. You should have told him on the phone, she told herself angrily. You're a good liar, you could have thought of something convincing. A few words would have done it. Better to hear him broken-hearted than to see him.

But he had been so fast on the phone – just 'It's Matt. I'm on my way. I love you, darling' – that she had had no chance.

He buzzed again and she moved like a sleepwalker towards the intercom on the wall. She stared at it. If she picked up the phone piece she would hear his voice. If she did nothing he would eventually go away, but then he would call her on the telephone, over and over unless she took the receiver off the hook. And he would be worried, she thought suddenly. He would wonder what had happened to her: why she had been there when he telephoned but forty minutes later she was not answering the door. He might even call the police.

She picked up the handset.

'Zoe! It's me! I thought you'd changed your mind and gone out.'

Her throat constricted and she could not speak.

'Zoe? That is you, isn't it? I've pressed the right buzzer?'

Oh Matt, she thought, I love you so. How can I do what I'm going to do? 'Yes,' she said. 'Yes it's me.' She pressed the buzzer and heard the answering click of the outer front door. What seemed to be just a moment later, she heard Matt's rat-a-tat-tat on her door.

She opened it.

'Hello, gorgeous!' His face was hidden by the biggest bunch of red roses that she had ever seen. 'I brought these,' he leant sideways and grinned at her, 'for the most beautiful girl in the world.' He held them down by his side, took a step towards her and kissed her full on the mouth. 'That's you by the way.'

He presented her with the flowers and she took them automatically. They were peachy-red with raindrops on the petals. She stared down at them, unable to speak.

Matt smiled at her. 'Well, are you going to ask me in, or are we going to make love here on the doorstep? Don't get me wrong, I'm as much an exhibitionist as the next man, but I thought you were the shy, retiring type.'

She looked at him. All her love and wretchedness were in her eyes and the laughter vanished from his face. 'What's wrong, angel?' he asked softly. He shut the door behind him and took her by the hand.

'Are you having a bad time again?'

Tears hovered on the brink of her eyes; his kindness was too much. She nodded dumbly.

'Give me those silly roses.' He dropped them on the floor and enveloped her in a great hug. The touch of his rough wool coat and his cheek soothed her. He smelt of the outdoors and of rain. He put his hand under her chin and raised her face so that he could see her eyes.

'You're in pain, aren't you?'

Her tears began falling.

'I'm not going to ask you to tell me what's wrong, so don't worry. But if you tell me where your sitting-room is, I'll take you in there and we can sit together. Just sit and I can hold you and tell you it's going to be all right because I'm here. All right?'

She led him into the room where she had been sitting staring at nothing since she had got back from Sir Magnus.

He switched on the light and set her down on the sofa so carefully that she might have been made of thin glass. Then he walked over to the windows and drew the curtains. At once the room, which had seemed much too large since she had got back that afternoon, was more manageable, more like her own.

'D'you want me to sit next to you?'

She nodded. He pulled her towards him, tucking her into the crook of his arm and laying her head on his shoulder.

'I can't ...' she said. 'I can't ...' She could not find the words.

'Sssh, ssh. It doesn't matter. Don't even try.'

For a long while after that he said nothing. He stroked her head gently in the way that she remembered her nanny doing when she had woken frightened from a dream. And gradually she felt herself begin to relax and cuddle in closer to him. This is madness, said one part of her, but the other part said she did not care; being with Matt was the only thing that mattered. He touched her face.

'Are you feeling a little better?'

'Yes. I'm so sorry Matt.'

'You've nothing to be sorry for. Have you eaten today?'

She frowned: she had been too nervous to eat at Sir Magnus' and, as for the rest of the day, she could not remember. 'I ... I don't know.'

'How would it be if I ordered us an enormous takeaway pizza? With pepperoni and olives and anchovies and lashings of extra cheese. Or anything else you fancy. How about it?'

She smiled wanly. 'It sounds like a lot of eating.'

'Well, I'm ravenous and I bet you'll be hungry when you see it. Have you got a number for a pizza delivery place?'

'There's a leaflet by the toaster in the kitchen.'

She heard him ordering on the phone – a long list of things ending with 'two lots of pepperoni and double tuna. Yes, that's what I said, tuna' – and wondered what such a concoction would taste like. Did he always have pizzas this way, or was it a diversion created for her sake? What did he imagine was wrong with her, anyway? However wild his imaginings, he would never guess the truth.

He came back into the room. 'The bike should be leaving in five minutes. D'you know we get a pound off if it's not here in half an hour? That must be why all their drivers ride like maniacs.'

He sat down and put his arm around her shoulders again. It felt comfortable there, as if it belonged. 'Did you ever have a moped?'

'No. My father thought they were too dangerous.'

'I had a 250cc as soon as I turned seventeen. I'd saved all my Saturday job money for a year so I could buy the right gear and then on my first outing I wrote the damn thing off going under a lorry.'

'Matt! How awful! Were you badly hurt?'

'A broken ankle and concussion. But the worst thing was my mother was able to say, "I told you so", and she did – over and over again.'

Zoe laughed and he kissed her temple. 'That's better. Now I know how to cheer you up, just tell you about one of my misfortunes.'

'Oh Matt.' She turned to him and saw his concern and she knew suddenly that she could not be without him. One day, she promised, when I get stronger I might be able to let him go, but not now, not when I need him so much, when I'm halfway down the staircase and I know there's something terrible at the bottom.

Live for now, said the voice in her head.

'What're you thinking?' he asked softly. 'You look as if you're fighting a great battle. You don't have to be alone, darling. I'm here and maybe I can help.'

I must divide myself in two. Whenever I'm with him, the other stuff must not exist. He'll be my reality. There's time enough for them when he's not here.

'Zoe? Can you hear me?'

She focused on him and smiled. 'Yes, I can hear you.'

'What were you thinking? You were so far away.'

'Nothing important.' She put her arms around his neck and

hugged him tight. 'I do love you,' she said. 'Thank you for looking after me so well.'

'Think nothing of it.' He stroked her hair again. 'You happier now?'

She nodded.

'D'you think that maybe after a while of being with me, this thing that makes you sad will go away?'

'Mmm. Maybe.'

'Hey, I haven't asked! How did your job interview go?'

'I got it,' she told the back of the sofa.

He twisted around so that she had to look at him. 'But that's brilliant!' He studied her more closely. 'Isn't it?'

'Yes,' she said. 'I suppose it is.'

'So what's the job?'

'I'm a temporary researcher at the House of Commons.'

'Bloody hell!' He sat up and stared at her. 'You're a dark horse, aren't you? I'd imagined you were going for another bookshop, or maybe publishing. Which MP are you working for?'

She told him.

'Sir Magnus! He's a good old boy. Still living in the dark ages of course but his heart's in the right place. Hey kid,' his eyes narrowed on her. 'You could be really useful to me, you know.'

She could not tell if he was being serious. She half-smiled: 'Matt Anderson, I can see your antennae waving. Put them away.'

He grinned and shook himself. 'Sorry. But your new job's terribly tempting. Sure you wouldn't like to be bribed? How about a bottle of champagne per secret document?'

'I'm not a spy.' Her voice quivered on the last word and she got up quickly. 'I'm going to put those beautiful roses you gave me in some water and stick some plates in the oven to warm up. And I suppose you're the sort of man who likes tomato ketchup with his pizza?'

'Please! And go on, make my day. Tell me you've got some mayonnaise?'

Chapter Twenty-Six

Barney had known that the meeting was going to be bad, but in this instance foreknowledge was not making it any easier.

They wanted to call off Operation Beauty two days early.

The Deputy Director was speaking kindly: 'There really seems little point, Mr Turl, in continuing at the present pitch when all the girls have been interviewed – bar the one living in Greece and Interpol will deal with her – and eliminated.'

That morning at eight-thirty, McGuillam had telephoned. Their best hope, the mysteriously-absent London girl, had returned late from her skiing holiday the night before. She had only come home, she told the officers, to borrow some money from her parents and then she was off back to France to work as a chalet girl. Both the Brighton and Sheffield girls had been interviewed the previous night and discounted.

'Perhaps if we weren't all so stretched,' the Deputy Director was saying, 'but with the amount of work that's been generated by the new government ...'

Barney had to interrupt: 'Sir, I really feel it's far too early to curtail things. There's so much that hasn't been covered; we've only just started.'

'If you had your way, Turl,' Hargreaves put in with a sniff, 'there'd be a state of emergency and roadblocks on the motorways. One must try to be rational, however difficult one finds it. For the last five days we've done exactly what you demanded. We've all been running around chasing our tails and it's come to naught. Surely you can accept that?'

The Deputy Director hastened to soften her blows. 'No one's criticising you, Mr Turl. Just the opposite in fact, and I can appreciate it must be very frustrating not to have found this person. The prospect of her was pretty terrifying, I think we're all agreed. The thought of someone sitting in our midst, so to speak, then one day having her timeswitch pulled, shooting the

Prime Minister or blowing up Buckingham Palace or whatever other ghastly scheme Never Again might have had in mind – well, it's the stuff of nightmares, isn't it? An undetectable timebomb – it makes one shudder.

'But I do believe that we've given it our best shot . . .'

'The ferries haven't been checked,' interposed the Number Ten woman.

Bless you, Barney thought. 'Precisely so,' he said out loud. 'The girl could have got to Corsica via Italy, France or Sardinia.'

'Or she could've been parachuted in, or swum. Or gone by bloody submarine,' said the Special Branch co-ordinator unpleasantly. 'We don't have the manpower or the time to check every route to the damn place.'

'But we could get the French and Italians to do it,' Barney insisted. 'We could get Corsican immigration to check their data for girls fitting the description and the dates.'

'Needles in haystacks,' sighed the Home Office representative.

'We can still do those things,' said the Deputy Director firmly, 'as long as we're prepared to wait a little. I shouldn't think it'd be a frightfullly good idea to let other countries know of the real reason for our, ah, enquiries, so something would have to be thought of. Something innocent-sounding, and certainly not along the lines of "We need this tomorrow."'

'Tell the French that and you'd get it next year,' muttered the Interpol man.

'Ah, is that so? Well, I'm sure you know best. How does that sound to you, Mr Turl?'

Barney took a deep breath. 'Well, I suppose it's something. Sir.' He looked round the room. The Number Ten girl was the only one who met his eye. They exchanged smiles and it gave him courage. 'But I don't see why we can't use the two extra days that were originally set aside for this operation to send a couple of people to Corsica to speed things up, maybe smooth the way with the immigration people there . . .'

'Turl . . .' grumbled Hargreaves.

'. . . and also do another sweep of at least some of these girls.'

'Bloody nonsense,' snapped the Branch co-ordinator.

'Mr Turl,' said the Deputy Director, still kind but with a slight edge entering his voice, 'we shall have to call a halt to this. There's a limit to the number of times police officers can be sent to interview perfectly innocent girls without at least one of them claiming she's being harassed and running off to her local newspaper.

'The first stage of the Operation is over; no results I grant you, but there we are. I think perhaps we have to consider some alternatives.

'We must bear in mind the calibre of our informant.'

'Quite so,' agreed one of the Intelligence Liaison men.

'Absolutely,' drawled Hargreaves. 'A little thug who shot an elderly gentleman in the back and kept shooting with every intention of killing him. A thug who hasn't shown one shred of remorse since his capture . . .'

'You don't know that,' Barney put in.

She glared. '. . . not one shred of remorse since his capture, chooses, for some reason, to make these allegations. They are unquestioningly believed . . .'

'Miss Hargreaves,' the Deputy Director interrupted swiftly, 'I've read a transcript of Valente's statement, as you have I think, and I'm not doubting that he was telling the truth to Mr Turl.

'What I meant by the calibre of the informant was more to do with his understanding of the English language – a point you made, Mr Turl, at our very first meeting. He heard the girl say something about golden eagles. Well, that sounds pretty strong, I grant you. But he could have misheard what she said.

'We have to look at that possibility. We have also to consider the chance that he got her nationality wrong. He thought he was hearing English but it might have been . . .'

'Greek?' someone suggested.

'Well, yes, or Dutch. Never Again is predominantly European, isn't it?'

Barney kept his eyes down.

'But let's say that Valente was right. The girl was British and she was trained. But who's to say that she passed her training?'

There was a general mutter of agreement. Barney did not look up.

'From everything Valente said, the training was pretty tough. Maybe not everyone made it. And this was a girl, remember, a young girl. Her physical frailty might well have disqualified her. She might well have been tossed back by Brunelli . . .'

'More likely had her throat cut,' muttered the Interpol man.

'And told to keep her mouth shut or else,' continued the Deputy Director. 'Or she could have completed the training but opted out of the group of her own volition . . .'

'Highly likely,' commented the Interpol man.

'Or,' continued the Deputy Director with a fleeting frown, 'she may have been planted somewhere else. For all we know she's fluent in Italian or German and she's biding her time in Rome or Berlin.

'Now,' he went on more briskly, 'I suggest we implement Mr Turl's suggestions of asking the French and Italians and so forth to check their records for the girl. Perhaps also ask the ferry companies – if they keep records, that is?'

'What shall I tell the Prime Minister about risk to VIPs?' asked the Number Ten woman.

'Ah. I think that's a question for our Special Branch co-ordinator?'

The Branch man looked bored. 'You can reassure him that every Special Branch officer in the country has been briefed on the potential danger, and all VIPs will continue to receive our utmost attention.'

'Good. And we can step down the security code from Amber to Special Black. And call a halt to the telephone taps that were put on last week.'

'That'll include the journalist that Turl had told of the Paris bombing will it, sir?' Hargreaves asked sweetly.

'Oh yes, I think so. The fewer taps the better. Right then,' he gathered up his papers. 'I'd like to thank everyone for their diligence in this matter, and of course please pass that on to your various departments and staff. Thank you all very much and good morning.'

* * *

The taller of the two policemen looked down at Zoe.

Their appearance had startled her; they had been half hidden in the gloom of the entrance porch.

'May we help you, miss?'

Her mouth felt dry but she spoke clearly enough: 'I'm meeting Sir Magnus Donnahue in the Central Lobby at two o'clock.'

'Lucky Sir Magnus, eh?' said the policeman to his colleague. He turned back to Zoe, bending down slightly to her level. 'Up these stairs, through security, straight down the Hall, up a few more steps and you're there. If he's not waiting for you, ask for him at the desk on your left. And, Miss?'

He was frowning at her. What had she done to arouse his suspicion?

'Don't look so scared. Give us a smile.'

'Aah, isn't she lovely?' said the other man.

She climbed the stone steps. She was inside the Houses of Parliament; she was here for Never Again. She felt sweaty and a little sick. Stop it, she told herself. You're going to meet your new employer, that's all.

In front of her were three airport-style security scanning machines, manned by uniformed guards. One of them smiled at her.

'A customer at last! Business is pretty slow during recess. If I could have your bag, please. Thank you very much.'

She surrendered it reluctantly. She knew it contained only the most ordinary items, but she feared, illogically, that something would give her away. A moment later she saw the contents on the TV screen – her keys, her address book, cheque book and purse.

The friendly guard said: 'And if you'll just step through here, please.' She passed through a bomb detector. 'Thank you, and here's your bag back.'

She walked through St Stephen's Hall, acutely aware of the sound of her own heels clicking on the mosaic floor. The place was deserted. If only there were more people about, she would not be so obvious. With half an eye, she took in the splendour of her surroundings: the great oil murals, the

vaulted, beautifully carved ceiling that seemed to stretch for
miles above her head, but she was too tense to be much of
a sightseer.

She mounted the steps at the end of the hall and found
herself in the Central Lobby, a vast octagon lit by an
enormous chandelier. She stood and gazed. There were
mosaics everywhere, beneath her feet, over her head and
on the walls. Dead ahead was a mosaic of St Andrew over an
archway to another corridor that led deeper into the building.
There were four such corridors, she saw, leading away from
this hub, and everywhere, on the walls, on plinths on the floor,
were statues of statesmen, of kings and queens and saints. It
was both impressive and intimidating.

'Zoe! Two minutes early! A girl after my own heart!'

Sir Magnus had emerged from the arch on her left. His
voice, in these surroundings, boomed and bounced but he did
not seem to notice or care. 'Afternoon!' he called, in passing,
to a black coat-tailed figure whom she had not seen standing
behind a desk.

Sir Magnus was wearing a peculiar assortment of clothing: thick tweed trousers with what looked like an old
dress-shirt. He shook her hand warmly. 'The Serjeant-at-
Arms said he could see you at quarter to three, so would
you like a quick tour? Of course you would. Right, let's go
into the centre.'

He led the way. 'Now we're at the very axis. Look left
and you're looking down the Peers' Corridor into the House
of Lords. Look right and its the corridor leading to the
Commons. You'll have good eyesight at your age. If you look
down there,' he pointed down one of those dark corridors,
'you maybe able to see the Speaker's Chair.'

She was not sure what she saw; it all looked like dark wood,
but she nodded and smiled.

'Impressive, don't you think?'

'Very.'

He smiled at her. 'Come along, I'll take you through into
the Chamber.'

Once or twice, channel-hopping in the afternoons, Zoe had
watched a debate on TV. But she had always been more

fascinated by the baa-ing sounds that the MPs made when one of their side was speaking, than by their surroundings.

The chamber was much smaller than she had imagined, and much less grand than what she had seen of the rest of the building. The five tiers of green benches on either side looked worn in parts and the plain wood panelling of the walls created a stifled, enclosed atmosphere.

Sir Magnus walked her around the Speaker's Chair. 'Gift from Australia,' he said. 'The Speakers used to take their chairs home with them when they retired, but this thing's been here since 1830 something. Can't imagine anyone wanting to take it home, can you?'

Smiling, she shook her head.

'What else can I show you? The despatch boxes. See how they're worn at the sides? That's from the sweaty palms of nervous Ministers. And this is where the Mace goes when the House is sitting.'

He came to a pause at the end of the table. 'Government benches on the right; Opposition on the left. I sit up there on the left. The Press Gallery's above the Speaker's Chair,' he waved one arm in that direction, 'and the Hansard reporters sit just below. Must have amazing shorthand, these Hansard people. They get down every word, you know.'

He laughed. 'And some of the words are pretty damn boring, let me tell you!'

In his presence, Zoe's fears were slipping away. Almost she felt that she had become the part she was acting. After she had been working for Sir Magnus for a few weeks, all this would be commonplace to her. It gave her a thrill of excitement.

Sir Magnus, she could see, was enjoying himself too. 'You see the microphones hanging down on wires? That's for TV and radio. Remarkable how people's appearances have smartened up since they've allowed the cameras in here! I used to be a right scruff, but now look at me.'

Zoe looked, and looked away again.

'Up there,' he went on, flinging his arm up suddenly, 'and over there are the security cameras. They'll be switched on at the moment, but not filming, so you're not on Candid Camera.'

He began walking back down towards the Speaker's Chair. 'They keep trying to tighten up on security, but it's a sticky problem, you know. They send in tracker dogs every day, but you can never be sure some lunatic won't get in. Every citizen in the land, including lunatics, has the right to walk in here and see their MP. So how d'you safeguard the place without infringing the rights of the citizen?' He glanced back at her. 'I tell you, young Zoe, no place like this can ever be a hundred per cent watertight.'

They were outside the Chamber now and in a wood-panelled corridor. Zoe saw that there were several doors spaced out along it.

'Are those meeting rooms?' she asked.

'No, they're Minister's offices. That one's the Prime Minister's and that one down there is the Home Secretary's. There are more Ministers' rooms all the way down that corridor, and the Opposition's got its office up this end.'

They walked past the doors and a security guard came towards them, nodding at Sir Magnus as they passed.

He looked at his watch. 'We've still got twenty minutes. Plenty of time. I'll show you the entrance you can use as soon as we get your pass. It's much easier, for members and staff only, so there's none of that being frisked and made to stand in line with the public. Can be awfully time-wasting.'

They turned into another corridor and he increased his pace, not appearing to notice that Zoe was having trouble keeping up. 'The other good thing about this entrance is you can get into the House straight from Westminster tube. That's the way you'd be coming in, isn't it? Yes, same as me. Well, you'll just be able to walk straight through. Wonderful privilege; you'll appreciate it on cold days like this.'

Matt tried the fourth telephone number that the Political Correspondent had given him. It was an Oxford exchange. On the second ring, it was answered.

'Seven-four-one-eight-three-six.' A man's voice, rather cautious.

Matt glanced anxiously at the recorder in front of him.

It was supposed to be voice-activated, but it was the first

time he had used the thing, and he could not see the spools turning.

'May I speak to Sir Hugh Leigh?' he said loudly. The machine began releasing its tape.

'Who's calling?' The caution had increased.

'Matt Anderson, from *The Clarion* newspaper.'

'Leigh speaking.' He was distinctly suspicious now.

'Sir Hugh,' Matt unconsciously adopted his telephone-manner: conversational and intimate, as if the two of them were facing each other over a pint. 'You may remember that I interviewed you last year about the new immigration regulations?'

'Many people interview me. I can't remember you specifically.'

This, thought Matt, is not going to be easy. 'I wonder if I could meet you again? I could easily come to you, and my questions wouldn't take very long.'

A pause, then: 'What's the subject-matter?'

'Uh, it's rather awkward on the telephone like this. I'd much prefer to come and see you.'

'I'm sorry but unless you give me some idea of what this is about, I really don't think that'll be possible. It's a policy of mine not to have my time wasted.'

Arrogant bastard! 'I assure you, the questions I have to put to you are not in the least time-wasting.'

There was a lengthier pause; the kind of pause that suggested someone weighing things up. Then, quite briskly: 'I've already stated my position, Mr Anderson. Now, I'm just getting over a bout of the 'flu, and I've got plenty to keep me occupied . . .'

'It's about the talks between the government and the UKN. About flying flags and doing deals.'

Matt heard the sudden intake of breath. The machine recorded it too, then, in the silence, stopped. Clive had been right, and Leigh knew about it.

'Sir Hugh? I could be with you in two hours' at the outside.'

'I . . .' A wheezing sound. Maybe the old bugger really did have the 'flu. 'I don't know what you're talking about or

where you get your information from. I'd have thought that
The Clarion was too respectable – if any paper can be said to be
that any more – to go flinging unfounded allegations about.'

'Maybe if we met up we could have a talk? Entirely off the
record, of course. A background briefing.'

'Mr Anderson, I am not foolish. Briefings and off-the-
record chats are only possible when there are facts to be
discussed. Which in this instance does not apply.'

'So you've no comment to make?'

'How can I comment on a figment of press imagination?'

He had recovered well; he was giving a good impression
of being back in the driving-seat. He had, after all, been the
Home Secretary's confidant and adviser as well as close friend
for over twenty years.

Matt gave it another shot. 'I understand that segregation in
schools is being discussed?'

'I refuse to listen to any more of this! Good afternoon.'

Matt held the phone away from his ear and switched off
the recorder. He had got more than he expected but it was
no use for the story. He would have to rely on the interview
he had set up with the UKN MPs for the following morning
and hope they were in the mood for bragging.

As soon as he replaced the receiver, the phone rang.

'Matt Anderson? It's the front desk here. You've got a visitor
in reception.'

Matt groaned. He was not in the mood to deal with a
member of the public who had walked in off the street.
One in every fifty might have a story to tell; the rest were
time-wasters, generally verbose and laden with documents
that had to be read.

'Can't you say I'm out?'

'He says that he knows you and it's important. It's a Steve
Carrington. I'll tell him you're on your way down, shall I?'

Steve was not looking forward to the meeting. He remembered
only too well that on the last two occasions Matt had called, he
had put the phone down on him, knowing that the calls were
being monitored.

If Anderson told him where to go, he would not blame him.

'He's on the way,' called out the dark-haired girl at reception.

Steve nodded curtly. The time and effort he had spent on Operation Beauty had taken its toll on his temper: his girlfriend rightly claimed that she had hardly seen him and, when she did, he was good only for sleep. There was a limit to how much overtime pay could compensate for other things, especially when the end-result had been negative.

But what was really eating away at him was the knowledge that he was being treated as a mere messenger boy once more, Mr Turl's pet dog. And just to rub his nose in it, this was not even 'official' MI5 business; he was doing his boss's mate a favour.

Steve's relief the previous afternoon on hearing that Operation Beauty was finished, had been short-lived. At five o'clock, McGuillan had called him into his office and told him that he had a little job for him: re-establishing contact with Anderson. 'Re-opening our Never Again channel', he had called it.

'It's a bit late for that,' Steve had remarked. 'The scare's off, isn't it? False alarm. Everyone stand down, phone-taps off, including Anderson's. You said the decision had been made at the highest level.'

'Don't be naive, Carrington. You know there are levels and levels. Looks like our Mr Turl might need him again. And that's why he wants you to soften him up.'

'But I've already started working on the UKNs,' he protested.

'Well, this won't take you long will it? A friendly chat with a mate.'

'He's hardly likely to be friendly, sir.'

McGuillan had pulled open a drawer on the right of his desk, taken out a buff-coloured document-file and tossed it over. 'I should think he'll be bloody friendly after he's got a load of what's in there.'

Steve had picked it up. It was marked 'Strictly Confidential'. He had opened it, read the first page, and flicked slowly through the others. There were eleven pages of closely typed A4 and a photocopy of a postcard, front and back.

'This is legit?'

McGuillan had nodded.

'You want me to hand this over to him?'

'Use what God gave you, Carrington. We're not even meant to see that stuff, at least not yet. We'll sort out what you can tell him.'

'Can I make notes?'

'If you must. But shred them afterwards, OK? The source can't be identifiable.'

'He'll guess anyway.'

'I don't give a damn what he guesses! I only mind what he's told.'

The 'ping' of the elevator made Steve look up. Matt approached and stopped. He was not smiling. 'Well?'

'Hi! Is there somewhere we could talk?'

'I shouldn't think we've got much to say to each other.'

'Look, Matt,' Steve lowered his voice. 'I'm really sorry about last week – and thanks for not running that balls-up over Paris.'

'Yeah? I might still. You really landed me in it, old chum.' He stared down at him 'So are you just here to apologise, or is there more to it? Your friends want to pump me again or dole out some more crap in my direction? 'Cos I can save you the effort; I've got nothing to say and I'm not interested.'

The receptionist looked up. She was interested.

Steve said urgently: 'Matt, I can guarantee you, if we can go somewhere to talk, you won't regret it.'

'Got another Exclusive for me, have you?' The journalist viewed him coldly.

'Yes,' Steve spoke as quietly as he could. 'It's about Gibraltar.'

Matt kept staring. 'All right,' he said wearily. 'I'll give you two minutes. We can use one of the interview rooms down here. But it'd better be worth hearing.'

The room was stridently pink: blush walls, deep carpet, pale sofas – the newspaper's management must have believed it would induce people to talk.

Steve sat down and took out his notebook. Matt stood, arms crossed, looking as if he might walk out at any moment.

Steve found the page. 'Anton Valente is to be brought to

Britain on Sunday afternoon to stand trial for the attempted murder of Sir Angus Delton. On Monday morning, he will appear before magistrates and be committed to stand trial at the Central Criminal Court.'

He looked up. Matt's arms had dropped to his sides and his expression was wary rather than hostile. 'But that'll be generally press-released, won't it?'

'Not till Sunday lunchtime. It's for you.'

Matt considered him narrowly. 'Why me again? They must know I'm pissed off with the whole lot of you.' But he sighed and sat down on the adjoining sofa. 'This is genuine?'

'If it isn't, I'm being screwed, too. Look Matt, I can't tell you much about what went wrong over Paris. I don't think anyone knows, actually. But take it from me, MI5 was given duff information. Major shit-flying scenario. They weren't playing games with you.'

'Why haven't you been able to tell me that before?'

'It was . . . difficult. There was a complete media ban.'

'But it's OK now, 'cos they want to use me again?'

'Yes, if you like. But why not use them? Have the story; it's no skin off your nose.'

'As long as it's true.'

Steve flicked over a page. 'During his interrogation, Valente sang like a canary. He was no ordinary member of Never Again. He was a Sleeper.' He glanced up: that had done it, thank God.

'What, like the KGB? False ID, set up in an apartment, wife and three kids?'

'Not a false ID, not in his case, anyway. And he was a bit young for the wife and kids. His orders were to keep his head down and wait.' Steve consulted his notebook again, though only for show. 'He was trained by an Italian terrorist who's been on the run for nearly thirty years. Sergio Brunelli.'

'Isn't he the guy they thought the Libyans hired for that hijacking?'

'Yeah, that and about twenty murders and a few kidnappings. He's not a nice man, Signor Brunelli.'

'Shit! What a set-up, huh? Kessler running the outfit, a shrink recruiting, and Brunelli training the kids up? I didn't bring any paper with me. Give me a few sheets of yours. Thanks.'

Completely won over. The cost of a journalist's soul.

'These people cost money, mega I should think. Where's Never Again getting its funds from?'

'No idea. Valente went into some detail about his training; commando stuff, very professional. All done on a ranch in Corsica.'

'Corsica! That's where people go on their holidays, isn't it?'

'This was some place up in the mountains. Remote. By the way, all this is for use after Valente's trial. For your background piece OK?'

'Sure.'

'After his training, Valente's told to go to ground. Four months later, he gets his wake-up call. A postcard of the Citadel in Calvi. That's a town on the north-west coast of Corsica.'

Matt raised his eyebrows. 'But someone could genuinely have sent that to him!'

'True. The thing about this postcard is it wasn't posted in Corsica. The postmark was Amsterdam; it could have been any of the European capitals.'

'Smart.' Matt looked impressed, then he frowned. 'Maybe you can answer the question I asked last week. Whether the Gibraltar shooting marks the beginning of a campaign here?'

'I can't, and I don't think anyone knows – well, apart from the other side, of course.'

'But MI5 and Special Branch have been working their bollocks off to find any home-grown Never Again commandos. I was right in thinking that, wasn't I?'

Steve shook his head. 'The answer to that's still no comment, I'm afraid.'

'Worth a try.' Matt grinned. 'This Valente, did he say if he was the only Sleeper, or were there others?'

Steve turned a page of his notebook. 'Nothing concrete on that,' he said smoothly.

'But it seems likely, doesn't it? They wouldn't get someone

like Brunelli in, and set up a commando school for only one pupil, would they?'

Steve shrugged. Thin ice, he thought.

'Valente didn't describe any fellow-Sleepers?'

'Throughout his training period he was the sole pupil.' He studied his notebook. 'There are a few names and addresses of Valente's family – you like that kind of thing, don't you? Parents saying how he was always such a good little boy, helping old ladies across the road. And there's quite a lot of detail in his confession about his recruitment by the Dutch psychiatrist.'

Steve shut his notebook. 'You can have a transcript of Valente's confession after the trial. And pictures.'

'You bastard,' Matt was smiling, but shaking his head. 'You think you've got me eating out of your hand, don't you?'

Steve smiled back. 'Well . . .'

'Yeah, well you have. So what's in it for you? Or should I say MI5?'

'I don't what's in it for them, but if I were you I'd milk it.' He gave Matt a shrewd glance. 'And I think there's more where that came from.'

'Oh?'

'Yeah.' He yawned widely and stretched his legs. 'There's a pub near here isn't there? Will it be open? Let's go and have a pint.'

Zoe was finding her first day in Sir Magnus's employ quite exhausting. Not because of the volume or the quality of the work that she had been given, but because of the large, grey-haired lady who sat at the desk opposite: Claudia Fuller, Sir Magnus' personal assistant for twenty-three years, and his most devoted fan. Although she was not being paid extra, she told Zoe, she had come in during recess to sort out some filing.

In a breathy but quite audible undertone, she related an astonishingly full and detailed account of Sir Magnus' life – from schoolboy anecdotes, through to his days at Cambridge, his early struggles in the political field, a very quick and dismissive account of his marriage – and her own pivotal role in securing and maintaining his current position in the Party. She also appeared to run his home life, to the extent of buying his family's birthday and Christmas presents; only to be snubbed in return.

Zoe attempted to let it flow over her but it was like trying to keep back a tidal wave. She would just have started to unravel a table that showed higher mortality rates among black families when a phrase from across the room would seize her attention.

'A pink brushed nylon nightie! That's what she gave me this Christmas! Can you believe it? I didn't think they still made them. Lord knows where she dug it up from. And she hadn't taken off the OUTSIZE label either. I'm a big girl I know, but there's no need to hurt someone's feelings, is there?

'I wouldn't think of saying anything to him, though. Oh no, there'd be no point in upsetting him. And he would be upset; he thinks the world of me. And he wouldn't believe Petunia would be spiteful; he thinks all ladies are lovely, you know. Always the gentleman: opening doors, lending you his brolly if it's wet, and he won't let me carry anything heavy even it means he's to do it himself, and him an MP! No, you take one look at him and you know chivalry's not dead.

'And Petunia, of course, being the sort she is, knows how to twist him round her little finger. It makes my blood boil at times, it really does.'

Zoe smiled wearily and went back to her report. It needed all her attention. Its author, as Sir Magnus had said, was good on facts, but awful on presentation. 'Number of Households with Extant Lavatory in the Rosewood Estate' she read. 'Of the nine hundred and fifty-one occupied dwellings, eight hundred and nine were working to a degree . . .' It was going to take all her concentration to make something readable out of it but that could be a very good thing. If she had to focus so much on her work, she would have no time to worry about other things.

She left at five-thirty, half an hour after Sir Magnus had departed, but with Claudia still declaring she had a mountain of work to get through before she could possibly think of going home.

As Zoë walked quietly through the maze of corridors and past stately rooms, she realised that Claudia's verbal battering had made her feel much less of a stranger. Why, those desks in the corridor must be like the ones where Sir Magnus used to sit when he didn't have an office; that's the Library he goes to when he needs to think, and those steps must be the ones Claudia said that led down to the cafeteria.

At the underground entrance, there was a different policeman on duty from that morning.

He smiled at her as she took out her pass, swiped it through the holder, then pressed the green button and pushed her way through the plate-glass turnstile.

'G'night,' he called.

''Night.' She started through the subway leading directly to Westminster tube-station.

Matt telephoned her at eight o'clock that night. He was still at work, he said, trying to finish a story so that he could leave at a reasonable hour the following night. 'But I must confess I had a couple of pints earlier on.'

'You don't have to confess it.' She gave herself over to the warm glow that came whenever she spoke to him. She wondered when that feeling would go: never she hoped. 'So you're working late on a scoop?'

'On a little scoop for this week and a dirty great big one for the future.'

'Tell me what it's about.' She smiled at the enthusiasm in his voice.

'No, it's work. I don't want to talk shop when I'm talking to you.'

'It's not that you think I'm too dim to understand? That I'm just your bimbo?'

'Zoë, come on! Let's remember whose degree's the third and whose is the 2:1. And you can read my story on Sunday. But hey, how did your day go?'

'It was . . . interesting. I could tell you an awful lot about Sir Magnus' private life.'

'Good girl! Now I want you to write everything down in your diary and I'll look over it when I see you tomorrow night.'

'Matt!'

'Well, why else am I letting my girlfriend work for a pittance? I want you to keep your eyes and ears open. Every little bit of scandal counts. If you find something really juicy we could flog it and retire to a Caribbean island.'

'My father's right. Journalists are awful.'

'Very true. So tell me, what else've you been up to? Sir Magnus didn't take you out for lunch or a sherry after work?'

'Certainly not. I went to the gym.'

'How revoltingly good of you. I know that's how you keep your spectacularly wonderful body while eating over half of a boy's deep-base pizza . . .'

'I did not!'

'And two-thirds of the garlic bread. So what did you do – a hundred sit-ups and five miles on the running machine?'

Double that, thought Zoe. It had amazed her how out of condition her body had become until she had counted back and realised it had been nearly three weeks since she had been to the gym. She had been bright red in the face after her workout, but she had felt exhilarated as well. It was good to be alive, she had thought. One evening next week she might go to the gun-club – just for fun, she had told herself quickly, just to see if she still got the same thrill from holding a gun.

'If I can get this story finished tonight, I can force the back-bench and the subs to look at it tomorrow afternoon when they come in. But I still probably won't be able to leave here much before seven tomorrow night. When they let you have a Saturday off at this place, it's with parachutes attached. I'll have to take my bleep with us when we go out. Have you decided what you want to do yet?'

'No. I don't mind, but I'd like to be at your place, at least for the day. I love the river.'

'A wise child, as well as a beautiful one. Why don't you come up here tomorrow night? You won't have to wait very long, if at all, and I can show you off to the boys. Then we can drive straight back to my place. I might give some friends a ring tomorrow and see if they're up for lunch on Saturday. There's one couple I think you'd really like; they're very nice.'

'I'm sure they are. I'm easy to please, so long as you're there.'

'What a smoothie! OK, go and sit in front of the box and remember your beloved as he slaves away over a hot terminal. And don't forget, my pet, if you see any secret documents lying around on his desk . . .'

'I'm putting the phone down.'

'Don't. Everyone does that to me. I'll see you tomorrow. Sleep tight.'

It was nine o'clock that night before Sir Hugh Leigh was able to contact Rodney Lewis. When he had first tried the number, just after that disturbing call from *The Clarion*, it had been unobtainable.

He had very nearly panicked: the journalist had clearly known far too much; he had been fishing, but with the confidence of knowing that he was in the right waters.

Someone had obviously talked, but Leigh could not imagine who. He was fairly sure that it must have come from his own side, but so few people knew about it. A secretary perhaps?

It simply did not make sense for the UKNs to be spoiling their chances, but they were new to the game and possibly easy fodder for a smart journalist. If a story came out, the whole deal would be off, end of talks, and the end, probably, of him. Brunelli's face had floated in front of him as he had picked up the telephone again: he had to warn the UKNs off.

This time, on the same number, he had got a recorded message. 'This is the headquarters of the UK National . . .' An awful twangy voice: Lewis's, South London, ill-educated.

He had hung up. He had known, sitting there in front of the old telephone, that it was his clear duty to inform the Home Secretary of *The Clarion*'s questions; indeed, it was the first thing he should have done. But if the Minister knew, he might call the talks off himself.

He had got up and left the house. Sarah was down in London at the Sales and both the kids were staying with friends. In the state of mind he had been in, he could not bear to stay in an empty house; better to be moving. And there was the fear, unformed but there nonetheless, that his phone might not be safe.

It had only taken him an hour and forty minutes to drive to London. On the journey he had kept trying Lewis on the carphone but it was either engaged or he got the message again.

If all else failed, he had the man's address in Millwall, but he did not want to be seen going there. Imagine if a photographer was waiting!

He had parked the car in a side street in Chiswick and sat there, trying to calm himself. He had not been able to go to the flat because Sarah would have been there. From seven-thirty onwards, he had called every twenty minutes, until:

'Rodney Lewis speaking.'

'It's Leigh here.'

'Oh yes? And what can I do for you?'

He had an oily, arrogant way of speaking. Leigh had always hated having to deal with him. 'Have any of your people been talking about . . . the meetings? To the press?'

'I'm the only one that talks to the press. I'm the only one who knows how to handle them. Why?'

'A journalist from *The Clarion*'s been rather nosy. And well-informed.'

'He isn't being informed by us, matey. What's his name?'

'Matt Anderson. He's an investigative reporter; he's interviewed me before.'

'What d'you say his name is?'

Leigh repeated it.

'I thought so. Good job you called. My PR man's fixed up for him to interview me tomorrow morning, so I'll be prepared.'

'No! You mustn't see him. He's only looking for confirmation, and one slip from you . . .'

'Slip, Sir Hugh? You suggesting I'm about to be stitched up by some snotty-nosed reporter? I'd say you're the one who'd better mind about slipping, you being so friendly with him and all.'

Leigh took a deep breath and exhaled slowly. 'I simply feel that at this stage of our negotiations it would be inadvisable for either of the parties concerned to speak to a journalist who, by whatever means, has been acquainted with very sensitive and crucial information.' He paused and watched a boy on a push-bike coming towards him. The boy passed. 'I think "No comment" is the best approach.'

'I'll bear that in mind. Thanks for calling.'

As he put the phone down, Sir Hugh Leigh, the Home Secretary's confidant and the British financier of Never Again, was deathly afraid.

Even on her second day Zoe was beginning to feel much more at home.

It had helped that in the morning, as she had been walking towards the Underground entrance, she had heard her name being called. Turning, she had seen Sir Magnus, striding along behind her in a voluminous black raincoat and deer stalker.

'Nice and prompt for work! That's what I like to see. What's this great load that's weighing you down? Let me take it for you. Off somewhere for the weekend?'

Zoe had surrendered her overnight bag gratefully. It was ridiculous that she had felt it necessary to take quite so much to Matt's for just one night, but then, she had reasoned, she did not know what they would be doing and the two outfits and two pairs of shoes would cover all contingencies.

The policeman had been the same one on duty as the previous day. He had smiled at them both. 'Morning, Sir Magnus; morning, miss. Can you manage through the turnstile with that bag, sir? I can hold it for you.'

'Not at all, not at all. It's only suitcases that're difficult through here. Thank you officer.'

They had walked side by side.

'Do many people bring suitcases in here?' She had asked. She could not imagine why; it seemed most peculiar.

'Good heavens, yes! Monday mornings and Friday evenings it's like checking in and out of the Dorchester. Everyone going away to their constituencies for the weekend. They want to get off early on Fridays, so they bring their cases in. Beats me, mind you, why they need to lug stuff all over the country.

Keep your constituency stuff there and your London stuff here, I say, but most of 'em don't. No organisation, that's their trouble.'

Zoe had noticed as they passed other people, how many of them smiled and greeted Sir Magnus. Secretaries, researchers, security men and policemen, the messengers – everyone had spoken to him. She, trotting along in her Kosack coat beside him, had been invisible. It was a strange feeling, she decided, and rather fun.

But later, on her own, she received plenty of attention. When she went to the library for one of the books that Sir Magnus had recommended, a messenger and two security men chatted to her. 'Finding your feet all right?' one asked. 'What're you up to tonight?' grinned another. 'Fancy a drink?'

In the afternoon, Sir Magnus asked her if she would 'run along' to the Home Secretary's office with some papers. Her heart was in her mouth as she walked along the dark pannelled corridor, with the Speaker's Chamber on her left and the offices of statesmen and women on her right. Then, a door to one of those offices had opened, and someone she recognised as a very well-known Minister, emerged.

'Hello,' he had said, smiling at her. 'Those papers look heavy! Mind you don't strain yourself.'

All in all, she thought, it was a friendly place, in spite of its grandeur and importance. Given time, she knew she would be happy there.

Chapter Twenty-Seven

Matt found a parking space quite near Zoe's block and began reversing into it.

'I'm dying to go to the loo,' she said.

'I know.'

She had told him that at least three times in the last ten minutes. 'As soon as I've stopped the car, you get out and run up and I'll bring the bags.'

'Matt, you're an angel.'

'Out you get.'

He watched her run off, her blonde hair bright in his head-lights. They had had a perfect twenty-four hours together. Everyone he had introduced her to – both at work the previous night and at lunch that day – had been impressed. Some of the back-bench had been positively drooling and even Lomax had muttered 'Nice' to him. Sue and Daniel, the friends they had had lunch with, had been quite amazed and had said so.

'She's stunning,' Dan had whispered when Zoe had gone off to look at the Sweet Trolley. 'And bright, and nuts about you, you jammy sod.'

'She's such a nice girl, too,' Sue had added, sotto voce. 'You'd have expected someone with her looks to be a bit spoilt and demanding, but she's not at all, is she? If anything she's shy . . . It's all right Matt, I'm not criticising her. Don't glare at me like that! I think you're very lucky.'

Matt pushed the passenger seat forward and pulled out their two overnight bags. Soon, he thought, they ought to start leaving a change of clothes at each other's places. Or maybe staying at one flat in the week and the other at weekends; a place in the country and a place in town.

Grinning at the prospect, he carried the bags into the lobby. Both lifts were busy; one still up on the top floor, presumably the one that Zoe had used. He pressed the button for it and watched as it descended with painful slowness.

The week that had started so badly was turning out so well.

Lomax had been justifiably pleased with the Valente exclusive; it was running across the attic of the front page in the paper. He had been even more pleased with the snippets that Matt had given him of background detail for the trial.

'Sure this is just for us?'

'So I'm told.'

'Mr Deep Throat coughs up at last, does he?'

Matt had let that one pass and they had parted on amicable terms, but he had the warm glow of knowing that the slate had been wiped clean.

Having a few good stories to look forward to was as satisfying as stocking a cupboard full of winter provisions. Apart from all the Valente material, he still had the cracker that Clive had given him.

The abrupt cancellation of the interview he had set up with the UKN leader for the previous morning had only served to convince him that the story was true. All he had to do now was prove it.

He had considered asking Steve about it, and perhaps in the end he would, but he was also a little wary of doing so. He had no wish to alert MI5 to a situation they knew nothing about. He was a journalist, not a policeman, and besides MI5 would feel it was their duty to save the Government any embarrassment. He wanted the story published, not repressed.

Once it was, it could prove fatal for the Government. Matt grinned at the prospect. 'Watergate,' he thought, 'public outcry, General Election, new government, Pulitzer Prize.'

The lift clunked to a stop and the doors opened. Stepping in, he pressed the button for the top floor and checked his appearance in the small mirror beside the emergency handle. Tousled, he decided, smoothing down his waves, before remembering that Zoe had said she liked his hair that way and mussed it up again.

They were supposed to be going out to the theatre in an

hour; a new musical that had been brought over from Broadway and variously hailed as 'A genuine triumph', 'Outstanding' and 'Unmissable'. In fact, according to *The Clarion*'s theatre critic, the show was entirely missable, but Zoe had wanted to see it and that was all that mattered. Tomorrow they were going to lunch with her brother and his girlfriend and he was slightly nervous at the prospect, he wanted so much to make a good impression.

The lift stopped on the sixth floor and he got out, a bag in either hand. Zoe had left the door slightly ajar for him and he pushed it fully back with one foot.

She was standing in the dark at the bottom of the hall, still wearing her coat and with her back turned three-quarters turned to him. The bathroom light was on, although the door was nearly shut. He could just see her profile; her face was in shadow.

'Hi,' he called but she did not answer; she was lost in thought. There was something white at her feet, an envelope.

He put the bags down, switched on the light and walked towards her. She gave no sign of being aware of him and he was suddenly afraid. 'Zoe?'

Nothing. Just that fixed stare. He had seen someone like this before: the mother of a child who had been killed in a road accident. Catatonic and rigid.

He put out his hand and laid it on her shoulder. 'Zoe?' he tried again, gently.

She blinked and turned around.

Thank God, at least she can hear me, he thought. Then he saw her face: drained of all colour, her eyes enormous, the picture of terror.

'Darling?' He took her by the other shoulder and tried to pull her towards him in an embrace, but she resisted. 'What's wrong, darling? Whatever it is, you can tell me.'

The look she gave him was as cold as death. Moments passed, then: 'Nothing's wrong,' she said brightly and the corners of her mouth turned up in imitation of a smile.

'Zoe, for God's sake!' He was very frightened now. She had never been like this before: icy and remote, staring at him as if he was an obstacle in her path. He tried to hug her again but she took a step backwards, out of his reach.

'Please, let me help you, Zoe.'

'I'm fine, Matt, really.' She put a hand to her brow and held it there. Her voice was stilted as if she was fumbling in an unfamiliar language. 'I've got a headache or something. A migraine! I sometimes get them.'

'Do you?' He watched her closely. 'You've never mentioned it before.'

'Well, I'm mentioning it now!' Her voice cracked at the end and she blinked furiously.

Please come to me, he begged silently. Please don't shut me out. I love you so much. 'D'you have anything for them?' he asked.

'For what?'

'For your migraines. What d'you usually take?'

She stared. 'Aspirin,' she said eventually.

'Are they in the bathroom? You go and sit down, and I'll get them for you.' He made for the door, but she moved quickly in front of it, panic on her face. 'They're not in there!'

'OK, OK, calm down. Are they in the kitchen?'

'Yes, no. Oh I don't know.' She swayed slightly on her feet. Maybe she really was ill; he touched her hand, it was icy.

'Come and sit down.' He took her into the sitting room and switched on the table-lamp. She was sitting rigidly, her eyes downcast.

'Zoe,' he said urgently.

She shifted away from him, but he held onto her hand.

'Zoe, I don't know what's brought this on, but it's much worse than the times before.' He swallowed; she would not look at him. Was she hearing anything that he said?

'I don't know what's happened to you in the past. All I know is that I feel I can tell you anything, and I hope that maybe one day you'll feel that way too. But until that happens, and even if it never happens, I'm always here for you.'

A little moan escaped from her. 'Oh Matt!'

'Can I hold you?'

She shook her head. He could see tears in her eyes but they did not fall. She took a great heave of air and

turned towards him, but would still not look at him directly.

'I'm probably better on my own just now,' she said.

'I'm not leaving you; not like this.'

'Please, Matt.'

'Zoe, I'm scared for you! I can't leave you alone.'

She looked straight at him. Never had he seen someone
look so desolate, so full of despair.

'All right,' she sighed, 'but I've got to go out tomorrow on
my own. Early, and I won't be back till late.'

'But where . . .?' He stopped himself. Instinct told him that
if he was to have any chance of keeping her, he had to let her
go. 'OK,' he agreed quietly. 'Will you need a lift anywhere?'

She shook her head.

'Will you call your brother and cancel lunch?'

'I . . . I don't know. Could you?'

'Yes. If you give me the number. What if your brother asks
to speak to you?'

She gave a despairing shrug. He wanted to hold her so much
that it hurt. 'I'm going to stay with you. If it makes you feel any
better, I won't touch you.'

She flinched but did not speak.

'If you're in bed with me in the morning, fine. If you've
gone, I'll just leave when I wake up. Is that a deal?'

She nodded. Then she said dully: 'I'm going to take a
shower. You can put the TV on if you like.'

He resisted the urge to follow her into the bathroom or
ask her to leave the door open. Instead, he pressed the
TV's remote control. But he saw and heard nothing. He
felt so powerless. 'Please God,' he prayed, 'help me to know
what to do.'

Sergio heard the sound of the motorbike and moved over to
the window. The surrounding French countryside was flat
and the road fairly straight, so he could see them approaching,
even on such a dark day when the sun seemed never to
have risen.

She was coming to him. She had made contact with the
go-between; she had got the flight from London. Now every

moment was bringing her nearer . . . He grinned: he was looking forward to seeing the young British girl again. The only girl he had ever trained and his only crackshot. He remembered how she had destroyed all his targets. Gun after gun he had given her, and she had learnt all their tricks like a clever child. And like a truly clever child she had been unaware of her talent and was thus unspoilt.

He looked out of the window. She and the boy were slight, and on the big machine they looked like children, brother and sister out for a ride.

The bike turned off the road and onto the rough track leading to the cottage. It had been a peasant's hut; originally just two rooms, side by side. Someone had added another floor and a bathroom. It was basic, but adequate.

In the first floor room he had set up an easel, very prominently in the front window. If anyone came snooping, they would see it and, if luck was on his side, be satisfied. Not that anyone had come near. The cottage was a long way out on the old road from the village; no one but a crazy artist would choose to rent it. The boy fetched him food and drink; all Sergio had to do was wait.

His only problem had been the enforced confinement. Every night, under the cover of darkness, he had gone walking in the moonlight. Even so, in the last two days, he had begun to feel caged. He would be glad when the next thirty-six hours were over and he could be gone from the place.

The engine cut. Light footsteps, then a tap at the old wooden door. He said nothing and, after a few seconds, the door opened.

He had expected her to be trembling, the same as the old politician. She was not. Her face was paper-white but quite composed. He could see the pupils in her eyes contract but she came calmly towards him, stopped and waited; she was playing his game. Just how far she was prepared to play, and how much he would have to make her, he was about to find out.

He smiled slowly. 'We meet again, my little friend.'

She gave a tiny nod.

He did not remember her being this cool. Standing there in her faded blue jeans and a heavy black donkey jacket, returning him stare for stare.

'You've kept yourself fit?'

Another little nod.

'And shooting? You've practised?'

'Yes,' she even sounded a bit bored, sulky, like a teenager faced by too many questions.

'Sit down,' he told her abruptly. He switched on the overhead light and took the chair opposite at the long oak table. Level with her, and in the light, he studied her more closely. Her eyes were a little fixed, slightly glassy. It was all right if she lost her head afterwards, but not before. Too much depended on her.

'Are you still afraid of me?' he asked conversationally.

She focused clearly on him. 'Afraid?' she repeated, like a foreigner with a new word.

'Si. Once you were full of hate but you were also very frightened. Like the rabbit with the wolf. Now, maybe you have lost that fear. That can be bad, very bad, Zoe. I hope you haven't lost your fear.'

Still she did not respond, beyond an almost imperceptible shrug of the shoulders.

'Your mama and papa, and your brother, they are well?'

The head jerked up at that. The necessary line of communication was reopened; Sergio smiled. 'Mama and papa live in a small little place, I think, called Newtonmore . . .'

'All right,' she broke in quickly. 'I'll do what you want. I would anyway. You don't have to threaten my family.'

'Oh? You think that I, Sergio Brunelli, threaten an old man and his lady who like dancing?'

She flinched, quite noticeably, and began chewing at the nails of her left hand. 'I'll do it, I said.'

'Good girl. The Leadership sends you greetings. For you they've selected a very great honour. You wish to know what you shall do?'

She stared at him. 'Yes,' she whispered.

He outlined it quickly. He saw her hand tremble slightly

when she moved a lock of her hair out of her eyes: a good sign.

'Four days,' he repeated. 'You have four days to choose. Tomorrow or Thursday; next Monday or next Thursday. Everything will be supplied but how you do it is your affair, and when. Maybe late at night; or early in the morning is best.'

'No,' she said slowly.

'What?' His voice became very still. 'You refuse?'

For a minute she said nothing, then she frowned and looked at him. 'No, it won't be necessary to go in out of hours. There's a much easier way; less suspicious.'

He gazed at her, letting none of the surprise he felt show. 'All right, tell me,' he prompted.

Ninety minutes later, after she had departed, he replayed her plan to himself with wonder; the plan that she had told him with such coldness and clarity, that had been so simple and yet so perfect.

All he had had to do was call the man in London and tell him to be there with the stuff at the right time.

Undoubtedly, Sergio thought, she was not the same girl he had trained last summer. That one, he had been able to read like a comic-book: he could punch her emotional buttons and be certain of the response. The only thing he had not been sure of was whether she would have the guts to kill when the time came.

This one, though! A snow-queen; nothing there to give her away. He drank his wine and stared out into the darkness that engulfed the cottage so early. What had wrought the change? She had only done one action; her first, the blooding in Turin, and that had been three months ago.

He glanced at the time; he should have called Axel ten minutes before, but Axel could wait. He was enjoying himself too much with the enigma that Zoe had become. He was much more excited sexually by her than he had been last September. She was so much more of a challenge now; a challenge to break the ice that she had formed between herself and the rest of the world.

Naturally, he could take her by force, but the idea of making her want him, of hearing her cry out his name, appealed. Maybe, just maybe, he would not do what Axel wanted. Maybe Zoe was an interesting enough proposition to be kept alive afterwards. It might mean he would have to find another body, and make it look like hers, but nothing was impossible.

He grinned: he might even take Zoe with him for his house on the beach . . .

Chapter Twenty-Eight

At passport-control they waved her through without even taking her passport. At Airport Security there was a small queue of three persons, with one man arguing loudly that the X-ray machine would damage his films.

Zoe let her eyes wander. Over to her right was another queue, only a little longer, and beyond that, another. On her left, was a partition wall with several windows of darkened glass. Zoe imagined hidden eyes watching her, tapping at keys on their computers, talking fast into phones, knowing.

She dragged her eyes away. The uniforms that the French security guards wore were so stylish; even down to the holsters slung around their hips. What would they do if they knew? Bang, bang you're dead?

The woman in the sweeping cloak in front of her stepped forward. Now Zoe had an unrestricted view of what lay in front: the bright lights and beckoning displays of the Duty-Free shops. Boring, nothing to keep her attention. She looked down at her feet; her ankle boots were scuffed from setting her feet down on the road before the bike had properly stopped. She had to keep her mind off that, and occupied: she looked up, and it was then that she saw them.

They were less than three feet away from her: their two faces neatly sanitised in matching oblongs. Someone had stuck the poster on the side of the X-ray machine. Pieter and the woman from the Leadership. Zoe stared at the name, Beatrix Kessler. She felt her stomach turn to ice; Kessler the Killer, a figure of terror from her childhood; the woman who got a kick out of killing people; who killed children. The same woman who had warned her that this was not a game for children.

She and Pieter were wanted for a lot of francs; any information leading to the discovery of their whereabouts . . .

'Mademoiselle?' The guard was waiting.

She stepped forward, placing her bag on the black moving rubber. It was a sign; they were watching her; their eyes following every movement, willing her on, making sure that she remembered who she was. She was not her own being any more and not Matt's; not her father's daughter. She belonged to no one but them and she had her duty to perform.

That knowledge, the knowledge she had chosen to bury down deep in her mind, had been reawakened the previous night. Holding the postcard in her hand, letting the envelope float to the floor, she had known the truth again. The Cause was what mattered – exterminating the Nazis so that never again would any man, woman or child be terrorised where they lived, or led to a pit and shot because of their colour or religion. The love she felt for Matt, she had realised, had been a selfish love, leading her from the path and making her forget her purpose.

It had been a sham – her being with him, the happiness she had shared with him, the feeling of belonging. The reality was this: orders being given; orders being carried out. There would be no flinching now, as there had been in Turin. She had not been ready then, but now she was. All that remained now was for her to perform her duty flawlessly. She was the Sleeper awake.

She walked through the metal detector and collected her bag. The woman in the cloak was being searched but Zoe passed unmolested. It would have surprised her to have been stopped. She felt beyond herself; beyond her surroundings; on a different plane to the rest of mankind.

On board the aircraft, her seatbelt buckled, she remembered how she had felt after her blooding. She had many of the same sensations now, but there were major differences. She was not frightened; Sergio had been right in that; she felt that nothing could ever frighten her again. And this time she was in control. She had taken an iron-grip on her emotions and crushed them.

Last night, tiptoeing out of the shower and standing in the hall of her flat, she had watched Matt through the crack in the open door. There was real anguish on his face, and fear and just for a moment she had wanted to run to him, bury herself

in his arms, and sob it all out to him. But it had only been
momentary weakness; the remnants of emotions that were no
longer hers to have. Matt could never rescue her: how could
he? The only amazing thing had been that she had been able
to fool herself and him for so long. All the same, the death
of that last hope, the knowledge that if Matt could not save
her, no one could, had been hard. As if she was standing by
watching while part of her was killed.

She did not notice the flight. At Heathrow, she did not see
any 'Wanted: Terrorists' posters. The man at Immigration
control took her passport: flip, flip, flip, a jerk of the thumb
and she was passed. Outside the terminal she stood in line for
a taxi. The cabbie wanted to chat, but she froze him out.

He stopped outside the hotel.

'That'll be . . .'

'I'll be five minutes. I want you to wait,' she ordered.

She went in through the revolving door. At the Porter's
desk, she handed over the yellow ticket that Sergio had given
her and received a black briefcase in return. She smiled at the
girl who served her. 'Could you tell me where your lavatory
is?' she asked.

In the cubicle, she sat down on the lid of the toilet and
adjusted the briefcase lock until the six numbers were correct.
She pressed the brass studs and the case popped open. She
lifted the papers out, and saw the package underneath,
wrapped in white tissue and sealed with Sellotape. She tore
it all off: a little Beretta, loaded, and with a spare cartridge.
She slipped both items into her handbag, picked up the case
and walked out.

The traffic was fairly heavy on the way back to London.
For a time, they were stuck in a jam. She stared at the cars
on either side: an elderly couple in one, the wife doing the
crossword; a gang of pre-school-age children in a muddy Volvo
in the other.

She closed her eyes. She was beginning to feel slightly
muzzy; her thought processes were less sharp and the resolve
that had carried her through the day was not so strong now. I
owe everything to the Cause, she tried telling herself, but her
mind was letting in other things, like a dam punctured with

tiny holes: Matt's face, his grin, his tenderness; the sense of being complete with him, bereft without him; life being unimaginable without him.

You're tired, she thought, but you must not give in to weakness. She had not slept the previous night, although she had had to pretend that she had. She had told Matt she was going to lie down, 'to try to get rid of this headache', and she had lain on top of the bed with her eyes shut, breathing slowly and deeply.

He had checked her twenty minutes later, and again after half an hour. That time he had sat down on the bed, and it had been so difficult to carry on with the charade. She had wanted so much to see his expression; whether he believed her or not. She had moaned a little and turned her head into the pillow, then, with effort, relaxed the muscles in her face.

Very gently, once, twice, he had stroked her hair and then left her, but with the door ajar and the hall-light on. She had heard the sound of the TV, with its volume turned low so as not to disturb her, and the clink of glass against glass as he poured himself a drink.

An hour later he had come back and she had sensed him standing, looking down at her before very carefully wrapping her round in the duvet. He had lain on the bed beside her, still fully dressed, with no covers for himself. For hours, it seemed, he had kept awake but eventually she had heard his breathing slow and deepen. After an hour she had turned over slowly, waited, then opened her eyes and looked at him. He was asleep, hair all over the place, one side of his collar pulled out of his jumper.

She had lain awake, her mind blank, staring at the false cornices on the ceiling. At five, she had crept out of bed, taken the clothes that she had put out on the chair, and crept into the bathroom. She had not dared put on the light, had washed quickly, brushed her teeth and pulled on the clothes in the darkness. All the time she had been waiting to hear a movement from Matt: the creak of his feet on the floorboards, the calling of her name; a light going on in the bedroom.

There had been nothing. She had jogged in her unsuitable boots up to the tube station, arriving just as the security gates were being opened. At Heathrow she had telephoned the number of the go-between and relayed the appropriate message. She had wondered, in the long three hours before her Paris flight, what Matt would think when he woke and found her gone: whether he would worry about her all day, while he was out walking by the Thames near his flat, or messing about in his boat, or whatever he would do to fill in the hours.

She frowned: she must not imagine things. His worry was not something she could cope with; it was too much of a burden. It dragged at her, pulling her back.

'We're in Battersea now, miss.' The cabbie's voice startled her. 'What road d'you want?'

When he set her down outside the flat she paid him and added a generous tip. She could tell that it surprised him and that he had marked her down as a cold fish. It was sometimes amusing to do the unpredictable, she thought, although at the moment dealing with anyone at all was a strain.

She was looking forward to getting inside, closing her front door, and being alone. There was nothing that she had to do; nothing that she had to think about. All that she needed was sleep.

She inserted the key into the lock and pushed open the door. The flat was in darkness, or almost. From the sitting-room came the glow of the standard lamp: Matt must have left it on. She moved towards the doorway to switch it off . . .

He was sitting in the low velvet armchair that was at right-angles to her as she now stood. In his hand, he was holding the postcard and slowly he turned his head towards her.

She acted by instinct; her hand reaching quickly for the gun in her bag . . .

Chapter Twenty-Nine

Matt had woken a little after nine that morning, cold and stiff on the bed. He had put out his hand and patted the place where Zoe should have been. Nothing but quilt. He cursed himself: he had not meant to sleep at all, but he had been so tired and so certain that the slightest movement from her would have woken him, that he had lain himself down on the bed to keep watch. Then after a long while, he had surrendered to sleep.

'Zoe?' he had called, then again, louder. No, she had gone. He sat up. His head felt thick from drinking too much whisky and his stomach growled with hunger. He got up, went into the kitchen and checked for eggs and bacon in the fridge. Then he went into the bathroom and turned the hot tap on full. He would soak in the bathtub, have breakfast and get out. If he could manage it, he would not call her tonight. But he would be sitting waiting by his phone at home.

'You do pick 'em,' he told his reflection in the mirror above the sink.

He wondered where she had gone: the thought of her visiting an old boyfriend played heavily on his mind, but he barred his imagination from taking that route. He was not going to dream up problems that might not exist; from the look of Zoe the previous night she was going to need all his strength to help her deal with very real ones.

He went back into the kitchen and made himself some coffee. It was so strange being in her flat without her. His hands lingered on some of the things that he had seen her use: the little Krupps coffee grinder that sounded like a power-drill, the mug with Father Christmas smoking a pipe on the side. I mustn't lose her, he thought desperately. I've only just found her. I love her. Calm down, soothed his calmer self. Give her time.

He carried the mug into the bathroom and set it down carefully on the side of the bath. It was a great old-fashioned tub on little claw feet – very picturesque, but it took ages to fill, no doubt because the flat was on the top floor. The bathroom was one of the main reasons that Zoe had decided to rent the place; and he could understand why. It was as large as the bedroom, with pot plants by the tall window and thick creamy mats on the polished wood floor. Beside the bath was a large ottoman and beside that was a bookcase.

He remembered her laughing when he had exclaimed over that. 'Why not?' she had asked. 'What could be better than having a whole bookcase to chose from when you're in the bath?'

He walked over to the books now and squatted down to see their titles. A shelf of modern thrillers, most of which he had read, and below that some romantic, girl-makes-good sagas. He shuddered: to think that a girl as intelligent as Zoe could waste her brain on such rot. The bottom shelf appeared to contain several of her course books: poetry and plays from the last century. There was a handsome looking volume of Browning's verse; remembering how much she loved the poet, Matt pulled it out.

A white envelope fell out onto the floor. It must have been wedged in beside the Browning and the Yeats. Matt picked it up. It was typewritten and addressed to Zoe. It had been sent express and he could not make out the date but the postmark read Rome. Odd, she had never mentioned knowing anyone in Rome, but then, he reminded himself wryly, there was a great deal he did not know about Zoe.

He turned the envelope over and saw part of a postcard sticking out over the flap. It looked like a beach: an Italian Riviera scene probably. He warred briefly with himself: a postcard could not be personal; on the other hand, the writer had sent it under wraps, so to speak, and Zoe had squirrelled it away. It was probably nothing at all; on the other hand it might help him understand her a little bit, and she need never know . . .

In the foreground, the postcard showed a beach, pleasantly half-full with blue-and-white striped sun-beds. Very regimented, not like an Italian beach at all. On the left-hand side was what looked like a sheer cliff, but right at the top were the turrets of a mediaeval fortification. He turned the card over. There were three words only, sprawled across the card in uneven black capitals. 'PARIS. NOON. SUNDAY.' Matt's eyes travelled up to the top of the card. There, in small grey print, he read: 'The Citadel at Calvi, CORSICA'.

It all came at him in a rush, words and phrases jumbled together, everything that Steve had told him. Not just the card but the postmark. He saw his hand was shaking: it must be a coincidence, but how could it be . . . No, there must be a mistake.

Zoe could not . . . he saw her face, the smiling lovely girl, but then it changed to the ivory statue she had been last night, and again back to the girl in the shimmering blue dress at the Ball; the one with the darkest eyelashes he had ever seen, and the great grey eyes that seemed too big for her face; too sad and knowing, eyes that had seen too much.

He moaned. His skin was hot and clammy; everything was spinning, going black; he made it to the toilet just in time and retched into the bowl.

Afterwards, he stood up slowly. He moved like an old man over to the bookcase, stooped and picked up the card, took it with him into the sitting room and sat down in the armchair nearest to the door.

It made perfect, horrible sense.

It explained Zoe's behaviour: the sudden bouts of depression brought on by God knows what memories. Had she killed someone? Had she planted a bomb? He saw the child's bobble hat in the rubble of the Paris church; heard the mother's voice screaming out her dead son's name . . .

He closed his eyes but darkness was worse; darkness brought on darker thoughts and he must think clearly; he must sort out what he had to do.

Other pieces slotted in. Her secrecy; her reluctance to talk about the past . . . My God, he thought wildly, remembering what he had said to Steve about Sleepers being set up with an apartment, Zoe could never have afforded this place! He had assumed that her father was footing the bill but now he recalled her saying that she liked to be independent; her father had offered and she had turned him down.

She had slipped up there, he thought. If he had been sharper, he would have wondered how a bookshop assistant could have paid the rent . . . if he had not been so much in love with her, so absolutely accepting of everything she said.

He felt suddenly chilled through to his bones: had she been using him, he wondered. Had she known about his Never Again stories; had she been put on his trail to find out what he knew . . . had all that loving been an act?

'No, no, no,' he whispered. It could not be. She could not have pretended that light in her eyes, or the softness in her being as she yielded to him. Could she?

For the second time in fourteen hours he prayed to God for help, but no voice spoke to him. He sat there, not noticing the time, not being aware of the darkness of the day outside, until finally hunger made him move.

In a trance he fixed a meal of eggs and bacon, and a jug of new coffee. The food revived him. Gradually he became aware of what he had to do.

He went back into the sitting room, switched on the lamp beside the chair and picked up the card that he had left on the arm. Just after seven, he heard her key in the door; her footsteps coming nearer, then stopping in the doorway. He could half-see her, but he needed to look into her eyes. He turned to face her . . .

Chapter Thirty

The man rubbed his cold hands together, blew on them and looked over at Big Ben. The minute hand jumped upwards. It was fifteen minutes to one o'clock. He saw the girl emerge from the tube station, carrying the black saddle bag on one shoulder and the red telescopic umbrella in her hand. She was on time, and she was walking straight towards him although of course she did not know that.

She had nice blonde hair and she was quite petite: he liked small girls – he was only just regulation height himself. She passed within six feet of him. A pretty face he thought; maybe a bit hard-looking but that could well have been nerves. She had looked calm enough; she was a professional, like him.

He waited four minutes before following her into the coffee shop.

The policeman on duty at the Underground entrance saw her approach and felt his spirits lift a little. It was a dull job, checking passes; most people barely gave him the time of day, but this girl was new and had not yet learned to ignore him.

'Good afternoon!' he called out, as she produced her ID card and swiped it through the machine. 'That was a quick lunch! The old boy's working you hard, is he?'

She smiled and nodded and he saw a faint blush on her cheeks. He liked shy girls; better have them that way than too bold like his own daughter. 'Don't let him push you too hard,' he said to her departing back.

It was fifteen minutes past one. The meeting was due to begin at two, twenty minutes before the sniffer-dogs would be led past the Home Secretary's room on their way to check out the Commons' Chamber.

Sir Hugh Leigh said to his secretary: 'I'm just slipping out for a bite to eat.'

'Don't forget your meeting,' she told him. 'He does hate to be kept waiting.'

'I'm quite well aware of that,' he told her sharply, then smiled, a little awkwardly. 'I'll be back in plenty of time for the meeting.'

He left the building via the Underground entrance. On his way out, he passed a girl with fair hair and a long black coat, but he scarcely saw her. He was praying that no one would stop him for a chat: he had a tube train to catch and after that the first flight he could get to somewhere far away.

Sir Magnus was surprised to see Zoe at her desk. 'Shouldn't you be at lunch?' he asked.

'I've already been. I met a friend. She had to get back early, so I thought I might as well, too.'

'Make sure you go half an hour early tonight then.' He paused on his way out for lunch at the Commonwealth Club. 'You're looking rather pale, my dear. Everything all right? Or am I just being an old nosy-parker?'

'I'm fine, Sir Magnus, absolutely fine. Have a good lunch.'

It was twelve minutes to two. The secretary on duty in the Home Secretary's outer office looked up from her keyboard. 'Come,' she boomed, in answer to the knock.

A young girl with fair hair, and carrying a small cardboard box topped with two Hansards, entered. The secretary recognised her; she was new, she had brought in something last week, but one could never be too careful. She frowned at the security pass around the girl's neck.

'Yes?' she said bossily.

'These are from Sir Magnus. It's his report on discrimination, with the relevant pages marked in Hansard.'

'Oh is it? Well, the Minister's far too busy to bother with that now. Put it over there.' She pointed to a table, overflowing with papers, boxes and books. 'And shut the door behind you. These MPs,' she muttered to her computer when the girl had gone. 'They think he's got nothing better to do than read the drivel they churn out.'

She glanced over at the new box on the table and thought, with satisfaction, that it would be the end of the month before the Minister had time to open it. He was in his office now, working away at something when he should have been at lunch.

1.55 . . . Sighing, the Home Secretary gathered up the papers on his desk and shuffled them back into order. He thought of himself as a good man, a Christian. He had always believed in individual responsibility and the potential in everyone to achieve greatness. And now he was getting into bed with such monsters . . . He would be remembered as the man who had legalised racism.

He put his head in his hands. They would be here soon, swaggering in as if they owned the place, taking their seats and smirking at each other, knowing that they had the Government eating out of their hands. And he and his old friend would have to sit there and endure it . . .

It was intolerable! There was a limit to how far a man could submerge himself in wickedness and remain untarnished himself. Ambition had brought him thus far, but it would take him no further.

He made up his mind. That very afternoon, as soon as he could after the meeting was over, he would ask to see the PM and explain that he had had enough. Either the PM must be willing to forego assured victory on the House Tax or he would proffer his resignation.

Resolved, he went to open his door for his visitors.

Zoe knew that she had to keep calm: that the bossy secretary could have been in their employ, or the tail-coated messenger who had stared after her as she walked past the desk into the Central lobby. She knew that everything depended on her looking natural.

She made it back to the office and was putting her coat on when Claudia returned from lunch.

'You off out?' she asked, looking a trifle piqued.

'I've got to get something from the chemist.'

'Oh. Oh right. There's one on the corner by the coffee-shop.'

'Thanks. Won't be long.'

She went down the steps, down again, across the Lobby and into St Stephen's Hall. Now she was passing, down below on her right, the vast, ancient Hall of Westminster; on her left the security guards and the bomb-detecting devices.

She shifted the bag on her shoulder. It was lighter now.

The last hurdle, the two policemen, were both occupied with visitors. Zoe walked through the doorway and out into the street. She turned left, towards the Lords and away from the Commons, going past the gardens, moving well, eyes forward, keeping going.

A car breaking. A door slamming. Don't look back. Feet behind, hard on the pavement. Just keep going. A hand on her arm, two hands under her arms, lifting her up . . .

All she had time for was one tiny scream before they threw her into the back of the car . . .

From outside, the house still retained the aura of grandeur that it must have once had. It had been built in the Gothic style at the end of the previous century, so it was a little gloomy-looking but impressive with its turrets and pointed roofs.

It was set at least a kilometre back from the road in the middle of its own dark pine woods. When the black, wrought-iron gates were not heavily padlocked and chained, the house could be reached by a private drive.

Inside, the building was in a considerable state of disrepair. The roof leaked in several places; rotten window-sills let in more rain, and dry rot had been allowed to take hold and run through much of the upstairs woodwork. In the spring, the bank that now owned it intended to have it pulled down. In the meantime the agent had been delighted to accept the rent he had been offered.

Downstairs, Beatrix, Axel and Leon sat in the kitchen. Pieter stood by the sink, his back to the window, his right arm resting on top of the sub-machine gun. The kitchen was one of the few rooms that could be heated to any degree of warmth and it was the only room in the whole place that had a table and four usable chairs.

On the table were three objects. Another machine-gun – on Pieter's advice, they were now armed, or at least had a couple of weapons within reach at all times; the radio, tuned to the World Service – there had been some argument about that, but it had eventually been decided that the World Service would carry it first; and a modern, plastic telephone.

The four of them stared alternately at the radio and the phone. Either might tell them the news: whether Zoe's mission had been a success. Later, if all was well, after Zoe had landed at Frankfurt Airport and found the number in the envelope on the Messages Board, she would be calling them direct on that phone. But now it was three-twenty in the afternoon in Germany; allowing generously for delays they should know one way or the other within the next twenty minutes.

On the wireless there was a Sherlock Holmes play.

'I'd like to get some air,' said Pieter.

Axel looked round. 'Feeling queasy are you? All right, but don't be long. You don't want to miss it, do you? Oh, and leave your gun.'

Pieter laid it clatteringly on the stained steel draining-board and went out.

'I say, Watson,' said Holmes. 'There's another footprint here. Look, by the bay window!'

Axel tapped on the table with one finger. 'Come on, come on,' he muttered. 'Oh stop that!' he snapped at Leon who was rocking back and forth in his chair.

Beatrix sat opposite, head bowed, unfathomable. While she waited, she was remembering the summer when she had been six years old and her parents had rented a small chalet in the Black Forest. She and her mother had gone walking every day . . .

Another minute passed, and another. Axel glared up at the kitchen clock. It was twenty-three minutes to four. He heard a slight noise outside; Pieter coming back.

The telephone purred and he snatched it up. 'Yes,' he said breathlessly.

'Ah,' said a man's voice, 'to whom am I speaking? Mr Axel

Shiner or Mr Leon Kleineman?'

'Uh?' Axel held the instrument away from his ear and stared wildly at it.

The pleasant voice – not English, but with such good command of that language that it was difficult to tell which country its owner had been born in – could be clearly heard in the room.

'Greetings also to my countrywoman, Ms Kessler.

'My name is Horst Gemmer. I'm acting as the negotiator on behalf of the GSG-9, counter-terrorist unit. Through cameras and listening devices we can see and hear everything that you're doing. Your comrade, Pieter Van Hoeffen, is already in custody.

'Please avoid bloodshed. Please give yourselves up peacefully. An assault team has already entered the top floor of your house and has taken possession of your armoury. There are four more teams of very expert marksmen surrounding the house. They're extremely well-trained, I assure you.

'You have one minute in which to open the window above the sink, pick up the two weapons and . . .'

Axel screamed and dropped the phone. He stepped towards the draining board, his hand reaching out for Pieter's gun. Leon made to grab the other weapon, but Beatrix's hands had already closed around it.

Like Kessler of old, she took aim.

Gone were the happy childhood memories; the ones that had been blurring her mind. In their place were the two men before her: Shiner who had destroyed the last remnant of her life, who had stripped her of all dignity and freedom, who had kept her from her father and driven her, with his torments, to the very edge of madness. Shiner who had ordered others' deaths, who had washed his hands clean in their blood and who now, for the first time, was trying to hold a weapon.

GSG-9 would not have him. She laughed out loud and squeezed the trigger; it had been so long since she had been in control.

'Noo . . .!' screamed Axel as much in rage as fear, as the bullets hit, making him drop his weapon and sending him flipping backwards over the sink, splattering blood and flesh.

She heard a shout coming from the phone crackle; she did not have long. She turned to Kleineman, quivering and whimpering on the floor. Too gutless to defend himself; only strong enough to stand behind a tyrant, sniggering and applauding, urging him on to inflict more pain.

She opened fire. He bucked and squirmed like the little snake he had been, and then lay still. She laughed again, feeling the power surge through her, and bent to retrieve the weapon Shiner had dropped.

'Scheisse!'

Gemmer tore the headphones away from his ears. The noise of the pump-action weapon bursting forth in the confines of the kitchen, magnified through the listening devices, was deafening.

Beside him the head of the GSG-9 unit yelled into his mouthpiece: 'Go, go, go!'

No one ever knew whose bullet killed Beatrix Kessler. When the four police commandos had entered the kitchen – one by the back door, one by the window, two tumbling in from the hallway – all they had seen was the woman that they knew as one of the world's most ruthless terrorists, standing with a machine gun in her hands, raising it in their direction.

There were two very dead men in the room. The assault team's bullets tore her body apart.

Her father, as next-of-kin, was not asked to identify her. He had become senile, which many said was a blessing.

Four weeks later, after the inquest, her body was burned at a public crematorium in Frankfurt and her ashes disposed of in an unmarked hole. Gemmer was there. Not out of respect exactly but more as a witness to her final passing; a stand-in for the father who had begged him to bring his daughter back all those years ago.

He had failed to return the pastor's daughter. But as he drove back to Wiesbaden that wintry afternoon in February, he knew that at least he had been part of the plan that had saved the lives of many other people.

That had, rightly, been a cause for celebration.

Epilogue

On the evening of the shootings, and for several days afterwards, the media had a bonanza. So, too, did the German Interior Minister who craved positive TV coverage. As a politician, he was used to fending off awkward demands for explanations, so he found it very easy, indeed pleasurable, to take all the credit for the destruction of Never Again without knowing any of the details.

Very few people did. It was nearly two days before Gemmer himself was able to form a complete picture of what had led up to that extraordinary telephone call he had received from Barney Turl late that Sunday night.

Thirty-six hours was the earliest that either he or Barney could set aside for a meeting and have any confidence that they would not be disturbed. Gemmer came to London, to the scruffy building beside Vauxhall railway station, and if he thought his friend's working environment not fit for a cockroach, he was polite and said nothing.

Besides, sitting in an ice-bucket on Barney's old wooden desk was a bottle of Bollinger and two glasses.

Barney looked exhausted, crumpled but jubilant. 'Horst! Take a seat, let me pour you a drink. We're not meant to have alcohol in the building – Hargreaves' rules – but I think the occasion merits it.

'Cheers! Here's to us; to the success of Operation Fawkes and the persuasive powers of a journalist.'

'A what?'

'I couldn't go into it all on the phone, there wasn't time, but we owe it all to that journalist, Matt Anderson.'

'The one you had briefed?' Gemmer frowned and set down his glass. 'What's he got to do with it?'

'A lot.'

* * *

When Matt had turned round and seen Zoe pointing the gun at him, her arms quite steady, feet apart, eyes narrowed, he had fully expected to die.

He cursed his stupidity, his arrogant belief that she would not harm him because she loved him. She was a trained killer, a Sleeper who had been activated; who had been taught how to deal with anyone who got in her way, no matter who it was. He was sitting there with her orders in his hand.

She would not hesitate.

'Zoe! It's me, Matt!'

She flinched as if she had been hit. The gun wavered in her hands but she steadied it.

Oh God, I'm going to die. 'I love you! I'm not your enemy! I'm not a Nazi! Please, Zoe! Please don't shoot me!'

She blinked. The face twisted in terror, the boy begging for his life, her fingers on the trigger, squeezing . . .

'Matt?' wonderingly. She dropped her left hand, took a step towards him, saw the gun still in her right hand. She stopped, staring at it, then back to him. 'Matt?'

He did not move. She could still turn; her training, whatever God-awful psychosis had warped her, could still win out.

She took another step, then another. She came into the arc of the lamplight; she was less than three feet away from him, two feet . . .

He looked up at her face, ghostly white, haunted by her eyes. 'Matt,' a whimper, childlike, pathetic.

The gun dropped to the floor with a thud.

'Matt hold me! Matt hold me! Please hold me!'

Barney took a sip of champagne. 'I wouldn't normally say this about Special Branch, but on this occasion, they got their fingers out pretty bloody quick. Immediate assessment, proper action. Which is more than can be said for my outfit.'

'Oh?'

'Hargreaves said it was all a hoax. A newspaper hoax and I wasn't to have anything to do with it. Her nose is a bit out of joint right now.'

*   *   *

Steve Carrington had been sitting at home that Sunday night watching TV when the telephone rang.

'Hope that's not your office,' warned his girlfriend.

'No, I told you. What I've been working on's been called off. It's probably your mum.'

'Oh, you get it, Stevie. Say I'm in the bath.'

He had picked up the phone.

'Steve? It's Matt. Look, something incredible's happened. It's to do with the British Sleeper. I've got to see you now, at once. You'll have to come here.'

'Hey, hey, hang on. You're not making sense. What about a British Sleeper? What've you found out?'

'I can't tell you over the phone. It's too ... complicated. But it's desperately urgent. She's ...'

'She?' Steve's heart hammered. He remembered McGuillan and himself filleting the MI5 file on the Gibraltar terrorist. 'We don't want him knowing too much; it's got to look as if the stuff could've come from a number of sources – the Gib police, or the Spanish. So nothing about the British girl; nothing about there even being a British Sleeper.'

'And if he asks?'

'Let him ask.'

'You still there, Steve?' Matt's voice had sounded close to panic. 'You've got to believe me, mate. It's all meant to happen tomorrow. She's got to do it tomorrow.'

'Where you phoning from? Give me the address.'

Barney stretched over the desk and refilled Gemmer's glass. 'Once Carrington got to the flat and saw her wake-up card, he called his boss. And he called me. By the time I got there the girl was in a bit of a trance, still talking and answering questions, but coming in and out.'

'Was she on anything?'

'No, I don't think so. She was just coming apart. We had to stop it, snap her out of it. She had to go through the motions the next day. If she hadn't, we'd never have got to the Leadership; never have got our hands on Leigh, or the backers, or any of it. They'd have gone on the same as before, maybe used another of the Sleepers for a "Spectacular".'

Four more Sleepers had been found and quietly arrested in their apartments in Florence, Berlin, Brussels and Rotterdam.

'So.' Through the blind that hung down at the window Gemmer watched a black crow alight on the sill, tilt its head to peer in at them, and then clearly disappointed, squawk, and take off again. 'How'd you convince her?'

'Blackmail and terror. I do a good line with them on little girls.'

At the flat, Barney had ordered everyone else out of the room. The journalist had to be hauled out by Carrington; watching him go, the girl had broken down.

'It's all right, I'm not going to hurt you. I need you looking unbruised tomorrow, because you're going to go through with this thing.'

She had lifted her head, grey eyes beseeching his.

'Don't give me "little girl lost", and don't freak out on me. You're in a lot of shit, young lady, a very great deal. The only way you've got a hope in hell of lifting yourself just a fraction out of it, is by doing exactly what we want. D'you understand?'

She had nodded dumbly, wiping away the tears with her fingers.

'Even then I'm not saying you won't go to prison for a very long time. It's not my decision. All I can do is make recommendations, got that?'

Another nod.

'Right, Brunelli told you you'd be watched from the time you picked up the bomb tomorrow till you got to Frankfurt airport?'

'Yes,' a whisper.

'Spies everywhere,' he had muttered more to himself than to her. 'Well, he's probably talking crap, but we can't risk it. We need the phone number that's going to be left for you at Frankfurt Airport too much. It's the only way we can trace where your friends are holed up.'

He had glared at her suddenly. 'Sure you don't know where they are?'

'No, no! I've told you I don't!'

'I hope you're telling the truth. You don't want to spend the next ten years inside, do you? Not with that handsome young chap on the outside, waiting for you and getting a bit bored after a while . . . finding someone else?

'No? OK, I thought not. Well, you're just going to have to go to Frankfurt tomorrow as they're expecting. They're not going to stick your message up till you've landed, or someone's seen you leave Heathrow.'

Barney grinned and rubbed at his forehead. 'I was wrong there, as it happens.'

'Ja, the message for Fraulein Grams was left at noon. We got it ten minutes later.'

'Good job too. I never liked the idea of her going all the way through. Too much risk of her cracking up on the flight, or doing a runner. We picked her up just outside. She was OK, actually, she only cracked up again when we let her see her boyfriend. I must say she went through with the whole thing like a pro.'

'Ah, you admire her?'

'Well, don't get me wrong, she's a pretty screwed-up kid but she's got guts.'

'All right,' Barney had told her after a while. 'I'm going to run through what you're going to do. You're listening to me aren't you?'

'Yes, sir.'

'You're going to go to work tomorrow with your black shoulder-bag and your red brolly, and you're going to look as if butter wouldn't melt in your mouth. You're going to work hard all morning and then at what time . . .?'

'Ten to one.'

'You're going to go and collect your "package" from the man in the coffee shop in Whitehall. You don't know who he is or what he looks like?'

'No, sir.'

'You're not trying to hide things are you? Because if you . . .'

'It's all right, sir. I want to help. You don't have to bully me any more.'

It was the first flash of fighting spirit that he had seen from her. He was pleased; she would need it all. He glowered at her.

'Bully! You think I'm bullying you? My God, girl, you've got a lot to learn! Just in case you're lying to me . . .'

'I'm not, sir. I'm truly . . .'

'Don't interrupt me! In case you are and you're thinking of having a quick word with your bomb delivery-boy, know that we'll have a dozen plainclothes men and women watching your every move, and I'm not telling lies. There'll be at least two of my people in your coffee shop, and they and the others outside will be armed. Got that?'

She nodded.

'What size is this package?'

'It'll be in a plastic sandwich box, inside a cardboard-box. Not very big.' She had indicated the size of a piece of A4 paper.

'Right. You take it and go back inside the House. Now, later on tonight, you're going to be shown plans of the Palace, so you know which ladies' loos you're to go to. They'll be closest to the entrance. Even if someone is watching you and they see you dive in there, they'll just think you've got the runs.

'You go in. A woman who you're going to be meeting later on tonight will be there, and you swap packages. Then you proceed with the fake bomb. OK?'

'Yes, sir.'

There had been a knock at the door. McGuillan had stuck his head round it. 'The car's here, Mr Turl.'

'Right, thanks. OK, you're now going to be taken to meet quite a few people, including a few shrinks. But I don't want you playing up to them, right? No freakiness, got it?'

She had flinched. 'Got it,' she said.

He had hesitated; it was not professional, he should allow her to be debriefed properly but he wanted to know.

'How did you get to Corsica last summer?'

'I flew to Nice and got the ferry.'

'Oh. Did you? And was it really a golden eagle that you saw at Brunelli's place?'

She had looked surprised. 'Yes, sir. A pair. I saw them several times.'

Gemmer raised an eyebrow. 'If your bosses had allowed you to check on the ferries, and port immigration, as you wanted . . .'

'Yeah, well water under the bridge now.' Barney drank again from his glass.

'How much damage would the real bomb have done?'

'Oh considerable. It'd have killed our Home Secretary, possibly the Prime Minister and another couple of Ministers who've got their offices in that corridor. Plus any of their staffs, anyone in the corridor, and it might well have got into the Chamber itself.'

'Scheisse!'

'Yep. A real spectacular. On the Guy Fawkes scale of things. Shiner would've been delighted. It would've also got the Home Secretary's four UKN MP guests of course, but I wasn't putting them in the same league as the others.'

'No,' Gemmer pulled a face. 'Deeply unpleasant people. Extraordinary that any British government would have considered dealing with them.' He sipped thoughtfully at his glass. 'You didn't tell any of them about the fake run?'

'We couldn't risk it. We didn't know if any of them were involved.'

Gemmer nodded. 'Leigh was the Home Secretary's friend?'

'Correct. Close friend and adviser for a good ten, fifteen years. Quite a bit older than the Home Secretary, seen as a father figure. Leigh was the only other person, apart from the Minister's PPS, who knew what was going on with the UKNs.'

'And he betrayed him?'

'For the good of the Cause. Or actually, I think, because he was shit-scared of Brunelli and knew he was in too deep to get out.'

'You got him?'

'Yeah, at Heathrow as it happens. Soon as we found out he hadn't turned up for the meeting, we knew he was our man and put out an all ports for him.'

'But why did he do it?'

Barney sighed and looked in the direction of the window. The day had become murky; too dark to see anything clearly.

'During the last war, Leigh was a young British officer working with the SOE and the Resistance. He was in Occupied France when he saw Jews being loaded onto a train. He was armed, he could have shot some of the SS men, but he was on a mission and he needed his ammunition for other purposes.

'But it tore him apart, the fact that he'd abandoned those people . . .'

'But so many others saw those things happening and did nothing!'

'Sure. But some are more affected than others. For years, he had bad dreams and tried to forget it. He joined various organisations, anti-racist and Anti-Semitic watchdog groups – quite unusual for a Tory, I can tell you; it might even have cost him advancement within the Party – and then about eighteen months ago he met the highly persuasive Mr Axel Shiner.'

'Who was looking for financiers?'

'Exactly. If Leigh really meant it about wanting to absolve himself of the guilt he had carried with him all his life, he ought to put his considerable wealth where his mouth was. Into Never Again's coffers.'

Barney topped up both their glasses. 'But Mr Shiner is the real dark horse in all this.'

Gemmer leaned back in his chair with his glass. 'Go on. Tell me.'

'I've never heard anything like it before. Leigh and all the rest of the group's backers – he coughed up their names in the first hour after his arrest – assumed Shiner was Jewish. He certainly made out that he was; talked about "his people" and the Holocaust. Said he was too traumatised to talk very much about it but that his father had escaped from the Warsaw ghetto uprising, and had fled to England as a refugee.'

'And he hadn't?'

'Oh, he was a refugee all right. But not Jewish. He came from Estonia where just about all the Jews were shot. Not by Nazis, but by Estonians working for them. Quite willingly working for them in Shiner Senior's case.'

Gemmer sat bolt upright, spilling some of his drink. 'My God! His father was a war criminal?'

'Yep. When he saw which way the war was going he changed sides, took a Pole's uniform, and, after the war, came to Britain as a displaced person. He married and settled in Kent. And along came Axel.'

'But,' Gemmer looked truly shaken, 'how did Axel come to ... how did he become what he did? Did he know about his father?'

'No, not at all. Thought he was a war hero. It was only after his father died a few years ago when Axel was going through his things that he came across a German medal and some documents of commendation for his services carried out in Estonia. Axel wasn't stupid; he did a little digging, and soon found out what his father had really done during the war.'

'So it was massive guilt that turned him? Some idea that he ought to fight for the people his father had killed?' He shook his head. 'What a terrible mess!'

'Yep, pretty awful.'

They both fell silent, suddenly sombre. After a while, Gemmer looked up. 'Your girl, is she going to be charged?'

Barney smiled. 'She hasn't actually committed a criminal offence.'

'She was going to blow up your Parliament!'

'But she didn't and she helped us find those responsible.'

'I thought she shot those two men in Turin!'

'She says she didn't. Those who did are dead. Anyway, whatever she did wasn't on these shores.'

'It doesn't seem right that she should go free,' Gemmer frowned.

'Oh, I don't know. I think she'll straighten herself out. She'd got screwed-up, and then misled, by your Mr Van Hoeffen.'

'He's not mine! He's Dutch. But you're right, he'll be tried in Germany. At least he got out of that hell-hole alive.'

Gemmer had been sitting jammed into a corner of the GSG-9 surveillance van that had been rolled in and parked at the top of the drive of the Frankfurt safe-house, when the sound technician had turned to him and whispered:

'One's coming out.'

A second later, he had seen Pieter on the tiny TV screen, opening the kitchen door and closing it behind him.

'He's not armed,' murmured the GSG-9 commander.

Gemmer had hesitated for only a moment, weighing up the

risks of a snatch going wrong against the cachet of a live terrorist. Then: 'Get him!'

Two minutes later, Pieter was lying spreadeagled on the floor of one of the back-up vehicles, with one commando kneeling on his back, shoving a gun into the nape of his neck and another standing over him.

'What are the names of the men with Kessler?' Gemmer demanded.

Pieter grunted and moved his head; he said nothing.

Gemmer nodded. The kneeling commando brought his knee up and ground it into Pieter's spine, at the same time jabbing the weapon harder into his neck. The combination was agony; Pieter screamed.

The standing commando kicked him in the ribs. He moaned.

'The names?'

'No . . .'

'Another movement from the kneeling man; another scream.

'Shiner! Axel Shiner!'

'And?'

'Leon Kleineman!'

After that initial reluctance, Gemmer remarked, Mr Van Hoeffen had proved most co-operative. 'He told me about Shiner's plans for your girl and Kessler. An appointment with Brunelli, who we think, by the way, was actually parked near the house when we went in.'

'What!' It was Barney's turn to jackknife upright in his chair. 'Say again?'

'Ja. When we were going to the house, one of the team noticed an old red Renault parked at the corner of the road with a man sitting inside reading a newspaper. Could've been innocent, but he took the number just in case and sent it through to Control. Car had been bought, cash, from a garage on the outskirts of Paris a week ago. We sent someone to ask a few questions but the car had gone.

'It was definitely him?'

'Oh yes. Van Hoeffen gave us Brunelli's phone number and we got a unit down to the place he'd been renting in Picardie . . .'

'Ah, is that where it was? The girl claimed she didn't know where she'd been taken to meet Brunelli. Said she'd flown to Paris, been picked up by a boy on a motorbike and driven off into the countryside, north she thought, but she couldn't remember. I pressed her a bit about it, but she kept to the story that her mind was a blank.'

'Ja, Picardie. Very remote cottage. Empty of course, except for an artist's easel he'd left behind. One old man in the nearby town remembered that the "artist" who'd just moved into the cottage had a red Renault, about nine years old. He'd seen him arrive in town . . .'

'So Brunelli's gone again?'

'Ja, looks like it. He's out there somewhere. Did you tell your girl what Shiner had organised for her?'

'No, not yet and I probably won't. Don't want her demanding protection.' Barney stretched consideringly. 'On the other hand, I might keep it up my sleeve if she ever steps out of line and shows any inclination to talk.'

'You really think she won't?'

'It's hardly in her interests, is it? And we're supplying plenty of listening ears and a shrink for her to unburden herself too. I don't think she'll say a word.' He picked up the bottle; there was not much left and he poured it into Gemmer's glass.

'This bloke, Van Hoeffen. You think he'll do a deal on keeping his mouth shut? About our girl and the whole operation here?'

Gemmer nodded confidently. 'Ja, he's full of guilt about recruiting her in the first place. He's happy that she's not going to be charged. He won't mention anything about her, or her mission, and in return I'm going to pull some strings and get him a reduced sentence, somewhere not too bad.'

He swigged back the last of the champagne. 'You know, he's an interesting man. Intelligent, perhaps too intelligent. And so remorseful about all the kids he recruited, not just your girl. He said it was curious, but he had only realised in the last month or so that nearly all his recruits were white, and very few of them Jewish. He had automatically discounted coloured kids, without even thinking about it. "I saw them all as victims," that's what he said to me.'

'Yeah, well it was the sort of group that was always going to appeal to white bleeding hearts, wasn't it?' Barney stared at his empty glass.

'What are you going to do about Valente? He's already here, isn't he?'

'Yep, and committed to stand trial at the Old Bailey. I'm going to do the same as you, Horst, have a friendly word in his ear, tell him to keep his mouth shut about the girl he thought he saw in Gibraltar and that, if he ever mentions her, I'm going to have him committed to an insane asylum or maybe to one of those nasty Spanish prisons where they torture people.

'But it shouldn't be necessary. Valente likes to please me.'

There was a knock at the door and Gregson entered bearing another bottle.

'Ah, in the nick of time. Nicely chilled, I trust? Good, shut the door after you, will you?'

Gemmer grinned. 'You're risking it if your director bans alcohol!'

'Oh she's taken a few days off sick. We're all hoping it's something permanent.'

The champagne cork popped and the liquid fizzed out over his desk. 'Hand over your glass.'

Gemmer did as he was told. 'So is no one going to stand trial here, apart from Valente?'

'Nope. No one wants it. We certainly don't want anyone knowing how close someone came to blowing up the Commons and half the cabinet. The Government don't want it . . .'

'No, I can see they wouldn't!' Then Gemmer frowned. 'But your Home Secretary was going to do a deal with those Fascists . . .'

'Well, he's resigned. And the Prime Minister's decided to shelve the whole idea of being friendly with the UKNs. In fact, I think he's due to make a speech this afternoon about political integrity and knowing that his precious House Tax Bill will get the votes it needs on the day.' Barney grinned: 'I think the whole thing's been a bit of a shock for him.'

'A shock!' Gemmer laughed. 'A classic example of British

understatement.' He took a mouthful of the new champagne. 'So all the villains except Valente and Van Hoeffen have escaped justice?'

Barney screwed up his face. 'None of them'll ever get banged up – well, so long as they behave themselves – but I wouldn't exactly say they'd escaped scot-free.'

Sir Hugh Leigh, ingloriously detained at Terminal One, resigned later in the week. In return for his silence, he was allowed to retire to his house in Oxfordshire from where, a year later, his wife ran off with his accountant.

The man who had made and delivered the bomb to Zoe had been followed to a rented house in Notting Hill. Later that afternoon, as soon as they had got the go-ahead, six armed men had broken down the door and dragged him out. 'Bank robber,' they had explained to the handful of neighbours who had come out to watch. They had chucked him into the waiting dark van and taken him off to a low building on Salisbury Plain. There, he had been told what the deal was: silence and a one-way ticket far away with quite a fair bit of cash to set him up.

'Or,' the snub-nosed, grey-haired man had told him, 'you'll be standing trial for murder next month.'

'But I haven't murdered . . .'

'Shut it, scum! The evidence against you will be overwhelming.' He had considered his captive carefully. 'But perhaps you're right. Perhaps you'd be less trouble if we shut your mouth for good.'

The bomber had chosen liberty and life.

Junie Carson had been fairly simple to deal with. The morning after the bomb should have exploded, a lady had visited her at the insurance offices where she worked in Holborn. She had told personnel that she was Junie's aunt and a family crisis had come up.

'I don't have an aunt . . .' Junie had started when the lady was ushered in to see her.

'Junie, it's about young Zoe. She asked that I come and see you personally.'

In the teashop around the corner, three specially selected large men had joined Junie and the woman.

'Keep your mouth shut,' the lady had said as she poured milk first, 'for good. Or else your parents will get a letter.'

'A letter?' Junie had asked, quaking.

'Saying that you are involved in Satanic child abuse and that you're about to be arrested.' The woman had smiled. 'And then we'll arrange that, too.'

Gemmer nodded his head slowly. 'You've been pretty thorough.' Then a gleam came into his eyes. 'How about that American, Zimmerman? You said on the phone that he knew Leigh, that's how he'd got invited to speak at that conference!'

'Yeah, that's right. But Leigh's not going to tell him anything, is he? All Zimmerman knows is the group's finished and if he's sensible he's going to keep quiet about his own involvement. It was pretty minimal anyway, that one speech and knowing Leigh.' He sipped again. 'Are the Russians going to co-operate with Kessler's minder?'

'Don't know. Now that Kessler's dead, Janke isn't the great prize he was, is he? Still useful for the historical record of what she did, and a few others like her, but that's about it.'

'So, everyone's sewn up.'

'Yep. I think so.'

'No one was suspicious inside your Parliament?'

'There was nothing to be suspicious about.'

The gleam re-entered Gemmer's eyes. 'How about your journalist? You can't expect to shut him up!'

Barney put his head on one side. 'Horst, you sadden me. Have you not heard "Love Conquers All"?'

Two months later, on a gloomy Friday night when the rain lashed down at the windows of his flat, Matt pulled Zoe closer to him on the sofa and kissed her tenderly.

'Ssh,' he whispered.

She was crying softly. She had just finished reading the evening paper's account of the outcome of the Valente trial: an eight year prison sentence.

'He could have got much worse,' Matt said.

'But it could have been me!'

'But it wasn't. You chose differently. He could have done, too.'

'But he didn't have someone like you! If it wasn't for you ...'

'If I hadn't whimpered for my life, you mean!'

'Oh Matt!' She snuggled in nearer to his chest, her tears making his shirt wet. 'When you cried out, I saw that boy, the one in Turin ...'

'I know, I know.'

'How can you still love me after what I did?'

'Oh, I'm a glutton for punishment.'

'You're wonderful.' She sniffed, staring down at the paper from which Valente's thin face stared back. 'You'll do all the articles you've got about him for the paper on Sunday?'

'Yes.'

'You weren't ever tempted to write about me? It would have been a great story, real insider stuff.'

'Stop that!' He frowned down at her, tried to hold it, then smiled. 'Of couse I wasn't! I've told you, not even for a moment. D'you think I'd have done that to the girl I love?'

That, he knew, was what that bastard Turl, and McGuillan and Steve Carrington, had banked on. He would never have done it, but to have gone along with anything that they had wanted him to do had made him sick.

He still hated himself for the way in which he had allowed himself to be hauled out of the room that night, leaving Zoe alone with Turl, to be threatened and co-erced into going through with that nightmare, while he had sat crying out his shock in the kitchen.

Oh yes, he had been bloody wonderful! A real tower of strength for her! Calling in MI5 and then abandoning her! 'What else could you have done?' the rational part of him sometimes asked. Zoe herself had told him repeatedly that she had been glad that she had gone through with it; not so glad about the deaths of the Leadership but so relieved that she had helped stopped all the other killing ...

But that was not the point, he had raged at himself: he should have protected her!

That afternoon, while she carried a live bomb along Whitehall, he had sat shaking in the Operations Room in Parliament Square, trying to pick up what was going on from the bursts coming in on the watchers' handsets.

'She's taken the bag off! She's taken the bag off . . . It's OK, repeat OK, she's just moving it to the other shoulder.'

'A man's watching her, by the newspaper stand, red bobble-hat, jeans, late twenties . . . he's following her, still with her . . . She's turned onto Bridge Street. He's going with her; he's a yard behind. Action?'

'Leave it,' ordered Turl, 'leave it. Where's he now?'

'Still behind her, going down the Underground steps . . . Out of sight!'

'I have them, I have them!' Another voice. 'He's right behind her. She's going under the tunnnel now. He's stopped, he's reading the No Entry to Public sign, he's turned. He's going back to the tube station.'

Turl had laughed and turned to him. 'Sounds like he just fancied her, huh?'

Matt had glared. Afterwards, when they had brought her back to him, she had collapsed and he had held her, trying desperately to soothe her and praying to God that she would be all right.

It looked like God was answering that one, at least. She had been seeing a psychiatrist – one of theirs, unfortunately, but maybe just as well; who else would have believed her? – for the past two months. At first every day, but recently it had been cut to once a week. Matt had seen the same person, a woman, a few times. It was going to take time, she had told them both; Zoe had a lot to work through, all that horror in Lithuania and Germany; the damage that Never Again had done her; her guilt and then the much earlier stuff, the loneliness, the feelings of not belonging.

If only she had talked to him, told him the whole thing! But she had been so confused, she said; she had wanted him so much; had felt he was so right for her, but all the other stuff, all that conditioning and terror and belief in the Cause had stopped her. She had tried to hold both parts of her life together and separate at the same time. She must have been torn to shreds inside: no wonder she did not say anything!

He should have talked more to her. But it had been his stupid belief that he should not talk about work, fearing it would drive her away, making the mistake of thinking she was like Louise. If he had only spoken once about Never Again, she would have broken down and he would have known, he was sure of it.

They had made a pact, seven weeks ago, when she had properly moved in with him, that they would always tell each other everything in future.

'You really want to know about Lomax?' he had queried.

'Everything!'

'About all the people who come in off the street with their tales of woe?'

'Yes! Well, you could condense it a bit.'

He smiled; she was so lovely. The brightness that he loved so much, which had seemed to vanish in those dark days immediately afterwards, had now returned. It was even better now because she had nothing to hide.

The Security Services had fed him titbits, the bastards. 'And there'll be more where this came from,' Steve had told him loftily as if expecting him to be grateful, 'so long as you keep your nose clean.'

At first he had been sorely tempted to tell Steve where to put it, but sounder, less noble reasoning had won out in the end. The stuff was bloody good; it would keep Lomax off his back and give him plenty of time out of the office to look after Zoe.

And that's what he had done. In one day, he had checked out the Shiner stuff, visited the man's mother who had, on Turl's advice, wisely moved to Sevenoaks to avoid the media, but had been told that she had to talk to Matt. He had spent a second day in the office, the rest at home with Zoe.

The Shiner revelations had been one splash. Lomax had been stunned. 'This is fantastic stuff! Where'd you get it?'

'Ah, that'd be telling.'

'Deep Throat again, huh? Bloody marvellous, Matt. Keep up the good work!'

A week before, Pieter Van Hoeffen's trial had finished in Germany and Matt had written an excellent background piece on the man. He had spent two days working flat-out in Germany, calling Zoe every couple of hours. She had been fine; she was really getting better.

And he had already written the articles on Valente for that week's paper.

After that, he thought, he would like to have a rest from Never Again. Maybe go back and have a look at the UKNs; maybe with his new-found 'contacts' find out some dirt on those four MPs they had and exposé them before the next General Election.

It did look as if there was going to be one. The Government had lost the debate on the House Tax and the Prime Minister had made such a pratt of himself over it that the Party had lost confidence in him. In consequence the public had lost confidence in the Party.

Clive had called him only that day to say that the latest MORI poll showed support for the UKNs was rising at an alarming rate. And not just in the big conurbations; some of the market-towns and rural areas too.

Matt shuddered and looked down at Zoe. She seemed to have fallen asleep. Never Again had gone horribly wrong, but it was easy to see why they had started.

Yes, he thought, he would do something on the Fascists; something to answer Clive's demand for a story. He felt he owed him one.

On the day that the Government lost the House Tax Bill, Clive had called. 'Did you ever find out anything on that tip-off I gave you about the UKNs and the Home Secretary?'

'No,' he had lied smoothly. 'I had a dig about, but nothing.'

'Oh well, maybe it was a bit unlikely.'

Zoe stirred and woke up. At first she had not been able to sleep at all, then only with nightmares, now even those were fading.

'Matt?'

'Yes, darling?'

'D'you think our phone's tapped?'

He started; he had not thought about that, but: 'Probably, in fact, almost certainly.'

'How long do you think they'll do that for?'

He stroked her hair. 'Oh, till they get bored with us.'

She seemed to fall asleep again, considering that one. Then: 'Do you know what one of the worst things is?'

'What?'

'Never being able to tell the truth to people like Alasdair or Kerry.'

'Mmm.' He sighed. 'But it's better they don't know. It's over, so why terrify them?'

'I didn't want to terrify them.' She sat up, quite indignant. 'I just don't like them not knowing the truth.' She lay down again. 'What did you tell Al that Sunday when you had to phone up and cancel?'

'Oh, that you'd got the 'flu and lost your voice.'

She giggled. 'I bet he was suspicious.'

'I don't know, he sounded very concerned. God knows what I'd have done if he'd come over to see you. Probably I'd have stuck a bolster in your bed and said you were sleeping.'

'But suppose he'd looked!'

'Yes, suppose.' He smiled and played with her hair. 'Oh what a tangled web, huh?'

She turned on her back and gazed up at him, her pupils huge in the darkness. 'Not any more, Matt. I promise.'